Where I Can Breathe

Hays Blinckmann

Hays Blinckmann

Where I Can Breathe

Copyright © 2020 Hays T. Blinckmann
ISBN: 9798600376793
Cover design by Irene de Bruijn
Author photograph by Stephanie Mitchell

For my sister, Buffy

"The past is the present, isn't it?
It's the future, too.
We all try to lie out of that
but life won't let us"

Eugene O'Neill
Long Days Journey into Night

PROLOGUE

It's the semantics people use, that's what gets to me. When someone dies, they say you have suffered a *loss*. Loss can imply it was out of your control, whatever you had is gone by whatever force. You lost your job, your sunglasses, your best friend in a car wreck. There was a cosmic intervention in your life. But the act of grieving? That supposedly involves *letting go* and suggests you have control, like you are freeing a bird from its cage. As if letting go of your loved one is as easy as the decision to push your dinner plate away and declare you are done. You see? To have control but to not have control, both circling back to the catastrophe that is somehow now your life. Semantics.

Death is fucked up like that, not to be crass. It's an uncontrollable virus that invades your life and says *deal with this shit motherfucker*. It is loss that is so vast and huge and ugly that we, as humans, can fail to recover. You don't rebound from death like a sports game or a movie ending. It's a cliff. There is no control over it.

So humans opt to say they are *letting go* as some sort of

therapeutic washed down version of *fuck you right back death, I have power, bitch*. But really, death just wins, death will always win. It's in the word loss, you are the loser. It's a game of roulette and black is going to succeed whether you call it or not. I wish I knew the therapist who coined *to let go*, fucking brilliant. It's a powerful statement but is it true? Oh hell no, it's magic fucking beans from a carnival.

Nobody ever really lets go of someone they love. Those people are a part of them like a seam in their soul, stitch after stitch keeping them together. Without them, the people left behind unravel and fall apart. It will take others, new loved ones to sew them back up again, if at all possible. But to truly let go of the people they lost? That's like losing your name, losing your DNA, losing your history. That ain't ever going to happen, folks.

A lot of people have gone over all this before; it just happens to be my turn now. What have I learned? Death is horrific, messy and sad. I am in awe of the whole situation. But death is just a part of my story, not the whole story. The whole story is an epic shit show.

Abby Williams O'Conner c. 2010

ONE

The air was tighter, different once the doors shut. Ansel Williams felt his lungs adjust and cool as he walked along the corridor. *So many people*, he thought. How could there be so many people rushing past each other, nameless and determined? Looking around, he kept losing his bearings; the greeter at the front desk had said down the hall, past the coffee cart and the elevators would be on the left. There was an immense line of people at the coffee cart, all shapes and sizes waiting quietly, too quietly. No one was impatient or rude. It was that kind of atmosphere: fellow passengers on a Titanic of sorts, staying calm and helping one another. The coffee line was the least of their worries.

What is it about doctors, nurses, people who work in hospitals? Ansel could tell them by the purpose of their gait. They were the ones in comfortable shoes, lab coats and scrubs relaxed and chatting at ease. Their pallor was a pale unblemished color. It was their own special hue created by years of traversing these hallways, skin unpolished by pollution or sun. It was the sanctimonious side effect to spending a lifetime saving others. Then there were the others, visitors to this fluorescent realm, with drawn faces and jerky movements. They were unwitting guests, skin stressed by multiple tints, clothes out of order, not calm or belonging. That was Ansel.

At the elevators, a great rush of people flooded from open doors and a tide of bodies pushed him onto one. Hospital elevators were unusually large and septic smelling. People actively avoided touching one another, fearing germs. There was no eye contact. No one curious about one another.

Ansel sighed, thankful no stretcher appeared with someone in a gown, arm jabbed with rubber tubing. At 36, he was squeamish enough about hospitals and actively avoided them. Being a hypochondriac would've been Ansel's worst nightmare. Just convincing himself for a checkup took months and, even then, his blood pressure soared at the sight of a doctor's office. He was going to die eventually, but had no desire to know beforehand.

The elevator opened after an eternity on the eleventh floor. Ansel followed a labyrinth of doors and corridors until he found the nurse's station. It reminded him of the Starship Enterprise run by quirky people in playful scrubs. The nurses wore fleece coats and cardigans and gossiped in front of a matrix of beeping machines. Ansel, not quite knowing what to do, stood confused.

That morning Ansel had entered his art gallery on Collins Avenue in Miami's South Beach, a happy man. Kerry, his assistant, had a double latte and Cuban cheese toast waiting for him on his desk. They were celebrating a successful show of a new artist from the night before. He had gone to bed over $50,000 richer with the smug satisfaction of running his business extraordinarily well. It was one of the few things he had in common with his father, business sense. Now seven hours later, he was in a Connecticut hospital corridor thinking about Miami air conditioning. It felt colder here and his linen shirt felt weightless, no defense against the geriatric floor climate. Ansel's soft brown hair with natural sun highlights flopped over his forehead out of place with the New England crew cuts. His blue eyes dulled by the harsh lighting, and out of his element in every way, he stood, dazed, until he heard his name.

It was his older sister Abby calling him. He recognized her squat stance, hands anchored on her hips. Her messy ponytail and flannel shirt seemed as familiar as light. He thought she looked the same as in high school. At 40, Abby was still girlish and pretty. With broad cheekbones, wide smile, hazel eyes and platinum blond hair, Abby was a natural beauty. She would have been a perfect model if she was a foot taller. The family genes stopped her short and she was slightly rounder than most. Having two kids probably didn't help the situation, but regardless, he always thought she was the loveliest girl in the room.

And there was his oldest brother Arthur, hard to miss towering over Abby. At 42, Arthur, tall, broad-shouldered, loomed in any room. With kind blue eyes, dark eyebrows, and trimmed chestnut hair, Arthur looked like Robert Redford if he happened to play football. Arthur was the fastidious accountant whose clothes were impeccably tailored and ready to have lunch with Wall Street at a moment's notice. He looked the opposite of Abby if not for their similar smiles.

The "accidental" third child, Ansel completed their sibling trio. Each different, each the same in many ways but only when together did all three feel whole. They had their roles. Abby cared for them, Arthur protected them, and Ansel adored them. He brought commitment and nonjudgmental love they both desperately needed in the wake of their parents' chaos. They were better together.

Abby and Arthur's expressions scared him. His brother and

sister looked tired, nervous, anxious and terrified. He waited for one or the other to say something. Instead, the doctors grew silent as he neared and Abby pointed with her eyes for Ansel to look inside the hospital room.

When he did, his heart fell. There were monitors beeping, the lines and tubes crisscrossed like an electrical nightmare. She was a limp body mass of wrinkled skin and sparse hair. Agnes Williams, their mother, the beauty and tyrant of their lives, pooled in the middle of a generic hospital bed. Stripped of all her power and life, her eyes were closed and her mouth rasping for breath. It was an unnatural sleep.

Agnes's stomach protruded like a basketball, out of proportion with her tiny frail limbs. *She looks so old*, Ansel thought, reminded of that awful moment in the movie *E.T.* when they found the alien gray and swollen in the river. He always hated that scene. But his mother wasn't gray, she was tinged a vulgar yellow. This was chronic liver failure. Ansel was seeing it for the first time and it was not some stupid hospital show. This was real life.

He thought if she was an animal they wouldn't be doing this right now, they would put an end to this. *It was impossibly cruel,* went through his mind, *no one should be alive like this*. He searched Abby and Arthur's faces with pleading eyes. Death was here, all around them, and it made Ansel colder than he could imagine. The siblings had never done death before – lots of other life-altering events, but not death.

"They cauterized the bleeding, and stabilized her," said Arthur, in his authoritative voice. "Apparently they can do that since she got here in time." Their mother had vomited a tremendous amount of blood the night before. The blood vessels in her throat had erupted because her liver was unable to function from scarring and damage. The liver diverted blood to smaller vessels, forcing them to erupt and bleed out. It was textbook.

"What does that mean?" Ansel croaked.

"They fixed her up and she's okay at the moment," said Abby, blowing hard out of her mouth.

"How is she okay?" said Ansel in disbelief. "Look at her. I mean look at her. How is she not dying right now?!" His voice was shaking. He pointed to his mother, lifeless in bed, and turned to the doctor, who was puffed up like superman, happy with the results.

"We've got your mother under control for the moment. We'll detox her from the alcohol and go from there. We are waiting on test results right now, but we are going to go ahead and say it's her liver. Lots of time, there can be some recovery from these situations. We just can't say right now. Starting a treatment program, changing lifestyles, there are lots of options given that she is willing," said the doctor smugly. His dainty little name tag read Dr. Adam Cooper. Ansel cringed at the doctor's thick tan shoes. He bet Dr. Cooper had a $4,000 mountain bike he only rode in the city. He irritated Ansel immediately.

"Oh you have got to be shitting me," said Ansel without masking his annoyance. "You mean this goddamn nightmare isn't ending right now? This is going to go on?" He was near tears. The three Williams siblings looked at each other and without saying it out loud, they all simultaneously thought *fuck*.

TWO

The story of the Williams family starts like any other. It's nothing special or out of the ordinary, just a string of rather normal events that resulted in some abnormal circumstances. Maybe it was the time, maybe the culture, the generation, but for whatever reason, the Williams story isn't far off from anyone else's – although perhaps it is tinged with more desperation and sadness than most. As a family, they carried on, made adjustments, improvements but mistakes as well, just like generations before them. This isn't an innovative story or particularly earth-shattering, but it is theirs and, in a strange way, ours.

We were all creatures once who rose from the sea and morphed into humans. Then humans became people who eventually socialized into colonies and shepherded themselves around the world. And not too long ago some disgruntled pilgrims dressed in burlap cloth and funny white and brown angular hats, climbed upon a sailing ship and left one old country to start a new country. On board that ship was Eli, 36, and Elizabeth, 19, Williams, now formerly of Surrey, England. Settling in Boston, Elizabeth dutifully provided her husband, a wealthy cargo trader, with five healthy children who went on to procreate and populate New England for generations.

Asher John Williams was born in 1945 to Eli and Mary Williams of Hartford, Connecticut. Eli, a mechanic by trade and Mary, a part-time secretary, welcomed their rosy cheeked son with the excitement of a to do list. The couple were not known for their personality but a resigned dutifulness to living exactly as told. They were New Englanders who carried on the hearty persona of their ancestors. They toiled. They went to work, paid their taxes, kept their two-bedroom clapboard house neat and intended to raise their only son Asher to be a quiet, obedient child.

But Asher was neither quiet nor obedient. From the moment he pulled himself up to walk on his first birthday, Asher created havoc wherever he went. He did so with an abandoned glee so foreign to the staunch Williamses they would lie in bed at night and wonder whether he was really theirs. Asher had an inherent intellect that made him curious and question everything and most of his questions were beyond the scope of his parents' ability to answer. *What's in a fingernail? How far does the galaxy go? How do crabs have babies?* As his vocabulary grew, so did Asher's taste for knowledge. The smartest thing Mary Williams did was go to the library and bring home volumes of the Encyclopedia Britannica. It kept young Asher quiet for a time. But he grew and grew more restless. Eli taught his son the finer points of car mechanics, hoping he could busy himself building car engines. But that wasn't enough. They signed him up for the track team when he was twelve and after he won every race quit a year later. He did the same for swimming the next year, and tennis after that. Nothing kept his attention. Then the girls started distracting him when

Asher's dirty blond hair and high cheekbones began to take shape on his slightly short but athletic body. He never did surpass six feet but confidence alone set him above the rest.

Mary worried. She knew Asher was intelligent but also very arrogant. Knowing he was the smartest in the room did not make him the kindest. He was impatient and gradually withdrew from his parents, not respecting or understanding their own limitations. Asher's disappointment in his father was palpable. Eli didn't wish for more money or more anything like Asher did, and that gave them little to nothing to talk about.

Asher turned industrious. Not wanting to be limited by his parents narrow view on the world, Asher found a way to provide for his own wants and needs. Mary wasn't stupid, she saw his new clothes and noticed the time spent away from home. He was earning money somehow, but she didn't want to ask, fearful the answer may lead to more problems. Instead she peppered the house with college applications, talked about college all the time as the best choice and Asher did not seem opposed. They discussed scholarship options but as Asher so quickly pointed out, he didn't want to be beholden to anyone for his education. He did not want limits or boundaries. Instead, he reassured his parents he would manage to pay for it, and he did.

Asher was different from other kids, he knew that. Ambition drove him toward a bigger picture. He didn't like to be confined to anyone or anything, or any social class. Asher loved his parents the best he could, but he didn't admire them. Unlike them, he read the newspaper daily, devoured television and sought ways to escape the confines of surburbia. The outside world felt big and glossy and he wanted a part of it, he wanted to be the one making it bigger and glossier. He studied men who were successful like Rockefeller and Ford, moguls. Even the word itself, mogul, felt attractive to Asher and he wanted to follow the step by step process to becoming one. First he needed a college education; he knew he couldn't do anything without that damn piece of paper.

Asher never wanted to be judged as the mechanic's son from the suburbs of Hartford. His plan was to save all his money during college for business school, one with a flashy name. He was already running a couple of scams in high school, getting kids beer and charging them double. He would steal from friends' medicine cabinets and sell their parents pills at triple the price. Ladies diet pills were just like speed. From selling petty drugs, Asher fell into an older crowd of less than upstanding gentlemen. From them, he learned to gamble, and gamble well. Poker came easy to him and he could win more often than not. Out in the hills of west Connecticut, tired husbands and desperate family men flocked to poker games for a quick fix hoping for a good night. Asher learned how to move from game to game, winning just enough to increase his own coffers. He learned never to feel guilty from whoever he beat out of their hard earned dollars. If they sat at the table then they were fair game.

That's how the great Asher Williams began. He felt flush, ready to become the man he always dreamed he would be: tailored, rich and, above all, respected. His philosophy set that there wasn't a fine line between truth and lies; it was just about what you believed. This would serve him well. The world was going to be his so when he kissed his parents goodbye in the fall of 1963 and entered the University of Connecticut, he felt invincible and didn't want to look back.

THREE

Arthur took the lead. Maybe it was his size or that he was the oldest, but Abby and Ansel obediently followed. Their big brother was the maypole they danced around with confidence and certainty. Most likely it was because of Arthur's quirks, his distinctive habits that they knew and loved. Since a child, he lay his pencils all facing the same direction on his desk and ordered his toys according to size and color. With religious certainty, Arthur made his bed, brushed his teeth and folded his clothes. He trimmed his nails and kept them neat and free of dirt. Outsiders would call him an old soul, but in the Williams house they joked about his tidiness and predictability. But it was exactly that, the idea he was the most predictable out all of them, that made them love him more. If Arthur was home, they felt better, like the day was going to go as planned without surprises or upset. If something bad happened, Arthur could fix it, put it back into order.

So his siblings followed him down the elevators and outside into the Connecticut dusk. It was a drizzling November night but they felt clearer outside than inside the hospital. The three instinctually took gulping breaths like they had come up for air.

With his soft manner and large peaceful eyes, his presence suggested there were answers to questions and order in the world. In the dim light they stood, looking to him for a solution that did not exist. Their mother was dying. They knew it without a doubt, but what were they supposed to do?

"What's the plan?" asked Arthur outside the hospital, his gaze going back and forth between Abby and Ansel. Ansel wrapped his arms around himself, shuddering at the thought of living through a Connecticut winter ever again. Florida warmth suited him fine. Opposite, Abby was comfortable with the chill and her foggy breath. Dreary days like this made her happy. She felt calm in the dullness.

"I've got to go home to the boys," responded Abby, foraging in her purse for her keys and avoiding eye contact with Ansel.

"How are they?" He said back too quickly.

"Fine. I'll come back tomorrow after I get them off to school." The chill emanating from her was worse than the wind.

"School already? Aren't they too young?" asked Ansel.

"It's Montessori, or in other words, expensive day care. They learn how to drink water instead of soda and make hug circles. But yes, they take them at two years old. Felix is two by the way." Abby shot out the last sentence.

"I know Felix is two, I sent him the trucks, remember? On his birthday, July 5."

"Yes, well I suppose I should thank you. *So thank you, Uncle Ansel.*" Abby would have spit venom along with the last two words if she could.

"Stop it Abs," said Arthur sternly. "Ansel will come home with me. I don't need you tar and feathering him right now. And we will meet back here tomorrow; doctors make rounds at 10."

Arthur, being Arthur, made the plan for them.

"Abby, how many times can I say I'm sorry, could you not be so Dad and let it go?" Ansel pleaded.

"You literally just insulted me while apologizing. How very *Mom* of you," Abby hissed.

"Enough, stop talking," said Arthur putting his hands on Ansel's shoulders and pushing him toward the shiny, black Mercedes.

"Smell you later, Ansie Pansy," Abby said loudly under breath.

Ansel cocked his head and sing songed, "Okaaaay, Crabby Abby."

"Good Christ," said Arthur "You two grow the fuck up."

———

Leaving the hospital, Abby only had a 20-minute drive home from Yale medical center to her house. She lived in a sleepy, quaint Connecticut village called Branton, with a town square that hosted Halloween and Christmas pageants. Large cities weren't Abby. Trees, grass, the rustle of leaves, that was her world. Peaceful. As she drove, Abby turned on her music. She missed being a teenager with a Diet Coke between her legs and a Camel Light drifting in her fingers. She always drove too fast, irritating anyone with her, and turned the volume up. She preferred singing in the car to talking on the phone, which no one did nowadays. Why did people even want to talk on the phone in a car? But the convenience of plugging her iPhone in instead of stabbing the car with broken cassettes or scratched CDs was really cool. It was all so easy. Playlists replaced albums and all her favorite songs were at her fingertips. Now, driving home the car filled with her favorites, Modern English, New Order and Yaz. The words familiar and comforting; it had been one helluva shit day.

Her own doctor's appointment had not gone well that morning. Dr. Santiago informed her bluntly she had a fibroid the size of a grapefruit seared up against her uterine wall. When he said grapefruit with his Spanish lilt, every part of her cringed. How could something have been growing in her for that long to become that big? *Gross.* He informed her it wasn't urgent but she should think about a hysterectomy. Abby was only 40 but that made her feel old, and she hated the idea of surgery. Like her brother, Ansel, hospitals freaked her out. When she had her two boys she could not believe she made it through each and every hospital visit. Thank god for C sections because the drugs were fantastic.

After hearing the news, Abby cried in her car. She felt tired and defeated, the idea of surgery like a wet wool blanket on her brain. The kids needed her, her mother needed her, Jake needed her. How was she going to deal with this shit now? The universe had a funny way of piling it on.

Moments later, Yale medical center called. Her mother had called 911 while bleeding out on her bathroom floor. She had been vomiting blood profusely but they got it under control. If a telephone had not been near, Abby would be talking to the funeral home instead of them. Forgetting her own news , she raced to her mother, Agnes' pain trumping all else.

Ansel was right: when would this nightmare end? Their tormenting, alcoholic mother chain-smoking Parliaments with the demeanor of Joan Crawford seemingly was meant to walk the earth forever *Jesus Christ, get off the ride lady. Get off the fucking ride,* Abby screamed in her head.

"Hi, I'm home," she tried to say cheerily walking through her front door. Two-year-old Felix in a diaper was sitting in his toddler chair on the coffee table. He had a lollipop and was watching Bubble Guppies giggling. He turned and smiled, "Hi

Mama!!!!" Taking in the magnitude of his happiness, Abby almost cried. To be her son, she would kill to be her son. His brother, Eli, 4, was sprawled like a starfish on the carpet surrounded by the countless Matchbox cars their father bought from the grocery store. Her kids were in such bliss, boyhood spread out before them like a buffet of wonder. Their world was such a miracle compared to hers.

Her husband, Jake, rushed toward her. He was only wearing boxers and an apron and enveloped her in a bear hug before she could shut the front door. At least she had them, was all she could think. She had them and they were everything.

She met Jake O'Conner her junior year abroad when she was only 21. They both happened to be from the University of Connecticut and both spending a semester in Rome. The organization threw the weary-eyed students in a dank Italian hotel after their first overseas flight. About 30 kids from all over the U.S. huddled confused and Jake stood quietly next to Abby smiling.

"You go to U Conn?" he asked.

"Yes, you too?" she looked bewildered but so did everyone else. Her hair was in a messy bun and she was biting her nails.

"I think we were in a calculus class? Freshman year?" Jake was seeing if she remembered him but she didn't.

"Oh god, I hated calculus, who was that, Mr. Reynolds, he was such a douche." She smiled brightly at him and Jake melted. He had a crush on her then and now. Four months in Rome wasn't going to be great; it was going to change his life and he knew it. They fell in love over pizza and chianti and ancient ruins. Abby would always look back on those few months as the most perfect in her life. She was young, in love but more importantly she was the farthest from her family she had ever been.

"I'm okay," Abby reassured Jake, whose brow was furrowing harder than a Shar-Pei. He went back to the kitchen, where pots were stewing on the stove with pasta, and poured her a glass of wine. Jake did what she liked best about him. He waited patiently for her to tell him everything.

"You have to have the surgery immediately," Jake said seriously. "We don't know what will happen with Agnes and you have to be prepared. This could go on with her and we can't let your health suffer. Think about the boys." *Not fair,* thought Abby. There wasn't anything either Jake or Abby wouldn't do for Felix and Eli. She would have to have surgery for them. She hung her head and sipped her wine. Her mother was dying, albeit slow as molasses, she had a grapefruit in her uterus, her kids needed her, the wet wool blanket was smothering.

"Ansel is home," Abby told Jake. He waited and said, "Then this shit between you two needs to end now."

"I know, I know," said Abby as she lowered head on the countertop. It was the first time she had spoken to her brother in almost two years. *Ugh,* she thought, *could things get any worse?*

FOUR

For all of Arthur's calm personality his actual demeanor was kinetic. His leg tapped whenever he sat. His fingers drummed while he worked. He liked to play solitaire on his phone while watching television. It was in his rhythms that his heart pumped blood, he could not stop. The fidgeting drove people crazy, so he worked alone; in fact he spent most of his time alone. Arthur didn't care, he preferred it. But when Arthur slipped behind the wheel of his S Class Mercedes, his body went lank and limp. Arthur loved his car, it was an extension of him. Driving eased and comforted him like no other drug. His body stopped moving and allowed the highest rated engine in all the world do the work. It was the only true luxury he allowed himself. He purposely opened an office 45 minutes from his house just so every morning he could take the Merritt Parkway, and go up and down the Connecticut countryside at unnatural speeds.

"You look good," he said.

"Why? Did I look like shit last time?" Ansel laughed.

"No, you know what I mean," Arthur rolled his eyes. "So what did you think about Mom?"

"Holy shit, that was fucking awful! How has it gotten that bad? Christ, I was just here a few months ago. And how is she going to make it? Did you see her? She's a goddamn corpse. And what's with the doctor? 'She could find the road to recovery' uuuum, maybe he didn't read the fucking chart? I don't think someone who has been to rehab countless times before 62 is exactly going to change her ways. No, our mother will wake up and hand her Amex card to an orderly for a pack of smokes and some fucking cheap vodka. And what did they say about the cancer?"

"Confirmed, no cancer." replied Arthur.

"Knew it! Knew it! Knew it! Mom's greatest scam: masking high grade alcoholism with breast cancer. I wouldn't be surprised if she ran a meth lab somewhere in her sunroom." Ansel was bouncing in the passenger seat with fury. He was always so passionate and expressive about everything. If he was cut off in traffic a litany of sarcasm ranging from political views to social commentary all came into play based on make and model of the offending car. But Arthur, being Arthur, remained calm at the wheel. He loved his little brother to death for saying everything he never let himself even think. Their mother had scammed them with cancer.

Two years ago, Agnes found a lump in her left breast and had it removed. It actually felt rather ordinary since the huge advancements in breast cancer. It seemed a manageable problem. Abby went with her for the lumpectomy and had to inform the doctors of her tendency to not embellish but diminish her health problems. No, her mother did not smoke one or two cigarettes a day, try one or two packs. No, she didn't have one or two drinks a day, but one or two bottles. They were quite grateful for the truth.

But after the surgery, by all claims successful, their mother began to spin a weird web of half truths about her recovery. Agnes claimed she didn't need radiation or chemo but then said she was taking a pill version. She blamed the medication for her memory loss, vomiting and sleeping at odd hours. It made sense to those who saw her, she was looking worse and worse. But her stories kept changing. She told people the cancer had come back, she told people it was gone. She even went so far as to say it was in her back because her back ached. Everyone got a different version. But when Abby or Arthur or Ansel questioned what an actual doctor had said, Agnes would clam up. Her answers were vague or she would claim the doctors were wrong. Undeniably, the drinking got progressively worse. Not until today did Arthur finally understand. It was then, when she had the lump, the doctors most likely told her she would go into liver failure if she didn't stop drinking. Four years ago, while being poked and prodded for a lump, they warned her. They gave her a life ultimatum and she chose. It was her choice now to be in a hospital like this. Her choice to be found bleeding out on the bathroom floor, her choice to let her body decay, her choice to die. It hurt Arthur that he had not realized this before; this, above all, would go down as his mother's greatest contrivance.

Arthur's intelligence presented itself early. His mother put blocks with numbers before him as a teetering three-year-old and he would not only arrange them sequentially but also in various patterns like triangles and circles. Numbers wave his second language. Instead of reading books like "Goodnight Moon" and "Harold and the Purple Crayon," he and Agnes practiced flash cards with addition and subtraction. It was clear from the start how to connect with Arthur. He took the guesswork out of it for everybody, to the great relief of his parents. Arthur's natural ability with numbers got him all the way to Harvard Business School. Now he had his own company as an "asset manager". A money watch dog for the very elite and wealthy, responsible for estates worth well into the millions. Arthur hated risk, worked alone, and charged his clients a fortune. He rarely made mistakes in his business.

Arthur's personal life was another story. Eighteen years ago, when just 24, Arthur married Janine Burkowsky. She was a pretty, bubbly girl from a solid middle-class background. Set up on a blind double date, Janine came on strong and Arthur let her. Opinionated, high-strung women didn't intimidate him, that was what he grew up with – his mother. Janine had the same take charge quality. Arthur probably should have assessed the situation better: if someone had flat out said to him *you are about to marry your mother*, maybe he would have heeded the warning. But because Arthur rarely dated, because he was quiet and thoughtful and full of so many odd traits, and had the tendency to acquiesce, he thought Janine was a good deal. He thought anyone who could put up with him alphabetizing the refrigerator was good enough for him. And Janine was attractive, so there was that.

They married six months into their relationship and Janine promptly became pregnant. Their married life began smoothly until their son Harry was born. Her pregnancy was normal and their son, bless him, actually came on his due date. For Arthur, who liked to plan and schedule their lives, he was immensely pleased his son was already honoring his father's exactitude. Arthur was not in the room when Harry came; he wasn't one for that kind of intimacy. Janine insisted she could handle it on her own, not wanting her husband to see her in such a state. It's old-fashioned, but they both were more than comfortable with being apart for Harry's debut.

Their son was a perfect eight pounds and came out loudly crying loudly. It was the most relief Janine had ever felt. The months of waiting to make sure everything would be okay is a struggle for any new mom. The sound of his bellowing cry was music to an exhausted Janine. Until she saw the frantic movements of the doctors and nurses and instinctually, like any mother, knew something was wrong. She searched her newborn son's purplish face and thought he looked as expected. But as the nurse cradled her son and began to wrap him in a towel, Janine saw what frightened the doctors.

Harry had no left hand. His arm past his stubby elbow was just a malformed lump. It resembled a dull pencil tip. Janine quickly looked and saw his other hand and two feet and was relieved, but what had happened? Janine panicked, saying nothing as they checked him and lay him in her arms. He was perfect in every way and confusion clouded her face.

The doctor explained Harry had a congenital limb defect. He asked and no, she had not taken Thalidomide, the drug that caused birth defects in babies. She had not smoked or drank during her pregnancy.

Janine barely remembers the doctor saying, "There was a disruption in the womb" and "a small percentage of children … limbs can develop abnormally."

Immediately, Janine wanted Arthur. She wanted him to come and fix this, make this stop happening. Make her son whole and complete and not handicapped. She cried as she felt his fragile limb and looked at his beautiful sleeping face.

The nurse soothed Janine and assured her, her baby would have a normal happy life, but Janine could only feel the bottom fall out from her.

For Arthur, who was in the waiting room, he also remembered the doctor and his formal explanation about amniotic bands and percentages of deficits in children.

Still, he ran to Janine, anxious to see his son.

For Arthur, it didn't matter. When he saw Harry wrapped

in a bundle, with his tiny striped cap, nothing but pride swelled in him. His only concern was that every other part of Harry was healthy. He would buy him a damn hand if he needed to. He asked the nurse over and over if Harry was okay, would there be anything else wrong? She smiled kindly, and said no, not until he was a teenager. It took Arthur a second to get the joke. But he smiled and rubbed the stub of Harry's arm like it was a good luck charm. He had a son and that was all that mattered.

Harry's arm was the first crack in their marriage. Although Janine would never admit it, she always felt the defect was her fault. Everyone assured her, even Arthur, it was just the luck of the draw. But it changed Janine, it plagued her. She refused to have more children and Arthur couldn't help but also feel cautious and respect her decision. He was more practical than optimistic. But for Janine, who had planned a house full of children, it was a shift. Her life had changed direction toward a place she never planned on going and her personality followed suit.

Arthur finished business school and they moved back to Connecticut. He opened his financial office and through some client recommendations from his father, the money slowly began to rain on the younger Williams family. Arthur was able to buy them a large colonial house in Fairfield. Harry attended the finest private schools and was a perfectly normal boy in every respect.

Arthur and Janine were used to explaining Harry's situation to other parents, used to the looks and stares, and used to the fact it was beyond their control.

But Janine manifested her disappointment in a different fashion. With the money coming in, she upgraded not only her wardrobe but her breasts, nose and overall identity as well. Janine realized she liked money and liked to spend it. Sweet Janine turned into another version of the older Mrs. Williams, who demanded life be at her disposal. She forced Arthur to join country clubs he never used and vacations he never wanted to take. Janine loved wine lunches with the ladies. She was a good mother but a distant one. As if she had broken her son once and was terrified to do it again.

Years passed and Arthur remained Arthur - quiet, thoughtful, buried in his work. Opposite, Janine grew restless, argumentative, and resented Arthur's steady nature. But for Harry, Arthur was a fantastic attentive father. Nothing gave Arthur more pleasure than coming home and sitting on the floor building Legos with his son. His patience for Harry was a vast pool that had been built from reservoirs of his childhood.

Asher and Agnes demanded their older child handle life with an unwavering calm, and Harry benefitted. While Janine mothered on autopilot, came and went as she pleased, Harry became loyally attached to his father. All of Arthur's kindness and assurance was magnified in Harry. Thus Harry was by far the most favored Williams descendant, the best of all of them.

"How's Janine? Hasn't run off with the yard guy yet?" joked Ansel.

"No, unfortunately. And don't say it.."

"When are you going to div…"

"Ansel, I know I am a pussy. It just feels like a lot of paperwork and with Mom the way she is, I just can't deal right now."

"Harry wants you to, he's told me it would be the best thing for all of you. He's worried you're wasting your life with her."

"He's right. She did give me him though. Too bad that wasn't a surrogacy situation," said Arthur.

Ansel laughed, he loved his brother's wit. Too bad he didn't use it enough.

"Speaking of Harry, I have apologized to Abby enough. She is being so damn stubborn."

"You're right. It's the Dad in her," said Arthur, who unconsciously sped up when speaking about his father.

Two years ago when Abby was pregnant with Felix, Ansel made a big mistake. He flew up from Miami for Harry's 15th birthday and took Arthur and Harry on an exclusive five star fly-fishing trip in Canada. He did not invite Abby or Jake, but to be fair she was heavily pregnant. But worse, he never went over to say hello when he came up that week. Abby found out about the trip after the fact and blew up about how Harry was his favorite and how Eli didn't even remotely get his attention. Which was absolutely true. Ansel always had a soft spot for Harry who, again to be fair, had been his only nephew for 13 years. It wasn't about Harry's arm, or lack of one, it was Harry's spirit. He was so easy-going; life had knocked him down early on and he already knew how to get back up again. The kid was ahead of the game. So Ansel did everything he could to be around Harry and when the art gallery was making money, he wanted to treat his favorite nephew to a guys' trip. Not telling Abby, or at least going over with some form of gift for Eli, or even seeing him, was a big mistake. Abby went dark on him, like dark dark. No phone calls, no emails, no contact. It didn't stop Ansel from sending birthday and Christmas gifts, but his sister was like a polar ice cap. He could only hope she would eventually melt.

They pulled into Arthur's house. It was late, but Harry was there to greet them. Janine called out from the bedroom a quick hello.

"She can't even come downstairs?" Ansel looked pitifully at his brother.

"What can I say? You're not everyone's favorite," said Arthur, laughing at his own joke.

FIVE

It was the spring of 1965 when Asher, bored out of his mind, was sitting in his Economy 101 class. He was 20, full of himself and skating through college courses without even trying. Girls came and went, and so did the money, through various scams, cons and schemes. He was firmly earning and paying for his right to be bored in the classroom. He was arrogant, young and knew anything could happen.

And just like that, the classroom's metal door creaked open and a girl with yellow hair, round face and dimples strolled across the room and took a seat. She was dressed in a fashionable peasant blouse and colorful feathers decorated her hair. Asher's curiosity was piqued. She fiddled with her bag and swung her leg like she was bored too. *Well hello, kindred spirit!* he thought. Professor Brown paid no attention to the girl. Which was odd, because the old professor was irritated by most of the student body's petty habits like gum chewing or whispering. When class ended, the girl stayed. While students filed out, she tapped her leg, impatiently waiting.

Asher made no move to leave.

"Son, do you have somewhere to be?" Professor Brown called to the empty classroom. Asher pretended to fumble and responded *yes, yes*. The girl was now standing by the Professor and unpacking sandwiches, they were going to have lunch. *How intriguing* thought Asher, *the cranky professor with this fairly young girl.*

"Umm Professor Brown, sir?" he purposely positioned himself in front of the pair on his way out. "What percent of the grade is the midterm?" It was the only thing Asher could think of to ask. "25%, Williams, now go away, I'm hungry."

Asher quickly turned toward the blonde, "Hi. Asher, Asher Williams." She smiled with a row of perfectly aligned white teeth and beautiful blue eyes. Her dimples like moons bookmarking her smile, she looked him in the eye and said coolly, "Agnes."

Asher spent the rest of the semester looking for Agnes somewhere, anywhere on campus. He came early to Professor Brown's class early and left late, always disappointed. No one knew a girl named Agnes, but he didn't dare ask the professor, who would accuse him of being nosy.

It wasn't until the next fall that Asher would find Agnes again. Taking Brown's Econ 201 this time, he was pushing his business studies. It was junior year and Asher was doubling down, set on going to Harvard Business School. Wanting an A, he would check in with Professor Brown during office hours in hopes of correcting any potential mistake.

One Thursday, Asher showed up at his office and a note on the door read. *Twisted ankle come to my house, 40 Grove Avenue but not after 5!!* Asher knew Grove was two blocks away from campus and headed to the professor's house. Knocking on the door, the last person he expected to open it was Agnes. A smile spread across Asher's face, it was the same one that appeared when he won at poker.

Agnes Brown was the 18-year-old daughter of Professor Sidney Brown, a tenured professor at University of Connecticut. When Professor Sidney Brown received such distinction, simultaneously, Agnes's mother ran away and was never to be seen again. To be fair, Sidney had met her mother, Joanie, at a bar where she was waitressing. Without even a high school diploma, she had no idea what the life of academia was like. Joanie quickly grew bored with Sidney and motherhood in general, too young to be tied to a house and a toddler just steps away from a college campus. She took off with a wannabe country singer she met in the grocery store when Agnes was just five.

So it was just Agnes and the professor that fateful night Asher knocked. He couldn't believe his luck.

"Staying for dinner?" she asked him in the professor's study, as if there was no question.

"I assume the boy has better places to be, Aggie," her father said without looking up.

"No, I actually don't. I'll stay, that sounds great." The professor peered at him over the tops of his glasses, not breaking his stare. "It would be a nice change from campus food," Asher said grinning.

"Mmph," the professor relented and Agnes just smiled and went into the kitchen to make dinner.

When they were done studying, dinner was ready. Asher giddily swallowed without tasting. Agnes led the dinner conversation like a composer. She asked Asher thoughtful questions. She got him to reveal his business dreams and he sounded ambitious, independent and attractive in every way.

It turns out Agnes had started freshmen year at U Conn. And in turn, she talked about where she ate lunch, what classes and what times they were and loved going to the concerts on campus. Also, she hated that she couldn't live in the dorms but her father would not let her. Every detail like a trail of bread crumbs for Asher to follow. He read her clues immediately. She was giving him a map on how to find her on campus. She was a sneaky girl and beautiful to look at; he had to press hard on his erection forming under the table. He looked at Professor Brown who had mashed potatoes in his beard and that did the trick.

Then the hunt began. Every day was a challenge to find Agnes. Once he got into the swing of things, Asher was like a sharp shooter. He could pinpoint exactly when she would be in line for lunch so he could join her or walk with her across campus to a class. They spent more and more time together and the professor barely noticed.

Agnes was rebellious in a deliciously smart way. She didn't need to hurt or worry her only parent, didn't need to kick and scream for her freedom. Agnes navigated it, worked within her limitations. She loved her father but, like her mother, she wanted more than the life of academia.

She saw herself in Asher, ambitious and craving more than their parents had to offer. The world was a giant feast that she and Asher should enjoy while their youth and looks were enough currency to get them started.

"Aggie," Asher would say and stare at her. Then he would put his hand to her cheek just to feel her soft skin.

"What can I do for you Asher, Asher Williams," she would giggle, teasing about how Asher always introduced himself to people. He said repeating his first name made people remember it. He wanted to be remembered.

"What do you think about New York City? It seems everything is happening there, and that's where I need to be. I don't think I even want to go to Harvard any more. Boston just isn't the place. I feel like I gotta get in on the ground floor in New York. I'm thinking about business school there, forget Harvard."

Agnes knew well enough not to say *what about me?* Instead she said, "New York is so exciting. Magical. I went once with Dad and I fell in love with it. I think you should absolutely be there." That's what Asher wanted to hear and kissed Agnes hard.

"What would I do without you, Aggie? You are just like a star I can make a wish on." And Asher meant that, he truly believed Agnes was one of the pieces in his life he needed to fall into place.

It was an easy relationship. Agnes, a smart girl, had studied her father's own narcissism and penchant for selfishness and just imagined Asher's to be the same. Men just wanted to be men, do what they want, when they wanted and not be overly questioned for it. Agnes had spent her whole childhood altering her life to her father's needs and wants. His attention was focused on his academic life more than her life of Barbies and tea parties. In this way Agnes learned how to fend for herself without waiting, wondering when he would pay attention to her again.

It was the same with Asher. She let him study, run his scams, keep the rhythm of his life while managing to fold her into it without much upheaval. When he wanted her there, she was there; when he didn't, she went off and did her own thing. But this was all calculated. Agnes was in it for the long term. Without a doubt in her mind, Agnes knew that Asher Williams would, first and foremost, become a very wealthy person and, second, take her places she could never dream as a professor's daughter. In order to ensure Asher did not exclude her on his trajectory to bigger and better things, Agnes devised a plan.

Agnes was a strategist. While her father stuck his head into books during her childhood, Agnes learned the art of planning. At six she planned her outfits, by ten she planned her own birthday parties, at twelve she understood what a reputation meant. Agnes constantly calculated where and when she would be with precision.

She never dated the wrong guy or marked the wrong girl as her best friend. She did enough school work to never be questioned, but she also never stood out. She was home when her father was home so he never questioned her whereabouts but when Agnes was free, her freedom was measured so that she would never have to compromise it.

No one was ever going to run away from her again.

Agnes got pregnant Asher's senior year just before graduation. Although they had talked about marriage, Asher thought that would be later and was surprised by the baby. But Agnes had a way with him, flashing her blue eyes, giddy with excitement that made him relent and be happy. The professor was not happy at all, knowing full well his daughter was about to drop out of college. But there was little he could do to change his daughter's mind.

The professor didn't realize her foresight began long ago, that fateful day when five-year-old Agnes caught her mother packing a suitcase. Every detail of that day was as vivid as a marquee and seared into Agnes's memory like a brand. She had watched as her mother fluffed up her hair in a cloud of Aqua Net and reapplied her coral lipstick that matched her shift dress. For little Agnes, watching her mother primp was like watching a star before a show.

When the knock came on the door, Agnes's mother jumped and grabbed her suitcase, grinning. Before she left, she leaned down and looked Agnes in the eye while holding Agnes's chin between manicured nails. Her mother's last words were, "Do what you want, baby girl, don't let anyone else tell you what to do, okay? Take what you want and don't apologize. People will be all right, you're gonna be all right. It's your life, baby girl, and no one else's. Remember that."

Her mother shut the front door hastily and without looking

ran down the front steps to a waiting car. Agnes watched from the picture window and waved but her mother didn't wave back. She could see a man's hat as the car drove away. Her mother never turned around. When the professor returned home and found a note Agnes would never see, his response was to make dinner and never speak of her mother again.

Perhaps that's why children are so adaptable; they are forced to be for survival. For Agnes, the abandonment by her mother, the sheer savagery of her parents turning her world upside down from one hour to the next was Agnes's most important life lesson. She would need to be able to fend for herself, but also maintain control where and when foreseeable. She would be the one to wear the hat and drive the car.

A week after Asher graduated *summa cum laude* with an acceptance letter to New York University's MBA program, Agnes, with a slight belly, put on a loose white dress and coerced him to a Hartford courthouse on a sunny June day. The world felt impossibly large and exciting to the young couple. Agnes assured Asher it was meant to be and it would be wonderful. His own arrogance had no doubt.

It was on a rainy November day in 1967 when Arthur Williams came faster than a subway train in New York City. Literally, by the time swollen Agnes stepped off the F train at the hospital she barely made it through the hospital doors before Arthur appeared on a hospital gurney in the ER. Asher, who was in class at the time, would find out later his wife had a healthy baby boy weighing a hefty nine pounds. They were waiting for him at the hospital.

"I named him Arthur," she told Asher. "Having a name starting with A will put him at the top of every list; people will think of him first."

"But our name is Williams," he laughed at her logic.

"I don't care, he's going to be the first always."

"If you say so, love." Asher kissed her.

Agnes smiled and wept. Arthur was perfect. Asher couldn't help but be proud and vowed to double down on his studies. He wasn't just going to build a career but an empire for this family.

In Agnes's mind, everything was going as planned.

SIX

"Well, why can't I have wine for breakfast?" Abby said under her breath. "If anyone deserves wine for breakfast, it would be me." She was tired, really tired. The boys kept her up last night.

Eli had a nightmare and called for her, which then woke Felix up. Both boys were upset so she had get into one bed sandwiched between the two. Everyone always talks about sleeping with their kids but Abby thought it was a nightmare. Legs and arms kicked and bruised her. The boys breathed, hard hot breaths, and her body temperature would rise smashed between the two. Then she would think of Jake sprawled in their queen size bed and his inability to hear any of the situation two rooms over. He slept like a man with no worries. Then Abby would lie awake, resentful, her blood pressure bouncing and not sleeping. Somewhere around 5 a.m., she managed to extract herself and go back to her room, annoyed at having to push Jake off her side of the bed. She was in a foul mood.

"Can you take them to school?" Abby said curtly, without

looking up from the lunch boxes she was making.

They were not allowed to use peanuts or peanut products or anything with yellow dye number five or taste. Her poor boys had to subsist on string cheese and multigrain crackers because apparently Maria Montessori really had a thing against Cheetos and a PB&J sandwich, Abby's favorite childhood lunch. Now Eli won't eat peanut butter because at four years old he thinks he is allergic to peanuts because no one can have them at school. Thanks, Maria, and whoever made kids allergic to peanut dust.

Jake didn't respond immediately. She knew he was weighing his options, assessing the potential damage of his answer. He wanted to say he had a busy morning and point out Abby usually did this particular chore. But given the no-sleep factor, Agnes in hospital and giant fruit-sized object setting up house in her uterus, Jake caught himself.

"Sure, honey, whatever you need." They both let out an audible sigh, marital strife averted. "Can I ask, how are you going to handle the Ansel situation?"

Here was the problem: both Jake and Abby loved Ansel. Abby and Ansel couldn't have been closer as brother and sister, for years they called each other obsessively, talked about everything and proclaimed themselves the best siblings ever. Ansel could cheer Abby up, take her out of dark places, make her feel whole and normal in ways Jake never could. And Jake accepted that, happy to have the help because honestly, Abby was hard headed and just as hard to read sometimes. Plus, Jake liked Ansel.

He was Jake's only male friend who didn't force him to watch sports. They would actually talk about movies and books they liked and drank martinis. Jake loved the fact Ansel made him more of a male grown up. In Connecticut there were two types of men, business-suit-wearing who worked in New York City making up the "gold coast," or flannel loving New England men who drank beer and watched the game. Jake was somewhere in between.

"I think it's time we put this Ansel thing to bed, he fucked up, okay. But it's been two years," pleaded Jake.

"Well, it hurt. When I had kids Ansel acted like it was nothing. Like nothing I do is any big deal, all about them, the brothers."

"Okay, now don't kill me," Jake moved his arm over his face in protective stance. "But maybe, just maybe, it had a little bit more to do with Aggie than with the guys. Remember that was when the incident at the club happened and you had to go and deal with it? I think you were pissed off that Arthur and Ansel were leaving you with Aggie's messes. You never told them about most of it, so then the burden was on you and then you get mad because they were having fun...and you see where I am going with this." Jake said without sarcasm.

Abby was jabbing goldfish into reusable pouches and remembering her mother. She was seven months pregnant, up with a two-year-old every night, and she was the one picking up Agnes from the police station, not her brothers.

Agnes had been handcuffed at the country club for throwing a steak knife in the vicinity of Mrs. Tuttle, widow of James Tuttle, founder of The United Adoption Services of America. Basically, their mother chucked a Ginsu knife at the Mother Teresa of orphans. Agnes claimed it was an accident but the incident was in a long line of incidents fueled by her drinking. The Southport Country Club had been looking for an excuse to expel the untameable Agnes Williams, but due to the family's great fortune and reputation needed to do so without a shred of doubt in the community. It would be best if Mrs. Williams no longer used the dining services, a letter later read. She had been a member for 30 years.

Shoving the wholesome lunches into bags made of hemp and soy and bee pollen, Abby joked, she could admit now that her mother was the catalyst of her blow-up with Ansel. He was so free from it all down in Miami and she was jealous. He wasn't a Williams down there, he was an art gallery owner dating hot guys and not scraping his mother off the floor on a Friday night. He still didn't even know about her third DUI that resulted in an ankle bracelet and Abby driving her mother to the store for over a year. Arthur didn't have time for such things.

Abby felt like her brothers pigeonholed her into being their mother's caretaker. So when her own children came along, she hit a breaking point. Instead of telling Arthur and Ansel to step it up when it came to babysitting their mother, Abby just blew up. She had been pregnant after all, lots of raging hormones. She remembered calling Ansel a narcissistic asshole and Arthur, King Arthur – a moniker he had always hated. She was pissed and tired and fed up, a lot like now. But she hadn't been entirely wrong, just hurt – and hurt people do stupid things.

Now the siblings were together again and in a worse situation. Abby needed to apologize, maybe explain why she was so angry and that it wasn't really the fishing trip. She felt Jake's hands on her shoulders, rubbing her neck.

"No goldfish have been harmed in the making of this lunch," joked Jake.

Abby felt relief having made a decision. She knew what had to be done and she would do it.

"I really think wine for breakfast should be acceptable."

"Organic wine in a recyclable bottle of course, Montessori approved," Jake smiled.

—

Abby, Arthur, and Ansel sat in the teal chairs outside of their mother's hospital room. The air was chilly and there was an endless alarm situation going on in the other geriatric rooms. The atmosphere was all very needy and stressful. Blood pressures were dropping, small seizures, someone needed a Jell-o, then a red light went on over the door and beeping would ensue.

Agnes was still in the not-sleep-but-not-quite-a-coma state. Her tubes pulsated with liquids going in and coming out. Wired stickers stuck to her frail body, emitting sounds and signals on monitors with numbers that looked like the Stock Exchange. Her heart rate varied, her oxygen level varied, the whole system of the human body appeared delicate and imbalanced. Tufts of her blond hair lay flat and greasy. Her usually plump face was sallow and withdrawn. Her arms and legs were peppered with age spots and skin as transparent as tissue paper. Her stomach was a gross protruding mass that made Abby think of her fibroid.

"So we wait here for the doctors? Do we have the same Superman or do we have an option to pick and choose?" asked Ansel, who already had it out for Dr. Cooper, or Super Cooper as he had been dubbed.

"Let's wait and see what we get with rounds," said Arthur evenly.

"Why does everyone in here look like a doppelgänger?" questioned Abby. "Look over there, that nurse looks like Julia Sugarbaker from *Designing Women*."

"Ooh, I see Dorothy from the *Golden Girls*," Ansel chimed in, pointing to a tall, gray-haired woman at the nurses station.

"Really, do you two have to do this now?" said Arthur, patronizing.

"Just because you don't like TV and can't play, or have fun, or remove the abacus from your ass, doesn't mean we have to be bored to tears by your adultness," teased Ansel.

It was true Arthur was too serious and never liked regular TV. He watched old Westerns like a 90-year-old man, unlike Abby and Ansel, who devoured TV. Characters and shows immediately became their best friends growing up, and they loved to annoy Arthur talking about it.

"Look, George Clooney, circa *Facts of Life*, not *ER*," Ansel pointed so Abby could see.

"For Pete's sake," sighed Arthur. Luckily, a group of doctors was rounding the corner and they all sat a little straighter hoping it was their turn.

The greasy Dr. Cooper was back, along with a smaller, older woman with kind eyes and pretty shoes named Dr. Moore, and three younger, obvious residents looking eager and shiny. Ansel fought the urge to smack one of them for fun.

They discussed Agnes. There hadn't been much improvement since she was brought in; her oxygen levels had stabilized and now she was in the throes of detox.

"Cirrhosis is a medical term you may have never heard of, it's the liver going into acute failure," the patronizing tone of Dr. Cooper stunned his audience. "Are any of you familiar with AA?" When none of them answered he said slower, drawing out the syllables, "It's called Al..co..hol..ics A..no..ny...mous?"

Ansel looked like someone had just served him fecal matter on a platter. Abby rolled her eyes so badly she almost fell against the wall and even Arthur brought his palms up to rub his eyes needing a moment to compose himself.

"Doctors, as we have tried to explain, our mother is a known alcoholic. She has been in and out of treatment centers for three decades. A.A. was like a trip to the theater, very entertaining but she thought very little about it after the show was over. She has zero desire to be sober," Arthur said evenly.

Super Cooper interrupted, "But now that she knows her life

is in jeopardy, we find patients can have a change of heart." Ansel gasped so loudly even Dorothy from the *Golden Girls* looked up from the nurses station.

"That would re…qui…re she act…u…ally have a heart," said Ansel said as slowly as humanly possible.

Abby held her hand up to Ansel and took over, "Tell us about her liver. What happens now?"

Dr. Moore gave an eye signal to Dr. Cooper to be quiet, "Well, it's in failure. And given what you have said about her history, she would not be approved for a donor. At this point, it is deteriorating, but at what speed we cannot say for certain. It could be a month or it could be two weeks, or two years."

"Two bloody years!" Ansel yelped.

"Yes, unfortunately these circumstances, we just can't give you anything more than that." Dr. Moore tried to deliver the blows softly.

"But this gives your mother an opportunity to make a change!" Cooper could not let this go as the three Williams children glared at him like he was an outstanding idiot.

"So what now?" asked Arthur, only speaking to Dr. Moore.

"Well, detox will take a few days. We've got her heavily sedated so she won't feel the worst of it. Then, depending on how the body is processing oxygen, if we can take her off of it, and if she's stable and coherent, she can go home."

"Like this?!" Ansel's emotions were not helping, Abby shushed him.

"I know it looks bad but the body can do amazing things when given time to heal. For right now we wait and see. Now is the time to discuss palliative care."

"I don't want to sound stupid but what is palliative care?" asked Ansel, to the relief of Abby, who also didn't know.

"That's okay. So palliative is care for long-term illnesses that may take a while, or hospice. There are minor differences between the two but there are options. We aren't there quite yet. Let's just get Agnes out the woods first."

The residents just stood there as though watching a tennis match, their heads bobbing back and forth. Abby could read their thoughts; they were grateful not to be in their shoes. Now she wanted to smack one of them as well.

After the doctors left, the siblings felt defeated. No news wasn't always good news. They had wanted something more concrete like yes, your mother is dying and this nightmare will be over in exactly two weeks, three days, 40 minutes and 21 seconds, *there you go.* Instead they were in freefall not knowing what to do or how to do it. Without their mother's guidance, instructing them, comforting them, they felt childlike. They were lost.

But they spoke too soon, forgetting they had another parent. Barreling down the hallway, coming toward them like it was the Pentagon and he was their chief, was Asher Williams.

"Oh Christ, who told Dad?!" Abby said fiercely under her breath.

"Sorry, it was me. I drank Arthur's gin and got all drunk and weepy and wanted to tell him because he's the asshole who put us all in this. To be fair, I just texted," said Ansel as fast as he could. "Oh shit, I fucked up, I'm sorry," he got out before Asher planted himself right in front of his three children.

Asher, with his full head of thick gray hair, chiseled cheeks that seemed far too tan for November and clear eyes, was huffing and puffing. They could smell his expensive French cologne, and his bright Hermes sweater and shiny Italian shoes stood out like he was Nancy Reagan in a pawn shop.

"Hi Dad," they all said in unison.

"Why in the good goddamn didn't any of you so smart children let me know what is good god's name is going on with your mother?!" Asher nearly shouted.

They didn't respond. He followed their gaze and looked inside Agnes's room. Usually the man was never at a loss for words, but he stopped short and hung his head. The crush of emotions was visible, from fear to sadness to shock. He turned and said, "Fuck," then "You three all right?"

"Yeah, we're fine, Dad," Arthur said, defusing the situation.

"Well, what in the hell did the doctors say? She gonna come out of this? Do I need to move her? I know this is Yale and all, but if she needs better doctors I can get them for her. Is it the cancer?"

Ansel snorted. Asher rolled his eyes; he never had the patience for Ansel. 'No, Dad, no cancer; liver failure."

"Liver failure! What?! How? I mean, that takes some serious time and damage," Asher looked back into the room bewildered. He was trying to understand.

Abby gently said, "Yeah, Dad, she has been drinking herself to death for quite a while now. Liver failure makes sense. She hid it from us, pretended to be sick from cancer."

"What? I just don't understand!" Asher was a man who did everything to fight death. He ingested vitamins, ran marathons, kept marrying younger and younger women, all in a quest for youth.

"After she had the lump from her breast years ago," explained Arthur "she was fine but I think that's when doctors got scared for her liver. Instead of doing something, she just kept changing doctors, ignoring the prognosis and when she started to look sick, she blamed the cancer for coming back."

"Good god," said Asher. "Your mother certainly had to control everything, now, didn't she? What do we do now?"

"Well Christ, Dad, we don't know," said Ansel, annoyed. They stood there in a stony silence. "Fuck, I hate to say it, but can we get a drink?" said Ansel, waving his hands like he was warding off an evil spirit.

Abby invited them back to her house. A bar felt too public and Arthur's house had Janine sitting in it like a spider. She poured Arthur a scotch, her and Ansel some white wine and they all just stood sipping like they were drinking under a volcano waiting for an eruption.

"Okay, I fucked up," Abby blurted. "I'm sorry, I am so stubborn. I'm sorry I got so mad. I'm sorry I let it go on too long. I was pregnant, in a bad place with Mom and so fucking pissed you two didn't have the burden of her constantly needing you. You two, off on your fishing trip, not a care in the world, meanwhile I had to bail her ass out of jail. I was angry, so there. I admit I took it too far."

"You through? Got it out? Couldn't you have said that two years ago?" Ansel just stared at his sister and she shrugged.

"Okay, I just admitted I fucked up too. We both did."

"Then are we good now. I mean good good?" asked Ansel. "Like am I allowed to see my favorite brother-in-law and nephews again? Can I watch reruns of *MASH* and call you? Like we are never going to mention this again, that kind of good?" Ansel was smiling.

Abby grinned back. "Yes, I'm sorry, I'm a twat."

"Duly noted, Abby is a twat. Checkmark."

"Wait, what do you mean you were the only one taking care of Mom?" questioned Arthur.

"Well, a few years ago, she got arrested outside of Pierre's, you know the French restaurant? She was dead drunk and they were trying to stop her from driving. But she got in her car anyway, so they called the cops. They let her sleep it off at the station but I had to come pick her up, then it kept happening. And then before your fishing trip, it was the Country Club. And Mom kept saying,

'Don't tell the boys, the boys can't handle it,' and she would beg me to keep all this a secret."

"Umm, Abby it wasn't a secret," said Arthur smugly, looking over his scotch. "Guess who had to hire her lawyers and go to pretrials to make sure she kept getting off."

"Oh, I didn't know that. So wait, you knew all along?!"

"I wasn't off the hook either, not even in Miami," said Ansel "I got all the drunken phone calls. She never wanted to call you to upset the kids and Arthur was too rational to talk to. When she got drunk and sad and weepy and angry she would call me over and over until I answered the phone. She would tell me not to tell you guys, so you wouldn't worry. I wanted to turn off my phone, even thought about changing my number. Then I would get all worried she would fall and hit her head or not wake up, so I would leave the phone on. And it would happen over and over."

"No shit?" Abby looked from one brother to another.

"Yes, but unlike you, our stubborn sister, Ansel and I shared notes," said Arthur.

"Crap, guys, I'm really sorry," she felt awful.

"Abby, Mom had a way of separating us," said Arthur. "Not meanly, she just didn't want us to compare notes on her. She didn't want us to see how sick she was really getting. So if she told you one thing, then she told Ansel another and on and on. And lately, I think she actually began to forget who she told what, which was really confusing."

"That's so true," said Ansel. "I would get different versions of the same story. It was like 'Wait, what?! Why didn't you say that before?'"

"Mom was sick, really sick. I guess she didn't want us to see it, but it was so obvious? Imagine how desperate she must have been trying to hide everything these past couple of years."

"She used her anger to drive us away," said Ansel.

"Fuck, it worked," said Abby. They all sighed and felt a range of emotions. Their mother had orchestrated this catastrophic event and they couldn't help but pity her and hate her for it.

Trying to lighten the mood, Abby pulled a joint out the drawer. "Anyone want a hit before Dad gets here? If he even shows up…"

If Asher showed, he showed; if he didn't, hey, they were okay with that too, they were used to it. Their father for their entire lives had been sidetracked by making money. If it was a business phone call or an email, it always came first. A meeting, a conference, or an event, as long as it had to do with his career or his bank account, it came first. So when he didn't appear at their school conferences or sporting events as children, none of them thought to worry or ask; they already knew where he was.

"Here take this," said Abby, trying to push the joint in Arthur's face.

"No."

"Seriously? Times like these is why this stuff was made; it's nature's valium," said Abby, who always loved pot, something about its mellowness, and the fact she laughed and ate with abandon. Pot was good. She and Ansel smoked as soon as he was old enough, too; in fact, it was probably Abby who gave him his first hit. They would watch television and eat weird pizza combinations like pepperoni and jalapeño or pineapple and tomato, just to freak Arthur out.

"Harry smokes," Ansel blurted while a puff of smoke came out of his mouth.

"A, I did not hear that, and B, stop baiting me. I'll stick to scotch but if you found some cigarettes that would be mighty kind." Abby went to the kitchen junk drawer and tossed him a pack of American Spirits.

"We aim to please around here." Abby was always good at

anticipating everything just like their mother. Keep the house stocked with alcohol and party favors and everyone will love you. Agnes might have that needlepointed on a pillow somewhere.

After the high kicked in, Ansel asked, "Is that a car," his pupils dilating a little too fast.

"No, you are just paranoid," said Arthur, pulling a deep drag on a cigarette.

Abby got up and looked out the window, "Fuck, it's Dad. We forgot about Dad."

"Let's get him high," Ansel fell off the couch giggling.

"Shit, oh god, Christie is with him." Abby circled her hands like air flow would make her less high.

"Wait, was Christie at the hospital?" asked Arthur, holding his cigarette like a cigar and enjoying it immensely.

"He probably left her in the car," Ansel answered. The three of them erupted in laughter. When they looked up, their father and his third wife, Christie, were standing in the doorway like the weird twins from *The Shining*.

"Children," Asher said in a tone trying to tame his own feral sperm. "I take it that scotch is for anyone." He walked to the bar near the kitchen and poured himself a glass like he had just come home from work. Christie stood awkwardly waiting for direction.

Christie Kalinsky was the last of the "Christies". As if a fateful summit of the gods declared their father would only be in relationships with Christinas, Chrissies, or Christie. After he and Agnes divorced there was Christy (One) whom he married, Chrissie (Two) whom he dated, and now Christie (Three), his now third wife.

Christie (Three) was only 30, their dad 64, when they met in a spinning class. She was a spin instructor, as well as a personal trainer and Pilates expert. Taller than Asher, she modeled on occasion to show off her perfect physique. Small hips, long legs, ample breasts, and a pretty all-American face, she was like bait on a hook for someone like Asher. Their "meet cute" story consisted of her not being able to adjust her bicycle seat to her correct height and Asher swooping in to save the day. *Thank god her father believed weddings were a waste of money*, Abby always thought, *they didn't have to relive that nightmare of a story in front of 300 guests.*

"Hi guys, how ya doing?" Christie did a head tilt like cat listening to high pitched sounds.

"Fine, Christie. Would you like a drink?" Ansel purred in her direction. One of his favorite pastimes was playing with the Christies like a cat with string.

"Gosh, it's like only one in the afternoon, so I just don't think I should." She grimaced.

"Are you being judgy, Christie?" Ansel said with wide eyes. He waggled his finger. "No judgy."

"No, no, like you guys are in like a bad place with your Mom and all, so no, you do what you guys need to do," her voice cracked, panicked. She often thought she said the wrong thing in front of them.

"So like crack cocaine, would that be acceptable? Or Molly? I might have some Molly." Ansel called out, "Hey Dad, want some Molly?!"

Asher looked at him, "Who the hell is Molly, I don't know a Molly." Abby burst with laughter.

"Ansel, play nice," Arthur said with a grin and whispered, "*He only does Christies.*" Tears streamed down Abby's face, she couldn't breathe from laughing so hard.

Arthur's phone began to ring with Darth Vader's Imperial March. He didn't move and all of them just stared while *Duh duh duh dun da dun* echoed through the room from his pocket.

"Who that, bro?!" Ansel said in street twang.

"Just Janine," said Arthur, sighing and looking into his scotch. Asher, Abby and Ansel erupted in a new stream of guffaws. It went on for an uncomfortable minute or two. Arthur looked at Christie, "Wait it out, they will stop when they forget what they are laughing about."

Asher nestled himself on the couch without offering his child bride a drink. "So what do we do now?"

"This isn't a 'we' situation Dad, you got out a long time ago," said Ansel sternly. "This is an 'us' situation and we have to deal with it."

"Now, son, we're still family and I'm going to help."

"I have always associated you with 'helping,' Dad." Ansel's sarcasm was dripping but Asher ignored him. Abby put a hand on Ansel's leg; the gesture said 'not now.' She grabbed the joint and forced it back into Ansel's mouth.

"We don't know right now, Dad," said Abby softly. "We don't know anything. It's like a ball rolling slowly downhill. We know where it's going to end up but we just don't know when it will get there." They all thought about Agnes lying alone in a hospital bed, her body breaking down, machines beeping, and none of them felt good about it because none of them could help her.

SEVEN

Their first apartment in New York City was tiny and cramped in a way Agnes wasn't used to, coming from a lofty two-story house. Although she was just a professor's daughter, their house has always been more than enough for the two of them. Agnes always had a large childhood room decorated with pink garlands and posters of Katharine Hepburn and Spencer Tracy. With light-filled windows and a walk-in closet, it had been her haven. Now, older, married and a mother at the age of 19, she lived in one of the biggest cities in the world. While fantasizing about it back in her girlish bedroom, it didn't seem like it would be such a leap. But reality was setting in. This was her life, their life, the young Williams family and it was hard.

Agnes did her best with what limited income they had. She made sure Arthur was well cared for; he got new clothes before she did, and the good cuts of meat on the dinner table. Surprisingly, she had not realized how thrifty her Dad had taught her to be. The professor was naturally frugal and he instilled in Agnes a sense of how much a dollar really meant in the world and, in New York City, it didn't go far.

Being poor kept Asher home. She didn't realize it at the time, but their lack of funds was the glue to their sapling marriage. He couldn't afford nights out with the boys from school. He didn't seem to mind. He had studying to do and focused on the bigger picture. Agnes made dinner every night and swaddled a loved Arthur. In turn, Asher loved her domestication. He would marvel at her ability to make a home from seemingly nothing.

"I promise, one day, love, I will get you everything you deserve." He would whisper in her ear at night.

She would whisper back, "I have what I want." But she knew, in her heart, he would forge the path for their lives.

Agnes rarely questioned his studies or invested too much in his school work; that was his part. Her part was Arthur and, soon, Abby was on the way. When she became pregnant a second time, she was more relaxed, more confident. The second baby didn't incite as much fear, especially since Arthur was so easy. Asher wasn't the most attentive father, but Agnes didn't want him to be; parenting was her job.

Asher decided they needed a new apartment but always it was a question of money.

"What if I borrowed some money from my Dad?" Agnes asked.

"I don't like it. I have never been in debt to anyone; it's not the way I do things, Aggie." He didn't say it unkindly but it had always been a source of his pride to be independent.

"Yes, but what if you take that money to a poker game, win and then pay Dad back as soon as possible," Agnes gently pushed him.

"I haven't played in a while," Asher mused.

"Does that matter, love? The money would be a short-term

loan, and then you could use it to earn so much more." Agnes knew how to plant ideas in his head like seeds to grow. Asher leaned over and kissed her forehead. It wasn't the worst idea.

He slept on it and said yes. "How do you know I will win," he asked, showing a hole in his pervasive male armor.

"You will, I know you will, now let me go talk to my father."

Agnes left that day with Arther swaddled and an infant in her belly. Happy to see her, the professor, while skeptical, could not say no to his only daughter. He loaned her $5,000 with no intention of ever seeing it again.

Asher found an underground game through two of his school buddies. That Friday night Agnes fixed his tie and helped him brush his hair. She could tell he was nervous.

"Do what you do best, Ash," she said calmly, motherly.

"And what is that?"

"Convince people you are a winner, of course." She smiled at him.

He leaned in, kissed her hard. She really was his good luck charm and he left whistling.

Agnes couldn't sleep until he came home. She watched dawn approach and light filled their dim apartment. Her heart pounded fearing something had gone wrong. *If something had happened to Asher, to the money?* Her thoughts swirled and her hands shook with fear.

It wasn't until well into the next afternoon the front door burst open. Asher's left eye was swollen and his lip busted and bleeding.

She gasped.

Smiling, he dumped a bag full of cash on the table, it was thousands of dollars.

"Don't ask, love. But we won, we won." And he kissed her, bloody lip and all.

They were able to move into a new apartment with four whole rooms and a full bathroom. With pride, he set up cribs and bought their first proper couch and chair. He was happy. He was a man who could provide.

After Asher went back to school busted up, the other men had a new respect for him. He wasn't some trust fund kid swinging by on Daddy's dime, he was a man's man. Asher was able to invade more inner circles of the elite and swindle just enough money to go unnoticed. He never thought of himself as a con man, just a smart man who knew how to play a game and win.

Agnes went into labor with Abby when Asher was at a game. Not knowing where he was, all she could do was leave a note at home and go have the baby herself. Their neighbor watched Arthur, who was two years old.

Her second birth wasn't as easy as as her first. The labor became difficult as the baby girl twisted in the birth canal. The pain seared through her; any drugs they had given her were useless. Agnes writhed and persevered with no one but a nurse as her cheerleader. Although she felt her insides had been torn in two, her daughter was healthy and relief flooded her like any new mother.

The next day, when the sun was high in the sky, Asher burst through the door pulling an ambling little Arthur. Agnes was so happy to see him she overlooked that he never apologized for the circumstances. Of course, she thought, why should he? He was on a winning streak. They were a family and each had their part, this was her sacrifice.

Agnes chose the name Abigail meaning "a father's joy." She wanted another name starting with A but she also wanted Asher to cherish his daughter. By labeling her right from the start, Asher wouldn't forget to love his children as Agnes did. That day, she watched him grin and hold the baby tenderly, cooing over her. He whispered "Abby" and it stuck.

With two children, Agnes's life became a blizzard of activity, Arthur toddling around, Abby nursing or crying, both in her care the majority of the time. Asher was out at school or god knows where. But when he was home, he was generous and sweet. He would grab fashion magazines from the Korean coffee shop or, on occasion, roses for no reason. Agnes was grateful for his attention, the kids clamoring for her all the time; she needed someone to care for her.

The young parents could never predict the cost of two young children, not financially but emotionally. Those newborn days were a struggle of sleeplessness, exhaustion and deprivation on all levels. Asher stayed focused on school and the finances; it was easier. The wails of the children, seeing Agnes near tears, frankly scared him. His childhood had been so quiet and serene, and now he lived in a chaotic symphony of desperate noises. Agnes felt the same. They both were only children and this world where they were the providers, the caregivers not the attention seekers, was disconcerting.

Agnes suppressed any anger into the form of crying. It tore through Asher to see her wiping away tears whenever she turned away. But she couldn't help it, it was her only form of release. For Asher, he either escaped to school or was quiet, catatonic. He was clueless how to stop infant Abby from screaming – she was a colicky baby – or Arthur from pulling apart the house. As parents, they operated like soldiers, in fear from one explosion to the next.

After a year, it subsided and they adjusted to family life like generations of parents before them. Abby's colic decreased and she became a fat, dimpled, smiling baby. Asher liked to make faces and get reactions from her. While he couldn't change a diaper, he could look into his daughter's eyes and feel protective, love. And as soon as Arthur could speak, Asher would read to him from the Wall Street Journal. Who knew if he understood, but patient little

Arthur was mesmerized by his father's voice. That was all Asher needed as encouragement.

Agnes grew stronger. The laundry, the constant meals, the daily grind became her rhythm. She used the city as entertainment, taking the kids on long strolls through the parks, and sought any free adventures museums had to offer. It was as if she had accepted a challenge the world placed in front of her that she was determined to win.

They lived in a bubble of sorts, but Agnes wouldn't realize it until she looked back years later. She and Asher had a strength to them that both never knew existed until the children. When Abby was a little over a year old, she developed pneumonia. Her fever was high and watching her red-faced and wailing crushed them both. They splurged on a cab and raced to the hospital in the middle of the night, Asher holding Arthur and Abby in Agnes's arms. Both were quiet, as was Arthur, sensing the danger to their family.

Abby was admitted and they were sick with worry. Asher didn't go to school and wouldn't leave the hospital. Then Arthur became sick and vomiting at home. Agnes was torn, desperate to be with them both. Asher and Agnes truly felt on their own with no family to help. Asher had distanced himself from his parents, making the occasional phone call. His father was unimpressed with Asher's ambition. And the Professor couldn't help other than some words of comfort over the phone. It was a time of needing. Their children needed them and they needed to be strong.

They would switch, Agnes going to the hospital while Asher came home. Taking turns, one parent for each child, both depleted, exhausted but full of love. The incident only lasted a few days before both children were on the mend. Like the heavens opening, by the time Abby could come home, Arthur was up again.

Asher went off script from his usual determined ways. He

took a few more days off from school, just so the four of them could be together. The overwhelming relief and happiness that everyone was safe reminded Asher and Agnes of their frailty, their own and the children's. None of them was invulnerable to hardship, to sickness or forces out of their control. But those few days following, as Asher watched his children play happily on the floor and eat their dinner, he kissed his wife often. They held hands and hugged each other in bed at night. They were partners, they were a family.

During that time, Asher was more motivated than ever. He graduated second in his class at business school behind Eric Bartor, whose family had a long history with the school. This Eric Bartor was the third, behind Eric Bartor Senior and Eric Bartor Junior, who also had graduated number one at NYU. The Bartors were steeped in New York distinction. Eric Bartor Senior started the first media wiring company that installed telephones as well as electricity throughout Manhattan. The Bartor Wire conglomerate eventually operated throughout upstate New York, Connecticut and New Jersey and amassed a fortune before 1935. The Bartor family was heavily regarded after the 1929 stock market crash for not only keeping all their employees but continuing to build the company. Those who were loyal were rewarded. Eric Bartor Senior had built a family company with American values of hard work and ingenuity written all over it. The son of a Hungarian immigrant, his original surname was Bartók but that was changed upon arrival in the U.S.. The family still had Eastern European looks: roundish faces, thick broad shoulders and strength in their hands. Centuries of tilling the soil in harsh weather had evolved the Bartóks into healthy, strong humans. As the Bartor wealth grew, they attempted to diminish the inherited genes by marrying lithe blonde debutantes, hoping the curved nose and long limbs would take shape in the next generations. While his shoulders were broad and his nose stern, Eric Bartor the third was tall like his mother and more attractive than his father.

Like all Bartors, Eric married an heiress of the highest degree, Sabine Dupont. She was educated and worldly but best of all, beautiful. Sabine had the French kind of beauty with radiant skin, fragile arms and legs, and long brunette hair that flowed in waves over delicate shoulders. She was tall, lithe and graceful from years of reaching across tennis courts and ballroom dancing. Sabine was the perfect match that satisfied both families. It was more or less a business arrangement between family-owned companies to ensure future generations more wealth and beauty they could ever imagine.

The exact moment she met Sabine often played in Agnes's mind; she was unable to forget it. There was a mixer of sorts for the NYU business school and it was always encouraged to bring wives and girlfriends to such events. It wasn't unusual for most of these men to be married because that was something their families had already arranged years in advance. Agnes, by Asher's side, was listening to a group of these soon-to-be titans of Wall Street when she turned ever so slightly and caught a glimpse of the doorway. Standing on its threshold, Sabine filled the space like a trophy, light illuminating behind her. Her cream silk blouse draped on her delicate clavicle, her hair in a beautiful low-lying messy bun, her makeup so delicate she stood out from all the heavy black eyeliner the other wives relied on for definition. Agnes was in awe and jealous. She watched Sabine move about the room on Eric's arm, feigning gaiety; Agnes could smell her boredom. This soiree was beneath her, a mandatory requirement of marriage. Agnes relished her newly discovered secret.

Eventually the Bartors came to Asher and Agnes.

"Hello, Asher you scat! Is this your wife? Jesus! Who knew you had taste!" Eric bellowed as he eyed Agnes up and down. She wore a formfitting dress that was a Dior knockoff. They didn't have much money but Agnes was good at scouring second-hand stores to look the part.

"Dear girl, who are your family?" said Eric. Rich people questions, Agnes and Asher used to laugh about them. Like, "What's your alma mater?" instead of school or which do you prefer, Palm Beach or Naples? As if everyone went to Florida in the winter.

"Sorry, they were gypsies and have no known address," said Agnes with a flirty smile. She was always prepared with a little joke to avoid answering the questions.

It took him a second but Eric laughed heartily.

"Pretty and funny, Ash, you don't deserve her." Eric and Asher started talking business and Agnes grabbed the opportunity to get Sabine's attention.

"So far I have met 14 couples, two professors and described my children, their names and ages, at least twelve times. You?" Baiting Sabine into a conversation.

"I'd rather be cooking dinner and I hate cooking dinner." Deadpanned Sabine.

"Reading a bedtime story for the fourth time." Agnes.

"Washing diapers." Sabine.

"Talking to my mother-in-law," Agnes.

"Oooh, good one, can't stand mine," The two women grinned at each other. And that was it, the two most beautiful and most likely intelligent women in the room found each other.

Sabine called Agnes the next day, asking her to lunch. Agnes could not afford a nanny, so she was grateful when Sabine insisted the children come as well. Eric and Sabine's apartment was grand. Four bedrooms on the Upper East Side, high ceilings, rich moldings and heirloom furniture. Agnes for the life of her couldn't understand why Eric even needed a business degree; they had it all already.

Sabine greeted her like they had always been friends, no fussy getting-to-know-each-other phase. That was too common for Sabine; you were either in or out with her socially. It was Sabine's nature to be casual and accumulate people into her life as easily as ordering a gin and tonic.

"Don't mind my children, they are little pets with voices," said Sabine nonchalantly. She was impeccably dressed in a chiffon dress, tight ponytail and looked like a dewy cover of a magazine. Eric and Sabine had two boys and Agnes could hear them in the other room. Arthur and Abby went to play while a nanny watched them. Sabine poured her a glass of wine without asking and set two plates heaping with salad and fresh bread on the table.

"Eat, dear, no sense in starving to death. And besides, what's the point of all this if we don't relish what few pleasures we can have." Agnes was mesmerized. Sabine had a healthy appetite for everything before her. Agnes could not imagine where it all went with a size 4 figure.

Sabine asked pointed questions and Agnes could tell she had already figured out her lowly background. Agnes was not the type with an artist fund or a debutante dress but that suited Sabine. She was tired of the same girl from the same old families anyway.

"Follow me," said Sabine after lunch, leaving the dishes on the table for some unseen maid to clear. Agnes, after two glasses of wine, would have followed her anywhere. Mazing through a labyrinth of gorgeous rooms, they ended in a room full of clothes. It looked like a mixture of a museum and Bergdorf's showroom. Racks and racks of designer clothes, color-coordinated. There were deep blues, light blues, fuchsias and greens. All so beautiful, Agnes stared with her mouth open.

Sabine pulled pieces down and urged Agnes to try on blouses and dresses. Although Agnes was shorter and bit curvier than Sabine, some fit perfectly. Everything that did, Sabine stuffed in a garment bag.

"I couldn't possibly..," Agnes gasped.

"Why not? They are just going to sit here taking up space while I waste my time buying more and more." It seemed so logical to Sabine, she was making more room for more clothes. Agnes hated feeling like a charity case but Sabine didn't make it seem that way. It was simply one friend giving another some clothes. And they were beautiful clothes that Agnes could wear at events. Time and time again, she knew Sabine recognized her own hand-me-downs. But she would only smile, kiss her on both cheeks and tell her how lovely she looked that evening. Never once did she say anything otherwise and humiliate her.

The two became inseparable. Sabine was incredibly lazy. Agnes on the other hand could never afford to be. She dragged Sabine and her kids, nanny in tow of course, to Central Park, to the movies, and museums. Agnes had to get her kids out of their small midtown apartment or she would go crazy. Sabine just let Agnes lead the way and followed, happy to have some fun. Meanwhile, Eric and Asher were getting closer at school, making weekend dinners and perfunctory school events much easier for all four of them.

When they graduated, Eric had already been recruited by McMillon and Company, an investment firm. Old Mr. McMillon was friends with old Mr. Bartor and that's how business arrangements were made and jobs bestowed. Eric decided to bring Asher along and got him a job offer as well. Asher was the personality and spark that Eric wasn't – he was more creative and savvy. Eric knew securing him a position would be a good bet and make him look good, not just daddy's boy.

So the Williamses and the Bartors were able to continue their close friendship. Agnes learned from Sabine the most rigorous society and social graces. And Asher smartly hitched his career to Eric's. Their mediocre beginnings faded as they ascended the social ladder.

EIGHT

Arthur, Abby and Ansel felt like Huey, Dewey and Louie when they showed up daily at the hospital. For a week, their mother had been sleeping, but they would be there for doctor's rounds. Dr. Cooper was oblivious to Ansel's constant smirking, unlike Dr. Moore, who all three of them confided in secretly. Dr. Moore's father was an alcoholic and she had lost her mother-in-law to the disease as well. She understood and didn't bullshit them.

Dr. Moore sympathetically explained how unpredictable cirrhosis was and how she couldn't offer concrete predictions. But that didn't stop them from looking at her like she had a crystal ball. There was no way of saying if their mother would live a week, a month or a year. There was a possible chance she could recover some to be on her feet, or not at all, but inevitably, their mother would need constant care in a facility or hospice at home. Given the diagnosis, they learned hospice would be available up to a year. None of this made them feel better; the uncertainty and unknowing tore at them, zapped their strength. Ansel and Arthur worried about their businesses, Abby about her family. Nothing was normal or routine or predictable. Now, every day had become a guessing game of epic annoyance.

"This is hard," Abby started with her brothers after meeting with Dr. Moore.

"No shit," said Ansel.

"No, not that, I need an operation," she confessed. Abby confided in her brothers about her own surgery and the worry became tenfold across their faces. She did her best to reassure them but they were all so fragile at this point. It was just another problem piled on top of all the others.

"It wasn't supposed to be this hard," said Arthur.

"What?" asked Ansel. "Mom dying? Or Abby getting old..."

"Hey," squawked Abby.

"You know what I mean," Ansel punched her arm. "It's called 'adulting' and it sucks."

"You know what I weirdly imagined," Abby and Ansel were gripped thinking how Arthur could *weirdly* imagine anything. "That it would somehow get easier. Like all the shit she ever put us through would add up. Like there was some sort of universal scale that tipped and said *okay, that's enough*. But no, this is going to play out to the end isn't it?" Arthur sadly mused.

"It's okay, brother, we are used to it," responded Abby. They all shook their heads resigned in agreement. Maybe they had been through worse, maybe this would get worse, who knew? But they at least knew one thing, they would survive not like Agnes.

When Agnes finally woke, they rushed to the hospital. Groggy and out of it, she was a shell of herself. The alcohol, the detox, the trauma had affected her brain and no one knew at this point how much of her they would get back. When Abby arrived,

Agnes was asking for her purse.

"Hi darling, where are my cigarettes. Can I have a cigarette?" Her usual strong and forceful mother sounded childlike.

"Hi, Mom, no, you are in a hospital. You're on oxygen, so a cigarette would be like *kaboom*," Abby said sweetly.

"Oh, okay," she mildly said. "Where is my bag?"

"No, Mom. No bag." Abby tried again. Ansel and Arthur appeared in the doorway.

"Ansel, what are you doing here? It's not a holiday. The house isn't decorated."

"Hi Mom, just came to see you." He kissed her head.

"Well could you be a dear and take the hamster off the bed? I never did like them and it's tickling my feet." With that, Agnes fell asleep again and they all looked at each other.

A resident explained their mother was still detoxing and now that she was awake she might be hallucinating. It was common. Their mother was wearing nicotine patches, so needing a cigarette was more a habit. Agnes wasn't in any pain and she was slowly progressing. Her internal bleeding had healed, but her breathing was not out of the woods. As long as she needed oxygen, she needed to stay.

"What about her stomach?" Abby was referring to the terrible basketball-size bulge protruding from her mother's body. It was unnatural.

"Unfortunately, we can't do much about that. Her body cannot process toxins and fluids like it did before without a functioning liver. And we can't drain her stomach because it will just build up again and sometimes that makes it worse." The three hung their heads. This was a nightmare.

"Can I just say it?" said Ansel later staring into a glass of white wine. They were back at Abby's house.

"Yes," said Abby, knowing full well that it was the same

thing on her mind.

"I wish she would just die. It's just cruel to watch her waste away."

"She was so beautiful," said Arthur, pulling open kitchen drawers trying to find another cigarette. They all were frayed. "I hate seeing her like this; it doesn't seem right." His hand was shaking as he lit the cigarette. Abby got up and lit it for him. She gently placed her hand on his arm. "It's okay, big brother, it's okay." He looked away, full of tears he kept trying to control.

"Who talked to Dad today?" asked Ansel, to change the subject.

"I did, he's going to visit again tomorrow," said Arthur.

"Will he leave the window down for Christie this time?" said Ansel and they couldn't help but laugh.

Arthur went home and left Ansel to play with his other nephews. He knew his baby brother and sister would smoke pot later and watch reruns on TV, it was their coping mechanism. The two together had a way of making each other feel better.

Arthur wanted silence and the comfort of his study and his son. The sight of Harry always made him feel better. But Arthur missed the days he would scoop his son up and hold him tight. Harry would nuzzle into his neck like they were one. If only a father could feel that way again; it went by too fast.

Coming down his own driveway, Arthur always thought his house looked slightly sad, no life to it. A five-bedroom house with one child and an unhappy wife. Her car was in the driveway, the sporty white Porsche she wanted. Harry's car was there too, a simple Volkswagen – they were German car people. Arthur always hesitated before getting out of his own car. Years of the unpredictability of his mother and his wife always cautioned him before going in the house. He never knew what he might find.

Tonight Janine was in the kitchen shoving random items in

an overly priced Birkin bag his secretary had picked out for her for Christmas.

Without looking up, she said, "How is she?"

"Better, stable, awake," he mumbled, hanging up his coat.

"So what's next? "Janine asked bluntly.

"What do you mean?"

"Is she going to die?"

"That's a bit crass, even for you darling," Arthur guessed it was Agnes's house Janine was after since he provided more than enough for her. His mother's was a gorgeous stone mansion right on the water in Westport. They still lived "in the woods," Janine told people, even though it was the exclusive Fairfield County. But Arthur didn't want his mother's house; the three siblings had wanted to sell it for years. Bad memories were like wallpaper there and none of them wanted to be reminded.

"Nope, looks like she is good to go," Arthur just blurted. He rarely ever lied but his subconscious just did not want to deal with Janine pestering.

"Well," Janine said. He could tell she was annoyed with the answer but she changed the subject. "Harry is locked away in his room. Lord knows what that boy does."

"He studies, Janine, he studies." Arthur felt exhausted.

"Well, could you make sure he eats? He is too skinny. I am going out to a book club meeting," She paused. "Did you hear me, Arthur?"

"Yes Janine, loud and clear."

Arthur poured himself a scotch and went to Harry's room. He knocked but his son laughed, "You don't have to knock, Dad." He was the best thing that ever happened to Arthur.

He found Harry engrossed in an advanced calculus book, his shaggy surfer hair flopped over to one side. Arthur never failed, not once, to notice Harry's arm. A pointed stub Harry used so deftly and with such grace, the same as any other limb. For Harry it wasn't deformed, just an extension of himself, and he didn't regard it with shame or pity. But for Arthur, a parent, he couldn't help but wish for it to be different. But Harry did have Janine's good looks and Arthur's personality, thank god, so the gene pool did some things right.

"How's Aggie?" Harry said, full of concern. Arthur had to remember a grandchild had a different view than a child. Agnes was Aggie to him and she was always sweet and loving to Harry. She made him feel special about his arm, like the universe had chosen it for him. Arthur admired his mother for her straightforwardness. When it came to children, she had natural affection. It was an untapped reservoir of patience. Too bad she couldn't apply that to adults. For the most part Arthur had shielded him from Agnes's drinking but Harry wasn't stupid. He loved his grandmother the same way she loved him, broken parts and all.

"Be honest, Dad."

"Okay, it's pretty bad, could be days, weeks or months. It's not great. We are just taking it day by day."

"Can I see her?"

"I don't think you want to see her like this, maybe in a week or two when she can go home. Right now, it's rough, just trust me."

"Sure." Harry was never one to argue, but Arthur could see the sadness spread across his face. He was losing someone close for the first time and it added more pain to Arthur's already overfull plate.

"Can we order pizza? Mom's not home and we can get the meat lovers," asked Harry. Arthur laughed, the kid knew how to work an angle. That night, the two of them ate a sodium-riddled pizza and loved it. They talked about work, Harry's college prospects, and Ansel and Abby.

Eventually Harry interjected, "When are you going to leave

her, Dad? I don't think she will leave you."

Arthur just wiped grease from his face, "I don't know. And you shouldn't worry about such things."

"Yes, I can. It's ridiculous. I've only got one year left, there's just no point in living in this castle of misery." It stung Arthur to hear the phrase but he couldn't argue.

"Well, Aggie is dying and there's just a lot going on." It was all he could say.

"I'm going to stop you right there. Right now, Uncle Ansel is in town, it's the perfect time. If you found a place, the three of us could move you out and you could give the house to Mom. And you would be done. I have a car, I can drive wherever whenever between here and wherever you go. It's time, Dad. God, even Aggie thought it was time a decade ago."

"You knew about that?"

"Dad, half the town knew about that."

———

Arthur knew it was mistake to be a part of the same country club as his mother. The Southpoint Club was the most prestigious around, so it was one of the few things Janine actually agreed with Agnes on. The "clubhouse" could have been mistaken for a colonial southern mansion. Looming on a perfectly manicured hill, the menacing columns and an opulent carpeted stairs could deter any carpetbagger (at least that's what Arthur joked). It had playgrounds, pools, a golf course and tennis courts. Agnes wanted to watch her handsome grandson excel at everything and beat all the other little wealthy spoiled kids in town and urged them to join.

It was no secret in the family that Agnes never cared for Janine. She tolerated Janine. Arthur was her first and shining child, and Agnes was old-school. She had hoped he would meet a girl from an established family who had ties to society. Someone from Harvard or the club, not a blind date of all things.

Agnes did not suffer fools. Intelligence ranked high on her standard of associations and Janine, as Agnes would say, was the dimmest star in the sky. Agnes equated narcissism with dullards. She could tolerate Janine if she was a Rothschild or a Gillette, but she wasn't and Agnes's snobbery would always hold that against her.

His mother would never tell Arthur how disappointed she was in Janine and her reaction to Harry's deformity. She thought she should have been stronger for son and grandson, less affected by it. Agnes saw weakness in her early on and that certainly was not the type of woman she wanted in her family.

Of course, it all played out on a national holiday in public. It was Easter and Agnes invited the family to the club for brunch. Ansel had just moved to Miami, so it was Abby and Jake with Arthur, Janine and Harry, who was now seven. Harry was still young enough to enjoy the Easter egg hunt and Agnes beamed as she watched her only grandson speedily whip across the putting green and gather more eggs than the rest, even with one arm.

"Agnes, he is so handsome," cooed Mrs. Lucja Rice. Agnes admired Mrs. Rice, a Polish beauty who had gone to Columbia University and married the son of a steel magnate. Brains, looks and money, and she gave generously to the community. She was exactly who Agnes liked to keep in her company.

"Thank you, dear, still waiting on the next round of grandchildren, though," Agnes whispered loud enough for Abby to hear.

"Mom, would you care to place an order? I'll just go rustle up two or three for you," Abby said snarkily.

"My dear Abigail, they will come in good time and you will

be blessed," said a gentle Mrs. Rice.

"Thank you, Mrs. Rice." Abby smiled politely and glared at her mother.

"Hi! I'm Janine!" Abby couldn't help but laugh as Janine pushed through and stood right in Mrs. Rice's face. Abby choked on her wine as she watched her mother's body go rigid.

"Yes, Janine. You have already met Mrs. Rice at my house, on several occasions."

"Oh sorry, oh yeah, that's right!" Janine said exactly what she thought, no filter, and it drove Agnes crazy. "In my head I call you the beauty queen. I mean for your age, you are gorgeous. I would kill for those cheek bones."

Abby thought she would see her mother's head explode.

"Thank you, dear, that's very sweet." Mrs. Rice visibly uncomfortable and when she saw Mrs. Beth Fisher, she shouted "Beth, dear, so lovely to see you! How are the children?" in order to move away from Agnes and Janine.

"What the hell was that, Janine? Can you even remember your own last name?" Agnes spit the words out as quietly and sternly as possible.

"What?!" Janine again said a little too loudly. "What did I do wrong now, Mrs. Williams?" Janine was getting mouthy right back.

"You are impossibly rude," said Agnes.

"So I didn't remember her at first, what's the big deal?"

"The *big deal*, Janine, is that it's impolite and disrespectful to not remember. The Rices were at your wedding, for god's sake."

"Yea and so were a bunch of your other friends too. You all look alike with your stretched skin and diamonds. Can't tell you people apart from your different shades of pink lipstick, so sue me."

Agnes took a deep breath and clenched her hands. *Uh oh,* Abby was thinking.

"Janine dear, would be at all possible if just for once, just for the sake of my son and my grandson, you could possibly fake intelligence? Give it a go perhaps? And throw in some manners too, I am sure there is some soap opera you enjoy that perhaps could teach you the finer points of human interaction." Agnes was enunciating a little too hard.

Oh boy, thought Abby.

Abby grabbed Janine by the elbow and forcibly whisked her away to the bathroom. The club had a restroom like a walk-in master suite. Lined with mirrors, and tables filled with extras like hairspray and lotions, it was a miniature clubhouse for the ladies with the toilets discreetly tucked away.

Inside Janine let it rip.

"Your mother has no right to talk to me like that. I have been married to Arthur for years, and every time I am around her, I am not good enough. I wear a goddamn tennis bracelet, I take golf lessons, I come when she beckons. My shoes are Gucci," she wailed. Abby tried not to laugh at the absurdity.

"Listen Janine, Mom just gets touchy about her appearance in public. We always had to take her lead. When in these situations, just try taking a back seat when she's around. Can you do that at least?"

"I swear, all you kids are just wussies against her. Arthur wouldn't dare upset the great 'Aggie,'" Janine was pouting. "Not like she hasn't been drunk in public. Yes, you think I don't know about that, your Mom has her own reputation."

"Listen," Abby was getting frustrated and defensive, "Don't even pretend you know because you don't know shit, Janine."

No one got to go against their mother except her children. While it was easy for people to criticize her mother, Abby felt only she had the right to do it. But in this moment and for the sake of her brother, Abby calmed herself. No matter how impossibly stupid

Janine was, she was Arthur's wife and Harry's mother.

Changing her tone, Abby pleaded. "It's just best to respect Mom, stay quiet, maybe stay away from her? Would that be so bad? And then you can do whatever you want. That's not such a bad deal, right?" Of course Abby knew her mother could be mean, but Janine really was annoying. But then again, she was a part of the family, whether anyone liked it or not.

Inevitably, things went from bad to worse that afternoon at the Southpoint Country Club. Janine and Agnes matched each other drink for drink during brunch. The waiter couldn't tell whose glass to refill first, with both ladies beckoning him constantly. Agnes, annoyed, got up to greet friends at other tables and Janine, of all things followed her.

No! Abby wanted to scream, but of course, Janine did not follow Abby's advice, not even a little bit. *She really was stupid,* Abby fumed, watching the circus play out in the dining room. The two women were like howling cats making a spectacle. At one point Janine hip-checked Agnes out of the way in front of Dr. Alisa King, the famed psychiatrist. Agnes dropped her drink and almost slapped Janine in front of the whole dining room. If high society did not know before, they knew now, very publicly, that Mrs. Asher Williams and Mrs Arthur Williams firmly hated each other.

Eventually, Abby leaped toward her mother and Arthur did the same with Janine, and they separated the two. The women were taken home. Harry was disappointed because he didn't get dessert but that couldn't match the disappointment his father felt, in his wife and his mother. Family dinners were never quite the same after that.

—

Arthur went to bed with indigestion after pizza with Harry.

Exhausted, he lay there with so many thoughts about Agnes and Janine. His mind kept going back over the years and the bitchiness between the two. He thought about himself in all of it and one word popped into his head. Coward. Arthur had been a coward. He hated conflict and those two women brought it tenfold. Why did he put up with it? Why was he so scared to stop it? To make a change? Maybe he couldn't when Harry was a boy, but now? Was his son right? Did he have to get his son's permission to stand up for himself? He thought *I guess so* and laughed. Yes, his mother was dying but he was still living. Or, in other words, he better start living.

It was late but he texted both Abby and Arthur and made a "group text" as the kids called it. He was feeling closer and closer to them, more so than in years. He wrote "If I left Janine right now would you guys help me?"

Abby wrote, "Now? Do you have boxes and white wine?"

Ansel also immediately replied, "Brother, you have seen the light."

NINE

The retreat was in Maine on a beautiful lake. The cool autumn air rustled the browning leaves and electric golds and oranges swirled like confetti in the air. When Agnes stepped out of the wood-paneled station wagon, she felt her breath escape in awe. Even Asher stopped for a moment to look around, a rare calm moment shared between the two of them. The loons drifted over the glassy water and the log cabins had little smoke rings coming out of the chimneys. It was picturesque fall New England that November day in 1974. The Williams children loudly exited the car like a pack of animals, pawing and scratching, sniffing the air as the three young faces looked warily about, as though taken out of a shelter to a new home. They were city kids unused to such vast earth not bordered by a metal fence or concrete sidewalks. Sticks were under foot and the breeze came low and deep from the lake.

"Let's find our cabin!" said Asher with a spring in his step. McMillon Investment was hosting the retreat for its top executives and their families. Three days in Maine so the boys could drink whiskey, hunt deer and congratulate themselves for being the titans of Wall Street.

The idea was Asher's. He had the ear of his boss's son, James McMillon Junior, and casually suggested the getaway over drinks. Agnes was getting antsy at home with three kids and Asher didn't want to plan a week away for the Thanksgiving holiday. A weekend away would make her happy, and if he could do it with his colleagues, then all the better. Asher was not a great family man. At this point in his career, he was all about work. He didn't know how to relate to his kids other than patting them on the head when he arrived home and buying them toys they didn't really need. Agnes assured him that when they grew up a little more, he could relate to them better. She didn't hold it against him, instead mothering them enough for both of them. Asher could see a glimmer of hope with Arthur, who was now seven. Arthur liked to come to Asher's office and read tables of numbers. The boy asked questions that were thoughtful and curious about the stock market. Arthur had a good head on his shoulders and Asher's first fatherly feeling was pride. Abby and Ansel were still too young, erratic and messy for him to understand.

For three crisp glorious days, Agnes had Sabine and the other ladies to talk to while Asher pursued his upward spiral in the company by ingratiating himself with the McMillon clan. Friday went by without a hitch. The families settled in, children played and wives chattered about schools, nannies and living in New York City. There were no actual events planned until Saturday, when the men woke early and went deer hunting with guides. The women and children were taken to pick the last of the autumn apples, peruse pumpkin patches and take hay rides. It was a flawless day. By late afternoon, the men returned to nap off the morning whiskey and get ready for a grand black-tie dinner that was to take place in the center dining hall cabin. Nannies were on hand to watch the children and the adults would cap off the weekend dining and dancing as if they had never left the city.

"You look stunning," Asher said, admiring his wife. Now that they had money, Agnes could finally buy her own couture dresses. She shopped with Sabine, who styled her beautifully. Tonight, she was wearing a light blue Halston halter dress, and the diamond dew drop earrings Asher had given her for Christmas. Unlike the stodgy, '60s updo, Agnes liked her blonde waves to sail around her dimpled face. She was only twenty-six and still youthful after three kids. Asher was proud to show her off. Most of the wives, especially those of the older executives, already had drawn faces from too much gin and tennis. While Sabine was the exotic beauty meant for Vogue covers, Agnes had a classic beauty that people felt comfortable and privileged to be around. The women were fine pieces of porcelain of different size and color but equally valuable.

Asher felt like a lucky man when they entered the hall. The caterers had done a magnificent job of turning the large wooden building into a winter wonderland. Decked with green garland strands and twinkling lights, the room was transformed into a magical oasis secluded in the chilly, smoky fall air. Asher and Agnes entered like royalty, circling the room and mingling with everyone.

Addressing his colleagues by their last names, Asher shouted, "Dawson, how's it going? Cleaver, you old goat you, that shoot was pretty spectacular, huh?" Asher didn't forget to address the wives with a sly smile, "Irene, I have never seen you so lovely. That dress suits you to perfection." Agnes wasn't jealous; it was a part of the game.

They had both honed the routine over the years. To be a power couple you had to be powerful. To be powerful people, you had to be liked and respected. Asher and Agnes played to others' egos, remembered names and nuances like whose children went to what school, the name of the mother-in-law and, always, compliments. She followed Asher's lead and for years, their polite banter had worked. Their reputation was preceding them in New York. Eric recommended Asher for McMillon and McMillon recommended the Williamses for the University club and so on and so forth. They were a shining example of social climbers, the son of a mechanic and the daughter of a university professor, if only anyone knew. But they were pretty, smart and savvy and could play the game better than anyone.

"The meat is delicious," Agnes cheerily said at the table. Eric and Sabine sat with them, along with the younger James McMillon and his wife Sara. Their table comprised the younger set in the room. The rest of the guests were McMillon Senior's partners and CEO and CFO, all much older, scattered throughout the room. Agnes had grown used to Asher flirting with Sabine. He had always walked that fine line of putting his hand on women's backs and leaning in too close to tell a joke. In turn, Eric was flirting with Agnes and she didn't mind either.

"One day we should all go to the Bermuda together; I hear it is just breathtaking," said Eric.

"I adore sunshine, sounds wonderful," responded Agnes.

"I bet you look smashing in a bathing suit." Eric licked his lips a little.

"Not as good as Sabine! The kids would love to play on the beach all day. I can't imagine how much fun that would be versus Central Park in winter." Agnes deftly ignored the innuendo.

"Yes, too much fun." Eric was leering at Agnes's cleavage. Her radar went up; he was on the dangerous edge of drunk. And not the nice kind because he had been swinging back whiskeys all night. His eyes were getting glassy and his hands had moved from dangling on the back of her chair to rubbing her back. It made her nervous.

"Would you excuse me? Ladies room," she whispered. "Sabine, care to join?"

She didn't hear her over the din of the tableware but Sara jumped up and said she would come.

The reprieve gave Agnes an opportunity to pull herself together and assess her own sobriety. It was always important to have fun but never come across too dramatic. *The dutiful wife*, she thought, and laughed a little.

When the ladies returned, plates had been cleared and a band had struck up, playing Motown hits, again Asher's idea. Instead of returning to her seat next to Eric, Agnes put her hands on Asher's back and tilted her head towards the dance floor. Asher jumped at the idea, knowing full well they would break the seal on the dance floor. He needed the band to be a smash so both father and son McMillon would attribute the success of the night to him.

They were dazzling. Asher and Agnes lost themselves to the music. They forgot about the children, the work, the life they had to carve out every day with a pickaxe. Instead they moved and swayed in expensive clothes like expensive dolls brought off a shelf. They came from nothing and now in the spotlight they were everything. Agnes glowed from sheer achievement. Her vision had come to life. Asher laughed and moved his arms and legs to the music, the center of attention with his gorgeous wife. This was it, they had almost made it.

Couples followed, entranced, wanting to exude the magic that music and food and wealth and privilege could afford. The caterers brought dessert and more and more wine. The champagne and dancing were delicious and Agnes forgot how much she drank. It was the most fun she had ever had. Husbands danced with other wives, wives danced with other husbands, swaying to Smokey Robinson and Marvin Gaye, Diana Ross and Gladys Knight. These whiter than white people found their soul and sweated and laughed into the late hours without a care in the world.

Exhausted and tipsy, Agnes went to find Asher. She had been dancing with McMillon Senior but was tired now. The kids would be up early and it was time to go to bed. But she wanted to find Asher and hoped he would go back to the cabin with her. Agnes looked around the room and downed the last of her champagne. Not seeing him, she left, but outside was a kick to her system, the fresh air made her spin.

Steadying herself on the railing, she couldn't navigate the wooden steps in high heels. She pulled them off and made it down safely but couldn't decide which path to take to the cabin. Outside was too dimly lit. Agnes went left when she should have gone right. She stumbled only a few yards from the building. "Dammit," she blurted, the trees and branches all swimming in front of her. She went back to the main lodge and steadied herself against its side, telling herself to take deep breaths. She could see the crescent moon reflecting off the lake clear as glass. The sound of the music was faint and sprinkled with people's laughter. The smell of the fireplace smoke tinged the cold air and Agnes wanted to stay right there, taking in all the wonderment. Thinking of her cherubic little children and the icy little puffs of breath coming from them back in the cabin, she pushed off the building and set off on a path.

Before getting too far from the main cabin she saw two people leaning against a tree. There was no space between them. His hands were deep between her legs. Her dress draped over his arm. Hair falling on her face, Agnes could see the woman's body rocking and swaying, lost in ecstasy. The man's face was burrowed in her hair. And for just a brief second, Agnes was turned on. With barely enough light from a cabin, it was erotic. The couple was undoubtedly in love, she thought, they were so passionate. Because all the men were in tuxedos, it was hard to tell who they were. Until the man pulled back orgasming while the woman's hand moved rapidly in his pants. It was Asher.

His eyes were closed and knowing him too well, Agnes could see he was coming. The woman's hair flipped back and Agnes watched as Sabine was coming as well. Lost in their euphoria, they did not see her. Motionless, Agnes thought this kind of passion doesn't happen the first time. This was planned, this was calculated, this was familiar to them.

She stumbled but caught herself. All of a sudden there was a hand beneath her elbow holding her upright and moving her quietly forward. Relief flooded her to be getting away.

The cabins were just down the path but each one only had a single bulb outside, barely enough to see. The blackness was stony. From her drunkenness, to her shock, she could barely make out Eric at her side.

"You didn't know, did you?" he said kindly.

"No," she whispered embarrassed.

His hand circled her back and led her down a different trail to the edge of the lake. The embankment was mossy, free of sticks. Agnes didn't care about her designer dress and sat down with a thud. Her head was spinning.

"Asher has slept with other women, I know that. All you boys have your side flings, no big deal." It was true. Agnes was annoyed about the other women but they were one-time dalliances. Trips to Boston for business or nights out with his colleagues that went too late. All Agnes ever asked was never to know, never to be humiliated. But this was Sabine.

"But you didn't know it was your best friend."

"No," said Agnes. Anger seeped in on top of her humiliation and trickled through her pulsing veins. Sabine, lovely Sabine, who let Agnes into her world of trust funds, clubs and finer things. Agnes should have known there was a trade. Her husband. That was the trade. Everyone must pay their debts, that's what her father used to say.

Eric handed her a flask of whiskey and she took a big swallow. She coughed but liked the burn in her throat. Staring at the lake's calm water, her head reeled. She lay back onto the cool earth and watched the moonlight dance between the branches. Agnes will never remember drifting off. Her mind will always go back to the moon and then nothing, like a black cloud had washed over her.

"No, no," Agnes began to say urgently, her closed eyes fluttering open. Something was wrong and all she could say was "no," with increasing urgency, as her senses came back to her. It was his weight on her, she felt pinned by a heavy moving object. His hot breath smelling of stale cigarettes and old food. Heaviness and thrusting, heaviness and thrusting and grunting. She heard him say, "oh baby."

She couldn't breathe, choking on the word "no" over and over again.

Agnes's hands were fighting to get under his chest to push him off. She felt her dress bunched up barely covering her. The moss under her naked back wasn't soft like one would think but scratchy, breaking her skin. Fine sharp rocks were like tiny knives sawing into her. His dick was short and wide stretching her inside. It tore the minute fibers of her most private part bit by bit. Sweat dripped off his face onto hers. It smelled too.

Again she tried to push him off but gravity worked against her. His contorted face haloed by moonlight grunting inches above hers. Desperate not to see his expressions, she craned her neck to the side as far as it would go. Tears flowed quietly from her eyes, and then she stopped fighting. Limp, she relinquished control until he came. It was a strange moment to feel gratitude but she did. His own rigid body went slack as he rolled onto the moss to zip up his pants. She breathed again but didn't dare move except to push her once lovely dress over hips.

He sat up and calmly patted her on the leg, "Thanks, it was as good I hoped." Eric wasn't talking about the sex, he was talking about the revenge. Asher had taken his wife so now he had taken Asher's; the score was settled. He was satisfied in more ways than one. Agnes tried not to watch as he combed his hands through his hair, primping himself to go back to his wife. Both cheats, both liars, both far too selfish for even Agnes to understand.

After he left, she lay there and cried. They were soft tears, exhausted bits of her life, everything she had worked towards ending like this. Maybe she did deserve it, she wanted a better life and this was her payment. Her own selfishness got her to this point.

She had no one to blame but herself. All of it, her doing.

Agnes had trapped Asher with a baby, she let him do whatever he wanted all the time. She willingly played second fiddle to Sabine. She had flirted with Eric and all those other important, powerful business men.

She only had herself to blame and the weight of that crushed Agnes in a way like no other.

At that very moment, Agnes stopped liking herself. The lake mirrored more than the moon but the life Agnes had chosen, and she didn't like what she saw.

Eventually, a headache began to form. She lifted herself up and wiped the heavy mascara she knew had pooled under her eyes. Her underwear was nowhere to be found. What did it matter? Stumbling, Agnes was able to pick her way back slowly toward cabin number seven. *Ha*, she thought, *lucky seven just for the Williams family*.

Asher was snoring when she returned, instead of a shower she changed, wiped her face and used a wet towel in the bathroom to wash herself before going to bed. It was late. Arthur roused a little and she told him to go back to sleep. While some might stay awake reliving the horror, Agnes did not. All she wanted to do was sleep and forget the entire night.

The next day Agnes, numb and disoriented, did exactly as she would have done on any other day. She packed their clothes, fed the kids and loaded the station wagon without looking back. Asher was oblivious to her state; he just chalked it up to fatigue from such a grand weekend.

Then in the weeks following, she continued to sleep. Agnes would pull herself together for the kids, making sure they were fed and looked after. She even hired a nanny service. The only people she would let touch her was the children, not Asher. Often she would go into bed with one of them and fall asleep in their room, leaving Asher on his own in the master bedroom.

Agnes would lie awake, watching shadows dance across the room, recalling that final moment when her mother called her "baby girl" and walked away without looking back. Then she would hear Eric's "oh baby" echo behind it. She had no control over her life; other people were changing and altering it. The injustice tore through her like acid. She blamed herself for the rape but also she was angry, deeply angry that this was the chessboard of life and she was losing. Asher on the other hand seemed to be winning, and Sabine and Eric. She would wake every day and vomit, sick with all the thoughts.

But in the cruelty of life, it wasn't her mental state making her sick. Six weeks after the retreat Agnes knew she was pregnant. Having been pregnant three times before, she felt it with certainty. The hideous catch was it could have been either Asher's or Eric's, she would never know.

For weeks she hadn't left the house, only to go to school for the kids or food shopping. Asher assumed she sick, perhaps a virus and urged her to go to a specialist. Agnes decided for the first time in their marriage to flat out lie to Asher. He had been lying to her, so why not? She said she had seen a doctor. She made up symptoms between mononucleosis and lyme disease. It wasn't hard for Asher to believe because he genuinely didn't pay attention. He was so focused on work, and probably Sabine, he would just kiss her on the forehead and told her he hoped she would get better soon. With the nanny in place, not much about their lives changed, except Agnes stayed in bed and had a perfect excuse to not go out to any of Asher's functions.

Sabine called but Agnes just ignored her. Eventually, Sabine stopped. Agnes didn't really care. No one mattered to her except her children.

Agnes felt more and more comfortable with her ability to lie. Fiction formed easily, bits of candy she doled out to people to make them happy. No one questioned her as she kept them at bay.

"Mrs. Aston," the receptionist called to the waiting room. It wasn't hard to find a clinic now that abortion was legal. She went to Brooklyn not to take any chances of being seen in Manhattan. She didn't give her real name and had $500 in cash on her. The nurse was kind, an older black woman who rested her hand on Agnes's shoulder when she was lying on the table.

"Tell me your real name, sweetheart, I know it's not Susie. No white girl wants to be called Susie," the woman laughed and squeezed her shoulder.

"It's Agnes."

"Okay Agnes, lucky for you this isn't 1958 any more and we can do things properly. We are going to give you a sedative, make you feel all nice and fluffy. The doctor will come in, you will spread your legs and he will do the business we need to do. There will be some discomfort and after cramping and bleeding. Your chart says you had three children before by natural childbirth? Then I have no doubt you can do this. Three, that's a lot, they must be cute and quite a handful, Agnes," the nurse chuckled. Her voice soothed

Agnes as the sedative took effect.

"They are my everything," said Agnes.

"Then we will get you patched up and home to them before school gets out," the nurse made her feel like this was a dentist appointment and would all be over shortly. Tears fell from Agnes's eyes, she couldn't help it, kindness and understanding had become foreign to her.

After the abortion, Agnes took a cab home. She had already lied to Asher that she was having a treatment to help her fake illness, so he shouldn't bother her tonight. He probably wouldn't even come home. The nanny was set to watch the kids so all Agnes had do was slip blissfully back into her bed.

When the taxi pulled up to their East Side building, Agnes wasn't paying attention. She only was counting bills for the driver and the twinges of pain in her abdomen kept her from looking up. She was headed to the front door when she heard her name, "Agnes. Agnes, wait." Sabine was standing on the sidewalk.

She was beautiful in her Chanel top, tailored pants and hair in her signature messy bun. Diamonds dripped from her ears and her fingers. The sight of her sent fury through Agnes.

"Agnes, why won't you talk to me? Asher said you were sick?" Sabine voice sounded concerned, motherly. But unlike the nurse from earlier, it set Agnes off. Sabine had no right to care, to be there, especially now. Agnes looked down and realized she was a mess. She was wearing old elastic pants, a stained sweater; she couldn't remember the last time she showered. All her jewelry was upstairs; she had removed it before going to the clinic. The humiliation rose like bile, choking her. Images of Sabine with Asher, of being raped, of the clinic crashed through her thoughts. Agnes had been betrayed, and now standing here, she looked the part. Raw, dirty, unarmed, the only thing left to do was focus her hatred on Sabine.

"How is fucking my husband, Sabine? Good? Great? Must be better than your own husband, he's a real brute, isn't he?"

Sabine went pale, and horror registered. She bit her lower lip. "Agnes ..." was all she could say.

"Here's what you don't know, Sabine, I saw you two in the woods that night in Maine. Yes, wasn't too hard since both of you were out in the open. Who knows if anyone else saw you, aside from your husband, because Eric did too. Yes, that's right, Sabine. And how do you think that made me feel? Us feel? One word, starts with an h, Sabine, a capital fucking H. That's right humiliated. So thank you Sabine, thank you for that. But that wasn't quite the end."

Sabine stood there motionless unable to get away from Agnes's venom.

"Question, Sabine, how do you think your husband takes being humiliated by his wife and partner? What does a rich, selfish, arrogant man do to exact revenge? Why, he takes his friend's wife, that would be me, Sabine, and pushes her down and rapes her on the dirt. Climbs right on top of her and unleashes all his anger on her instead of his own wife. So Sabine, forgive me for not calling you, not making you feel better, not being YOUR friend, Sabine."

Sabines face flushed with fear.

"Now if you will excuse me, I just had an abortion. A doctor just had to clean me out so that I wouldn't have the child of my rapist on this earth. Again you are welcome, so very welcome, Sabine." Agnes turned and stormed through the building door, ignited.

The most glamorous woman in New York woman stood on the sidewalk for a long time, her body shaking, whispering meekly. "I am so sorry," before turning and walking away.

Agnes worried Sabine would tell Asher everything, but for whatever reason she did not. Like an unspoken code among certain women. Keep secrets secret because they are not worth the trouble of explaining. The next day, a very large arrangement of peonies arrived, Agnes's favorite flower, but no card. Agnes knew they were from her and she put them in her bedroom with strange satisfaction that she knew Sabine's darkest secret. She had the power and control now and it made her feel slightly better.

Soon after, Eric Bartor joined his father's business and did not ask Asher to go with him. The relationship between the Williamses and the Bartor's dissolved naturally without either side questioning it. Asher rose to vice president at McMillon and with his own investments, was amassing a great fortune for their family. Agnes could not want for anything.

But for Agnes, it was time for a fresh start. Many wealthy families were moving out of the city, up the coast to Connecticut to raise their kids in lavish houses surrounded by rolling green hills and private schools with apple orchards. Asher thought it was a splendid idea, returning to their home state, wealthy, important people. While he still kept an apartment in the city for weekdays, Agnes was able to close the chapter on the city for good.

TEN

It wasn't that Ansel was keeping a secret, he just didn't want to mix situations right now. He wanted to focus on his family in Connecticut, not his life in Miami. The three siblings were either at the hospital or thinking about the hospital day and night. They operated as a crisis team navigating hour to hour, emotion to emotion. Tired, frayed and scared, the world felt fragile without their mother whole and well.

Ansel felt like he had been in Connecticut an eternity. When Abby and Arthur were not around, he would cry quietly in the shower. Losing his mother made him feel vulnerable because he had so few relationships in his life. For all the rotten things she had said and done, the hurt she had inflicted on them, she was still their mother, the one constant in their lives.

Regardless, Ansel loved his mother deeply. And he knew she loved him. Her drinking just masked that person, took the sweet mother he once knew and made her loathsome. These past few years he couldn't help but answer her phone calls, open her emails, hoping and wishing for a glimpse of the old Agnes. But her alcoholism robbed him of that, it made her cruel and unbearable. And toward the end, there was barely anything left.

Ansel loved when she told the story of him being born and forced her to tell and retell it over the years. For him, it was less about his entrance into the world than his mother's ingenuity. His mother, he proudly thought, was a clever woman.

It was a warm April in New York City and Ansel was due any day. Bored by waiting at home, Agnes took Arthur and Abby to Central Park to get some fresh air. That day they were offering free rides on the local horses at the barn. Abby, at only four, was already smitten by the animals and the grooms let her feed them carrots and apple slices. Arthur naturally stayed ten feet away, cautious of the two-ton beasts and wrinkling his nose at their musky smell. Then Agnes had an idea.

"May I ride one of your horses just for a bit?" she asked a young groom who immediately looked at her swollen belly with concern. "Oh, it's fine, I am not due for a while," Agnes lied. She flashed one of her convincing smiles full of joy and the young man blushed. It was 1973 after all; nobody really obsessed about lawsuits or safety concerns like the world unfortunately did today.

"Are you sure?" The groom said and Agnes just patted him on the back reassuringly. "Darling would you question your own mother?" Agnes kept smiling.

The groom shrugged and led a brown mare over to a box so Agnes could climb aboard. Abby was clapping her hands with glee as Arthur scowled at the event. Agnes told Arthur to watch his sister while she gently trotted away down a path. She was gone for a while, enough to make Arthur start to worry, but then she came back smiling.

Agnes got off the mare and handed the groom a ten-dollar bill, thanking him. She grabbed Arthur and Abby by the hands and led them to a taxi. "Guess what?" she said "Your little brother or sister is coming!"

Asher did make it in time for Ansel's arrival, which luckily was easy. He was smaller than Arthur and Abby, only seven pounds but healthy. Agnes had already picked out his name after seeing a photography exhibit at the Met. The photos were beautiful black-and-white landscapes of national parks and Agnes had been mesmerized. She thought only a true artist could see the world with such wonder. The photographer's name was Ansel Adams. She wished if she had a son that he could create such beauty, such magic, and her mind settled on that prophecy in the name Ansel.

Agnes had been the type of mother who let Ansel stay home from school for no reason, who forced him to swim class to be strong and encouraged his artwork. Every birthday he awoke to streamers and balloons and piles of presents in the living room. His mother loved birthdays better than any holiday.

"It is the only day of the year that is all yours," she said gleefully. She never could bake a cake right so she would pile donuts as high as she could and put candles all over them for breakfast.

She kissed them every night before bed and took them to their favorite movies on weekends. There was no doubt for any of them: Agnes loved them.

But when she drank, it was if she wore a hideous costume. Recently, she would call Ansel and he was always drawn to answer. Fear that she would hurt herself enveloped him like a shroud. They were phone calls filled with drunken tirades, bashing her friends or Abby and Arthur. She wasn't just unkind, she was cruel. She called Arthur weak for marrying Janine and Abby a show-off for loving her husband. She loved to talk about Asher with such hatred, and Ansel pleaded with her to forget him. No one was good enough for her any more. Good days were getting fewer and farther between and Ansel stayed in Miami, visiting less and less.

It's not that he didn't want to see his family. He was just scared at what he would find. Each visit, Agnes looked older and older, more bloated from the drinking. She was aging rapidly and her beauty became a lifeless, distorted shell. It pained Ansel to see her fraying hair and watering eyes. She shuffled from room to room like she was a hundred years old. His mother forgot names easily and got angry about the simplest of things. So Ansel answered her calls. He listened while she raged until she went to bed and he knew she was safe. They didn't often talk about Ansel's life, which was all well and good; he wanted to keep it private anyways.

Maybe because of his parents' marriage, Ansel never truly believed in love, or perhaps he just didn't believe in it for himself. He had long ago resigned to the single life, bruised and battered by his parents' inability to be in a committed, loving relationship. It was a relief to be gay because there wasn't the outside push for a relationship. The world seem to accept Ansel to be well enough on his own. He felt bad for women in their 20s and especially 30s who were made to feel like spinsters without a man. Only Abby asked about his love life but only Abby had defied natural forces and found true love. Abby knew deep down, Ansel needed love.

When Ansel came out as gay to his father at 18, Asher's response was mediocre at best. Sequestered in his home office on Sundays, it was one of the few chances for Ansel to talk to him alone.

"Dad," he interrupted while his father tapped away on the computer. "Dad!" He said again to get his attention.

"Yes, son," Asher barely looked up.

"I'm gay. I just thought you should know that, like one of those things if the police found my lifeless body. He had blue eyes, brown hair and was gay."

"Don't be so dramatic, Ansel, it's really not necessary,"

Asher looked up and just stared at him. "Son, if I didn't know you were gay already, then I don't have eyes in my head. Is that it?"

"Well, yeah," Ansel said, disappointed. The silence blanketed the room.

"Do you need anything else?" asked Asher.

"Sure, some cash. I'm going out." Ansel didn't need the money but he felt spiteful and wanted to take the only thing he could get from his father. Asher pulled two hundred-dollar bills from his pocket and waved them at Ansel looking back at the computer screen.

Was it because Asher was a womanizer and simply could not relate to a gay son, thought a hurt Ansel. *Did it make him uncomfortable, did it mean anything to his father at all?* It disappointed Ansel not to know, he would have preferred anger or any emotion to just nothing, no reaction at all.

His mother, on the other hand, kissed him on his forehead and said, "You do whatever the hell makes you happy." She was secretly thrilled and promptly bragged about it to the ladies at the club. It was terribly progressive to her. Abby and Arthur, of course, knew it all along. Abby said, "So what? You get a special VIP card or something?" and Arthur replied, "I am still older and smarter than you, don't forget it."

As the third child, Ansel always felt on his own. Everyone was preoccupied with their lives, all of them older and more complicated. They never took enough notice how complicated Ansel's life was. While his brother lived to order things and his sister sought chaos, Ansel was somewhere in between all the time, navigating his way the best he could. He rarely asked for help for any matter. He quietly mused to himself about everything. His mind was in constant motion. Art was such a clever field for him. It spoke emotions that he was incapable of ever putting into words. When he looked at paintings from different cultures and different eras, he found a connection. The glorious thing about art was that it was an emotional language that Ansel understood. He found a place for his anger at his absentee father and for his deep-seated love and worry for his mother and his siblings, who he could never admit he couldn't live without. Ansel rarely told his family he loved them, because he felt he loved them too much and he wasn't sure they felt the same. Miami was his only shield against all the memories and sentiment at home.

A few months back, Ansel finally met someone in Miami. It was still new and more frightening than he would admit but now thousands of miles away, Ansel thought of Hector more often than not. Hector was the antidote to all the sadness. He was funny and kind and cared about Ansel without the pain or chaos of his family.

It began on a rainy, dull day in the gallery when Ansel and his assistant Kerry were moving heavy sculptures in preparation for an exhibit. Although they worked together, they were also good friends. From Connecticut as well, Kerry Garner was a funny, no-nonsense girl who understood Ansel. Like him, she had ditched stodgy suburbia for sunshine and a life free of family and obligations. At 34, she was being harassed by her family about marriage and kids, the Connecticut way. *Tick tock*, her mother would say. But people could care less about such things in South Beach, where life was always a party. Ansel intended on making Kerry a partner soon if she planned on staying in Miami, because it was so rare to like and trust someone in his life. They were two peas in a very distorted pod.

"Oh look!" Ansel said as he pulled a bottle of Patron Silver tequila from behind his desk with a bow on it. "This this was a gift from Mrs. Bowden for the De Kooning sculpture, how thoughtful of her. Let's have snitch."

"It's 11 a.m., Ansel," said Kerry, grabbing two glasses. "But as Einstein said, 'time is an illusion.'" They drank a shot and began moving the cast iron sculptures again.

"God, these things are heavy." Ansel grunted.

"Do you think the artist got like really stoned, like really really stoned, looked at a forest and said 'Bingo?'" asked Kerry.

"If he didn't, then there is no reasonable explanation," sipped Ansel.

"I feel like I need a red cape," giggled Kerry.

"During the opening just keep running through the trees and asking about a wolf." Both of them were getting a quick buzz on. Nothing else to do on a rainy Tuesday. In Miami, rain meant no one went outside; apparently they were all made of sugar. But then again, a Miami downpour could be like Niagara Falls on steroids.

An iron tree toppled and struck Ansel. "Oh shit." They said staring at Ansel's foot trapped under a silver trunk. The pain hit a good thirty seconds later and Ansel howled. Even though they were acutely tipsy, Kerry swiftly got him in a cab and off they went to the urgent care clinic. Ansel had begged not to go to the ER, hospitals terrified him, so Kerry poured him more tequila.

It was June, off-season for South Beach and few people were at the clinic. "No drunk tourists," Kerry said, looking around, "just drunk locals." She was amusing herself.

They were ushered into a bay. "Nurse, can you get him one of those backless gowns, he would love one," smirked Kerry. The nurse was unfazed as she took his blood pressure. A doctor would be in shortly.

Didn't they know not to leave two drunks alone in a hospital bay? By the time Dr. Hector Diaz drew back the curtain, Kerry was repeatedly taking her temperature and punching buttons on a beeping machine and Ansel was making a gauze and popsicle stick head band.

"I dropped a metal tree on my footie," Ansel laughed.

Another doctor poked his head in to see the ruckus and Ansel shouted, "Doctor, Doctor," nodding to each of them, hardly containing his laughter.

"Seems someone has seen 'Spies Like Us,'" Dr. Diaz said without looking up from the chart. "Never heard that joke before."

"Yes!" Ansel was pleased the reference didn't go unnoticed. "Really hurts, Doctor, pain chart twelve. I don't handle pain. She did it." Ansel pointed to Kerry who was now wearing the gauzy popsicle headband.

"I did not," Kerry shouted. "It's his fault, he's a damn dandelion."

"I'm a dandy dandelion," and Ansel burst into fresh waves of uncontrolled laughter. Dr. Diaz assessed the two of them like an amused father. He promptly placed a hand on Ansel's foot and pained seared through him. "OOoooow," said Ansel. Hector smiled.

"So tell me a little bit more about this accident?"

"Well, we had to move the statues. Trees, iron trees, not the Iron Throne, that would be silly. Game of Thrones is so good. Anyway, what was I saying? Oh, damn things weigh a ton but they do go for an awful lot of money. She is little red riding hood by the way."

"I'm his assistant," Kerry vaguely explained. "It's an art gallery."

"What gallery?"

"Williams," Ansel hiccupped. "Williams Contemporary Art on Collins."

"Mmmm, I see and was it a slow day at the gallery?"

"Yes indeedy, very slow," Ansel slurred.

"He's cute," Kerry whispered and pointed at the doctor. Hector pretended to ignore them.

"So cocktails were in order?"

"Yes," Ansel shouted too loudly. "Tequila. Patrón from a

patron." He mispronounced Patrón and patron.

"Mm, okay we are going to get you an X-ray, but I think it may only be a fracture. Your hangover may hurt worse later."

"Then can I have drugs?" Ansel asked with a chipper voice.

"Oh can I have some too?" said Kerry, giggly.

"Let's get you that X-ray first, cowboy," Hector winked and smiled in a way Ansel would never forget.

Ansel left with an air cast on his foot and nothing stronger than ibuprofen, dammit. Afterward, Kerry called it a day and got Ansel home, so he could sober up and watch reruns of *The Golden Girls*.

The opening was Friday night for the trees and Ansel was annoyed to be shuffling around in a boot. Kerry wore a red dress, to which Ansel replied, "Touché." By 7 o'clock, the gallery was full with the usual patrons sipping cheap white wine and schmoozing the same people they schmoozed at every opening. Walking through the crowd, saying hellos, Ansel bumped right into Dr. Diaz. This time, without the lab coat and clipboard, he looked fit, thinner and even more handsome.

He was Spanish or Cuban, Ansel couldn't tell, but he had a lovely olive skin, bushy eyebrows, a thick head of black hair and glittery eyes. The two men were exactly the same height and weight, twins from two different cultures.

"*Buenos Noches*, Ansel," said Hector.

"Doctor, ummm," Ansel turned a deep shade of crimson, remembering how he and Kerry behaved.

"*Amigo*, call me Hector," he was enjoying watching Ansel squirm. "I live in the neighborhood and thought I would check out these trees slash weapons of destruction."

"Listen, I want to apologize, Kerry and I, we are not well." Kerry pushed through the crowd, "Doc! You're here, awesome." Kerry was never embarrassed.

"Got any Patrón?" Hector asked her.

"Of course, sweetie, I'll be right back," As Kerry turned away, she winked at Ansel. Ansel was clueless as to what was going on.

"How is the aircast?" Hector asked.

"It's like a Prada shoe, if it was knockoff, made in Taiwan, wrapped in cement and sold at Walmart. It's really stunning." Hector agreed.

"Only a few more weeks and then maybe your prince will show up with a shoe. I always thought the story would make more sense if Cinderella was drunk. Only drunk girls run away without picking up their shoe," said Hector, enjoying himself at Ansel's expense.

Was the doctor joking about him being a drunk Cinderella? Was he implying he was Ansel's prince? Wait, was the doctor hitting on him? Ansel turned crimson again and stammered about getting back to the party.

Eventually people left the gallery, Hector stayed and waited patiently for Ansel's attention.

"I have reservations at Casa Tua," South Beach's best and most exclusive Italian restaurant. "Would you care to join me?" Kerry was behind him and madly giving thumbs up behind the doctor's head like she was having a stroke. Ansel had no choice.

It was a perfect evening, aside from Ansel limping along like a toddler learning to walk. Hector was not only funny but very smart. He was Cuban from immigrant parents and had worked his way through medical school. He didn't date much because of doctors' hours, had never seen the snow, never done cocaine, and never slept with a woman. The doctor liked funny movies with anyone who was a former or current cast member of *Saturday Night Live* and loved rewatching old sitcoms. A perfect night for him was home in bed with take-out food and something on TV. He hated exercising and thought politicians should be forced to work in McDonalds before taking office. The more Hector spoke, the more Ansel not only liked him but admired him. The South Beach community could be vain and trite, a good time but not very sincere (that's how Ansel made his money, after all, selling to those people). It was the first night in a long time Ansel forgot about himself, his family, his mother and lost himself in someone's else's story. It was one of the best nights of his life.

———

Now the November cold made Ansel's bones ache and he missed his sunshine state and, admittedly, Hector. Abby and he spent more time at the hospital; Agnes was coming around. She still asked for cigarettes but had started eating solid food, toast versus just pudding – but only chocolate not butterscotch. As her demands grew, they saw her old self coming back. But when she hallucinated – things like her father coming to visit, he had died of a heart attack in his classroom years before and fluffy bunnies on the floor – it wrenched their hearts to see her so confused.

Ansel secretly called Hector every day, an outlet for all his sadness. It killed Hector to hear Ansel's voice lifeless and exhausted from the hospital. Life and death was Hector's profession but it did not make the situation easier. He walked Ansel through the diagnosis and helped where he could. Hector listened as Ansel told stories of Agnes, a loving mother, a tragic mother, a bitter mother. As the youngest, Ansel was the observer of his family. He noted all Williams behaviors, put them away like books in his library. He understood them and forgave them like no other. His role was the loving one.

So Hector didn't hesitate when he had three days off to fly to Hartford to surprise Ansel. His shock exiting the Connecticut airport was laughable, a Cuban in the arctic breeze. Clapping his hands together and breathing in the cold air for the first time, he got a rental car and headed to Abby's.

Only Jake was home. "Can I help you?" he asked as he watched the stranger turn left and right, confused on his doorstep. It was if the man had landed on a foreign planet and kept checking everything out.

But it was terribly new to Hector. Abby and Jake lived on two acres in the Connecticut woods. The house was like a Puritan farmhouse, white clapboard, green shutters. It was cozy and big enough for the family. There was an outlying barn with Jake's workshop and, upstairs, a renovated apartment for guests, and that's where Ansel had been staying when he wasn't at Arthur's palace. The place was dotted with trees and lawns like an idyllic meadow.

For Hector, the place looked like a movie set, something with Jimmy Stewart. Even handsome Jake in a flannel shirt looked like a catalog. Nothing could have been more opposite than Miami.

"Yes, hi I'm Dr. Hector Diaz? A friend of Ansel's?" Jake looked confused.

But Jake let him in and assessed the situation. "Ansel doesn't have friends, doctor, or friends he lets us meet…" Hector smiled broadly and Jake knew this was going to be good.

"Yes, I know. I feel like I am a Cuban unicorn in this whole scenario," Jake laughed out loud and offered him drink.

Abby and Ansel were all still at the hospital and so he was left alone to grill Hector about his relationship with Ansel. By the time the brother and sister returned home, Jake was beaming with man crush.

When Ansel walked into the room, Hector stood and they just stared at each other. Abby, confused, looked at Jake, who shook his head and ushered her out of the room. Ansel welled with tears so happy to see him and fell into his arms.

"How did you..." Ansel stammered.

"Well, it's not *that* difficult to find the Miami airport," teased Hector. "Ansel, although it pains you to admit it, you are not alone, *mi amor*."

Ansel called from the living room, "You two can come in now, and bring drinks." Ansel didn't like touching people and he didn't like people touching him – as though affection was a spark of electricity, causing him to recoil. Abby couldn't help but notice Ansel had his hand on Hector's leg and sat as close to him as possible, almost afraid he wasn't real. She had never been so thrilled for her brother. If Ansel could find any happiness in all of this, she would take it.

ELEVEN

Westport society in the '70s wasn't as exclusive or hard to enter as it is now. Sure, the money was old and the families were even older but there was still plenty of space to share. Wealthy New Yorkers were just getting on the suburban bandwagon and the appeal of large houses with swimming pools was enticing. Asher and Agnes were new to the area but not to Connecticut, which helped them easily acclimate. Westport was far fancier and snobbier then where they had grown up, but the landscape was the same.

Asher took great pride in purchasing a sprawling four-bedroom stone house nestled on two acres of prime Westport real estate. The front hall was as big as their first New York apartment. It was a newer home with modern amenities and it felt grand to the Williamses. It was a big change from apartment living, but Agnes liked it. Looking out windows at trees, not buildings, reminded her of being a young girl. Although Asher had to commute to the city, he felt satisfied to be returning to his home state a wealthy man. They still kept a smaller apartment in the city for when Asher didn't want to commute home. He had the best of both worlds and praised Agnes for the idea to move.

Secretly, Asher loved roaming through his big house, looking at the fine antiques and artwork they purchased. He gave Agnes unlimited funds to decorate and she did so with the taste and elegance of someone who had always had the finer things in life. He agreed with everything she did because she made them look as important as he felt.

Agnes liked making their home; it gave her purpose. Away from the city, the fresh air and new environment seemed the elixir she needed, at least for a while. She pushed the memory of Maine further down into her consciousness. Every time it itched, she didn't scratch but distracted herself the best she could with the children.

The children were elated with the move. The large backyard was covered with soft grass and elegant trees that Arthur and Abby took to climbing. Agnes immediately purchased a playground set so she could watch the three of them without having to go anywhere. In the suburbs she had no need for a nanny. She wanted to spend as much time with them as possible.

After a few months, the kids settled into their exclusive private school and Asher adjusted to going back and forth from the city. Without Asher home every day, Agnes felt more insecure, not less. She called him often at the office and regretted when he stayed in the city for the night. As safe as she was, surrounded by large hedges and crickets chirping in the night, Agnes wasn't safe from her own dark thoughts. The question of happiness was formidable. She had it all now, but was she happy?

Agnes had everything, didn't she? Did she have a right to complain? Young, pretty, rich, her children were perfect, how could she wake every day and feel so alone? It was hard for her to be close to people, especially in their world. Sabine had been her closest friend, and look what she had done. At night Agnes would toss alone, sweating in her sheets, as her mother filled her thoughts. The only women she had ever been close to betrayed her, abandoned her. The memories went around and around in her head and she could only wonder why.

Desperate for some kind of answer, Agnes went to her father. They didn't see each other often; he came for holidays but wasn't much of a grandfather. He didn't respond to small children and Agnes didn't know how he made it through her childhood. The irony was he and Arthur were so alike.

Still living alone on Grove Avenue, still teaching five days a week, the Professor was older, more frail, but his mind was still active. He often wrote about economics and the markets for major publications; he was well respected in his field.

Agnes knew how to find him. His schedule rarely altered. She bought lunch and entered halfway through one of his classes just like she had the day met Asher. The professor didn't show a hint of surprise when she interrupted his class. Radiant in a summer dress and expensive jewelry, he was proud of her, although he never said so.

They sat in the classroom and had lunch quietly together after his students left.

"To what do I owe the pleasure?"

"Just checking on you Dad; it's easy now that we are in Westport." He was only an hour away.

"Well, that's nice isn't it? How are the kids adjusting? And Asher?"

"They are all fine and love having a yard. It's true, the city isn't the best for kids."

"And Asher?"

"He's good."

"I read a lot about him and his, what did they call it, 'upward mobility,'" the professor said with a hint of sarcasm.

"Yep, he has certainly made a name for himself, for us, I guess." They both were silent. The professor ate his sandwich and waited for Agnes to continue.

"Dad, how come we never talked about Mom?"

Her father put his sandwich down, taken aback a little. He wiped his face with a napkin, taking a moment to collect his thoughts.

"What's there to say?"

"Why did she leave? Why don't we talk about it?"

"Aggie, if I have taught you anything, at least by example, it is hard for a man to admit when he is wrong." That sat in the air between them.

"I need more, Dad," said Agnes honestly, not letting him off the hook.

"I suppose you do. Maybe I do owe you that," he sighed and said, "I probably shouldn't have married your mother, she was too young, too wild, I was older and should have been wiser. I was smitten, as they say. I thought she could be the spice to my dull life. But you can't tame someone who doesn't want to be tamed. I was too bullheaded to take "no". Men do that, they think they know what women want without ever asking them. It's stupid, but men do it generation after generation."

Agnes took that in, surprised. Her father was very perceptive.

He continued, "It was me that convinced her to have a baby, she didn't want to, she wanted to wait. But I thought it would be good for her. How arrogant of me. And it was my arrogance," the professor paused and hung his head, "that cost you a mother."

Tears welled in Agnes's eyes.

"And it was my arrogance that wouldn't talk to you about it

after she left. I just thought we could move on. I thought I knew what was best for you without even asking. Aggie, I am so sorry."

"Did she ever love me?"

"I think she did, as much as she could, but sometimes loving someone can feel like your own prison, if that makes sense. And she wanted her freedom." Agnes was crying now, and even the professor had watery eyes.

"Again, Aggie, I am so sorry." He wouldn't look at her, but she could feel his shame.

"It doesn't feel right not to be loved by your own mother." Agnes surprised even herself by saying that out loud.

"But the good news is you aren't her. Aggie, I have seen you with Arthur and Ansel and Abby, you love those kids more than I think you even know. Focus on them, what you have, not what you don't."

"What about you Dad, all these years alone?"

"Who says I'm alone?" The professor smiled and laughed. "I guess I should have told you, but you and Asher always are so busy. Do you remember Mrs. Brady? Anita?"

"Wait, my math teacher from high school?"

"Yes, we have been seeing each other for about three years. I am thinking about asking her to move in."

"What?! Dad, wait, Mrs. Brady, Anita was married ..."

"Yeah, that was a little bit of a scandal, thought I would keep you out of it."

"Oh my god, Dad." And Agnes laughed for the first time in a long time. She gave him a kiss on the cheek and left. She knew that was all he had to say, and she understood.

They settled into Connecticut life. The kids made friends, the Williamses joined the Southport Country Club and The Cobb Racquet Club. Agnes got on the board of the kids' school. On the outside, everything was picture perfect. Asher was now partner at

McMillon, renamed McMillon and Williams, one of the most powerful investment firms on Wall Street. The Williams name was stretching far and wide and people Agnes had never met clambered to be their friends.

But her life, her real life, was empty, shallow. After the kids went to school, she often went back to bed. Agnes had never been one for hobbies, but she did read. Novels were her great escape, and there were never enough of them. Whenever the topic of literature came up, people were always impressed by Agnes's vast mental library. She could recall in great detail the most intense books like *Madame Bovary, Crime and Punishment, Sophie's Choice*. She could recite who was on the New York Times bestseller list that week. It was a habit she had formed living in a house with a single father who was preoccupied himself. Books were her best friends.

But even the best of novels could not take away her gnawing melancholy. It was far too late to be postpartum. The years of supporting Asher's career, building their reputation, she had some purpose, but now? Now what was her purpose, aside from getting the kids to piano lessons on time and scheduling a school fair? Was this it? Was this what she had so dreamily thought would be the greatest life? She listened to a maid vacuum hand-woven carpets that once she never dreamed she could afford, and all she wanted to do was hide. Outside, gardeners came to trim the hedges, a man showed up to service their car and Agnes hated it. There was no privacy.

When Asher was home, he had nowhere to go, not like the city. He took up space in the house with loud footsteps and he always was bellowing into the phone. Either it was eerily quiet without him or too loud with him. Everything frustrated Agnes.

With no other options, she went to a doctor. She chose the friendly general practitioner, Dr. Larry Black, who serviced all the wealthy Connecticut housewives from school. He had a reputation for prescribing diet pills that thrilled the ladies. Later they would learn it was simply a low dosage of speed. He also prescribed a healthy amount of valium, mother's little helper, as the simple cure-all. Westport housewives were convinced Dr. Black could fix any ailment and highly recommended him.

He asked general questions about her health and asked if she needed more energy, more pep? No. Then do you need to calm down feel more relaxed? No, none of that. Agnes explained she felt sad for no reason.

Dr. Black was going to prescribe something new for Agnes called a tricyclic antidepressant. She had never heard of it and accepted the drug without question. Dr. Black was using Agnes as a guinea pig. Antidepressants did not gain popularity until the late '80s when Prozac hit the market. For now, altering the brain's chemistry was new territory to both doctors and patients.. Also, the late '70s saw very little oversight on general practitioners and their prescriptions.

Agnes didn't tell Asher about the drugs; she just wanted all her problems to go away. It wasn't until a week or two after taking the pills she began to notice changes. A drowsiness overtook her and any activity caused a certain level of dizziness, even getting up from a chair. But the good news was Agnes didn't feel sad any more, that was true. But she also felt nothing, like someone had numbed her brain. Watching her kids eat or sleep or play usually caused a surge in her heart. When they giggled or hugged her, she would spontaneously smile, but now, nothing.

Days slipped by where there was neither joy nor pain. Her belly began to get thick, and she blamed the lack of exercise. No get-up-and-go in her, she laughed. But she didn't really care if she got fat, in fact she didn't really care about anything. Sometimes she could just feel a slight tingle on the side of her brain but that was all.

The kids began to notice and tried to tell Asher. But they were so small, Arthur was only 9, Abby 7 and Ansel just 3, they couldn't describe it. Mommy just wasn't being Mommy anymore.

They asked Asher if Mommy was sick. They told him she spent a lot of time lying in bed. In turn, Asher would question Agnes but she was unfocused and gave answers like don't worry, I've seen a doctor.

One Saturday on a sunny June day, Asher was going to the club for a round of golf. Agnes hadn't gotten out of her pajamas yet but she had fed the kids. Asher stopped himself going out the door.

"Aggie, are you all right? Should I stay home today? You don't look well," he was concerned but he also wanted to take advantage of a day of golf.

"Ashh," Aggie's speech was slightly slurry. "I'm fine, just didn't sleep well, you go, I'll be fine." Asher hesitated but went anyway.

Arthur and Abby had gotten good at chasing after little Ansel. Agnes didn't worry when they played outside without her so she went back to her bedroom to lie down. She must have drifted off when Arthur began shaking her.

He was crying saying something about Ansel. *Ansel broke something? That couldn't be right?* Her vision was blurry and when she got up, she almost fainted. Arthur was crying and hitting her. Why was he hitting her? And then he was pulling her arm. She followed, her only thought *Ansel*.

Arthur pushed her and pulled her outside. It was bright and sunny and Agnes took a deep breath. Abby and Ansel were in the back seat of the car both crying. Agnes shook her head violently trying to clear the fog.

Arthur grabbed her hand and put the car keys in them.

"Mom," he said slowly and clearly, "Take us to the

hospital." Agnes remembers the sunlight speckling the bright green tree leaves. The Connecticut road wound up and down and around. She breathed in and out hard, focusing on her task getting to the hospital.

Pulling up to the door, Arthur carried Ansel in while Abby stayed behind with their mother. All Agnes could remember was her sweet child screaming as loud as she could, "HELP! My mother needs help!!"

Hours later Agnes awoke in a hospital bed, the sun still bright as the summer days were long. "Ansel," she muttered. "The kids…" Asher was at her bedside.

"Shhhh, love, he's okay. Ansel broke his wrist jumping from the swing. It was a clean break though, he'll be fine. Doctors say it will heal fast."

"The kids, where are they?" Her thoughts getting clearer by the second, anxiety rose in her.

"They are at Leslie Johnson's with her kids having a playdate. They have a pool so the kids are happy. I think we need to get a pool." Asher was babbling, he was uncomfortable, scared to find out what really happened.

"What happened, Ash? I barely remember getting here." He didn't know and just shook his head.

The doctor came in, "Well Mrs. Williams, took a little digging but I think we know what happened." Relief flooded through her.

"Have you been taking a prescription? We called your physician, a Dr. Black, and he said he prescribed an antidepressant? Does that sound correct?"

"What the hell is an antidepressant?" said Asher loudly.

"Yes," said Agnes nodded.

"Okay, good. We know you hadn't been drinking, nothing was in your blood but this medicine is rather new and can be unpredictable."

"What the hell were you taking it for?" Asher was confused.

"Ash, calm down, I was just sad, that's all."

"Sad about what?!"

"Mr. Williams, we can get to that later. Mrs. Williams, how many were you taking a day? "

"One, sometimes two, sometimes I would just forget and take another."

"Okay I see, I think the first problem was you were taking too many and that led to today. The dizziness, confusion and sleeping were caused by incorrect dosage or maybe just a reaction in general. My recommendation is you stop taking them; I am not sure they are right for you. We want to keep you here a few days for observation. For the future, maybe, instead of medication, you should go see a psychiatrist and work out some other ways to feel better. I know being a mother of three can be stressful, so maybe as a family you can all work on that together."

"Well, she sure as shit isn't taking any pills any more," said Asher.

"No, Asher I won't, it'll be okay. I will figure it out; nothing is that bad, promise. I just thought they would make me feel better. I'll take up tennis, okay? I promise, it's fine, really."

Agnes stayed a few days in the hospital as her head cleared. Honestly, the whole incident was so scary that she told herself from that moment on to buck up. She willed herself to get stronger, happier the best she could. This was just the wake-up call she needed to finally put the past in the past and she could do that on her own. Couldn't she?

TWELVE

Agnes was coming around at the hospital. It had been almost two weeks and her mind was clearer. Her oxygen levels were good, her heart was strong and she was getting feisty about going home. Abby and Ansel along with Hector were standing outside her room, waiting for Dr. Super Cooper to finish examining her. Abby said "shhhh" to the guys to stop talking so she could hear the conversation between her mother and the doctor.

"Oh, yes Dr. Cooper , I think I will go back to AA again. You're right, it's time I did make a change," said Agnes sweetly.

"That's the spirit, Agnes, a lot of times, deciding to make a change, we can see a lot of progress."

"Yes, I agree, so I can go home soon? Promise no more drinking."

Abby turned to Ansel, "Do you hear this bullshit? She is playing him so she can go home. And he believes her?! What planet are these two on? Jesus." Abby was annoyed Dr. Cooper was even entertaining the discussion. She saw Dr. Moore and waved her down.

"My mother can't walk, let alone get herself to an AA meeting. What is this bullshit Dr. Cooper is talking about? This is ridiculous. She is dying, we all can see it. Her eyes look like fucking sunflowers and the itch has gotten worse. Sorry, I didn't mean to swear."

Abby felt guilty about her mother's itch, for months her mother had been complaining. Her arms and upper legs had an itch that seemed to be under the skin. But no one could see an actual problem. Agnes complained day and night that her arms were on fire. Abby bought her every lotion and potion she could find. Even ice packs didn't help.

Now Abby was kicking herself, if she had just googled liver failure she would have seen it as a symptom of cirrhosis. The toxins, unable to be filtered by her liver, build up near the skin and create the sensation. Abby felt stupid and ashamed for not recognizing it earlier.

"I completely understand. I was going to talk to you about options. Let's go to a private room." Dr. Moore led them away from Dr. Cooper. She was dismissing him too. They talked about home health care versus a facility. No way would Agnes want to go a home, Abby explained, they could afford to set up a camp in her house.

The doctor explained how the hospital would help facilitate hospice and a nursing association, they would bring all the necessary equipment to Agnes's house. Two nurses could live with her around the clock. Luckily, Agnes had the money for it. They made a plan, called Arthur, who was on board and would get his secretary to start the arrangements. In a few days' time, they could take their mother home. But as Dr. Moore reminded them, they needed to prepare themselves for the long haul.

First they had to get Agnes to agree to their plan. It would mean relinquishing control of her house, her life and allow others to take over. Abby and Ansel knew their mother was not going to take this well. Ansel, who was the least confrontational of them all, begged Abby to do it, so she went in to talk to their mother.

"Hi Mom," Abby busied herself shuffling blankets and arranging her mothers extra bedclothes. "Listen, Mom, good news, we are going to be able to take you home soon."

"I know dear, I'm fine, really, it's sweet of you kids to worry but get back to your boys, tell Ansel he can go home." Agnes was convinced life would be returning to normal.

"Well, Mom, here's the catch, in order to go home, you are going to need some help in the house," Abby said, waiting for it to sink in and there it was. She saw it that glint her mother's eye when she started to get angry.

"No dear, I don't need strangers in my house. I will be just fine." Agnes said firmly.

"Mom, listen to me, they found you in a pool of blood by yourself. I don't want that to happen again, do you?"

"Don't be so dramatic Abby, you're always so dramatic."

"Did this not happen? Have we not been in a hospital for two weeks?" Abby's sarcasm came out.

"I'm fine, Abby, go away. Just get me my bag and I will go home myself." The two women glared at each other. The showdown had begun.

"Mom, you can't even walk any more."

"I most certainly can." Her mother looked like an angry animal. Eyes darting left to right. Abby stood at the foot of the hospital bed not about to back down.

"All right, Mother, if you walk from this hospital bed to the bathroom, I will let you go home alone." Silence.

"You little bitch. You think you are so great but you're not, you had an affair with a married man, so disgusting." Agnes had turned vile.

"Doesn't matter, Mom, nothing you can say can get you out of this."

"Well, I have gotten you out of plenty of situations. Without me little girl, your life would have been a disaster. You remember that! Ungrateful, that's what you are, so ungrateful for everything I gave you."

"Mom," Abby's heart was racing but she was trying to stay calm, "this isn't about me, it's about you. You cannot take care of yourself any more."

"I most certainly can. You are not some Mother Teresa, sweetheart. Your husband can't make a dime, you just want me to die so you can get all my money. That's all you kids want from me, my money." Agnes was growling.

"Stop it, Mother, stop it!" Abby waited for her mother to stay quiet before saying, "Fine, if you won't have nurses at the house, then Windemere it is." This was Abby's trump card. Windemere was the old folks home near them. Abby and Agnes went there once to visit an older friend of Agnes's and it was awful. The home was a catacomb of depression with small cement rooms and old people drooling in wheelchairs.

"We can get you a room there and since you cannot walk, that is where I will have the ambulance take you." Abby just stared at her mother, waiting.

Agnes was fuming and would not look at Abby. Silence reigned.

"Fine. But I stay in my own bed, no hospital bed. That's ridiculous and these nurses better not bother me or I will fire them. Remember, it's MY house."

"I have no doubt. But you get to go home, Mom, you get to be in your house, with your garden. Okay? I think that's a pretty good deal." Abby fluffed her mother's pillow and told her she would arrange everything. Her heart was still racing from the argument but she had gotten through it.

Outside the hospital, Ansel said, "You did so good, Abs, so so good. How you can stand up to her like that? I could never, you just did so good. Don't listen to all those things she said, just forget them. Her brain isn't normal."

"Can you believe how she just twisted that on me, bringing up the past like that? She is so goddamn mean. Christ, she doesn't even believe she is sick." Abby was in disbelief over it all.

"Well if she had been able to admit she was sick then maybe we wouldn't be here right now," replied Ansel.

It wasn't that her mother was wrong, it was that her mother was right. That's what burned Abby. It was the way she twisted what had happened and threw it back at her daughter with such disgust. How could her mother be so cruel knowing how hard all of this was for Abby?

—

Because of her mother, Abby broke up with Jake before they graduated college in 1991. Agnes's unhappiness terrified her. It wasn't hard to see her mother's envy of women who had gone to college or had careers. Abby felt Agnes's bitterness like stinging nettles. Her mother had never even lived on her own, not until her father had moved out. Abby was only sure about one thing in her future: she wasn't going to repeat the mistakes of her parents, or at least she thought.

Like Asher, Abby had a stubborn streak. The only girl and middle child, she was good with people and a perpetual nurturer, but when it came to following through on an idea or sticking to her guns, Abby rarely caved. Like Arthur's orderliness, Abby was predictable when it came to being bullheaded.

"We are just too young," she told Jake. "I love you. I love you like no other human being but if I don't go try, if I don't go live on my own, then my mother will have taught me nothing." Jake was heartbroken. He was angry, too, at the Williamses for having such a screwed up marriage, angry Abby didn't choose him, and angry that for whatever reason, he understood what Abby was doing. He loved her that much. His own mother told him, if you let someone go and they come back then it was truly meant to be. Jake had waited three years in college for Abby to even notice him; he had reservoirs of hope.

After college, Abby moved into Asher's penthouse on the Upper East Side. It had four bedrooms, after all. All Abby had to do was tell her father what job she wanted and he made it happen. It was the epitome of privilege, but why not? Abby had enough dark scars from her parents to at least enjoy a few bonuses as well. Asher had so much pull in New York, it only took a phone call. She wanted to work for a newspaper; it appealed to her in a way she couldn't explain. Considering her paycheck didn't matter and all her living expenses were taken care of, Abby took a low-level job with the New York Chronicle. It was a weekly newspaper whose features were revered for being well-researched, incisive and subtly liberal. The Chronicle had been around since the Great Depression and its reputation was indisputable.

Abby would be assisting on research. Never had she been so scared or excited to finally be a grownup, out of sight of parents and teachers. She felt a little like Mary Tyler Moore. Entering the paper for the first time, Abby made a decision not to talk about her family. She did not want to be associated with Wall Street's Asher Williams and certainly did not mention the rent-free penthouse she was living in. She wanted to make it all on her own.

The newspaper business is like no other, not for the faint of heart or the unambitious. Abby learned quickly that newspaper people treat co-workers like human Google. Bosses ask a million questions and demand correct, smart answers. And everything is immediate. The business can be brutal, like an advanced game of Jeopardy or Trivial Pursuit, and if you lose more than win, everyone notices. It's about being the smartest in the room but also the most competent.

Abby caught on and never answered a question with "I don't know." It was always, "let me get back to you." And before she gave an answer, she learned to damn well double-check it. And when someone asked her to do something, even if she had no idea how to do it, she just said yes, and figured it out. After a couple months listening, paying attention and in general not being a pain in the ass, people noticed her. When they started saying good morning and her name, she knew she was making progress. Interns and other new employees came and went so rapidly, rarely making it past the trial period. Somehow she had crossed the finish line and the paper began to embrace her.

Abby loved the job. Ferociously, she started reading other papers, following the news, listening to politicians and paying attention to the world like she never had before. The city was so intricate and deeply connected, from the unions to the billionaires, mayors and corporations running the city. She had never considered important issues like taxes, the standard of living, or housing as it affected society. The Chronicle peeled back the layers of mankind's ego and defects - and for Abby - it was fascinating.

She upgraded her clothes, added makeup to her lifestyle and started going to important events with colleagues. It wasn't being the daughter of Asher Williams but an employee of The Chronicle that opened doors for her.

After two years, Abby was off minor ad copy and put on as a full-time researcher for Jonathan Upton, the paper's top reporter. He had won a Pulitzer at 30 and now at 40 was still on top of his game. Abby was 25 and could not believe her luck. Jonathan was an unusual man, son of a Jewish woman and Christian father. He had lived in New York his entire life, a city boy, and his father was a professor of World Religions at Columbia. His younger brother was a famous actor in Hollywood, and his sister was married to a TV mogul. They were part of the most elite social circles in the city.

Nothing about Jonathon was ordinary; it was extraordinary. He was stout, built heavy with a strong nose. His hair was wavy and peppered with gray and he had bright grayish eyes. He bounced excitedly from foot to foot when he had a good scoop, he charmed women easily, gave out compliments freely and his sarcasm was the best in the room. If he picked on you, it was a compliment. But in turn, Jonathon was known for his temper. If a story went wrong or another paper beat him, he could be seen in his office throwing magazines or yelling into the phone. The one quality everyone agreed to when describing Jonathon was passion.

"Williams!" He bellowed. It was her first day and she was sitting at her new desk outside his office. She raced in ready with a notepad; never go anywhere in a newsroom without a notepad.

"Williams, what do you think about the impending teachers strike?"

"The way I see it, Mayor Giuliani is going to head it off at the pass," she said. "Election season starts at the beginning of the school year and it's bad visuals for both Democrats and Republicans. He will conjure bipartisan funds to show up at the eleventh hour. But he will make the teachers sweat first. Can't have a bunch of underpaid, do-gooding women 'best' the all powerful, all-knowing male political figures, now, can we?"

Jonathan smirked. She could tell, he liked her. "That's good, Williams, write that up and put in on my desk, I'll see who to interview to make fit that scenario. Find out who the loudest teachers are, we need good visuals – not too pretty, not too old or ugly, believable, and if she has a family she is trying to support, all the better – you know the drill. Get on it."

And Abby did. For the first few weeks she sat at her desk, wrote things up for him and every morning they met to go over story ideas. He seemed to value her opinions. One day it came: "Williams, get your coat." From then on she was allowed to sit in on interviews and investigate alongside him. If it was after six, he bought her a drink before sending her home. Abby was mesmerized. More than once she fantasized about being with him; the more they were together, the more they were drawn to each other. They had a good rhythm.

But Jonathan was married to the novelist Katherine Upton, who had three best-selling books on the New York Times list. She was a brunette Jewish beauty whom Jonathon's mother adored. Jonathan didn't speak about her often but he called her at least once a day from the office. Abby only saw them together on the society pages of the New York Times and Vanity Fair. They were a power couple.

When Jonathan invited Abby to their home for a dinner party, she was shocked. "C'mon Williams, the old lady wants to see who is outsmarting me at the office. I am sure you have a party frock."

Abby got a new dress, terrified of her first impression. When she walked out in the penthouse, Asher did a double take because she looked just like her mother in a lovely Dior black cocktail dress. Abby left her hair down in waves and wore just enough makeup. She didn't want to look too old and or too young.

"Where are you off to?' Asher sounded suspicious.

"The Uptons," Abby replied coolly. Her father thought she should be reporting more about Wall Street, the backbone of America he would say, and didn't say much on Jonathon's more political articles.

"Careful now, don't let that Jonathan guy, you know, you know …" Asher was waving his hands and being vague. But he was realizing if he was still 40 and his 25-year-old assistant looked like Abby, no way would she be safe.

"Dad! He's too old and I am going to go have dinner with his wife. I think I am pretty safe," said Abby, embarrassed at the suggestion and even more embarrassed because she had secretly fantasized about it.

"Okay, all right." Asher kissed his only daughter on the cheek and for the first time felt a twinge of guilt and regret about how he had treated other men's daughters. But he dismissed the thought by pouring himself a scotch and watching a cooking show. Cable had started a "food network" and he thought it was brilliant. He even thought about buying it.

The dinner party was lovely and Katherine made her feel at home. For the most part, Jonathan ignored her for more important people. There were two politicians, a doctor and an actress.

"How ya doing, Williams, need a drink?" He said bluntly during a lull in the chatter.

"No, I'm fine. Katherine is wonderful."

"Yes, she is, isn't she? Glad you two got to meet." Jonathan seemed antsy; she noticed him dancing on the balls of his feet, a sure tell. "Well, thanks for coming," he said, rather blasé as he skittered off, leaving her to chat with the actress. She wondered if he did cocaine.

Monday morning was routine, no mention of the party. A few weeks slipped by; big stories were happening. It was political season. Jonathon said it was like deer hunting, they have to get up early, sit in the dark and cold and wait for the right shot. He was presently aiming for a religious conservative running for Senate. Jonathan just knew something was wrong with the guy, too clean.

The politician made the thumbs up gesture too often and his wife looked like a waxed Barbie.

"Keep digging, Williams, keep digging!" he urged from his own office as she did research.

Finally, late on a Thursday night, the break came with an anonymous call. The politician was seen entering a club in Chelsea through the back alley. Abby and Jonathon raced there to find a drag show and drag queens everywhere. They spotted Mister Thumbs Up. They almost missed him because he was wearing a wig, a sequined dress and eating a Big Mac at a corner table. Jonathan starting laughing as they moved closer. They could see a woman dressed like Jesus was giving him a hand job under the table while snorting a line of coke. "Jesus!" Abby exclaimed and Jonathon whispered "Yes, I do believe it is the coming of Christ." Instead of taking a picture, Jonathon slipped into the booth, presented his card and said "Let's talk."

Mr. Thumbs Up gave up three other conservative politicians for their money-laundering and drug habits. Abby and Jonathon stopped not one, but four, corrupt politicians from taking office with a ten-page exposé in The Chronicle. It was the most satisfied Abby ever felt. They wrote right up until press time on Thursday night. High from the thrill, Jonathan invited her back to his apartment. She assumed Katherine would be there. She wasn't.

The calm of the apartment was palatable. "Where's Katherine?" she asked.

"Book event in California." He poured her a drink. Abby thought of the cliché, older man, younger woman; her dad. Nothing about this scene was getting past her. Jonathan had orchestrated it, all men did. Abby sipped her wine slowly, her head reeling. Nothing about this was right or good. He was her mentor, he had the power, he was married. Katherine was probably suspicious; that's why she was invited to dinner. She felt so stupid.

But there was another voice inside her head, one that she would grow too loathe. It said, *who cares?* Two of the most dangerous words in the world. Abby had been good, always too good, despite her parents' lack of morality. She worked hard to be a good person but did she ever get much back? When was she ever truly happy? With Jake, but she couldn't have Jake because that didn't work either. Entitlement is a seed that grows with unrest. Didn't she deserve to be happy? Wasn't she entitled to be happy? If Katherine suspected them, didn't she already have a scarlet letter on her back?

That night Abby stepped off the cliff with Jonathon and spread her wings, thinking she could fly.

The affair lasted almost two years.

Their sex was passionate. Abby abandoned herself in cars, restaurant closets, spare bedrooms, and hourly hotels. Wherever they could find, she greedily took him. He couldn't get enough of her, every look tinged with some sexual invitation, every chance to be together taken. He ignited an intensity inside Abby she never knew was there. She unleashed herself, gave herself wholly to this experience and refused as long as she could to admit what it was, wrong.

But relationship issues eventually seeped in. Abby wasn't above jealousy and suspicion. They started to run hot and cold at work. Either they were the best of friends or bitter lovers, unable to work out how to be liars without lying to each other.

Jonathan was a good liar just like her father. He could make her feel like the love of his life but then turn around and do the same with Katherine. He loved both women, wanted both and he didn't like to compromise. But Abby felt like all she did was compromise and it made her feel worse. Hiding in hotels, wearing glasses and hats to go back and forth, ever cautious of Katherine or anyone in the city who would see them. They rarely spent one full night together. She felt dirty, cheap, used. She attempted to get angry but he would woo her back. The situation was reprehensible and she knew it.

Abby wanted out, but how do you get out of love? She had been able to walk away from Jake but why not Jonathan? Her drew her in again and again, her self-loathing only calmed by his attention.

Jonathan forced her to be around Katherine. Abby had to watch as he created spectacles at parties or events, making big affectionate displays with his wife. He wanted to show everyone Abby was nothing, a nobody to him. But she knew Katherine could smell the affair like cheap cologne. No longer was she sweet to Abby; she barely tolerated her.

After each meeting Abby would go home and cry. She fled to her mother's on weekends, anything to get out of the city and away from him or them. He would call at 2 a.m. and say, "I just wanted to hear your voice. Promise you will be back on Monday, promise, I can't go to work without you."

The more Abby pulled away, the more they would argue. Jonathan could be cruel.

"That's why I hired Asher Williams's daughter," he told her. "Families like yours think they are above everyone. You're not, your father is not. I only ditched my last assistant because she wasn't as pretty as you. Her ass wasn't as good as yours and her daddy not as rich. So get over yourself darling, everyone knows who you are and what's happening, we're fucking newspaper people."

After one of his episodes, Jonathan wouldn't speak to her for days. Eventually he would call crying and apologizing and afterward he would want to meet just for sex. It was a merry-go-round of his neurosis and she wanted off.

Abby became more paranoid at the office. How could she not realize they all knew? It was a fucking newspaper. All her coworkers were insatiable gossips; that's what made them good at their job. They pounced on anyone with bleary crying eyes, because they needed to know what was wrong. Reporters could be cruel and judgmental, battering about people's secrets like lions with mice. Abby realized she was nothing special. Her privileged life in Connecticut had made her think there was a shield around her, an invisible screen that kept her life private. No, in real life there wasn't. There had been people watching, knowing all along. They would say it was in Jonathon's nature to do what he did, a womanizer. They would use the word casually, without incrimination, like a valid excuse. In turn, Abby would be called naive and gullible. She was careless for falling into his trap.

The head secretary at the paper had delivered the final blow. One afternoon, when Abby sulked at her desk, the affair and her stupidity weighing on her like a billboard for everyone to see, Dolores, with her coiffed gray hair, plump middle and glasses on a beaded string around her neck, quietly approached.

"Sweetheart, listen, we would have all been amazed if you didn't sleep with him. Hell, if I was 30 years younger, I would have fallen for him too. But darling, don't you get it? They were going to assume you were sleeping with him no matter what. The cards were always stacked against you. Yes, we all know about your Daddy and with your youth, there was no way anyone was going to take you seriously. A good-looking girl with a trust fund? Jeez, you would have to climb Mt. Everest to get anyone's respect. Don't get me wrong, these men want you to work for their companies, of course, and by and large you educated debutantes do a damn fine job. You are a smart girl, but you will always have a safety net that others don't. And people are just going to resent that; they want to see you fail. You've already got the pot of gold at the end of the rainbow that makes you different and people judge. My advice?"

Abby was catatonic listening to her; never had someone

been as honest with her – and it was all true.

"The only way to win without Daddy's help, without a grown-ass man taking advantage of you, without the world seeing your looks before your brains, or your trust fund before your abilities, is to work for yourself. Leave this shit behind, get creative, start something of your own; only then will they even begin to respect you. My mantra – and I will share this with you because I do think you are one of the brightest girls I have met in a long time – *Fuck them*.

"Seriously, say it, say it as many times as you need to. Say it in the mirror, say it under your breath, say it when you see the smug looks on their faces, say it when you win and say it when you fail. FUCK THEM." Dolores looked for a long time in Abby's weepy eyes and patted her on the shoulder. Her last words were, "You gonna be okay, baby girl." Something struck Abby in the heart and she actually breathed a little easier.

As much as she tried, Abby could not remember which came first, Katherine finding out about the affair or revealing she was pregnant. It all happened so fast. Jonathon had been rubbing her leg under a table at a restaurant during lunch, when Katherine's best friend a few tables away saw it and knew instantly. Undoubtedly, Katherine had already been suspicious and alerted her friends. Jonathon tensed and panicked when he noticed the woman. Abby remembers actually wishing Katherine would find out so that it would be over.

Pounding on her door later, Jonathon rushed in and told her not to answer her phone. He said Katherine knew but he was handling it, he had an excuse, just to sit tight. He was going to try and salvage his marriage and their relationship. He never asked Abby if she cared.

That night, Abby lay on her bed for hours without moving. Did she really want Jonathon to talk his way out of it? Did she really want to be let off the hook? She didn't want to be the bad guy, the mistress, but she knew that ship had already sailed. So did she want the affair to continue?

If everyone knew, she would lose her job, but he wouldn't. Her life in New York, her reputation, would be destroyed. His would not. Is that what she wanted? Maybe she did, maybe it was the only way out. Some time around midnight, her phone rang. She didn't look to see if it was Jonathan or Katherine. She took her chances because at that point, she was out of options anyway.

Katherine was crying. "I'm having a baby, do you understand? A baby. This isn't about you, I don't care about you." The words were harsh and stinging. Abby never felt so alone and pitiful. "I'm sorry. I am so sorry," Abby wept.

"Get out of our lives!" Katherine screamed.

"Of course," Abby whispered softly as she hung up the phone. She lay on the cover of her bed dozing until the sun came up. She called her mother at sunrise. Abby sobbed and spit out the story in great gulps, Agnes just listened.

Within 30 minutes of finishing her story on the phone, a car was waiting downstairs to drive her back to Connecticut. Abby packed a suitcase and left a note for her dad that she had gone home. While in the elevator, her cell phone rang and rang; it was Jonathan. Before climbing in the waiting black sedan, she tossed the phone in a city trash can. Fitting, she laughed, she had thrown it all away.

At 28, Abby had crawled into the worst hole of her life. It was one thing to blame all of your life's problems on your parents; it's entirely another to be the cause of the problem, to ruin your own life as well as others. It decimated Abby. She still loved Jonathan, thought of every passionate moment they shared, and it broke her heart not to be with him. But she thought of his wife, Katherine, and their baby and how she had ruined a family. Her thoughts were a black pool she swam in where she wanted to slip beneath the surface and never return.

Agnes went into warfare mode and she was in the trenches with her daughter. The pain Abby felt all was all too familiar. Agnes was angry at her for getting involved with this man, but then she blamed herself for not teaching her enough to do otherwise. Agnes felt guilty; her daughter had been drawn to the only love she could find. Why? Because as parents they had failed. Asher wasn't a good male role model, Agnes was a bitter wife. She already knew Arthur was in a shitty marriage and Ansel thought of relationships like telenovelas that ended after 20 minutes. Agnes felt horrible for Abby, but goddammit she was going to get her daughter out of it. No one helped her but she wouldn't do that to Abby.

Agnes let her daughter wallow in bed for a week, watching *Designing Women* and eating a steady diet of instant mashed potatoes and gummy bears. Agnes didn't judge. Abby needed kindness. She flew Ansel up to help.

"Mom, what's going on?" Ansel asked from Miami.

"It's your sister she's had an affair with an older married man. She probably was in love with him and it's over. His wife is pregnant and Abby blames herself for everything. Okay, now that we are up to speed, when can you get here?" Agnes could be incredibly efficient with drama.

Ansel came home, climbed into bed with Abby and talked all night. For the next week the three of them ate take-out, watched sitcom reruns and bought a stupid amount of clothes. It had been awhile since Agnes's children had needed her like that and she loved it. They laughed, a lot. Arthur came over with five-year-old Harry and they felt good, like a circle. They were family and no matter who hurt them, they could recover and come together. Only true family can forgive your sins.

It was a year or so later when Agnes really worked her

magic. Abby had settled back into Connecticut life and had a job researching for a local author. Abby was still living with her mother but Agnes knew it was time for her to move on.

On a crystal spring day, Agnes asked Abby to go furniture shopping. It wasn't unusual for Agnes to expect her children to drive her places.

"Don't go so fast," demanded Agnes.

"Mom, I'm going the speed limit."

"Well, that's too fast!"

"It's like driving Miss Crazy," said Abby under her breath. She had been living with her mother for over a year and felt like some kind of handmaiden. She had so much gratitude for her mother for helping her, but now, it was Abby this and Abby that.

They pulled up to a big old red barn in a rural part of Connecticut. "Here," her mother stated and Abby slowly, very slowly turned the ticking diesel Mercedes into the drive. Agnes handed her Chanel bag to Abby as she got out of the car.

"What, do I have to open the door for you too? What the hell, Mom?" Abby was annoyed.

"Work with me, dear, I'm getting old."

"Lady you ain't that old, I've got underwear older than you."

"Don't be crass, I swear, the bad habits you got from that paper." Their conversation often sounded like this, Abby teased her mother relentlessly.

Abby slammed the door and marched ahead of her mother, but not before turning back and handing her $2,000 handbag back.

It was cool in the barn, Abby liked it. Neat rows of artistic hand-made chairs, couches and dining tables. Abby liked them all.

"Mom, why are you here? Are you buying something?"

"Well, I don't know, I thought you might like it." Her

mother looked suspicious, casing the gallery expectedly. Then Abby visibly saw her mother relax, exhale and smile. It was very un-Agnes of her. Abby followed her gaze and stopped short.

Jake didn't notice them. He was looking at a clipboard like he was doing inventory. Abby had nowhere to hide.

"Yoo hoo!!" Her mother began frantically waving at Jake and Abby thought she may actually die of embarrassment.

"Oh my goodness, is that you, Jake O'Conner?!" Agnes said like a southern belle in *Gone with the Wind*. Abby wanted to crawl under a table.

"Mrs. Williams?" Jake cocked his head in the adorable dog way Abby always remembered.

"Yes, it's me. So good to see you Jake, darling. Look who I have with me, it's Abby."

Abby went crimson. She regretted the forest colored flannel shirt and saggy ripped jeans she was wearing. Since New York she hadn't even put on mascara. She was going to kill her mother.

"You two kids talk, I just have to look at these chairs! Jake, did you make these? The design is wonderful."

Both Abby and Jake stood like deer in headlights. If it was a reality show then Agnes would have been narrating: "I just knew these two kids were perfect for each other, it was me who got them back together."

After some embarrassing small talk, Abby ran to the car. But Agnes knew she planted a seed in Jake to pursue. Agnes wasn't dumb; she knew about Jake waiting three years to meet Abby on campus. Jake would be like a dog with a bone. Agnes smiled. Her daughter didn't need a rich or powerful man. She would make sure her daughter had enough money. Abby needed someone to love her, protect her, give her everything Agnes had never gotten. Someone who would never leave her.

And it worked. Slowly, Jake came back into Abby's life. It

only took a year before they were engaged. Agnes helped them with the down payment on their house, the one they were still in today. While Agnes was happy for Abby, she also felt the stinging loss of her again. All her children were grown and flown, and the days started to get longer, her life lonelier.

THIRTEEN

Change upset Arthur and his routine and everything seemed to be changing so fast. His mother was dying, actually dying. It wasn't a cancer scare or fear of her driving drunk, she was actually going to leave them. A prospect too big and unknown for Arthur to wrap his head around.

He had talked to a lawyer about Janine. He was going to take care of the situation the best he could, damn the rest.

But Arthur was thrown off guard. It was his secretary, of all people, that upset him the most.

"What do you mean you are leaving?" Arthur tapped his fingers in frustration. Throughout the past couple of weeks Arthur had remained level as usual but this was the last straw. "You... you can't leave... no. Can I pay you more to stay?"

"Arthur, Arthur it will be okay, trust me, everything will be fine. You pay me too much as it is."

"No, this is not right, you can't leave right now." Arthur was starting to sweat and tapped his fingers compulsively on the desk.

He thought he was having a heart attack, but most likely it was a panic attack. Mrs. Forster called them "mantrums": a grown man having a tantrum.

"Arthur, I have a plan," she assured him. For 15 years, his beloved secretary Mrs. Forster had done everything for him before he even asked. She was the most competent employee he had ever had and knew him the best outside of his family. Older than him, she was at ease with Arthur and all his quirks. He felt she understood him more than others and he relished her more than an office assistant. He let her take as much vacation time as she wanted, come and go whenever, but she never did. Arthur had even started an investment account for her that was doing nicely.

"Michael's retiring, William is in college and the portfolio you made us, well, it's enough for us. We want to travel, see the world a bit before our backs give out and we have high blood pressure and all that."

"But now?!"

Mrs. Forster just stared at him with her "really did you just say that" look.

"So what's your grand plan?" said Arthur grumpily.

"My younger sister, Eve – Genevieve, but we call her Eve."

"You have a sister?"

Again, she stared at him. "Yes, the whole time I have known you."

"Sorry, I guess I wasn't paying attention."

Mrs. Forster squinted her eyes at him.

"Eve is just as good as me, I promise. Probably even better, she is a lot younger and more your age. She is getting a divorce and that idiot husband of hers is trying to not pay her. You will pay her, because you will value the job she does. Right?" She glared him.

"Of course, if she does the job."

"She will. She has two teenage sons and oh, she hasn't

worked in 17 years. Do you have a problem with that?"

"Mmm, I assume the correct answer is no? And I don't have a choice?"

"Ahh, grasshopper, correct. She will start training with me tomorrow. When's she ready, I will go to Paris and forget all about the great Arthur Williams," she teased.

"Don't you dare." Arthur couldn't help but smile. There were some really good people in the world and he felt like he kept losing them.

Arthur took a page out of Agnes's playbook. If he was going to divorce Janine, he would do it in the most civilized way possible. His lawyer wrote the sweetest deal he could offer Janine. He gave her the house, stocks, cash, the country club membership and most of their possessions. There was already a trust for Harry's college and the most priceless thing she would receive, his name and her freedom.

He sent Harry over to Ansel and Abby's for pizza and came home with a bottle of Dom Perignon. Janine was immediately suspicious.

"Did you finally break the law or something?" she said in her she thinks she's being funny but she isn't funny way.

"No Janine, we are celebrating."

"Really? What?"

"The fact we have made it this far. We made the most wonderful human being together and now we can part ways, happy, fulfilled and wishing each other the best." Arthur looked at her earnestly.

Janine had the champagne flute poised on her lips and took deep gulps processing the information.

"You want a divorce?" He knew she might get defensive if only because she didn't have the idea first.

"Janine, hear me out. You are an attractive woman, a vibrant woman, you have so much fun left in you – but us, this, is this fun, Janine? Are you having fun? Do I make you feel vibrant and attractive?" Arthur stayed earnest and calm while talking to her.

Janine weighed all of his words. He could see them begin to resonate like bells chiming louder.

"Janey," he hadn't used that term in years, "there is another chapter, in fact many more chapters for you, and I want you to have them all. And Harry wants you to have them too."

At the mention of Harry she tensed but he pushed the papers in front of her. "Just read this." He had Mrs. Forster outline the divorce terms in a list. She used the simplest and biggest font. Like a prix fixe divorce menu, Janine could easily scan the page.

She poured herself another glass of champagne and kept reviewing the list. Arthur remained quiet.

Out of the blue she said sweetly, "Are you sure, Arthur?"

"Yes, Janey, I'm sure." Janine wasn't an idiot; if she dared contest it, Asher Williams would come at her with an army of lawyers. That was why she was always so afraid to ask for a divorce. Janine had been terrified of the Williams family. If they cut her off, she would have nothing. But now, Arthur gave her everything. Relief flooded through her body like valium.

"Oh Arthur," was all she could say. She signed that night and Arthur called a real estate agent the next day. He thought, *why didn't I do this sooner?*

—

It surprised Arthur how easy it was to adjust to Eve. She was just as efficient as her sister but more mild-mannered. Softer. Eve was tall like Arthur, bigger boned than most women, but he found comfort in it. Delicate, slight women were too fragile, like breakable sculpture. She kept her straight brown hair neat and had lovely almond eyes hidden behind thick framed glasses, which Arthur rather liked as well.

Eve was set the task of finding her new employer a new home. Her sister had told her everything she needed to know about Arthur. From the soon-to-be ex, Janine, to his dying mother, Eve never had to ask too many questions. She caught on quickly to his habits, like placing his morning coffee on the right side of his desk, and learned never to interrupt a phone call, ever.

Eve picked three houses for Arthur. He didn't want to go alone and asked her along. Driving through the back roads of Connecticut was pleasant. She didn't chat unnecessarily and it relieved Arthur.

The first two houses were simple, stodgy Connecticut homes with clapboard and green shutters. They didn't appeal to him at all. He had done his life his parents' way and then Janine's and now it was time to live his own way, but what was that?

Arthur would never admit how jealous he was when Ansel moved to Miami. While he was not a fan of the heat, hurricanes or spicy ethnic food, Arthur admired his brother for making such a big change. It was unimaginable to him to actually leave Connecticut or the circle of his parents. But his brother did imagine it and did break away, far more courageous than cowardly.

He had visited Ansel once on a business trip. His brother's gallery was impressive in size and reminded him of a library for art. It was like a quiet oasis where people could come to worship beauty. And Ansel's apartment was polished and exceptional; he had their mother's flare for decorating. While it was modern, it was also homey, with bits of art and important, interesting things that reflected Ansel's gifted personality. Arthur's own personality was as stodgy as the green lamp on his desk and leather bindings on his books. His brother had created a home for himself that showed the world how interesting he was and Arthur was begrudgingly jealous. Then he saw the house he never knew he wanted.

It was the last home of the day and the real estate agent was waiting for them. Neither he nor Eve knew what to expect when opening the front door. From the outside the house was modern, sleek lines, flat roof, with heavy steel beams creating rectangles that formed the house. The landscaping was minimal and the straight gravel driveway did not have a lot of pomp and circumstance. But the house was sufficiently set back from the road and no neighbors were visible, which appealed to Arthur. Large trees bordered the property, giving it an enclosed, nestled feeling.

Inside the house, the ceilings were tall and it suited Arthur's physical appearance. Entering they had to walk past the bedrooms down a long hall and emerged into one sprawling large room. The living area took up well over half of the house. The breathtaking part was the back wall, entirely made of floor-to-ceiling windows. The impression was like living outdoors. Eve gasped because the effect was so dreamy. It appeared as if the house was welded with the lawn. The eye followed the grass that sloped down to a pond surrounded by a lush garden.

Eve turned to Arthur, "It would be like living in a Monet painting."

A few moments later, Arthur said to the realtor, "I'll take it." Arthur could see himself and Harry reading on Sunday afternoons on large leather couches while the snow fell inches away from them. The charming wood stove warmed the room and invited him to stay. Giddy, he leaned and kissed Eve on the cheek to thank her for finding it. She blushed.

For just a few moments, Arthur felt actual joy and forgot about his mother. He had never tasted much freedom, mostly beholden to his own chains. His acute sense of responsibility to others and to himself boxed him into the status quo. He followed all the rules and rarely even argued them – the complete opposite of his parents. Learning from them, he went in another direction but in doing so, never found his own direction. But now in his forties, it was as if he was relearning the fundamentals. As if he could shed his parents like a skin and finally live in his own.

FOURTEEN

At times, Agnes could be harsh with her parenting. Asher spent so much time in the city, barely making it home on the weekends, she felt the burden was on her to be both good and bad cop. She often sent the kids to school not believing they had a stomach ache or sore throat; she wanted them to be tough and figure out how to cope. Deep down, she wanted them to be stronger than she ever was and her parents certainly never coddled her. She navigated it alone as Arthur and Abby sailed into their teen years with gusto and quiet Ansel held onto childhood for as long as he could.

With Asher away, Agnes was ferocious about schedules. The kids were turning into teenagers and she was in charge. Arthur had squash team and extra math tutoring, Abby had tennis and dance classes, Ansel, the least competitive of all, went to art classes and she forced him to join the swim team for exercise. Keeping them busy kept Agnes busy.

The truth was, Asher and she were growing farther apart.

The money kept rolling in but so did the waves of depression. In the darkness of night, Agnes would return to the shame of her drug overdose because that's what it really was. In her dreams, she could hear her mother whispering "Baby Girl" and walking away without looking back.

Agnes no longer felt youthful and there was little wonderment to being Mrs. Williams. She did as the other housewives did, wrote hefty checks to charities and bought herself diamond jewelry. The house was swaddled and adorned in rich fabrics and expensive antiques. The lawns were beautifully manicured. People always commented on her taste; it was refined and enviable.

For the most part, the family was okay. Agnes held it together as long as she could. The cracks began to seep in when Asher got lazy with his extramarital affairs. He would be photographed in the Times or on Page Six and Agnes would fly into a rage. They could argue for hours.

"It's fine, Asher, just put your dick into anything," Agnes would scream. She inevitably drank too much when Asher came home for the weekend if he came home at all.

"Well, you won't let me put it into you."

"Why would I? I'd have to take a number to get on that ride."

"What do you want from me, Agnes? You act like you despise me but here we are, still together." Asher threw up his hands.

"I warned you not to embarrass me, it's not fair, not after all I have endured."

"What have you endured, Agnes? What? A beautiful home? Motherhood? A bank account you didn't have to earn?"

"I earned every penny, Asher Williams. I stood by you, I have raised your children and kept your secrets," Agnes hissed.

"That money isn't all clean. Think I like being a pawn for your 'overseas investments'? How many times have you used my name to hide your dirty money? I keep my mouth shut on a hornet's nest that could take us all down. So yeah, I've earned the goddamn money."

It was true, while Asher did find a profitable way to make clean money, it never was enough. As in his college days, Asher was a clever man and wanted to play with his power. He knew how to turn a trick and double a dime. At this point, it was way more fun than just sitting at a desk all day crunching investment numbers. Hiding people's money, filtering offshore accounts, gambling on maybe-not-so-legal ventures, that's how Asher got his kicks. It's what separated men from the boys, those who played their hands for high stakes. Asher never apologized for it. Agnes knew from day one he was that kind of businessman and she looked away. Neither had a lot of morals when it came to making money.

"Agnes, just stop. We have a good life don't we? What's missing? Nothing."

"Integrity, that's what's missing Asher, goddamn integrity."

"Agnes, that's overrated."

"Just stop embarrassing me, Asher, no more pictures, no more flaunting other women in public and we'll call it even."

It was Arthur who was the first to learn of their parents' dirty secrets. He would hear their raised voices and sneak downstairs to get within earshot. Staying quiet in the shadows, holding his breath, he took in every word. Their indiscretions exposed like raw sewage that made his stomach turn. His dad, dirty money, other women and his mom allowing it all to happen. Arthur resented them for being so callous and stupid with their lives, with their family's lives. What if his father went to jail? What if they got a divorce? What if the house caught on fire but, because they were arguing, no one noticed? So many what-ifs for a young boy.

Arthur decided they weren't his secrets to expose; if anything, he needed to protect them. His job was to store them away and pretend they didn't exist, at the very least for his brother and sister. His siblings couldn't know, shouldn't know, the depths of his parents' immorality. He never meant to be the jury for the family but as the eldest, he was impossibly forced to rule on their fate. As for Asher and Agnes, he would watch them too, make sure they didn't ruin it all for everyone. The burden felt like a swamp Arthur had to walk through, thick, muddy unknown. The secrets shaped and changed him; dangers lurked and he had to be vigilant. What people so often didn't realize was that most of the decisions Arthur made were to protect his family, so often he was like his namesake.

As a teenager, Arthur's habit of eavesdropping became his most reliable source of information. He waited behind doorways and listened to Abby and Ansel giggle in front of the TV or the maid complaining about his mother on the phone. He always hesitated before entering a room, hoping to catch his parents in their lies. For as physically big as Arthur was, he could be amazingly quiet. It was in the quiet he could hear his family's thoughts, feel their real intentions. If anyone was to predict Agnes' wavering, her slipping beyond their grasp, it would have been poor Arthur.

No one can actually look back and pinpoint the moment it started happening, only the moment when it was revealed.

It was as subtle as days clouded by his mother's erratic emotions. One day, she would be sweet, loving, shuffling her children from place to place, and others she would be dark and moody.

"What do you want?" she would say brutally to one of them if they caught her off guard. All three of them learned how to tiptoe, put on a smile and find reasons to stay out of the house.

Agnes's drinking was escalating, but she was very good at hiding it. She eventually developed a pattern the children could pick up on. They would come home from school and she would seem off, angry, sullen. Some nights she played music loudly and ignored them. They could hear her storming around her room and left her alone. The next day she would be kind and patient in the best way with them. It was her regret talking, the guilt.

As hard as Arthur tried to shield his brother and sister, they all became accustomed to Agnes' fluctuating moods. At ten, Ansel was perceptive enough to be overwhelmed with worry for his mother when she drank. He would wait outside her bedroom door until she fell asleep and sneak in to make sure she was okay in bed. When the house was quiet, Abby would soothe and console Ansel back to his own bed. But he would be the first to wake, return to his mother's doorway and sit vigilant until Agnes awoke. In the morning she would hug him and pretend it was a normal day. The three of them never turned on her. It was their unspoken code. Asher was hardly around, so without their mother who would they have? They were her guardians, not the other way around.

The breaking point came the fall of Arthur's junior year in high school. That day, he had met with a college counselor who was full of promise and hope that young Arthur would go to Harvard or MIT or any Ivy League school. It set off Arthur's anxiety to hear such lofty names. Could he really be one of those types of men, the ones he knew his father envied? The burden now felt real, to excel in ways his father never had. It would be what his father wanted and it weighed on him.

Arthur came home to an empty house, Abby and Ansel weren't home from school yet. He didn't know where his mother was, but there was no reason to assume anything wrong. Then a police car drove stealthily up their long driveway.

Arthur, confused, stood in the doorway not sure whether to let the officer in or not.

"Son, your mother has been arrested," the officer said kindly, seeing Arthur's bewilderment. They needed Arthur to come and get Abby and Ansel at the station. "Do you have a father, son? You need to contact him." Dazed, Arthur went to the phone and called Asher's office. Luckily he was there.

"What!?" Asher screamed and asked a million questions. But Arthur didn't know how to answer them, he just told his father to come home.

He followed the police cruiser to the station. Arthur's heart was heavy in his chest, he felt like they were all in trouble. Entering the station's swinging doors, Ansel and Abby ran to him. Abby's wide eyes ringed with smudged mascara from crying. Ansel's skinny arms and legs were shaking. They hugged and knew better than to say anything in front of the police. Their instinct was to protect their mother and themselves.

It had happened at their school. Agnes attempted to pick both of them up to go to swim or tennis or something and she was drunk.

"I knew when I got in the car, I knew she had been drinking. I should have stopped her," cried Abby, filled with guilt. The school parking lot was always a busy place, parents and kids not paying attention during pick up. They stepped out into the road without a care. Abby will never forget the Carpenter twins holding hands, each with matching backpacks and ponytails, coming out between two cars. Agnes didn't see them.

"I screamed," Abby told Arthur. She had been in the front seat with her mother. Instinctually, Abby grabbed the wheel from the passenger side and pulled it a hard right. Agnes's Mercedes swung and hit a parked station wagon, the twins jumped out of the way in time and thankfully everyone was fine.

"Goddammit, Abby!!" Agnes screeched and looked like she had bloody murder in her eyes. Ansel, terrified in the back seat, started crying. Abby had hit her head on the passenger window and was stunned.

"Mrs. Williams, are you all right?" It was Mr. Brown, the gym teacher who rushed to the car first. He pulled open the driver side door and was taken aback, smelling their mother. Her expensive perfume couldn't mask the sour stench of wine, her bloodshot eyes, and the slurring in her voice.

"You, who are you? Get the hell out of my car," shrilled Agnes.

"Mrs. Williams, I am going to need you to get out of the car. Abby, Ansel can you guys get out?"

"Leave my children alone, get the fuck out of here." Agnes was getting more agitated. Mr. Brown opened the back door and urged Ansel out but Abby was trapped, her door slammed next to the station wagon, tears rolling down her cheeks.

"Abby, honey, just crawl in the back and come out this door." Mr. Brown was so calm, ignoring their mother. Following his voice, Abby did as she was told.

"Where are you going?" Agnes yowled and tried to start the car as Abby crawled into the back.

Mr. Brown, a former Army man, calmly reached his long arm in and grabbed Agnes's keys. There was now a circle of concerned parents and interested kids watching the scene.

Abby made her way out and hugged Ansel, hard. They were both frozen. More teachers rushed around the car and Abby could not hear what was happening next. She saw glimpses of her mother, angry and pushing away the arms pulling her from the car. They got her out and their mother went limp. She slid to the ground like a deflated balloon. She had given up and Abby could hear her say, "Just call my husband, he'll take care of it."

Mr. Brown stood over her until the police came. They didn't handcuff her, just asked her to get in the back of the squad car. Thankfully, she complied. Another police officer asked Abby and Ansel to get in another car. And off they went like a royal family being escorted back to the palace.

They lost sight of their mother after that; she was taken to another room at the station. Police men and women were kind and tried to give them donuts and soda. They just waited quietly on a hard wooden bench, hoping Arthur or their father would come. Abby will never forget the relief she felt when Arthur arrived, as if the ride had finally stopped and she could get off. The police let Arthur take them home, happy to see them go. The sight of the two young, scared kids reminded them of the worst part of their jobs.

Agnes was never formally charged. She was Mrs. Williams, after all. Asher made it to the house in record time from the city with two lawyers in tow. He asked the kids each if they were okay and left them with one of the lawyers named Christy. She was in her 30s and newly hired at Asher's company. Extremely pretty, Christy looked just as scared as they were. But she was capable enough at ordering pizza and sitting with them while they watched movies, waiting for their parents to return home.

Christy tried to triage the situation. Phone calls kept coming in from Asher at the station but he never spoke to the kids. Instead, Christy became his translator for the night.

She would stop the movie and update them. "Good news, your Mom isn't in any trouble, okay? She wasn't really arrested and she won't go to jail." All three of them were relieved, having feared their mother would never return. Naturally, they had watched too many cop shows on television. "But in order for her to not go to jail, your mom, well, she has to go to a hospital for a bit. She's sick, and again it's good news, because now she is going to get better!"

"What kind of hospital? Is she hurt?" asked young Ansel. Christy wrung her hands. She should not be the one having the conversation with these kids she met two hours ago. They could tell she was obviously struggling with the situation.

"Listen, do you guys have an aunt or uncle, grandparents, cousins, someone I can call for you?"

Abby hung her head, "No, we just have us." The statement lay heavy in the room.

"Okay, well you guys are doing great," said Christy trying to sound upbeat.

Arthur coolly interjected. His leg was tapping so hard on the ground, all of them could feel it in the floor. "It's Mom's drinking, isn't it?"

"Yes, yes, it is," relief washed over Christy. "She is going to get some medical help for it. It's not really a hospital, not like surgery, more like a clinic. Does that make sense?"

"Where?" asked Ansel. Tears streamed from his face, he couldn't help it.

"Not far, just one hour away at a place called Silver Linings. Completely nice, kind of looks like your country club."

"How do you know what our country club looks like?" asked Abby.

"Well, I actually grew up around here, and your Dad and I have that in common." She was nervous and smiling awkwardly.

"How long will my mom be gone and who is going to take care of us?" Ansel's anxiety was palpable.

"I think two weeks? But I am not sure."

"I will, Ansie, I will take care of us and Arthur and Dad. Dad will have to this time," said Abby with confidence, wrapping her arms around Ansel's skinny frame.

"Yeah, Ans, I am not going anywhere," said Arthur, who

tapped his fingers against the chair frame.

"Everything is just going to be A-okay," said Christy, who turned on the movie again and wouldn't take her eyes off the screen to look at the kids.

Agnes was never charged. Asher and his lawyer quickly negotiated a deal that she go straight into the treatment facility. A very large donation was made in the Carpenters' name to the school, making them look like great benefactors and the school agreed the children could stay as long as Agnes never stepped foot on campus again. Asher immediately hired a driver for the sole purpose of driving the kids to and from school.

Their father came back home for the three weeks that Agnes was gone. It was the most they had seen him in years. He worked from his office and Christy came and went a lot from the city, bringing him his paperwork and such.

After two weeks in treatment, the kids were allowed to see Agnes. Jumpy, nervous, none of them knew what to expect.

Abby couldn't believe the thick wooden entry doors were for a hospital. Silver Linings reminded her of a stately home an old couple would live in with patterned furniture and wood paneling throughout. There was little light and the atmosphere was cold. Ansel was relieved the workers weren't in uniform and there were no hospital beds.

The family was ushered back to a room filled with sofas and a nice fireplace. No one was inside except their mother. Agnes looked clean and bright in the middle of all the heavy decor. She was without most of her jewelry, just her wedding bands and small earrings. Her hair was in a relaxed ponytail, a style she never wore at home. In jeans and a white sweater, she looked years younger. Ansel was the first to run to her and hug her ferociously. Abby and Arthur wanted the same and for a long time they just held each other. Asher remained to the side, respectful.

"First, I am so sorry, so so sorry," Agnes's eyes filled with tears as she again hugged Abby and Ansel. "I should have never put you two in that position. I know I scared you and I promise not to ever, ever do it again." Relief flooded the kids, that was what they wanted to hear, to believe that the nightmare was over.

Children can be forgiving to a fault. They take adults' *I'm sorrys* like medicine to make the pain go away. But no one ever asked the kids how they felt. No one asked if Arthur was now scared to go away to college and leave his brother and sister unprotected. No one talked about the embarrassment it caused Abby and how she stopped socializing at school. And poor Ansel would withdraw from people, living in fear they would get too close to him and loving them would be too hard for him. Loving his own mother was hard enough. Instead, that day after Agnes said a quick apology, they talked about a vacation they would all take when this was over.

Agnes managed to stay sober for six months, until a drink here and there began to seep back in. She avoided drinking at home for as long as she could, hiding it from the kids but her old patterns flared up again. Arthur was the first to notice.

Agnes referred to the arrest as the "hitch." Like the whole thing was a hiccup or minor interruption in their daily lives. If she didn't know Ansel won an art contest, someone would just say "Oh, that was during the hitch," and all would be explained. Arthur thought Agnes could handle things better now after the hitch. She couldn't let herself get out of control, he assumed; the hitch would have taught her a thing or two.

But the arguing with Asher started again and Arthur crept around corners and walls listening, gathering information to head off the storm. He could sense it was building, the rage inside his mother. She needed a release valve and none of them knew how to help her.

It started like a normal Friday night. Asher had come from the city and wanted to take the family out to dinner. They went to their favorite Italian place but Agnes already was moody and itchy. Since she had secretly started drinking again, she lacked calm and the children could sense it. They in turn were overly jovial and talkative trying to mask the situation. Asher, preoccupied as usual, couldn't see the metaphorical bomb that would eventually go off among all of them.

"You know who I ran into the other day? My old friend Eric Bartor. Can you believe it has been years?" Asher said making conversation. He failed to notice Agnes stiffen at the name.

"Not really a friend now, is he, then?" she replied coolly.

"Well, it was you and Sabine, that had that falling-out remember? What was all that about? Nonsense, probably. You women and your cat fights. Well, anyway, he is on his second wife. Sabine ran off with a younger man, lives in California, and he married some heiress from France. Says he might be running for Senate in New York. He certainly has enough money to do it. It's more for the power, I presume. Get inside the government to make policy he can benefit from. Smart move."

"What the hell does he know about government? Just another spoiled tycoon since birth. Ha. Eric Bartor 'serving the people,' the idea makes my skin crawl." Agnes grabbed the waiter and ordered a martini. *Enough with the charade* she thought. No one was particularly surprised; her mood was getting darker. Asher never dared ask or question her when she did order a drink. He always found it easier to stay quiet.

"Well, we had a good time once, remember? He helped me get my first job."

"Mm-mmm." Whenever Agnes didn't use words, the kids knew it was like seismic meter for something worse to come. Something about the Bartors was bothering her and Arthur quickly changed the subject to college applications. Dinner was finished, but not before Agnes had another martini. They went home in silence and the kids ran to their rooms afraid to set her off more.

Later that night Arthur heard the yelling start and a crash. He went out into the hall and saw Ansel sitting there rocking on the carpet, afraid.

"Abby!" he whispered loudly; she appeared quickly. "Take care of Ansel, I am going to stop this shit right now." Arthur was getting sick and tired of this scenario, the three of them held hostage to their parents' arguments. He crept down the back stairs but before bursting into the library, he stopped and, as usual, listened.

"How dare you bring up Eric Bartor," yelled Agnes. "Don't mention him or that awful Sabine ever again."

"What is your problem, Agnes? I don't understand. It would be really nice if you could finally tell me why you are such a cunt."

"Yeah, that's right Asher, I'm the cunt, not Sabine who you had pinned up to a tree that weekend in Maine. I seem to recall you were all up in her cunt." Asher went still, the silence was heavy.

"Yes, I saw you two, it was awfully passionate, Asher, like it was familiar? Like it had been happening all along." These words had built up in Agnes for almost a decade.

Asher tried to placate her. "Listen, Aggie, honey, that was a long time ago. Obviously it meant nothing, I mean, we were young, stupid. Not like you and I were having a lot of sex, you had just had Ansel and you know, I messed up. A one-off. "

Abby starting laughing. "You think it was just that, you had a 'one-off' with her because I had three of your children at home? That wasn't the game, Asher, not amongst you men. You can't just take another man's wife without him taking something in return."

Asher looked confused.

Agnes laughed, "You stupid men, while you count your money, your things, you never count the tab. There was a price to pay, Asher darling, and I paid it for you." Asher was silent. "I wasn't the only one who saw you that night. Your good old buddy Eric did, too. Tit for tat, he thought." Agnes was letting the story sink in for Asher, telling him slowly.

"I was drunk and an easy take. Alone in the woods, no husband to get me safely home. He pushed me down on the ground, he held me down, Asher. And while you were passionately kissing my best friend, your best friend held my hands over my head and raped me again and again until he was able to come just like you. So I paid, Asher, I paid your debt." Asher was stunned. He tried to hold his arms out to her but she swatted him away. "Even better was the abortion I had weeks later; at least I got drugs for that pain."

Agnes was sobbing now, tears streaming, she was drinking rapidly from a wine glass trying to kill the awful searing pain in her chest. Her anger and regret hot like a prod, branding her over and over again.

Asher moved toward her and she fought back, cursing, "Fuck you," and slapping him over and over. He took it and still moved closer and closer until he could wrap his arms around her. Like when she was arrested, Agnes wilted, all her strength gone.

Arthur could hear his father, who was crying now, saying "shhhhh, shhhh, it's going to be okay, Aggie, love."

Arthur, who had wanted to stop the fight, was paralyzed on the other side of the door. He knew this was information no child should know. It felt too private, too raw. He wanted to go back to bed and push everything he had heard into the far recesses of his mind. He closed his eyes, willing the last ten minutes to have never happened. But when he turned around to sneak back upstairs he stopped dead in his tracks. Standing there quietly shaking and holding hands were Abby and Ansel. There was no going back for any of them.

The days after felt perilous. Agnes wouldn't leave her bedroom, Asher looked terrible. He went in and out like a trauma surgeon. He was visibly worried about his family, which made the kids tremble more. They remained quiet, the unspoken agreement that they knew a truth they could never reveal.

For Asher, this was his biggest failure. His family had been invaded, attacked. His wife, for all their mistakes, was his wife. Agnes was still that dimpled girl with braided blonde hair and bell bottoms who smiled when he came in the room. He remembered how happy she was throughout business school when the children were small and swaddled. She had smiled like the sun toward him. He missed that smile, he missed being the center of her attention.

Where had it all gone wrong? When did he take his eye off the ball? Had he rejected Agnes the same way he had his parents? When they became of no more use to him, he abandoned them emotionally and now had he done the same Agnes? He had convinced himself that it was the agreement between them, that this was the kind of marriage she was fine with, that she wanted this too.

But it wasn't that at all, she was keeping a secret that could destroy what Asher had been building. One that could crush their family and their dreams. She had sacrificed herself for all of them and what had Asher sacrificed? He worked hard and had sacrificed his time with his kids. But he always thought they needed her more than him. He had created the same pattern with them, an agreement of sorts not to expect too much from him.

Asher felt tired. He was faced with not knowing what to do, a first for him. How could he fix the situation? Make her better? How could he get revenge on Eric Bartor? These thoughts weighed on him hourly. The house felt like a funeral home and the kids stayed quiet. They hunkered down together and braced for the storm raging with their parents, hoping it didn't turn on them.

"Are we going to be all right? Are Mom and Dad?" Ansel worried. Abby reassured him and Arthur kept an eye over both of them. None of them spoke about what they heard.

Three days later, it was decided Agnes would head back to Silver Linings. Asher said she just needed some rest and that was the best place for it. It was May and the kids could fill up their time with end-of-the-year school finals and parties. Asher made sure help was on hand to get them through and Christy was coming constantly from the city for business.

After Agnes left, Asher consumed himself with a new project – taking down Eric Bartor. He hired an army of private detectives to gather information. He looked into Eric's taxes, his companies and his family. Any blemish he could find was gathered like food for winter. He had stockpiles of dirt on Eric, from insider trading to a secret child he kept tucked away in New Jersey with a former maid. He might have raped her as well, but at least she was being paid handsomely for it. Asher kept just one file on his desk marked EB, and when the time was right he was going to release every last bit to the world.

The opportunity came in July when Eric made noises about announcing his candidacy for Senate. He made a big splash about being backed by the Wall Street community as well as New York City politicians. He went as far as to announce on the news his confidence that he would win.

The day Eric's campaign was to have a press conference to announce his running, Asher was ready and waiting. It was set up at the Waldorf Astoria for 5 p.m. At 4:45 pm, Asher delivered to three major newspapers every ounce of information and proof of Eric's comprehensive lying and treachery. He even had him on tape blasting unions, gays and veterans. It was all pure gold. So while the newspaper editors were watching Eric wave, smile and say God Bless America, they were churning out the most salacious political story of their lifetimes.

Asher took great pleasure in watching the announcement, knowing Eric's smug smile and fat fingers would never be put on TV again. He gave him that moment in the sun, his pinnacle, his peak, just so Arthur could be the one to push him off the mountain. By noon the next day, the entire Bartor family was disgraced across the nation. It was the best Asher could do because if he ever saw him again, he might kill him.

When the story broke in California, Sabine wept with tears of joy. She always hated that son of a bitch and he had finally gotten what he deserved.

FIFTEEN

Moving Agnes from the hospital was like a theatrical production. People hustled and moved and rearranged equipment and furniture like an orchestrated dance to get their mother home and settled. The kitchen was the center of it all and the refrigerator became a pop up pharmacy. Abby had them put a hospital bed in the dining room next to the kitchen, foreshadowing the eventuality of her mother's move.

Ansel had a hard time watching. Agnes had to be moved on a stretcher, put in the ambulance, then carried into the house. She wasn't capable of even a wheelchair. They initially settled their mother in her own bed, just to keep her calm. Too much change felt wrong.

"Careful!" Agnes would shout, but no one could decipher if she meant her or her house. It was filled with precious things, her safe space from the world. Abby understood how barbarous for her mother it was to let all these strangers in to move around her things. But they had no choice.

Agnes's bedroom had always been sacred. With large theatrical windows overlooking the water, who wouldn't want to spend all day in bed with a private view of nature? But the bedroom was looking the worse for wear and Abby cringed, finally acknowledging what really had been going on in there.

This was where her mother had been hiding and drinking. The white carpet that once had been beautiful and plush was stained with god knows what. Her bedding, some of the finest, was old and torn. Ashtrays were full on her bedside, bits of ash ground into the carpet everywhere. There were cigarette holes in the bedspread. The windows were dirty and clothes lay cast on the chair and closet floor. Abby guessed her mother had stopped the maid from going upstairs. It made the situation even sadder and Abby could only whisper, *oh Mom.* Ansel went back downstairs, not able to handle the extremity of it. It was like assessing the damage after a war, their mother a desperate casualty.

A nurse named Valerie, a native of the Dominican Republic, moved into Abby's old bedroom near her mother's and another nurse, named Bev, from South Carolina, moved into Arthur's room. They would rotate shifts so someone would always be on duty. Val liked nights and Bev liked days; they had a system.

It felt weird to have strangers in the house, let alone living in it. Abby tried to reassure her mother and ease her into the new situation.

"I don't like her," whispered Agnes conspiratorially to Abby upstairs.

"Which one Mom? They both look alike." It was true, both were fairly heavyset black women with accents. Valerie looked a little tougher, with large strong arms and heavy-lidded eyes. Bev, softer, had a rounded face that was pleasant to look at. "The Jamaican one, with the colored head band. She's rough. Make sure nobody is going through my things."

"Mom, they are trained at this, I don't they would be able to keep their jobs if they stole from clients." Abby couldn't believe her mother's snobbery had survived unscathed from the last weeks.

"Get me a cigarette, dear."

"You haven't had one in weeks, why start now, Mom?"

"Get me a cigarette or I start firing those women in my kitchen. And remind everyone that this is my kitchen and my house."

"Fine," Abby said like a sullen daughter. The sight of her crippled mother was the complete opposite of the ornery bitchy women barking orders at her ??? Would wonders never cease?

Abby wasn't anything if not the dutiful daughter. She went downstairs to find a cigarette. Her mother usually had packs of Parliaments everywhere. She never really finished one pack, it was more about having lots of packs placed conveniently throughout her life. It was easy to find a pack in one of her mother's handbags. Abby lit one for her and held it while Agnes puffed and closed her eyes, as though she was seeing an old friend.

"OOOOOh, lordy, stop that now, stop it. No smoking in this house, no!" Valerie came up the stairs shouting.

Agnes glared at her through yellow eyes. "This is still my goddamn house and I will do what I goddamn want. Get the goddamn out if you don't like it." And Agnes took another deep drag.

Abby looked at Valerie and shook her head, silently relaying, not now.

Downstairs both nurses were meeting about it.

"Mrs. O'Conner, it's not safe and it smells awful," said Bev, waving thick hands like shooing away a spider. "It's not good if your Mama wants to get better."

"Bev, I know. But she's not getting better, is she? I can't take away one of the few things left on this planet that she can do. I just can't. Now if she asks for a drink, no, but this and all the junk food she wants, we can do that for her."

"Yes, but we have to open the windows. I won't be helping her with this, lordy, no," said Valerie, annoyed. Abby hesitated over leaving the two women alone with Agnes for the night, but this was going to be the new normal for however long it lasted. She needed to go home to her boys.

After Agnes was settled, Abby drove Hector and Ansel back to the airport.

"Go home, get some rest, feel normal, take a break. It's okay," urged Abby. Ansel wanted desperately to go home to Miami, just to breathe hot air and see Kerry, who he really had realized was his best friend more than his assistant.

"I agree, and don't worry, I got him," said Hector with a wink. Abby loved Hector already. He had been great at talking to the doctors, getting their mother what she needed; he was the perfect partner for Ansel.

At the airport, Abby could feel the agony in her brother. He never left his mother, not when things were perilous. Abby knew that, but she also knew what was best for him and he needed a break. Hector made him down a valium and Bloody Mary at the airport bar and pushed him towards security.

Abby called out, "Hey Ansie Pansie, I love you more than my luggage," it was a line from the movie *Steel Magnolias*. He called back, "Drink your juice, Shelby."

That night, at home, Abby cuddled with Felix and Eli. Felix wasn't fully potty trained and smelled like poop, but he crawled on her like a bear cub. He held toys close to her face, trucks and cars for her to inspect, shouting words like "Toyota" and "Diesel." She had no idea where he picked up the terms but thought he was a genius. He always had a fistful of Goldfish or Cheerios, his breath a constant barrage of cracker and preservatives.

Eli, on the other hand, was a thin little chatterbox. He had already learned about airplanes and dinosaurs. He wanted to meet a dinosaur and fly the Concorde. Again, Abby had no idea where or when they became so smart or kind or fun. She couldn't help but cry. They would never know their grandmother. The good parts, not the bad parts.

"Mama, why you got water in your eye?" Eli asked, rubbing his dirty fingers roughly on her cheek.

"It's okay, it just happens," she tried to say with a smile.

"Like pee just happens? Like Felix pee happened in daddy's car today?" Eli grinned knowing that he shouldn't, but thought it funny all the same. It made Abby laugh. Felix giggled and said "Peeeeeeeeeee……"

She turned cartoons on the television and snuggled with them to watch Mickey Mouse. Holding her two sons, she thought of her womb and getting rid of it. She thanked it for doing a tremendous job. And she thanked her mother for teaching her how to love her children.

SIXTEEN

When Agnes left Silver Linings the second time it was the summer of 1984. Arthur, 17, had one more year in high school, Abby was 15 and little Ansel had just turned 11. Abby had become Ansel's full time caretaker, watching over him like a mother hen. They filled their time with movies to escape. *Splash, Revenge of the Nerds, Ghostbusters, The Karate Kid, Never Ending Story, Indiana Jones and the Temple of Doom, Gremlins, Sixteen Candles, Dune* and *Fire Starter* gave their lives a sense of adventure, humor and wonder. The greatest year in cinema was happening and it would take decades for the brother and sister to realize that they were there in the front row.

There was always the honeymoon period after rehab when Agnes felt renewed, happy, determined and guilty. As a family, they never addressed what sent her there in the first place but accepted all of her affection and charms like payment for their silence. That same girl who was 20 and full of spirit, would peek through her mother's stony veneer.

When Agnes came to the decision to divorce Asher, it was

with so much amiability that she was almost giddy with the idea.

"Kids," she gathered them all around one night, including Asher. Agnes had a catered dinner with all the fine China.

"Mom?! It's like a Tuesday, is it someone's birthday?" said little Ansel. "Hey, Arthur, did we forget your birthday?"

"Ha, little man, they would never forget mine, must have been Abby's."

"Okay I'm here, I'm here," said Asher, bursting through the door. "Whoa, Aggie, what's going on?" The whole family sat looking from one to another.

"Nothing my dears, I simply have very good news and I thought it would only be appropriate we all celebrate together."

"Mom, you aren't getting a facelift or something stupid like that?" asked Abby.

"Heavens, no. I'll leave that up to Mrs. White at the club, daresay she's had more than one."

"We're going on a trip?" Ansel was always eager to go on trips.

"Not a trip but there will be suitcases." They could tell Agnes was sober, she seemed so delighted with herself.

"I've decided to buy the Miller place on the water," she beamed.

"Wait, we're moving?" asked Abby.

"Well, Arthur is off to college and Abby next, so I thought I would downsize. And to be on the ocean will be fantastic." None of them could argue that.

"Well, let me see it and go over the paperwork," said Asher.

"No," said Agnes still smiling.

"No, what?"

"No you won't be seeing it or going over the paperwork."

Everyone stopped eating like the invisible shoe was dropping right before their eyes.

"It's my house, Asher, and I have taken care of it," Agnes replied evenly.

"Well, if my name is on it and my ass is going to sleep in it then I am going to see the paperwork."

"That's the thing, dear Asher, your name will not be on it and your ass, as you so crassly say, will not be sleeping in it." It was beginning to dawn on the family what was happening. The kids waited, holding their breath.

"What about this house?" asked Asher who was slower to realize.

"We are going to sell it and you can either give me the proceeds or split it, whatever. In the end, I think we both know you will be writing me a big check, so potato, potahto, as they say."

Agnes carved a large piece of filet mignon and shoved it in her mouth. "Ooh, this is delicious. Arthur, Ansel please eat. Abby dear, make sure you eat your greens, good for your complexion."

"Mom," pursued Arthur, "have you just announced you are divorcing Dad?"

"Yes, dear, I thought that was obvious. Does anyone have any objections?"

Arthur, Abby and Ansel all looked at each other as if to ask whether they all heard the same thing. "Oh, you three cannot ever make decisions without each other, I swear, you little ducks are so codependent." But Agnes wasn't chiding them, just laughing.

All three kids starting shaking their heads from side to side and shrugging their shoulders. When they thought about it, maybe this was the change their mother needed.

"It's okay with me Mom, whatever floats your boat. But can we go on a trip somewhere? I will be a child of divorce and I think I need some proper spoiling. You know, a split household affects a young soul," said Ansel, feigning sadness, shoveling in some potatoes.

"Do I get my own room? I won't share, Ansel's feet smell. And if he gets a trip, I get a car. It can be used one, I don't mind, but please, a car," whined Abby.

"Divorce isn't the drive thru at the McDonalds, guys," said Arthur, like the only adult in the room. "Dad, you're quiet?"

"Mmmmm, I guess, whatever your mother wants…" Asher mumbled like his mind was far away. "Is this what you really want Aggie, you don't have to…"

"Yes, dear, it's time this family moved on … from everything." Agnes said without leaving any room for further discussion. Asher was quiet for the rest of the meal.

In the end, they ate chocolate cake like a burden had been lifted and it was time to celebrate. Except for Asher: Agnes was the only person in his life who ever made decisions for him and for some reason, he could never argue.

Agnes rose from the table last, "I thought that went well, didn't you?" she whispered to Ansel.

That summer, Asher thought it best for Abby and Ansel to go to summer camp while the family moved. Arthur, too old for camp, stayed home and took extra calculus courses at the college. The kids were sent to Springbrook Camp near Lake George in upstate New York. Neither of them wanted to go. But Asher and Agnes thought it would be a reprieve from the family drama. Abby and Ansel felt ousted from their family. They didn't want to be farther away from their parents; in truth, they wanted to be closer. And separating them from Arthur was like taking away their most sacred security blanket. Too much change was happening and the world felt unstable. Their mother was sick in ways they couldn't understand and their father was like a feather they tried to catch in the wind. But as Williamses, they did as they were told.

T-shirts embroidered with the camp logo arrived in hideous

yellow and brown colors. Ansel held one up and looked at Abby, "Well, thank god we we'll look good." Both of them made faces and tried to hide the shirts. Agnes found them under the bed and put them back in their trunks. They had matching lockers. Ansel kept taking his clothes out and hiding in the trunk to scare Abby. He popped out like Dracula every time she came in his room. It scared her every time.

"I don't want to go," he confessed as they were brushing their teeth.

"It will be okay," she mustered some positivity for the sake of her little brother. "I'll be there, so don't worry." Without Arthur, she would be the oldest. She didn't like the feeling.

Of course her little brother annoyed her, but when it came to it they needed to stick together. Her family was different in a way they could not explain to outsiders and, at the end of the day, the one thing she and her brother had in common was that they were scared. They were terrified to leave their house in case something happened to their mother and they wouldn't be there to save her.

"Who knows? Maybe it will be fun." Abby didn't believe that, but looking at Ansel's soft eyes and floppy hair, she only wanted him to feel okay, never mind how she felt.

Agnes drove them to the bus that would take them to Lake George. Kids lined up in the parking lot like lost sheep. If Abby and Ansel had been older, they would have laughed at these mustard- and turd-covered children acting as if they were headed off to Normandy Beach.

Instead, Abby did her best acting and tossed off her mother while jumping on the bus. Ansel, shivering with dread, barely hugged his mother and raced on behind his sister.

Agnes was terrified to be without them but she knew they needed a break from her. That's being a parent, knowing what's best for your kids, not you. They needed nights without worry, fresh air and other kids who didn't have a mommy in and out of the hospital. Agnes cried the majority of the way back to Westport, for herself and them. She knew the divorce was her fault but she hoped the new house would be a fresh start. A beginning both for her and them; they just had to get through the summer.

The springy bunk beds squeaked and the other kids were excessively loud. Immediately, they labeled Ansel different. It was the first time he ever truly felt like an outcast. No one liked his quiet sullen ways. He shied away from anything competitive like archery or canoeing and they held it against him. Because he preferred the quiet of the craft room, they relentlessly teased him for his shyness. He could only see Abby at meals and she purposely sat with him in her own rebellion.

"See that girl, Kelsey? What a bitch. She stole my Depeche Mode t-shirt and ripped it just because that other girl Jenni liked it. Jenni is cool, and with that girl, Sas, but the rest of them are hose-bags. I hate it here, everything smells like wet dog." Abby tried to cheer up her little brother while it killed her to see him so miserable.

"Abby, dear, don't you want to sit with your friends from your cabin?" said Miss Clement coming up to the table. She was the young, pretty counselor Abby was pretty sure all of the other male counselors wanted to bang.

"No, my brother might go into anaphylactic shock if he eats the wrong thing, so I gotta watch him eat. This is chicken, right?" she smirked. Abby drew a thin line between lies and sarcasm.

"Is your brother allergic to something we don't know about?" A look of worry crossed the counselor's face.

"Well, how would I know what you know?" Abby deadpanned. She was really good at being a rude teenage girl. Ansel laughed. His appetite only returned when she was there.

Otherwise his stomach was in knots and he couldn't eat at the camp.

"How's your cabin?" Abby asked.

"There is a douchebag named Evan who thinks he can get laid at eleven years old. He smells and I want to punch him."

"Kid with the curly hair? Yeah, don't worry, no girl will ever touch him," said Abby "So I am thinking of a plan to get out of here," she whispered.

"How? We can't just walk back home and no one gave us any money," said Ansel, childlike, digging into a chocolate pudding.

"Duh, think about it, Ansie, who would save us?"

"Mom?"

"No, Arthur!"

It wasn't hard to convince her big brother. Abby called him, crying, and pretty much embellished the whole situation. She told him the girls were mean to her, which wasn't entirely true. Jenni and Sas liked her but they were having fun and she clearly was not. And the bitch Kelsey kept stealing her stuff and telling boys lies like she had lost her virginity in a Stop 'n Shop parking lot.

With Arthur, she played the Ansel card.

It wasn't as if she and Arthur never talked about Ansel, they knew long before their baby brother did that Ansel was gay. It had happened a couple years before when Ansel came home from school crying.

"The kids made fun of me when I quoted a poem," he explained, looking like they had killed his hamster.

"What poem?" Abby asked tentatively, already knowing how sensitive her brother could be. Arthur, as usual, remained quiet.

"I found it in Mom's room," Ansel said shyly and unfurled a worn piece of paper that had been crumpled and re-crumpled. It said :

"Hope" is the thing with feathers -
That perches in the soul -
And sings the tune without the words
And never stops - at all -
And sweetest - in the Gale - is heard -
And sore must be the storm -
That could abash the little Bird
That kept so many warm -
I've heard it in the chillest land -
And on the strangest Sea -Yet - never - in Extremity,
It asked a crumb - of me.
　　　Emily Dickinson

"I just thought it was cool, you know, the bird, he is hope, you know? We all imagine hope and what is better than a bird who can fly. I think we all want to fly." Ansel wouldn't look up at his sister, ashamed.

"That is a lovely poem, Ansel," Abby said. "It is so very true and we do all want to fly."

"Ansel, look at me," Arthur said with conviction. "They made fun of you because you are smarter than them. They might be able to add numbers and dissect a frog but you…are…smarter… than… them. Please, don't forget it. " Arthur looked at his brother in awe. He knew at that moment Ansel was special but also a burden; protecting him would be his lifelong duty.

Abby brought it up later that night. "Do you think?" she asked Arthur.

And he responded, "It doesn't matter." And from that point on they knew what they had to do.

So when Abby called from camp it was like sending a Bat signal.

"Mom and Dad will kill me," Arthur feared.

"Arthur, when have they ever killed you? When have you ever gotten in trouble? Trust me, once we get home, Mom, isn't going to do anything."

"Yeah, but…"

"Shut up and come get us."

It was fairly easy, Arthur came the next day. He drove up and explained to the counselors their father was sick in the city and their mother was with them. Arthur had been sent to get the kids. The camp counselors couldn't call their parents because they were at the hospital.

They loaded up the trunks in the back of Arthur's car and took off.

"Wasn't that a little too easy?" Ansel laughed. Arthur felt giddy with rebellion.

"So do we have to go directly home?" Asked Abby.

After some discussion, they realized for the first time in their lives the three of them were totally free. No one knew or cared where any of them were at the moment. They were tasting the actual bright side of adulthood.

"I heard over in Lake Placid, they have rides after the Olympics?" Ansel offered. The 1980 Winter Olympics had left Lake Placid with abandoned bobsled runs. Also, the lake was gorgeous in the summer. Arthur of course had money and they rented a cabin on the lake. For two days they ate, laughed and had the vacation their parents actually wished for them to have, just not exactly on the same terms. For the three of them, in just a few short days they saw the possibilities, they felt their world open. It wasn't in a camp but in their hearts with each other.

When Arthur drove them back to their mother's house, they all felt fierce and ready to defend leaving the camp. They had created valid arguments and would, at all cost, stand together against their parents so Ansel and Abby wouldn't have to return.

But when Agnes heard them all open the front door and bust in, she only smiled. She hugged them like they had actually been away at war. The only thing she said was, "So what are we all going to do tomorrow?"

Abby would remember those as the lighter years of her mother's life. Agnes, unburdened by Asher's comings and goings, was renewed. She took tennis lessons, traveled with Ansel and helped Arthur apply to colleges. She started campaigning with Abby also go to college.

"Mom, I'm not sure. I don't think I'm good enough," said Abby.

"Nonsense, you are far smarter than I was and I went to college, at least for a year." Abby, disguised in heavy black eyeliner and Doc Martens boots, was pretty but riddled with insecurity, unlike Agnes at that age. Agnes was determined to get it out of her. She wanted Abby to go to college to find herself and, unlike her, get a degree.

"I want you to think big, dear, big. I know, I haven't been the best mother but I am your mother and if anything, learn from my mistakes. Enjoy your youth, dear, it goes away so fast."

SEVENTEEN

None of the kids could quite pinpoint when Ben Reed came into their lives. They later would joke he magically appeared. But he entered into their mother's divorced life like sunlight into a darkened room.

Unlike them, Agnes does remember meeting Ben. It was at her friend Stella Blacksmith's cocktail party. Agnes had grown to love lunching with Stella, gossiping about people in town. She knew all about Agnes' past indiscretions and didn't care. She was one of the few women of Westport society who found Agnes's biting charm more humorous than threatening. Both women had time and money to burn, and Stella, her husband a hotel mogul, was damn well going to have fun doing it.

"Dearest," Stella whispered to Agnes at the party, "see that gentleman over there? Doesn't have a penny to his name. His father was an ambassador somewhere, can't remember, had the best education around the world and went to that Swiss boarding school everyone is always so chummy about. Anyway, he blew through his inheritance but somehow makes a living as an artist. He actually makes money selling his paintings! Imagine. Travels the world, everyone just raves about him."

"Stella, he sounds dreadful," Agnes moaned.

"Aggie, darling, he's like a modern Rhett Butler. Go have fun – and he is easy on the eyes, I tell you. Just keep your wallet in that Chanel bag of yours." Stella winked at her and started shouting, "Ben, Ben darling, come over here and meet my good friend."

Agnes couldn't have been more embarrassed. The truth was she had never been with anyone but Asher. She hadn't dated since high school and never flirted with any real intention. Standing there, middle-aged, in her expensive clothes and jewelry, she felt like a fool. She wasn't a teenage girl with all that naive confidence anymore.

"Hi." Ben approached with a lovely smile. He was tall and thin with dark wavy hair. His green eyes sparked and when he laughed he tilted his head back like he enjoyed no other thing.

"Hi, back," Agnes said, trying not to look him up and down. It would be rude. But he was handsome.

"Let me guess," he said, "your favorite painting is 'This Kiss' by Chagall?"

"Uhh, yuck. Is that what you assume of all women? That's rather rude." Agnes was offended. "Worst pickup line ever," she scoffed.

Ben laughed but was clearly embarrassed. "Okay, easy. That's just kind of my little test in these circles. Knowing what kind of artwork a woman likes tells a lot about her."

"Well, that's just barbaric. You've known me for thirty seconds and you're giving me a test." Agnes shook her head with disgust. "I'll give you a test."

Ben held up his hands, "Truce, I didn't mean much by it,

I'm sorry!" He was still laughing, not taking the conversation as seriously as Agnes.

"Name three abstract impressionist painters; one of them must be a woman," Agnes actually poked him. Never had she poked a person in her life.

"Pollock."

"Everyone says Pollock but okay."

"Motherwell."

"Go on."

"Agnes Martin."

She couldn't help but smile. Choosing Agnes for Agnes was very clever, and she was one of the lesser known artists. Ben smiled back, triumphant. And for the rest of the night, the two talked art, literature and even forbidden politics. Almost everyone had gone, while they were still talking. Agnes pulled herself away but before she did, she boldly asked Ben to lunch the next day. Stella laughed, knowing that would happen.

Ben was living at his cousin's empty house in Darien; the cousin was traveling Europe. He was painting for a show in New York but quickly started spending most of his time with Agnes. At 50, Ben had never married but had much to say about the world, stories that kept Agnes fascinated and occupied. He talked to the kids like they were adults. He had never had his own but was at ease around them. Ansel, only 12, acted far older than his age anyway and enjoyed having a smart man around the house. Abby admired Ben, she liked his worldliness. He bought them a French press for their house and played classical music on the stereo. Everything about Ben seemed to lift them up, take them all to a higher level of living.

Agnes let him sleep over and none of the kids minded. It was a happy time. Unlike Asher, Agnes wasn't required to be a certain way around Ben. They went to events together or separately. He respected her role as a mother; Ansel was in the thick of school and she always needed to keep an eye on Abby's comings and goings. Ben would disappear sometimes for days on end to paint. Agnes, used to being alone, never minded the time apart.

Was Agnes in love? She wasn't sure. It was hard to distinguish love after so many years with Asher. She knew she could be cold and indifferent but that was the way she always had been; she couldn't help it. But Agnes couldn't deny that she loved being around Ben. He teased and excited her, paid attention to her. If anything, when she acted aloof, he accepted the challenge to draw her out. He wanted her to be present with him.

Before long, eight months had passed and it was time for Ben's art show. Agnes was wary; going to New York didn't excite her. The old memories and despair were still etched in the pavement for Agnes to retrace. She wanted to be there for Ben at his opening but didn't want to watch others cling for his attention. She knew ladies would throw themselves at him, they couldn't help it. He would be the handsome star of the evening after all. It reminded her too much of the time when Asher held center court, circling the room, vying for the spotlight. Memories of having to play along reminded her of what she didn't want now. When they were at her home in Connecticut it was less exposed, easier. It was less like her former life, putting on displays as Mrs. Williams.

Her anxiety got the best of her. Ben kept attempting to make plans for the opening and a long week in the city.

"I don't see what the problem is. Abby can look after Ansel and we can spend a few days in the city? How about The Ritz or the Waldorf? I have loads of friends we can see." He was getting annoyed with her refusal to confirm either way. For weeks he had been going back and forth with her but the more he talked about the trip, the more silent Agnes became.

"Just give me a day or two to sort things out," she would vaguely say.

"Surely, the children can survive without you..." Ben was irritated with her using the children as an excuse.

"You don't know, you don't have any," she retorted. Agnes was done with being pushed around by anyone. As much as she liked Ben, her privacy, her space, her sanity came first and foremost. No longer would a man dictate where or when or how she did things. And she was at an age she didn't feel the need to explain herself. Agnes just twisted his words and found excuses like weeds in a garden not to enjoy this time with Ben.

She argued with him about their differences to excuse her bad behavior. She started secretly drinking, fueled by her anxiety. Agnes convinced herself the relationship wasn't meant to be. Men like Ben don't commit to women like her. She persuaded herself he couldn't really love her and would eventually leave anyway.

Ben did leave for New York and never came back. Not a phone call or a word, defeated by her stubbornness as she predicted. Agnes read about his art show in The New York Times; it was a big sensation. The photo of him included a young blonde on his arm, who Stella pointed out looked a lot like Agnes. It stung, of course, to be cast away so easily, but deep down, she knew it was her own doing. Over the years her walls had closed, not expanded. She liked routine and predictability, her house and her control. Agnes could never go back to pills again, the shame from that time was too painful. So Agnes managed her depression and anxiety her own way, with a solitary life and lots of vodka.

EIGHTEEN

The quiet was disconcerting, Abby noticed, walking into her mother's house. It felt like a movie set as Bev or Valerie shuffled about. They never quite said good morning, they just announced situations as they entered a room.

"Your mother was not good last night," said Bev kindly.

"How so?" as if it mattered.

"Her arms were itchy and the hallucinations were back. But she is eating, which is good news. She likes steak and popsicles."

Wonderful, Abby thought, *end of life reduced to steak and popsicles.*

"Hi Mom!" She cheerily announced, going in the dining room. Agnes only lasted two nights in her old bedroom before the nurses all but quit. She had to be in the hospital bed, they insisted, downstairs in the dining room. Abby suspected it was the smoking upstairs that got them; at least downstairs they could open the door to the garden.

The dining room was bright with large windows. Agnes had decorated it with a lovely yellow wallpaper adorned with muted white flowers. Heavy molding gave the room a regal feel and it had ample views of Agnes's gardens. Although winter had descended, the green grass and bushes were a better backdrop than the tops of trees upstairs. She could see her bird feeders where blue jays and cardinals came to eat. Soon it would snow and she would have a front row seat to winter nestled in her own bed. The room was next to the kitchen, making it easier for Val and Bev to get her medications from the fridge and serve her food. Also, they could sit in the living room near Agnes but give her space all the same.

"Hi, honey, make this work," said Agnes, shoving the phone in Abby's face.

"Who do you want to call, Mom?"

"Your father, he didn't pay the cable, it won't work."

"Yes it does, Mom, you just have to press this button." Abby showed her for the umpteenth time on the remote.

"Oh," said Agnes, childlike, delighted when the TV screen came on.

Abby sat there beside the bed. It was awkward. Her mother was changing before her eyes. Each day the decay was more visible. The hollowness of her eyes more predominant, the frailty of her limbs. Her stomach sat between them like a third entity in the room.

Her mental state came and went. The unfiltered toxins in her body were rotting her brain. Simple things like the difference between the tv remote and the phone came and went. Time was elusive, her memory a road of potholes. She repeated herself, she could be sweet and then angry. She would understand and acknowledge her impending death, and then pretend like it wasn't happening at all.

Every visit, Abby felt the pressure to have that last conversation with her mother. That heart-to-heart that is always in movies. But she didn't know how, when, or what to say. One minute Agnes seemed like her mother, demanding things, rolling her eyes, but then she was lost. There never seemed to be a time.

"That portrait, right there, it's of your great-great-grandfather Eli, make sure you take that, okay? Don't let anyone steal it."

"Yes, Mom, I know." Agnes did this every time they saw each other.

"And don't let your father have anything, he has enough, and one of those child brides, no, dearie me, no, she can't have anything of mine."

"Yes, Mom. I know." Abby said patiently.

"Can I have a tea party with the ladies? That would be nice."

"Sure Mom, who do you want to come?"

"Oh, I don't want anybody over here, let's do it at the club."

Abby would sigh. Around and around, these conversations, ending up nowhere.

Thanksgiving was in two days and they all agreed to avoid it this year. It was their least favorite holiday anyway. The past three weeks had been exhausting, from the hospital to getting Agnes home. Abby knew her kids were still none the wiser at their age, so Jake and she were going to have a simple meal with them. Harry had asked Janine and Arthur for one last proper holiday together and they would go to a restaurant. Ansel had gone home to get some sun and Asher would most likely never have Thanksgiving with his children again.

Abby thought about their last Thanksgiving together and laughed out loud.

"What's funny dear?" asked Agnes jabbing at the remote and messing up the TV.

"Mom, were we awful kids?"

"No, no you weren't awful. You were my little duckies. Arthur was so fat, like a baby koala I just wanted to hold. And you, when you had a tantrum, you would stamp your feet like an elephant. And Ansel, such a sweet boy. Who called you awful? Did your father?" Agnes made a noise like *humph*. "He never was around to see any of the sweet things."

"No, later when we were teenagers or almost grownups, were we awful to be around?"

Agnes got quiet. Abby watched her mother's weak arm, full of liver spots and bruises from intravenous needles, lift up to wipe her nose as she looked away.

"No, my dear, don't think about any of that. I want you to only think about what was good. Focus only on what was good. It was good, you three were so good. Listen to me, forget the other nonsense," said Agnes as she closed her eyes.

Abby couldn't tell if her mother was sleeping or wickedly ignoring her. But she sat there anyway and thought about how all of them were such emotional train wrecks in their youth. The Williams kids lashed out when they could, regardless of who was in the way.

Abby will never forget how in one swoop they not only destroyed a holiday but a marriage as well.

—

It was 1989 and Christy (One) had spent the week preparing for Thanksgiving. For her, buying new linens and meeting with the caterer was about as domestic as she could get. Now that the day had arrived, she was agitated and skeptical. She could not shake the ominous feeling that went with the Williams family gathered in one place.

Her whole life had been spent studying and working. Now

she was an accomplished lawyer and the great Asher Williams's wife, but the workload never ceased. Whether it was the papers on her desk or the emotional burden of being the second Mrs. Williams, everything felt like a job. Asher liked that part of her most of all and confided that maybe if Agnes had worked, maybe she wouldn't have been so unhappy. Christy always had a soft spot for Agnes and defended that raising three children *was* a job. It was a woman's catch-22: devote yourself to family or to work, successfully having both was the golden ring few could catch. It felt heartless to judge other women by their choices.

After Christy babysat the children that first time, Asher felt comfortable with her near the family. He would often send her alone to check on things in Connecticut. The romance didn't develop between them until after the divorce and by that time no one was surprised.

At first, Agnes scared Christy. They were alone in the Westport house one day and Christy had papers for her to sign. While sifting through them, Agnes casually said without looking up.

"Are you sleeping with my husband?" she asked.

"No, Ma'am, I am just his associate." Christy wasn't stupid; she knew about Asher's dalliances.

"Well, for now. But I am sure he has his eye on you." Agnes was looking at Christy not with hatred or animosity, more curiosity. "You're quite beautiful, obviously intelligent, he relies greatly on you with our" – Agnes made air quotes – 'family secrets.' Give it time, dear, he will get you."

"I just go to work," Christy stammered.

"We all do, dear, we all just go to work," sighed Agnes. After that, when Christy arrived on her doorstep, Agnes was sweet and kind to her. She offered her coffee and biscuits and encouraged Christy to stay and talk to the children. When the divorce did go through, Christy felt accepted by Agnes, which made it easier to succumb to Asher's advances. Later, she would look back and realize Agnes was just vetting and grooming her to be a part of the children's lives. For Agnes, it was the devil you know. Christy appreciated Agnes's astuteness and never underestimated her again.

This Thanksgiving was one of the few times all of Asher's children were coming, and they could be a contentious bunch. Dinner with them was like a live action chess game and debate rolled into one. Arthur at 22 was finishing up college. If he wasn't in a library or classroom, he felt nervous and out of place, like a loaded shotgun sitting at a table. Abby, 20, was trying to shake off the residue of being a teenager. College had a different effect on Abby; her clothes and hair got wilder and her mouth, mouthier. She felt the need to speak up about everything from politics to religion. She came in looking for a fight, especially with her tycoon father. And sweet Ansel at 16 had become a rather moody teenager. His clothes were unpredictable, as well as his manners. He was undoubtedly clever and chose his words wisely but they could bite all the same. They would never admit it but they were all still reeling from the divorce, their mother's ups and downs and Asher's absence. Christy felt for the kids, always had, since that first night years ago.

But she could never get used to the Williams dynamics. She was from a loving middle class home with parents who had been married 40 years. When Asher was alone with her, they rarely talked about Agnes or the kids; it was his way and she respected his privacy. But when she was surrounded by them, Christy felt outnumbered and, as a lawyer, unprepared.

Thanksgiving was Asher's idea, not hers. "Let's have the kids, let's do it right this year." They had gone to the Bahamas alone the year before, which suited Christy fine.

"Okay, can I ask why now?" but Asher didn't respond.

Asher couldn't explain about Sabine. It was so unexpected when he ran into her that it caught both of them entirely off guard. Asher was at the Waldorf Astoria for a meeting with Japanese investors. It was routine to have guests of McMillon stay there, and now that Asher was CEO he picked and chose who he dealt with. Often he sent the men under him to start the meeting, then he would come in halfway through, make a big statement and leave, wowing the client. Often afterward he would stop in the Waldorf's oak-lined bar to celebrate another win with a whiskey.

While sitting alone at a table he heard, "Asher, is that you?" Sabine stood, lovely as ever, in front of the table. She was older but it suited her; she was even more statuesque. Dressed in a beautiful French silk blouse and tailored pants, she still looked like the cover of Vogue.

Asher, taken aback, stood and kissed both of her cheeks. They stared at each other for a long time.

"May I?" she asked, pulling back a club chair and beckoning the waiter. Asher had no choice.

"I always…" said Sabine .

"Sabine, I…" said Asher. They both sheepishly laughed.

"Ladies first," smiled Asher.

"There is nothing I can say, I just have so many regrets. I'm sorry," she started. Asher curiously stared.

"Did you know, did you know what happened in Maine when we were…" Sabine asked. She lowered her head and when she lifted it, a tear was falling down her cheek. Asher understood.

"No, not then, I didn't. I only found out a few years ago," Asher said, also feeling the shame rise within him.

"Is Agnes okay? Tell me she's okay." Asher shook his head a little from side to side. "But that's not on you, Sabine, if I had only known, maybe I could have helped her then."

"I did that, Eric did that, I don't think I can ever forgive myself."

"Well, count me in on that shit show too. It broke Agnes but she never told me she was broken; she never healed. We are divorced now, the kids are almost grown."

"Did you see what happened to Eric when he tried to run for Senate?" said Sabine brightly. Asher looked at her and began to grin.

"Was that you?!" Sabine was aghast.

"Agnes had just told me. It seemed like a good opportunity to save the rest of the world from him."

Sabine let out a hearty laugh, "Oh thank you, Asher, thank you. I can't tell you how many times that prick did the same to me, just like Agnes, but it was in marital bed blessed by the pope." She couldn't suppress the bitterness in her voice.

"Well, Sabine, I took advantage of you too. Look at you, it was hard not to," said Asher, unapologetically. Making love with Sabine was and always would be one of the greatest personal achievements of the son of a mechanic.

"It was fucked up," said Sabine, the word sounding out of character with her beauty. "I was fucked up and poor Agnes with her naive ways. She entered a world maybe she was never meant to be in. I was born into it, I had no choice." Sabine sighed like she was carrying heavy truth. "Will you please tell her, just tell her how sorry I am, she didn't deserve any of it."

It stung Asher. No, Agnes didn't deserve anything he had done, either. "I will, Sabine, I will."

Afterward all Asher wanted was to see his family. He wanted to try and put the pieces back in the box, make them whole again. His idea was to have a family Thanksgiving and Asher invited Agnes. He campaigned for her to come, wanting everyone together, if only selfishly to erase his own past faults as a husband and as a father.

"Aggie, come, please, it won't be right without you," Asher pleaded. He wasn't going to tell her about seeing Sabine. Too afraid to hurt Agnes with her name.

"I think one Mrs. Williams in a room is quite enough, Asher dear," said Agnes stonily. He ignored her rebuff and said she was welcome.

Abby asked, "Mom, would you consider Thanksgiving with them?"

"I am not starving, dear, so why would I eat food I neither care for nor want," Agnes stubbornly replied.

Christy had been expecting Agnes to arrive, but when it was just the kids, she sighed with relief.

"Where's your mother?" Asher was confused.

"Did you really think she would come, Dad?" said Arthur.

"But why the hell not? This was supposed to be a family Thanksgiving!"

"I believe her exact words were 'Not a chance in hell,'" smirked Ansel. It was no secret whose side Ansel always backed – his relationship with Asher so distant, both unable to bridge the years they lost together.

The growing mood from all the children was resentment toward Asher. After the divorce, they saw him less and less and they felt neglected. While it was all Agnes's orchestration, they couldn't help feeling their father got an easy out. He made less of an effort with them, especially Ansel. They never held it against Christy, they still had a soft spot for her from that night long ago, but they certainly held it against their father.

"Well, we will just make the best of it, right kids, that's what we always do?" said Christy, trying to steer the mood. Her parents were in the other room, sipping their martinis, expecting a pleasant holiday dinner.

Nothing about this was going to be pleasant, the kids knew that like animals know when it's going to rain. When they left their mother that afternoon she had already started drinking. Either here or at home, there would be a storm.

"Oh my dears, don't worry about me. I will be just fine," Agnes said brightly at her door wishing them off. "You know how much I love you and a silly little holiday isn't going to stop that! I am just going to put on a movie and wait for you three, the loves of my life, to return home. As much as I would adore watching your father and his sweet sweet wife eat fowl, I will pass. He can pretend all he wants he has a family but I've got the real thing here." She hugged them and it made them feel even worse for going to the city.

"Hey Dad, so like do we pretend we have traditions like a normal family or do we just wing it? Like should I call you Daddy for more of an effect?" At 16, Ansel knew how to sneak wine and was getting surly. Christy shot Asher a look and Asher responded, "Now son, can you please save the sarcasm until the second course."

During dinner, the kids let the adults do most of the talking. Arthur quietly chewed the starter salad, Abby pushed it around her plate but Ansel loudly chomped and made a mockery of the dinner. It wasn't that they had anything against Christy but they had everything against the situation. Leaving their mother didn't feel right.

It was Christy's mom, Mrs. Carter, who started the unfortunate situation. It wasn't her fault. She was trying to be polite but had no idea what kind of mine field she was stepping in with the Williamses.

"Dears, where is your mother today? Is she having a nice dinner somewhere?" Obviously Mrs. Carter wasn't versed in the art of divorce. Asher nearly choked on a tomato. "Mom, she's home," said Christy, subtly trying to tell her mother to lay off the Agnes subject by shaking her head back and forth.

"Yes, home alone," chimed Ansel, looking sulky. Mrs. Carter, who obviously had had one martini too many for her small frame, continued filling the silence.

"Well, I am sure she is having a lovely day." All three William kids just stared at her like she was an idiot. "Okay, new subject!" she said, chirpy. "Did you hear about the new skyscraper on 60th? They promise it to be an architectural marvel. I just don't know how they do it!" No one was particularly listening to her. Ansel was rolling his eyes at Abby and Arthur was busy meticulously cutting his food into perfect bite-size pieces.

Mrs. Carter continued to babble, "I believe it's the Bartor Corporation, you know that Eric Bartor, the businessman who tried to run for the Senate? Dare say, he does have loads of money, not too far down on the Forbes list, I think. They really do a lot for the city, lots of charity, quite a family."

All of the Williamses became quiet and stopped eating. Christy, unaware, said, "That is interesting mother, do you know who the architect will be?" Asher put down his fork and just stared at the table.

"No response, Daddy?" sneered Ansel.

"Don't Ansel, don't," Abby hastily whispered. Asher looked up at them, pale and waiting.

"Weren't the Bartors friends of yours, Daddy? Good friends I thought, way back in the day?" Ansel was baiting him in an angry teenager kind of way.

"Ansel!" Arthur nearly screamed.

"What's going on? what's happening?" Christy knew immediately something was coming.

"Did your mother tell you?" Asher stayed calm and looked at Ansel.

"No, Mom didn't. Funny, it was you."

"Knew what, Abby? What are they talking about," pleaded Christy.

"Then Daddy dearest didn't tell you either? Dad, c'mon, she's your wife," shot Ansel. "Oh, but you like lying to your wives, don't you?"

Christy grabbed the red wine and began pouring it to the rim of her glass. Mr. and Mrs. Carter looked like audience members at the U.S. Open.

"How do you know!" boomed Asher.

"We lived in that house too, Dad. We heard you both fighting the night Mom told you," said Arthur evenly, wiping his face with his napkin.

"How could you do that to her? To us?" said Abby.

"What?! Do What?!" Christy pupils were overly dilated.

"Eric Bartor raped our mother," Ansel said out loud. "But Dad was too busy fucking Mrs. Bartor to notice. You see, Mrs. Carter, really rich people can also do really bad things."

The table went silent. Mrs. Carter hiccuped.

"It's not that simple, son, I know how much you love your mother and want to protect her, but it's not that simple. I loved her too, I love her, I didn't know! If she had told me sooner?! I didn't know," Asher started rambling.

"Save it, Dad. We can't go back and fix anything now," said Arthur. "But you have to realize, we love Mom but we had to live in the aftermath. You didn't. You got to live in the city. No offense Christy, but this ivory tower here with the expensive china and views, it's all a joke. All the money in the world can't save people from getting hurt, and maybe it actually causes the hurt." Arthur said and downed his own glass of wine.

"You were supposed to protect her, take care of her, but you didn't. But she still took care of us," said Ansel flatly.

"Goddammit, Asher. I knew you did some shitty things, hell, I have seen the paperwork. But this, this is why Agnes is the way she is ... and you were a part of it..." Christy was stumbling over her words, exhaling and beginning to cry.

The Carters got up and took their daughter, upset, from the room.

"So we having pie or what?" Ansel mocked.

"Stop it son, just stop it. I will say this once and only once. Your mother in no way deserved what happened to her, and yes, I was part of it but I didn't know! She never told me!" Asher's voice boomed off the walls. He had never shown them so much anger.

"Dad, she never told us, but we still stood by her," said Abby.

"Let's stop," said Arthur. "There is nothing we all can say or do now – no point in entirely blaming Dad."

"Why not?" said Ansel.

"Whether you like it or not, I am still your father and she is still my family," stated Asher sternly. "I will always take care of you."

"Well then, can't wait to see what that looks like," said Abby.

Not long after that dinner, Christy left Asher. She accepted so many of his faults, but this, she couldn't. He had failed his wife so spectacularly, Christy couldn't even name it particularly, just that he failed. Years later, Abby received a Christmas card from her, happy with a new husband and baby. Abby wasn't thrilled that she and her brothers helped destroy a marriage, but she was glad she got Christy out of the ivory tower – at least someone had escaped unharmed.

NINETEEN

"Hi Agnes, if anyone could pull this look off, it would be you," Jake said jokingly as he kissed his dying mother-in-law on the cheek. "You requested my presence, milady?" Agnes had Bev call him, relaying she wanted to meet with him alone.

"Jake O'Conner, stop that nonsense," Agnes laughed. For some reason, Jake made her feel girlish; he was the only one who could tease her.

"How are the boys? I am worried about Abby; this isn't easy on her," said Agnes seriously. "Jake, I am dying."

"NO! I had bets on forever. I am going to lose the pool."

Agnes giggled again.

"Funny, Jake. No, seriously, sit down. We need to talk." Agnes was clearheaded. "I wasn't kind these past few years, and I don't expect to be forgiven, but maybe we can forget?" she said.

"Have you said this to Abby? I think she should hear it."

"I can't, every time I see one of them, I just can't, you have to tell her Jake." He was surprised. Dying Agnes was nice and it was disconcerting.

"Jake, your wedding. My daughter's beautiful wedding," she started to cry. "I ruined it." This was something Jake had been angry about for so many years, but listening to her, he couldn't help but cave.

"I can't say she wasn't disappointed. I was disappointed too," Jake managed.

"Not as much as me. But Jake, dear, hold my hand, know this. You are the best thing for her. If I could have had just one of you in my lifetime, maybe I would not be here right now." Jake sighed as he thought if his mother-in-law had just been like this earlier, honest, so much pain would have never happened.

"It seems it's not too late for me to say I'm sorry, so this is it." Agnes looked hard into his eyes and he understood.

"Jake, my children are everything that I never was and when I go, I want them to be everything I never could be. Watch over Abby, make sure my baby girl does what she wants, the right way. Push her to follow whatever dreams she has and don't let anyone get in her way. Remind her to do it for herself. Remind her not to be like her mother. You are a good man, Jake, and I know my daughter, I know my daughter is in good hands. " Jake held her hand for a while, both of them unable to speak. Bev came in with Agnes's morphine shot and Jake stayed as she drifted off.

Bev said to him as he left, "Remember, there is always grace in goodbyes. It's in the humility of the dying we can go on living." He was struck that Bev was most likely the wisest person he had ever met.

—

It was late 1998 when Jake proposed to Abby. He was respectful and drove his pickup truck to the city to ask Asher for his daughter's hand. Asher looked at him a little condescendingly, but said yes, knowing he was in no place to tell him no.

Agnes called all the shots and their marriage had her approval. After the debacle at The Chronicle, she had "informed" Asher that Jake was the right choice for Abby. They couldn't complain because Abby and Jake loved each other and that's what mattered. Eventually Abby would inherit money anyway, so why did she have to marry a rich man now? Jake had a successful furniture shop and that was good enough, Agnes said. She was just excited to plan a wedding, a beautiful Connecticut country wedding, for her only daughter. She hadn't had luck with weddings. Hers was barely memorable and she shuddered at the memory of Arthur's paltry wedding with his generic bride Janine. And Ansel, well, no wedding there. Abby was her only chance to live the fairy tale. Her daughter would have a big society wedding with a lavish reception at the club. It gave her a purpose.

So with the Williamses' blessing, Jake proposed with a gorgeous two-carat diamond ring that he had designed and paid for on his own. No Williams money, no inherited rich boy's money, he was a man who could stand on his own and love a girl, and ask her to love him back. No compromises, no agreements, no bullshit, he was hers and she was his. "Will you marry me?" he asked as she lay in bed. She was reading a book and wearing an old flannel shirt, it was Jake's favorite version of her. It was the Abby he knew and that was why she said yes.

Looking back, neither Jake nor Abby could pinpoint when it went wrong during the wedding planning, just that Agnes slowly started to unravel. It was subtle but became more apparent with each decision that had to be made, from place settings to flower arrangements. Abby could feel the tide of her family's past coming in like a tsunami. Her mother became more agitated, a telltale sign that disaster loomed. And Abby knew her mother's anxiety was linked to all the hidden family secrets that threatened to bubble to the surface.

Was her family doomed never to have happy endings, just remorseful beginnings?

The wedding was set for June 1999 and the world was nervous enough with the new millennium approaching. The news was filled with Y2K and the end was coming for anyone who believed in god, the devil or a computer. Maybe it was the sense of change everywhere or the fear of the future but Agnes fell down the rabbit hole again.

The wedding put her on constant edge that winter. As much as Abby told her it didn't need to be perfect, Agnes was determined. When Abby thought back about what went wrong, there were so many reasons.

Asher had been dating Chrissie (Two). This Chrissie wasn't young; in fact, she was close to Asher's age. She was the ex-wife of one of his McMillon partners and owned a profitable handbag company. Honestly, the kids were all impressed with Asher's choice and hoped the relationship would last. Chrissie was an appropriate partner for Asher on paper, but they forgot, their father never chose a woman for her pedigree. But the idea of Asher bringing a smart, accomplished woman to the wedding made Agnes uneasy. She felt like they would be compared and it set off all of the insecurities Agnes felt when married to Asher. For Agnes, it was easier to hate a young wife than accept one of her peers as Asher's newest conquest.

"Is he bringing her to the wedding?" Agnes badgered her daughter.

"If they are still together, I would assume so." Abby said, rolling her eyes. In retaliation, Agnes started dieting and obsessing about her looks. She was not going to be upstaged by her ex-husband's girlfriend. As Agnes became more manic, the drinking slowly began to increase.

She and Abby began to fight over everything, starting with the wedding dress. Agnes insisted they go together to multiple stores even though Abby had already picked one. "Is it made of flannel?" her mother joked with a little too much sarcasm. Abby shopped with her mother anyway, just to appease her. She tried on tulle and princess dresses she hated and the whole expedition was forced.

"Mom, none of this is me," Abby moaned. Even when she was a child, she firmly was against any form of Disney-esque dress.

"Abby, everyone is coming to this wedding and you have to be properly dressed. Now stop whining." Agnes's tone was harsh.

"Wait, is the dress for them or for me? I'm a little confused, mother." Abby shot back. Later that week, Abby went ahead and bought the dress she wanted without her mother. It reminded her of something Rita Hayworth would have worn in the 1940s - straight, silky, sexy- and Abby loved it. She was sympathetic, her mother never had her own big wedding, but this was getting ridiculous. When she called to tell her, Agnes was livid.

"Fine, dearest, I see you can do what you want all on your own. What do you need me for? What do any of you need me for?" All three of the Williams siblings were getting used to this rhetoric since they were out of the house now. If Agnes wasn't getting angry at them, then she was guilting them.

They could tell her drinking was escalating by the phone calls.

"Your sisster wants these bigs fancy wedding," Agnes slurred on the phone with Arthur. "I don'ts know how I can do it. It's like a dog and pony show and I haves to put it all together, me, just me, Arthur." Arthur didn't tell Abby about the phone calls, knowing how they would hurt, but they got worse.

Abby was losing the one thing that was supposed to be

about her, not her mother. Jake was patient but frustrated as well.

"We have to do something," he implored.

"What Jake? What do I do?" Abby was on the edge about the whole situation and found it hard to even talk about. "Don't you think I am terrified that she will show up drunk in front of 200 people? Don't you think that is my worst nightmare? Then what do we do? How do I stop this whole thing from happening?" Abby was near tears. The pressure was building and something was going to give. She could feel it. She didn't want any of it, except to be married to Jake.

Ansel's 26th birthday was in May right before the wedding and that's when the dam broke. Agnes insisted on having a small party at her house and forced him home from graduate school in Boston for the weekend.

It was as if fate intervened just to save Abby and Jake.

"Where's Mom?" Abby asked when she arrived for the party. Arthur and Ansel just looked at each other and shrugged. No one knew.

"We thought she was with you?" It was six o'clock already, time for the party to start. Janine and Harry were there and Asher would be coming up from the city. Agnes always invited Asher to any event involving the kids.

"People are supposed to be here soon, what do we do?" asked a worried Arthur.

"Smile, take my gifts and send them on their way," Ansel chuckled.

"Are you high?" Abby whispered to him and Ansel giggled again.

"Oh Jesus, so Mom's missing and you're stoned. Well this ought to be fun," sighed Abby. "Ansel, focus, when was the last time you saw her?" He explained their mother got a phone call that morning and rushed out; he assumed it was Abby who had called.

Friends and neighbors began to arrive. Abby saw Mrs. Blacksmith and exhaled with relief and quickly pulled her aside.

"Mrs. Blacksmith, have you seen our mother?" Abby asked in a hushed voice. Mrs. Blacksmith was known to know everything that happened in Fairfield County.

"Dearie, please call me Stella. Yes, I'm afraid I heard she was at The Palm this afternoon and had quite a few martinis. It was Mrs. Kirwin who saw her and made the suggestion that she head home. The bartender didn't know what to do. She was alone."

"Was Mom angry?" Abby grimaced expecting an answer that would feel like a blow.

"No, quite the opposite. Your mother was crying." Stella looked worried.

"Mrs. Blacksmith, Stella, sorry, my mother does not cry and does not cry in public."

"I know dear, that's why I am worried."

Abby grabbed her brothers, "We have a situation."

"I can't handle a situation right now Abby," said Ansel going pale. "'I don't want realism. I want magic! Yes, yes, magic.' "

"Did you seriously just quote Blanche DuBois from *A Streetcar named Desire?*" Abby looked flabbergasted at her stoned brother and shook her head. She decided to ignore him and turned to Arthur. "It's gonna be okay, we just have to find Mom." Abby put Jake on Ansel duty, who promptly led him to the kitchen to eat.

"Ooh, canapés," Ansel said excitedly. "Happy birthday to me!"

Agnes still didn't carry a cell phone; she thought them rather stupid. But ironically, she urged the kids to have one so she could call them constantly. That was Agnes. Arthur called Asher, who was on I-95 headed to Fairfield. He told his father to drive around looking for their mother, he and Abby would do the same;

it was the best they could do. Ansel and Jake stayed home to man the party.

Asher was the one who found her. He knew to drive along the beaches, anywhere Agnes could look at the ocean. It was a cool May day; the sun was setting and the sky was bright bands of reds and oranges. He was thankful he had not brought along his girlfriend Chrissie. He pulled his car up next to hers and cut the engine.

He didn't see her at first. She was not in the car or on the beach and he began to panic. But Agnes was sitting on a small jetty, arms wrapped around herself. Asher walked slowly and approached her with caution.

She was shaking and he took off his jacket and placed it on her shoulders. The smell of alcohol was stronger than the sea. Asher was relieved but in disbelief she had made it to the beach.

"Aggie, what is it, love?"

"She came back Asher, she came back," she murmured.

"Who Aggie, who?" Agnes was silent. Suddenly, she stood like she had just changed her mind and fiercely shook her head.

"Never mind, Ash, never mind. We have a party to get to, right? I am the host and not there. Bad me. But I don't think I should drive; would you?"

It took Asher his whole life to realize the one mistake he made over and over with Agnes. He never asked her what she meant, never asked her what she was thinking, never asked her what had happened. She was right about one thing, he was a coward. He was afraid of the truth, his or hers.

Asher took her back to a house full of people and the evening went from bad to worse.

"Darlings!" Agnes entered the room like the movie character *Auntie Mame*. Her makeup was bleary and she was wearing a simple black sweater and pants, very unfestive. The

Williams children knew the look and went into panic mode. Luckily there were only 20 or so guests, but enough that Abby felt like this was a rehearsal to her wedding.

Her heart raced watching Agnes take glasses of wine and then knock them over, too drunk to even drink them. Her mother slurred and stumbled and looked like a fool. The guests were polite but the whole thing was a mockery at best.

Arthur tried to get her some food but she was unable to get the fork to her mouth.

Ansel went outside to get high again.

Asher sat mute on the couch; he had never been around enough to know what to do.

Janine took Harry home.

Guests politely left.

Stella did not leave Agnes's side. If Agnes wanted music, she played it. If she wanted a cigarette, she got it for her.

"Thank you," Abby said when they were alone in the kitchen. "I just...."

"Honey, your Mom is sad," said Stella squarely. "It's as plain as day. I don't know why and I don't know if she talks about it with anyone but she should. Some people have a sadness that can't be explained. But darling, she's not the first and not the last, so there's always hope."

Abby nodded and thought about the horrible story of her mother and Eric Bartor no one ever talked about.

"Women like us, we only get one story," continued Stella. "And we don't get to write it or get to tell it. Lord knows, I have tried with your mother, but she just can't put hers into words. It's not something she ever learned how to do, no one let her," Stella's kind brown eyes looked at Abby so dearly. "So we women get the houses, the jewelry, the nice shiny things but we don't get a lot of choices. We knew that, we signed up for it, but the reality, dear, is it's a lot harder to live with than any of us ever considered."

"But you seem happy?" Abby looked at Stella's bright colorful kaftan and thought of joy.

"Listen, I got my own secrets, my own casket of mysteries so to speak. But I went into this life with my eyes wide open. I came from these people, I know how they operate. Your mom, I don't think she was as prepared as she thought she would be."

They heard a crash. Glass had broken. The two women rushed from the kitchen.

Fortunately, everyone had gone except for Arthur, Asher and Ansel. Agnes had been trying to dance and had fallen through the glass coffee table. She was laughing, unable to feel the cuts and shards of glass piercing her skin. The sight was agony to all of them. Their beautiful mother pitifully writhing on the ground, unable to pull herself up.

Agnes looked at Abby, and said, "Do what you want, baby girl, do what you want…" Her eyes were dead and inanimate like a fish caught at sea.

The wounds were superficial, thank god. Stella and Abby took Agnes to her room where she promptly passed out. They applied bandages and removed her clothes, which had shielded her from most of the glass.

When Stella left, she looked at Abby and put her hand on the girl's cheek. "The difference between your generation and mine is, we were so afraid of doing things wrong that all we did was make mistakes. It's ironic." She laughed. "My piece of advice? Don't be afraid, be brave. Agnes would want that more than you know."

Abby returned to a room full of beaten men. Asher was pale and defeated. Arthur resigned. Ansel was so high, he was putting cigarettes like candles in melted brie wedges and singing Happy Birthday. Jake stood when she entered like a knight, ready to do anything she commanded but riddled with anxiety.

Abby sat down and looked at the people she loved most in the world. And she did; for all their faults and missteps, these people were her people. And now was the time to lead them, to be brave. She told them the plan.

The day after the party, none of them spoke to Agnes. They left her the mess in the house to clean. Abby insisted not a word from any of them until Monday, when their mother wouldn't be hung over. Of course, she attempted several times to call each of them the day before but they ignored her.

All four of them arrived back at Agnes's early morning, when she least expected it and would not have started drinking again.

"What do you mean there won't be a wedding?!" Agnes screamed. Abby had gathered everyone in the living room. It was an intervention of sorts.

"We are getting married, just not the way you planned," interjected Jake.

"Aggie, it's time. You need to get some help again," said Asher. He had found a recovery center in Palm Beach. A private jet was waiting at the airport to take her to the specialized clinic just for women with substance problems.

"No, I'm fine," Agnes said angrily. "You are just making a mountain out of a molehill. You can't do this to Abby, Asher."

Abby shook her head and went over to her mother. She sat at her mother's feet and took Agnes's hands.

"Mom, listen to me. I don't want this big wedding, I don't want any of it. I just want to be married to Jake. It's about me and Jake. But I also want you back. You are not well, and a wedding can't happen without you being healthy. Look how you behaved on Ansel's birthday." That hit Agnes like a dagger. She winced at the thought, her sweet boy's birthday ruined. She couldn't look at

Ansel because of the shame.

"Mom, don't do this to Abby, please, we are begging you to get help," said Ansel.

Agnes was quiet. She knew there was no way out, no way of winning this argument.

"Well, I guess all of you know what's best now. My opinion doesn't matter." Agnes was sulking.

"It's not about opinion, Mother," said Arthur sternly.

Agnes was too tired to fight and went to pack her things. Asher was taking her to Florida; none of them trusted her to go alone. Agnes barely looked at Abby when leaving, the thought of missing the wedding would forever be a thorn between them. Agnes would never forgive her daughter for going ahead without her and never admit she brought it on herself. For Abby, her wedding would always be tinged with sadness but also relief.

Three weeks later with the family and just a few friends, Abby and Jake married. Agnes, in rehab, didn't communicate at all that day. Abby wore the dress she wanted and for the most part was happy under the circumstances. But for years she would hide her wedding photographs, terrified of hurting her mother if she saw them. They never spoke of it again.

—

On the jet to Palm Beach, Agnes tried not to speak to Asher. Just a few hours ago, her world was in her control and now she was being shuttled off to some healthcare prison. She was fuming.

"Aggie, I know you are angry. But can you tell me who you saw the other day? What happened that started all this? You said there was someone, a woman who came back? Was it Sabine?" Agnes let out a cruel laugh.

"No it wasn't Sabine, Asher. That woman is nothing to me." Asher could hear the anger in her voice and thought otherwise.

Agnes stared out the window and started to cry.

"Who, love, tell me who?"

"It was my mother." Asher looked, visibly startled; they had never spoken more than two sentences about Agnes's mother in their whole relationship. Asher always assumed that Agnes was too young to remember her; at least that's what she told him. Again, Asher never had asked.

"She found me. Wasn't hard I guess, my name and address were in Dad's obituary at school."

"What did she want?"

"To see me, to say she was sorry, but she wasn't really sorry."

Her mother had called her out of the blue that Saturday morning of Ansel's birthday. Agnes was stunned. Joan Cooley was her name now and she was twice divorced since her marriage to the Professor. She was chipper and rather pert on the phone, asking to meet Agnes for lunch or a drink? Every fiber in Agnes told her to say no, but curiosity got the best of her.

They met at The Palm. Agnes, nervous, had a healthy glass of vodka beforehand.

She was surprised she recognized her mother after all the years, seated at the bar. It wasn't hard; Agnes looked a lot like her. Joan's blonde hair was short and neat but her large green eyes had too much makeup attempting to cover up the visible wrinkles and sagging skin. Her clothes were worn and her overly large handbag a tacky pinkish color. They both had dimples but Joan was an older, sadder version of Agnes. Life hadn't been easy for Joan; she had gone from one husband to the next, never quite winning the jackpot.

"Hello," said Agnes, not sure how to address her, mother or Joan?

"Oh my, you are lovely, Agnes, just lovely!" said her mother, who was certainly eyeing her up and down, taking in the diamond jewelry, neatly ironed clothes and expensive shoes.

"I have to admit, I don't really know what to say. I was just curious at best," said Agnes coolly.

"I am sure, I am sure," Joan nervously laughed and sipped her pinot grigio.

"Well…" Agnes didn't know what to say.

"I have grandbabies?"

"Yes, I have three children."

"Are they healthy? Cute?"

"Well they are grown adults but yes, they are healthy." Agnes was not about to let her mother have even a taste of knowledge about her children.

Joan was visibly nervous. "Oh my, maybe this wasn't such a good idea. I can see you are still upset with me."

"Why would you say that?" Agnes's tone was turning.

"Okay, fair enough. I admit, it's not right that a mother leave her child. Hallmark does enough movies on that subject. Reminds me all the time, *I'm the bad guy.*"

Agnes didn't argue.

"But baby girl…" those two words tore through Agnes's facade. It took everything within her not start screaming at her mother. "Baby girl, I just had to go, it wasn't right for me to be with your father, it wasn't right for me to be there. I was so young."

"I was younger," said Agnes indignantly.

"Yes, I know. But I knew your father would do a better job raising you. I knew he would be good at it. He loved you more than I could and he was far more responsible."

"Well, you let him prove that point."

"I was no good for you, no good for your father and maybe no good for myself."

"Why did you come? Just to make excuses forty years later? Why bother?"

"I'm getting old, I guess. I am at that time you start to look back and stop looking forward. When I found out your father had passed away, I thought maybe we should clear the air before I go as well."

"Big of you."

"Maybe this was a mistake. I should go." Joan turned to leave.

"You abandoned me," Agnes said loudly.

Joan didn't back away. "But look how good you turned out, baby girl. Not like me at all, you don't have want for nothing, that's obvious. Me, I just keep chasing something I'm never gonna find." Agnes noticed her mother's chipped, cheap nail polish. The latch on her purse was broken. Her earrings weren't real gold.

"I'm just glad you got the life I always wanted," Joan said, looking sincerely at her daughter.

Agnes turned away as her mother left and stared into a martini. The sadness that enveloped her was overwhelming. Her mother was so right and so wrong at the same time. But Agnes knew one thing for certain; she wasn't going to watch her walk away again.

TWENTY

The hospice doctor was a nice, elderly man with a subtle German accent. The work being fairly simple – it was always the same outcome – Dr. Becker was mostly retired. As far as the siblings could tell, his job was to come, reassure their mother everything was fine and whisper *two more weeks* to them before he left. *Death was in no rush*, Dr. Becker told them. He likened it to a holding pattern at the airport, just waiting for the go-ahead from the main tower.

Abby scheduled her surgery. Fibroid, uterus be damned. She was tired anyway, might as well heap this on top of her endless pile of other things to deal with now instead of later. All the men knew well enough not to argue with her.

Standing before her mirror, Abby brushed her teeth and stared at the wrinkles forming around her eyes. She had lost weight from the stress and her skin had the bluish hue that came with winter. It was December and the days were short and cold. Everywhere she turned, people were jolly with Christmas and they had barely celebrated Thanksgiving.

Abby was letting Jake handle Christmas this year. He had strung some lights and gotten a tree. They would go to the toy store and buy a bunch of useless plastic gadgets that the kids would love for at most an hour. They were too young to care. That was Christmas. Bah humbug.

Abby brushed her hair slowly and watched her forehead crease, thinking about the surgery. Jake and she worried it would affect their sex life; would she be the same afterward? Jumping on the internet they found reassurance, but they wouldn't know until later, after her uterus was gone. The bright side, she thought, was no more periods – and that could thrill any woman. It was a wretched thing the human body does to women, make it bleed and cramp. How did biology think that was a good idea?

"Hey, you in here?" Jake yelled, looking for her.

"Yeah, back here," she called to Jake. "Maybe I should put the surgery off? Now doesn't seem like the right time."

"I know, but I just don't like the idea of this going on and on. What if it, whatever it is, makes you sicker? We just need to get it over with," *So male*, thought Abby, he couldn't even use the term fibroid. If men don't get it, like periods or UTIs, then it just becomes a pronoun they squirm saying. It made Abby laugh. Women really were stronger than men; they just couldn't tell them.

Jake wrapped his arms around her and the two of them stood for a long time just breathing. Abby started to cry from the stress and he soothed her hair and held her tighter.

Jake always understood the magnitude of Abby's mother and her effect. It was a constant push and pull with Agnes. One minute she could be loving and kind, showering them with attention, and the next full of rage and hatred. Jake didn't understand how a mother could be that way but he had been around long enough not question it any more.

Like Agnes forcing Jake to do odd jobs at her house, he also stopped questioning it. "Jake dear, something is wrong with my refrigerator door, could you look at it please?" or "Jake, my car's engine is making funny noises, can you check it?" Before the kids, they used to visit her regularly. Every time, Agnes would find some menial chore for Jake to dutifully perform. Prepared for the inevitable, he kept a tool box in the car. He and Abby didn't understand it but he complied with his mother-in-law's demands as she hovered over the task.

"It's good that you can use your hands, Jake. Asher never could. His father was a mechanic and he can't screw in a lightbulb." Jake laughed. It was true. "Maybe if Asher spent more time touching things, you know fixing what was broken, maybe he would stop breaking them in the first place." Jake just listened; that was part of the scenario, listening.

"I like that you can do things, it's good for Abby to have someone capable around." Jake realized these were little tests. Agnes was making sure her daughter would be taken care of, that he wouldn't treat Abby like Asher treated Agnes. This was the closest Agnes would ever get to telling Jake she approved of him.

Jake got irritated with Agnes when it came to the subject of children. He and Abby had been trying but it wasn't happening. Abby had had two miscarriages and both were devastating. The first miscarriage, Abby made the mistake of telling her mother right away. She called her crying and Agnes rushed her to the hospital. All was fine and normal. But when Abby went back home to rest, Agnes got drunk and called all her friends about it.

"I can't believe you did that mother!" Abby screamed into the phone after her mother's friends called Abby and sent flowers. "This was private, not for all your friends to know about."

"But I'm sad darling, I'm hurt, this has really hurt me," Agnes whined. "I don't understand what the big deal is, my friends want to help. Some of them have had miscarriages and you can talk to them about it. Your father is devastated as well."

Abby turned to Jake, "Oh my god. Oh my god. She told the fucking world because 'she' was sad. Oh my god, If I had wanted my father to have known, I would have fucking told him." After that Abby stopped speaking to her mother for a few weeks, but Agnes ignored her silence and sent food and flowers, acting like nothing was wrong.

Her brothers sympathized, not so much with the miscarriage but more with the boundaries their mother crossed. They knew it was a cautionary tale. When Abby had her second miscarriage, they only told Ansel. Each month after became an emotional roller coaster of hoping and then disappointment. Abby got quieter and quieter. Agnes knew something was wrong and tried to ferret out information from her brothers, but they circled the wagons and protected Abby's privacy. It was her and Jake's business, not the family's or anyone else's, for that matter.

And then, as they say, everything happens for a reason. After they had started talking about fertility doctors and options, and had given up watching Abby's every move, she threw up. She began throwing up for days; even Jake thought it was gross. She thought it was a virus, but then she realized a virus didn't make everything smell so bad and her boobs hurt. Eli was on his way. While they were extraordinarily happy, Abby was too sick to even leave the house. But that was fine, they wanted to lie low until the three-month mark.

But Abby's absence took a toll on Agnes. Her daughter had pulled away from her and it made her angry. Her drinking was getting out of control again and she was doing her best to cover it up. Now that the kids were grown, she drank daily. She kept a bottle of vodka in her closet and wine in the refrigerator. When people came over, she just put the vodka in her diet coke can and no one was the wiser. If only they knew Agnes' heart was breaking.

Ansel drove Abby to the hospital for the surgery so Jake could stay home with the kids. Jake looked too worried and serious and Abby couldn't handle his fear on top of her own.

"You know how much I hate hospitals," said Ansel driving at 5 a.m. like an old lady, hands gripped at the wheel.

"You don't have to stay, just get me there." Abby was jumping out of her skin.

"No I'll stay, I'm a martyr like that. Like Mom, it's not about you, it's about me and I how I feel. " Abby laughed.

"Thanks."

"So will you grow hair on your face or some weird shit after this?"

"Oh, shut up," and Abby punched him.

An hour later she was in a cold hospital room by herself. Her clothes shoved in a plastic bag, her body wiped down with antiseptic. She thought Ansel was completely rational in his fears about the medical profession. It was scary and lonely in a hospital.

Eventually, she was wheeled downstairs. It was shocking how many people were scrubbed and awake at 6 a.m. Amid the beeping machines and curtains being slid constantly back and forth, they offered her a sedative. Abby knew from experience, the countdown to oblivion was the best part. Within minutes, the voices and beeping faded away into blissful nothingness. After two C-sections, she appreciated that it was the kind of sleep most could only dream about.

She awoke later in a new, equally cold room. Recognizing her bag of clothes on a table, Abby was confused by the clock which said 2 p.m. But the surgery was only supposed to take 2 hours? Ansel had run away back home after Abby was out of surgery but Jake was there. He looked drawn but happy to see her coming around. He explained her fibroid was worse than assumed. It was seared to her bladder and it took hours of laparoscopic surgery to get it out. Dr. Santiago came in; he was pleased with the results but ordered her to stay the night.

The drugs swam delightfully around in her system and she told Jake to go home so she could watch bad hospital TV. It was the first time she had been alone in months and she didn't want anyone to ruin her mini-vacation. She inwardly congratulated herself for surviving, let alone showing up. *Checkmark* as Jake always said. Funny, how some people needed family, needed their mothers or sisters to get them through this kind of female surgery. But Abby was content alone. She had stopped sharing with her mother a long time ago and now her life was filled with men, her husband, her brothers, her father, her boys. None of that sentimental womb lifecycle of a woman crap for Abby. *Good riddance*, she thought. Recovery and normal life would begin again tomorrow. And hallelujah, no more periods.

But still Abby couldn't push away the sense of loss. A physical part of her was gone and in its wake were five bullet hole-like scars on her stomach. They were adjacent to the C-section scars that ran horizontally on her midriff. For years after, the purplish ridges would itch like a subtle reminder there had once been a war in her body. Life and death situations had happened inside her. There was a time she created children. Now, she could no longer give a mother's love to another child. And the irony was soon she would no longer be able to receive it from her own. The loss of that maternal part of herself and her mother felt connected, interlaced. It was like being shot but still alive. Jolted, shocked, scarred, recovering, that's the real lifecycle of being a woman.

TWENTY ONE

None of them could avoid it, even Agnes knew it was Christmas. From the constant Christmas movies and incessant TV commercials streaming before the sick bed, even death couldn't stop that holiday.

Outside was thick with the smell of fireplaces and pine wafting in through an open door. The trees were bare and not much for Agnes to look at as she twisted in her bed waiting for her next meal or visitor. It had strangely become routine, her dying. The doctor came and went, giving his vague prognosis. The nurses doled out meds, rubbed cream on her arms for the itching and administered her scheduled morphine. Agnes complained and bitched, pushing everyone to their limit. Then she would become docile, childlike and couldn't remember the last meal she ate. It had been four weeks since she had left the hospital.

Ansel was back for Christmas. He was staying at Abby's but going to his mother's every day. Abby went every other day, needing to split her time with the kids. Arthur visited as often as he could and between the three of them Agnes always had someone coming or going. Her health deteriorated, from bad hours to bad days. She slept, ate and watched the sun move across the sky, not caring if it was day or night.

"No, I don't like that, take that away!" Ansel heard his mother shouting as he entered the kitchen.

"Oooh I tell you, she's in a mood today," said Valerie. Ansel thought it didn't help that Valerie's head scarf was bright orange. Agnes hated bright orange but he wasn't going to say anything.

"She said she wanted toast, I made her toast, but my toast wasn't good enough for her, humpf." The nurse said to no one.

Bev came in the room, "Pay no mind. You go and rest, I'll take over from here." Bev really was the better nurse, all three of them agreed. But Valerie was a good night nurse, able to stay awake and put up with Agnes.

"Ansel, you are too skinny, how about my fried chicken for lunch?" asked Bev. "Your mother loves it. Go tell her that's what I'm doing." She started pulling pans and Ansel slipped away.

"Ansel, dear, what is that racket? And fix the TV, it won't work." His mother had gotten very good at barking orders. *The queen on her throne*, he thought.

"Mom, stop fussing with the TV buttons, here..." he gently took the remote, turned on the TV.

"Oh turn it off, the sound is annoying,"

"Okay. Bev is making fried chicken for lunch."

"Is it my last meal or something?"

"No, mom, just lunch," Ansel sighed. Some days she was sweet and some days surly.

"So when do I get to meet this boyfriend of yours? Not like there is a lot of time left, darling, and I would appreciate you not keeping these secrets from me, especially now."

"Are you playing the death card, Mom?" Ansel laughed.

"Well, he's not my boyfriend. Okay, maybe he is … how do you know about him anyway?"

"I still bloody know things, I'm not deaf and you three have always been chatterboxes. Never could shut any of you up when you're together. What's his name, Hector? A doctor? Well, we could use another doctor around here, especially one who doesn't talk about quality of life all the time. Good lord, the terms they use. I'm dying, so just keep the pain meds coming."

"Yes, Hector."

"So? What are you waiting for? Call him now." Ansel didn't know what to do. *Okay, well fuck it, why not?* Ansel thought she did get a dying wish or two.

Standing next to the bed, Ansel called Hector. He knew he was at the hospital and expected the answering machine. "Hi, Hector, ummm. I am with my mother and she is requesting to meet you, preferably before she is in an urn. So I am being the good son right now and formally asking you to come and visit when you can, thank you — Wait, what, Mom? Mom, he has a job, Mom, stop it, he can't fly up here today. Hector, my mother says as soon as possible please. Yes, I told him, well it's up to him, Mom, god, you can't pull the death card every ten minutes! Sorry, bye, Hec, talk later." Click.

"Are you happy, crazy lady?" said Ansel.

"Yes dear, such a wonderful son you are. Now where is my fried chicken?"

———

When Agnes's friends came to visit, a visible horror spread across their faces when they saw her. To have known someone so pretty and vibrant and to see all that was left was a cadaverous shell. It was truly heartbreaking. They would casually ask about the cancer. Abby would politely shake her head and explain it was cirrhosis. More shock would register: no one knew.

Cirrhosis wasn't the most dignified of diseases, not something you would refer to in an obituary. People didn't like causes of death that sounded like cautionary tales. While the Williamses had gotten used to it, Agnes's friends and neighbors treated it like a communicable disease. Acquaintances, too afraid to come, sent flowers; others sent emails or left a voicemail with unsolicited advice. *Watch out for the nurses, they steal. Try vitamin A and D and a vegetarian diet. Wouldn't your mother be more comfortable in a hospital?* These supposed words of wisdom left Abby and Ansel bitter with resentment. Arthur, on the other hand, had a great aptitude for just ignoring people. He didn't care what they said. The siblings felt like they were doing the best they could and didn't exactly value the opinions of others.

Abby and Ansel came in one day to see a priest at her mother's bedside and three women singing hymns. *What the fuck?* She mouthed to Ansel, who just shrugged. It was Mrs. Robbins, one of their neighbors, a plastics heiress. She explained that she knew Agnes loved music and thought the ladies could cheer her up. People who inherited wealth tended to cross personal boundaries, having never heard the word no in their lifetimes.

"I thought Mom liked the bands Chicago and Steely Dan? I never realized she worked on the rails in the Midwest," Ansel whispered to Abby, who snickered. They let the women finish and enlisted Bev to shoo them politely out. Bev had no problem, she thought it was crazy how rich people handled death anyway. That day Agnes was higher than Neil Armstrong in space and was completely oblivious anyway.

Some days Agnes just slept. Bev or Valerie would show the kids the increasing chart of opioids knocking her out.

The plan for Christmas was to visit their mother on

Christmas Eve, no presents. They would just sit with her, that was all she could handle, and then the rest of the family would do the big deal in the morning with the kids. Hector was coming then and Ansel could introduce him to her as she had demanded. It surprised Ansel that he didn't feel more wary about the situation.

"Maybe you actually do like the guy," said Arthur.

"Yes, but meeting Mom like this, it's all so terribly weird and like some Lifetime movie."

"What's a Lifetime movie?" asked Arthur. Ansel rolled his eyes.

"I don't want it to be *meet Hector before you die because he is the love of my life* mumbo jumbo."

"But what if he is, and Mom should meet him before she dies? Sounds pretty simple to me."

Ansel glared at him, saying nothing. Arthur's matter-of-factness and rightness really could be annoying.

The day before Christmas, Ansel took Hector to visit. He was relieved he didn't have to explain his mother's appearance. Hector, a doctor after all, was more familiar with the maladies of the human body than most.

"Leave, Ansel, go chat with Bev and find out what my next meal is; could be my last, you know," Agnes said with a chuckle.

"That's still not funny, Mom," said Ansel, hesitating at the door. His mother was in good spirits and wanted to talk to Hector alone. Ansel didn't like it but left anyway.

"Hector, dear, sit near me, I can't see too well." Hector did as he was told and smiled sweetly at Agnes. It relaxed her and they began to talk.

"Ansel has never brought anyone home in the best of circumstances so you must be quite special," said Agnes sweetly. "But you should know, Ansel is far more special than you or I could ever imagine to be."

"I've come to realize that," said Hector.

"It wasn't fair that he had to be the baby. He got the short end from his father and me but he turned it around. Showed us, as they say, but he is not without his scars. I will always feel guilty about that. I could have done better, Asher certainly could have. Do you know why he hates hospitals?" asked Agnes.

"I just assumed like other people, needles, blood, etc."

"Not quite. Something bad happened when he was very little. He hurt his wrist and I wasn't there. Me, his own mother, not there to protect him, hold him while doctors and nurses poked and prodded. He was only four but I know deep down he remembers it. He had no one to reassure him. I screwed up that one. I stupidly overdosed on some medication. I'm afraid my kids will only remember me as being too sick at the most important times in their lives." Agnes went silent, her guilt washing over the room like a shadow.

"But also hospitals are where damaged people go," she continued. "That's where the neediest and most urgent people are crying out for help. All of humanity's worst emotions are on display: fear, sadness, pain in their truest form. You see, it hurts Ansel to be around hurt people. He is too empathetic, he cannot help but feel their pain and want to do something about it, even when he can't. That's what I did to him, because I was always hurt in one way or another. All these years, he felt my pain and he couldn't do anything about it. What a horrible thing to do to a child." Hector listened.

"It was me, and his father, but especially me, I was too messed up and he couldn't fix me. Every crack and tear, Ansel couldn't look away from and it became too much. Because that's how much he loves me. Letting me go will be the best thing for him; he can finally stop worrying, finally stop wanting to repair the irreparable. He thought his love could be like glue to put me back together, but it doesn't work like that.

"I know he loves Miami and I hope Miami loves him just as much. I hope you love him just as much. He needs to be away from this metaphorical hospital of broken people. He cares, we know that, but we care about him too. So when I am gone, dear Hector, will you heal him? Will you heal my son?"

Hector nodded and let the gravity of Agnes's love sink in. Every word she spoke, he would not forget nor would he ever tell Ansel what his mother asked. It was his promise to Agnes and it would be his gift to her memory long after she was gone. He would cure her son.

TWENTY TWO

Abby eased herself into a chair near the hospital bed. After the surgery, she was sore around her middle but up and moving. The doctor said it would feel like a gut punch; he wasn't wrong.

"Where were you?" Agnes asked her daughter. They never knew when Agnes was in reality or in morphine land. Today, she was in a good frame of mind. "You don't look good, what happened? And don't lie to me; I am still your mother."

"Had my uterus taken out, nasty fibroid." At this point, why lie?

"Oh honey, oh, are you okay? Are Jake, the boys?" Now that her mother had been sober almost a month, she had changed. Her edge was gone, she was the old Agnes. Agnes the mom.

"Everyone is fine, I'm just sore."

"Now, I mean it, Abby. You don't overdo it, let the guys do everything. They have no idea how strong you are, but you don't need to be. I worry about you. You can't take on so much all the time. Let other people help, Abby."

"I will, Mom, don't worry about me." Abby turned away, fighting back a tear. She loved hearing the care and concern in her mother's voice; this was the version of her mother she would miss. "So how are you feeling?"

"I'm itchy and I still don't like Valerie and she doesn't like me. Wakes me up all the time, who cares what my temperature is at 3 a.m.?"

"Well, Mom, you get a little feisty at times."

"It's my house until you bury me. Listen, see that portrait of great Uncle Eli, send it back to Asher, lord knows why I have it. Where is your father anyway?"

"The city. Do you want to see him?"

"Yes, tell him to come. I need to make sure my will is up to date and the house, you know it goes to all of you to handle. Can you three do that?"

"Yeah, Mom, we will be okay."

"And my ashes, no box for me, not your mother."

Abby started crying, she couldn't help it. Talking about her mother's death was horrible.

"Don't cry, sweetie, we have to get through this. I am having a good moment right now, so let's take advantage of it."

"I know." Tears flowed harder. "I know..." was all Abby could say.

"So my ashes: you know the Haven Jetty near the lighthouse?"

"Yes."

"Go there when there is a beautiful sunset, I want yellows and reds and the sky to be on fire. Walk to the end, and when you get to the point where can't see the land behind you, spread my ashes. Okay? Promise me? I want to spend my eternity swimming towards the horizon."

Abby could barely speak, "Why there, Mom?"

"Because that's where I can breathe, honey." Her mother's watering eyes looked into hers. "My whole life I went searching for things I thought I wanted but really, I should have been finding a place to breathe. The place that doesn't hold you, that doesn't squeeze the life out of you. The place that is endless and open and welcoming like the horizon. I should have been looking for that, searching for the people who made me feel that way, carving out a life that gave me breath and didn't choke me. You and your brothers, promise me, you will find that because nothing else matters. Find the place where you can breathe."

Abby lay her head down on the hospital bed and cried. Her mother's hand gently patted her hair. After a while it stopped and her mother was asleep. Abby rose slowly and went outside to the garden. The air was frigid and she wasn't wearing a coat. She sat on a stone bench and cried so hard, her eyes swelled. Eventually Bev came out with a blanket for her shoulders. The nurse's soft hands lifted and guided her back into the house. Bev made her lie on the couch and urged her to sleep. And Abby did, deeply, breathing in and out.

The true socialite, Agnes ordered Bev and Valerie to prepare food and decorate the house for Christmas Eve. It gave her some purpose, some feeling of the woman she used to be, entertaining. That night they all filed into the dining room, now her mother's sick room, except Felix and Eli, who Hector kindly offered to babysit. Harry insisted on coming with Arthur, saying he didn't care what Aggie looked like, he needed to be there. They were family. Arthur protested but the boy was close to manhood in so many ways and could make up his own mind.

Abby brought some champagne so they could feign normalcy with a drink. The house had been cleared out of any alcohol by the nurses, which Abby thought ridiculous since her mother couldn't even get out of bed. She assumed it was Valerie punishing them for letting Agnes smoke.

"I hope you people aren't this morose at my funeral," Agnes teased, trying to ease the tension.

"Abby and I plan on recreating the scene from *Steel Magnolias*. Abby is going to run around shouting about her hair looking like a helmet."

"My hair does not look like a helmet!" Abby shrieked.

"Guys," Arthur said.

"Harry, come sit by me, you were always my favorite," Agnes joked. Agnes even looked happy.

"Hellllloooo!!" They heard bellowing from the front door. Everyone looked at everyone, who could that be?

"Ahh, the brood." It was Asher. Dressed in a suit made for an opera at the Met, he looked too formal for the occasion.

"Hi, dearest." Asher stormed in and kissed Agnes on the head. She giggled. Everyone looked perplexed.

"Don't mind them Asher, nobody has quite accepted I can do whatever the hell I want right now. Kids, I invited your father." They looked at each other and shrugged, oh well. Like always, they never really knew what their mother was going to do.

There was small talk and Agnes insisted they eat some food. But shortly thereafter everyone could see her wincing in pain. It was hard not to notice.

"I'm sorry - I'm afraid- can you get Bev?" she whispered to Harry. Bev meant morphine, which meant sleep, they knew the drill. Kissing their mother goodbye didn't feel festive. It was her last Christmas, their last Christmas with her. Abby sniffled and tried to push those thoughts away. Jake held her hand and got her outside quickly. Ansel grabbed the half-opened bottle of champagne and Arthur glared at him.

"What?! I'm not driving." Arthur rolled his eyes at his baby brother. Outside, they could see Bev in the window, Christmas lights sparkling while she held up the morphine bottle and filled a syringe. Eerily, it felt like a silent night, as the song goes, until Ansel broke the sad reverie.

"Oh my god! Dad, is that Christie in the car?!" shouted Ansel. Jake, Abby, Arthur and Harry all turned to look at Asher.

"What? I didn't want to upset your mother."

Back at Abby's, they set two more place settings for Asher and Christie (No. 3); it seemed wrong not to invite them at this point. They were relieved the visit with Agnes was over and Abby was filling drinks and getting the turkey ready. They desperately pushed aside thoughts of Agnes; the holiday was a trial run of what it would feel like without her, as if she were already gone.

Christie, thankfully, pitched in to help Abby, seeing her in pain. There were some things women just didn't need to explain to each other. When Abby went to lift something, Christie appeared and did it for her. Not like her brothers were any help. Abby was beginning to see Christie's kindness; it was just hard to see past the perfect breasts and prepubescent waistline.

Felix and Eli were wound up. They loved having people in the house. Harry was on the floor playing with them and Hector and Ansel on the couch were making jokes. Arthur as usual was chatting about the markets with their father. It felt like Christmas.

But could they ever get through a meal without something happening?

Was it eating turkey or their proximity at a dining table that sent the Williams family awry? Just like a sinkhole, the argument opened up so suddenly and so forcibly nobody could circumvent it. But then again, the family was always a lethal combination of alcohol and strong personalities. It was in their DNA to erupt at a holiday meal like Mount St. Helens.

"Where's Janine, son?" Asher asked Arthur across the table. Abby and Ansel stopped chewing and looked at Arthur. *Did he not tell their father?*

"We separated a month ago, Dad. I've got a new place."

"What in Sam Hill? You mean you are getting a divorce and didn't bother to tell me?!" Asher's face looked hurt.

"Well, I didn't think it would be that important to you."

"That's wrong, right now everything is important," Asher almost shouted.

"Really, since when?" said Ansel. He always got defensive when it came to Asher telling them what to do. What right did he have?

"Don't take that tone with me, Ansel. I care about what goes on in this family."

Ansel set his fork down slowly. "Again, Dad, since when?" The room went silent.

"Oh are we gonna do that pity party thing where I was a bad father and not around enough. Again? It's getting pretty old, Ansel, especially at your age."

"Dad, stop," urged Abby.

"Well, Christ, Abby, no matter what I say or do, it's wrong, especially with that one." Asher pointed to Ansel with his fork. Ansel fumed.

"Dad, let it go," Abby implored.

"Let what go? It's you kids who hold on to everything. Like goddamn elephants remembering every little thing I've done. You are grownups now; move on." Asher looked down and lifted a forkful of potatoes.

"Little hard to move on when all your mistakes have caused our mother to rot to death in a bed down the road." Ansel shot back.

"STOP!" said Arthur, slamming his fist on the table.

"No, I will not."

Arthur put down his utensils and glared at Ansel. "I am your father and I brought you into this goddamn world, paid for everything you ever had, so I get to say something. This one thing. Your mother was no saint; she messed up just as much as me. Some of it was my fault, some of it wasn't. But I will say this, if she can forgive me, why can't you children?" Asher stood, threw his napkin on the table and stormed outside. The silence was deafening.

"He's right, you know," said Christie. "Yeah, I speak. Don't look so shocked." No one masked their astonishment.

"I know you guys need a bad guy in this story and your father is an easy one. He wasn't home, he loved business more than you guys, your mother drank because of him and a lot of other horrible stuff. But how long, like, can you keep that going around and around in your heads? Like, what's the point? He's right, you guys are grownups, so, like, maybe act like it?" *They were being chastised by a Valley girl,* thought Arthur. *Certainly a new family low.*

"Oh I know, you think I am just some dumb Christie, Christie Three, you call me? It's okay because I am the last Christie. I will be there when your father needs his medicine and I will call 911 when he goes downhill, just remember that. And it's not about the money. That's so, like, yesterday. Old men, they know what they like and what they don't like, and lying and cheating is boring to them. Asher is a what-you-see-is, like, what-you-get-kind of man and that's what I want. I really do love your Dad, he is, like, super cool for his age. Did he ever really tell you how we met?"

The whole family was gripped by Christie's every word. In four years she had never strung so many sentences together in front of them. She held her arm over the centerpiece and snapped her fingers at Ansel. She pointed to the wine bottle in front of him and waved for him to give it to her. He had no choice but to comply. Hector could not help but smirk; she was dishing it out and it was delightful to watch.

"Yes, we met in a spin class, like, you think I don't know how silly that sounds? But it was a charity spinning class," she took a healthy swig of wine. "My brother is blind, as in he can't see. I doubt any of you knew that. I was hosting the class to raise scholarships for other blind kids at his school. Your dad heard about it at the gym and he, like, had never even taken a spinning class before. He wrote a big check and came to the class. As soon as he walked in, he began helping anyone who was blind, including my brother. It was, like, so super cute.

"Your father is the sweetest man. Maybe he wasn't always the best when you guys were kids, but he has changed, you know?" She gulped some wine before continuing. "And don't make fun of me for sitting in the car. God, your mother is dying, she does not need to see me. Like gross, that would be, like, so mean. And Asher and your mom have been talking a lot lately, like, I want them to talk a lot. I don't want to spend the rest of my life with him moping around. Yuck, boring. So they have patched things up. Like, be happy for them, you guys. Be happy your Dad has changed, be happy I am here to take care of him, be happy everyone isn't, like, so sad any more. I mean, you three are blinder then my brother sometimes."

Stunned. Never before have all three Williams siblings looked so sheepish and felt so guilty. They were looking down, away, anything but admitting that, against all Vegas odds, Christie was most likely right. Asher came back in and sat down. Christie smiled at him and began eating her food again.

"Umm, sorry Dad," started Arthur. "We didn't mean, I mean, hey, sorry I didn't tell you about Janine. I just thought, well everyone expected it at some point, but I should have called."

Ansel coughed, "I'm sorry too, Dad. I shouldn't have butted in, just, sorry...." was all Ansel could say.

Abby brought over the platter of turkey, "Can I get you some more, Dad? You didn't eat enough." Christie was smiling at her husband; he looked around the room like aliens had landed. But he could accept that if everyone was getting along.

"OOOh can't wait for dessert, Abby," said Christie sweetly. Eli and Felix started chanting "Cake, cake, cake!" and banging on the table, reclaiming the title of children of the family. Holidays.

TWENTY THREE

"Arthur, I got to fall in love with you first," said Agnes, propped up in the hospital bed. "I know that was a blessing and a curse." Arthur sat with his mother.

"I never knew I could love like that. You were so round and chubby and you smiled a lot. You were such an easy baby. Quite frankly, you didn't prepare me for the other two." Agnes laughed. "I'm sorry you were burdened with so much. The oldest always is, or so I am told. But I always felt like it wasn't fair." Agnes looked dreamily out of the window. "I sometimes thought we, the family, were the anchor that was going to drown you."

"Mom, no," protested Arthur, even though he did feel that was true. He felt awkward talking about feelings with his mother; they never did. She expected things of him, things maybe his father or his siblings could never do, so he did them. But they didn't need to talk about them.

"I knew, Arthur."

"Knew what?" He asked naively.

"I knew you were around the corner, behind the door, listening." Arthur was shocked.

"I wanted you to hear and I hated myself for it." Arthur was stunned.

"But why? I was only a child."

"You were more than a child, always so much older and wiser than any of us. I was selfish. I wanted a witness to my pain. I wanted someone to know what I was going through so if your father ever said it didn't happen, you would know that it did."

Arthur thought for a minute and got mad. "That wasn't fair; I would never do that to Harry."

"But you have, son." That hurt Arthur, you were supposed to make things wonderful for your children, not engulf them in your own problems. He always thought he had protected Harry from his and Janine's animosity.

"It's okay, Arthur. I didn't mean that. In some ways marriages, good or bad, can't help but get the children involved. No one is immune to it, not even you and Janine." The truth stung but he could see it. "I wanted you to be on my side. If any of you knew the truth I wanted it to be you. I thought you could handle it; you would protect it and protect me."

"Still, Mom, I drowned in it." It felt good to be honest with her.

"I know, and I am sorry. I suppose I am confessing my sins," Agnes said dryly.

"Am I allowed to be mad at you?" Arthur asked.

"I am not dead yet, my boy; be as mad as you want. I can take it." Agnes changed the subject, "Do you remember Billy Fitzgerald? That shitty little liar," Arthur winced at his sick mother swearing. But of course he remembered, he would never forget it.

Arthur at 14 was shy, nerdy even. For him, eighth grade was a never-ending nightmare. He had one friend, Joe Catchell, from a

Canadian family who had moved to Westport. Joe was fun and funny but, like Arthur, didn't have a lot of friends. He was considered an outsider. The boys both liked math and became "math buddies." Whenever the eighth grade class split up or studied, they chose each other. While Joe could care less about what the other kids thought, Billy Fitzgerald was the opposite.

Billy was a bully and most of the kids in school hated him. His father was caught embezzling from Leslie Johnson's dad and well, everyone knew and resented him for it. So vengeful Billy started the litany of usual teenager shit. He lied to people and cheated in school. But Joe was nice to him, he was nice to everybody, and Billy took it too seriously. When he saw Arthur and Joe were buddies too, he became jealous. Billy decided to go after Arthur because he wanted Joe's friendship all to himself.

Agnes got the call she never expected, Arthur was in the principal's office and accused of cheating. He could be expelled. Before Agnes even left the house, she put on her best Chanel suit and the highest heels she could find. For women, clothes and makeup were armor and there was not a chance on this god's green Earth that her son Arthur, named after many kings, had done anything wrong.

Agnes arrived fifteen minutes late. Asher had taught her that trick. Let them all gather and wait. The fancy private school seemed eerily quiet. It was midday and Agnes walked in with Western showdown music playing in her head. This wasn't Asher's fight, this was hers, this was her son.

"Mrs. Williams, please have a seat." She could tell Principal Panico was annoyed at waiting for her. "I will get right to it. Billy has accused Arthur of cheating and looking at his math exam. He says Arthur distracted Billy and thus, he failed the test. Arthur has simply denied the accusation without any detail."

"Yes, I see," said Agnes, disengaged. Arthur was about to

dissolve into a puddle. Poor boy could not handle confrontation of any kind. He certainly did not inherit his father's confidence.

"Mrs. Panico, if you would indulge me for a second, may I ask some questions of the boys?" Agnes said, widening her eyes looking innocent.

"Mrs. Fitzgerald, would that be all right?" asked Principal Panico. Mrs. Fitzgerald had no answer except to nod. It was hard to tell any expression through her multiple facelifts.

"Billy, what is the square root of ... mmmmm, " Agnes tried to draw it out, "2500, give or take."

Billy looked around and then said, "We use calculators for big numbers."

"Arthur?" she asked.

"50," he replied.

"I knew that." Billy looked sullen.

"Billy, what's the Pythagorean theorem?" asked Agnes. Mrs. Panico leaned forward curious, waiting for his answer.

"Ummm, the hypnosis of a triangle is equal to each side?"

"So you can hypnotize a triangle?" Agnes asked.

"No, you know what I mean, stop trying to trip me up," whined Billy.

"Arthur? Care to provide an answer?"

"A squared plus B squared equals C squared, it's finding the length of the third side of a triangle or the length of the hypotenuse of a right triangle equals the sum of the squares of the lengths of the other two sides, if you want to get technical."

"Billy, is that correct?" asked Agnes. No response. "Billy? Okay another question, this is easy, no numbers, no math, who invented calculus?" Mrs. Panico stayed completely silent. In fact, if she had some popcorn she might have been happier. The Fitzgeralds had always been stupid and pushy. Mrs. Fitzgerald kept turning her Cartier watch over and over on her wrist like she was late for a hair appointment.

"Billy? No... Okay, Arthur?" Arthur was smiling, his mother was playing a game he only wished he was smart enough to start himself.

"Isaac Newton, but it could have been Gottfried Leibniz, it was kind of a he-said-she-said thing back in the late 1600s," said Arthur bluntly.

Agnes looked at Principal Panico. "Should I go on or can I take Arthur home where he can study without *distractions?*" Agnes said it so acutely, every syllable so pronounced, the room was silent.

"Thank you, Arthur," Principal Panico replied. "I think it's okay if you go home with your mother now. See you tomorrow."

Outside, Agnes said to Arthur, "Let's get some pizza and go to the movies, we deserve a little fun after that!" They saw *On Golden Pond* starring Henry and Jane Fonda. Arthur thought it was the best movie he had ever seen on the best day of his life. He never wanted to see another movie again and ruin such a perfect day.

"Arthur, I wonder whatever happened to Billy?" Agnes mused. She changed the subject. "I wasn't the best of role models. I know that. And your father knows he wasn't, either. I'm not sure if any parent goes into it thinking they will succeed more than others. I, at least, tried, Arthur, please know, I tried."

"Mom, we know you did, really." Arthur hung his head.

"Arthur, I am so very proud of you, so very, very proud of you. We didn't do enough to teach you to be a good man, but you are one anyway." He needed to hear that and he didn't know why. He wanted his mother to be pleased with him, to recognize that he had done a good job with his life, Janine and all. That Harry was the end result of him being a good man. And Arthur was a very good man.

After he left his mother's house, Arthur walked toward the water, not his car. There was a path that ran along a seawall and he stomped down it angrily. The wind bit at his face as he let himself cry frozen tears. Grabbing rocks from the beach, he threw them one by one hard out into the water, the salt air pungent with bitter seaweed. The winter mocked him as if to say, *I can be stormier than you.* There didn't seem to be enough stones for him to grab, each one a bit of his rage, his fear, his sorrow. He felt useless and pitiful. The shame he felt for not saving his mother, not doing more, not being stronger for her. But truth be told, they both were at fault. Neither one of them capable of saving themselves let alone each other.

Death was an awful mirror to life. It showed an ugly picture of his family's faults and flaws. And Arthur couldn't figure out what to grieve more, who they were or who they weren't.

TWENTY FOUR

"Bev dear, bring me another blanket," asked Agnes. She was agitated, tossing in bed, unable to get comfortable. "I don't feel right leaving them," she confessed.

"I don't suppose anyone feels right about leaving their children. Everyone always says it should be the other way around," Bev responded while fixing to change the bedsheets. She had always been very good at doing her duty without disturbing her patients.

"Do you have children?" asked Agnes.

"No, ma'am, not yet, or I guess I don't know if I will." Agnes didn't question it.

"It's a love you can't imagine."

"I guess that is what I am afraid of. I say goodbye to so many good souls, maybe I've forgot how to say hello," said Bev, startlingly herself with her honesty.

"Well, for me at least, it was worth it. I know they seem crazy, a handful. Lord, sometimes I want to tell them all to shut up.

But I love them. They are the only people I find perfect because of their faults, not in spite of them."

"I guess that's what you call a mother's love," said Bev. Both women chuckled.

"Well, if you do have children Bev…wait how old are you, damn, I can't tell."

"34, an old 34."

"Well hell, that's not old!" Agnes yelped. "Maybe you should take a break from all this dying business and start living, young lady."

"Noted, Agnes, noted." Bev smiled. She liked the sick rich lady, she couldn't help it. "Can I get you anything?"

"A clock, dear, " said Agnes. "One that can go backwards, preferably."

Bev left the room but Agnes didn't want to watch TV. Instead she sat and thought about her children long and hard. Motherhood had been her greatest feat and greatest accomplishment despite it all. She wasn't perfect, but she knew her kids – maybe sometimes better than they knew themselves – and they, in many ways, were.

Thinking back, she laughed. Agnes always knew when one of her kids was in trouble. She had a sixth sense for it. As they grew up she began to worry more, not less, for their well-being. As teenagers, they scowled and argued when she enforced curfews and made them tell her where and with whom they would be. They wanted freedom and she wanted the security of knowing they were safe and sound. Agnes wasn't afraid to argue with them; it was her way or the highway. No matter how old they were, Agnes would be there to protect them, save them from themselves. And she was. And she did.

It was Abby who tested her the most, especially after she

got her driver's license. Asher had moved out and they were in the new house in Fairfield on the water. Agnes tried to make the transition as easy as possible and it wasn't that difficult. Turns out the only thing missing of Asher in the new house was his office. His presence had long ago gone.

Agnes finally felt in a good place – well, at least in her own place. Unlike new divorcees, she did not feel bitter or angry, in fact quite the opposite; she had never had this kind of freedom before. Going from her father to Asher, finally the weight of partnership and compromise was gone. She focused on keeping herself healthy. Not necessarily sober, but she wasn't drinking heavily. Decorating her new home was a delightful hobby. She joined charities and worked at school events, much to the kids' embarrassment. In a way, Agnes had never been so alive and she wasn't even 40 yet, only three years away. The world felt open, possible to her.

Abby, on the other hand, was an unruly 17-year-old. Agnes didn't take it personally. She saw other girls from better homes than theirs act far worse. In fact, watching Abby revel in her world of hair, makeup, boys and parties felt normal to Agnes. But she was determined not to let her daughter hitch a ride to some boy like she did. Would Agnes have done it differently had she not met Asher? Yes. It was hard not to look at Abby and think about how naive and young she had been. More and more, it was on Agnes's mind not to let Abby go down the same path.

Agnes could never forget the night young Abby came running to her mother, not away, for help. It was times like those Agnes knew her purpose in her children's lives, their protector as well as their savior.

It was a usual high school Friday night, Agnes at home, while the kids were with their friends.

"Mom, Mom!" Abby shook Agnes out of her sleep.

"What?! What is it, are you hurt?"

"No, Mom. I'm in trouble, please, please, don't get mad." Agnes shot up out of bed.

"Tell me and don't lie about anything because then I won't help you." Abby began to cry and explain. She had taken the Volvo station wagon without her mother's permission. Usually she was allowed to drive, but Agnes put her foot down that night because Abby had failed a math test. So after Agnes went to bed, Abby stole it to go to a party. But her girlfriend Tricia had gotten drunk and there were two creepy older guys at the party stalking them. They decided to leave. On the winding dark Connecticut roads, Tricia felt sick in the car and began throwing up. Abby panicked, swerved and the Volvo ran off the road into a tree. The girls left the car and walked the half-mile home.

"Where's Tricia?"

"In my bathroom throwing up…"

"Wonderful. And you, dearest, were you drinking?" Abby nodded yes.

"No one saw you girls? How far away is the car?" Abby explained they left it just at the bottom of the hill.

"Are the police coming for me? Mom, I am so scared, I am so so sorry. Please don't let me get arrested. Help me, help me." Abby was stricken with teenage panic.

This was the first time Abby had really gotten into trouble. Sure, she didn't study enough and was perpetually late, but on the teenage scale, she wasn't criminal. Agnes would be the first to admit, it was her daughter who saved her far more times than in reverse. Now it was time for Agnes to return the favor.

"Go clean yourself up, and take off all that wretched eye makeup. You look like a raccoon. Tell Tricia to stay in your room, she can't come out at all, then meet me in the kitchen."

When Abby came in, her mother was on the phone using her country club voice.

"Yes, officer it's been a terrible night. Yes, oh you found it! Wonderful! And someone is on the scene? Oh thank goodness. Not there? Because I had to walk home in order to call you, that's why I am not there. Like I said before, my daughter is sick so I wanted to get her home. Oh, the officer is on his way? Great, we are here waiting!" Less than a minute later, a patrol car was in their driveway and two officers were approaching the door.

"Yoohoo! Over here! Hi, officers, good evening, come on in." Agnes could not have been more gracious offering coffee and giving them a seat at the table. She explained to the officers how she went to pick up Abby from a friend's house because her daughter called, feeling sick. But then Abby just began throwing up (look of shock) and it caused her to swerve and hit the tree. She decided to leave the car – they were close enough to walk home – and call the station.

"Mrs. Williams, I just have to be blunt here, have you been drinking?"

"No, officer."

"We have a file on you at the station and your history shows a drunk-driving incident." The police were solemn.

"Yes, that was years ago and I went to treatment for that. I am fully aware." Agnes stared bright-eyed at both officers. "This, honestly, was about my daughter throwing up all over my car," Agnes chuckled for effect, making it seem all so silly, "And oh my gosh, the smell was terrible! I just lost control and there are no lights at the bottom of the hill. They should really put in a streetlight there, don't you think? The road curves so drastically and you can't see and Abby was throwing up, it was all very … in the moment. " Agnes waved her hands like she was done with the whole thing.

"Yes, we understand, Mrs Williams, that is a bad combination."

"Would you like me to take an alcohol test, I'd be happy to." Silence.

"No, No, I think we have it, Mrs. Williams. We will let you know where the car's been towed and we will write it up as an accident."

"Well, miss, I hope you feel better," the officers looked at Abby who was sheet pale and shaking.

"Clams, I ate clams!" was all Abby could say. Agnes told her to go back to bed. She thanked the officers and sent them on their way.

The next day, Agnes dragged Abby and a hungover Tricia to the tow yard. The dented Volvo was in bad shape but the smell of night-old vomit was worse.

Agnes turned to Abby, "I am not happy about what happened; drinking and driving is no joke and you should have learned that lesson from me, young lady. But I do understand you girls and your instinct to get away from those guys at the party. Just next time, call me, call a cab? Just don't drink and drive, please. Promise me you won't drive." They bobbed their teenage heads and looked like they were 10 years old again. It pulled at Agnes, remembering how sweet and young they were once.

"Yes mom, and thank you, you are like the coolest mother ever. I promise, I will pay for the damages and clean the vomit."

"Well, you are grounded and no driving except to school and back, I have no desire to be your chauffeur. But dear we are not taking this car home, gag me, as you girls say." Agnes made a throw up noise. "This is the exact reason to have money, no way am I taking this one home."

Tricia giggled and said, "Agnes you are so cool."

They bought a new station wagon that afternoon in the same forest green color but a newer model.

Agnes couldn't help but come to the defense of her

children. It was in her nature. Her own mother never coming to her rescue, she couldn't imagine her children suffering the same void. Children are just that, children, and they need parents to mediate between them and the world, no matter how hard or painful the task may be.

She feared for all her children, but it was Ansel who first learned what cruelty and injustice looked like. There was no way she could have shielded him. The helplessness of watching him suffer shook Agnes and scared her much more than she could admit. She couldn't protect her children forever but she wasn't above trying all the same.

When Ansel announced he was moving to Miami, it was both exciting and agonizing for Agnes. She never held much hope for Arthur breaking from his norm; he would always stay close to home. And poor Abby failed miserably in New York, her fragile young heart got in the way. But Ansel, he was her last hope to break free from the family, no matter how much it terrified both him and her.

Back in the '90s a young, attractive gay man was still an anomaly in the Connecticut suburbs. Agnes assumed there were more roaming the gilded halls of the Southport Country Club, but they remained discreetly underground. There were strides in equality but not in every part of the country. The good news, AIDS had been declared an epidemic. The country and the medical community accepted the responsibility. (It still didn't stop Agnes from continually going on and on about safe sex with all three of them.)

"Ansel, safe sex isn't about not having children. Your sister has to worry about that. It's about diseases and you don't want diseases. Trust me." Ansel, who had heard the speech a million times, just rolled his eyes.

"Why, Mom, did you get a disease?" He was teasing her.

"Oh no, no, your mother only has alcoholism, that's more of dirty secret than, you know, a nasty virus."

"Jesus, Mother, your sense of humor is really twisted."

"I just want you to be safe. When it comes time, you have to push my wheelchair and not the other way around."

"I'm not pushing your wheelchair, that's Arthur. I get to draw in your eyebrows when you get old."

"That's my son, you know you are one of my favorites." She never would say who was her favorite, honestly she didn't have one – it was like her kids were just a litter of cute creatures.

When the incident happened, Ansel, 27, had been in Miami a few months. He had found a decent apartment and thanks to the trust fund his parents had set up, his living expenses were covered, barely. He waitered at the Newes Cafe during the morning shift and Friday nights at The Palm Club on Ocean Drive. Agnes called religiously twice a week; she wanted to call more but knew he would stop answering.

On their Saturday morning call, Agnes knew immediately something was wrong. Ansel was slurring and trying to get through the conversation. She could not tell if he was drunk or on drugs. Her heart skipped, not being able to pinpoint the problem, her mother's instinct in high gear. She repeatedly asked "Are you hurt?" and "What's wrong?' but he avoided the answer. After she hung up, agitated, she called Abby.

"Call your brother, something is wrong, find out what it is." Abby called back without any new information but agreed, something wasn't right.

Agnes called Asher. "I need a jet to go to Miami this afternoon."

"Agnes, why … is it Ansel?"

"Please just don't ask, I need to go. I have always taken care of everything with the kids…"Asher knew she had, always gave her credit; it was his place to support her in that and he knew when to leave her to it.

"On the way."

Hours later, Agnes pounded on Ansel's door and kept pounding. She was about to call the police when he finally opened. "Mom?" Ansel's face was battered and torn, an eye swollen shut. His arms were bruised. Hair had been torn out of his head and his lips were cracked, swollen and bleeding. Agnes all but kicked the door to open more. When he saw her, he began crying uncontrollably.

Agnes gently dressed him in a button-down shirt – nothing could go over his face. She got on her knees and delicately, put one foot and then another in flip flops. She had a car service from the airport waiting downstairs in case Ansel had kicked her out.

Wrapping her arms around him, Agnes slowly led him down the stairs to the idling black sedan. The driver kindly helped Ansel in and Agnes held him all the way to the hospital as he wept.

They were in the ER for hours. Ansel had two cracked ribs, some broken fingers and needed stitches for an abrasion on his back. When the nurse came in, Agnes was in the room.

"Mr. Williams, can you tell us what happened?" Agnes read the terror on her son's face.

"Ansel, love, remember what I always said, there are two people you never lie to, your lawyer and your doctor. Whatever you say does not leave this room." He looked at her and squeezed her hand. He began to tell his story.

It was 3 a.m. when he left The Palm the night before. At closing he had had a few shots with his coworkers, but was tired and decided to head home. The Palm wasn't a gay club, an anomaly in South Beach, but it didn't matter. That night, two white guys from the Everglades were outside waiting, ready to hunt. They drove a beat-up old Ford truck adorned with a confederate flag sticker and visible gun rack. They were parked and watching whoever left the club.

The first thing he noticed was the words Alligator Alley printed on the side and a hand drawn picture of a gator, as they would say. When the truck slowed alongside Ansel, he kept walking, head down. He was only a few blocks from his apartment.

"Hey faggot, you a faggot? You look like a faggot." Ansel walked faster, his heart racing hoping they would move along.

"Hey faggot, want one of us for the night?" The two guys were laughing and drinking Busch Light. Wearing mesh baseball caps and T-shirts with the sleeves ripped off, they were dangerous. Ansel knew he was underweight and not strong enough to take them. His only instinct was to run and that was a horrible mistake.

When Ansel took off, he heard them yell, "woohoo" as the truck sped up and jumped on the sidewalk in front of him. Ansel hit the hood.

"C'mon you little fucker, let's get to fucking," or that's what he thought he heard, he couldn't really remember. Fear invaded Ansel's whole body. The redneck with a missing tooth punched Ansel's face repeatedly until he fell down. Then the other one dragged him, half-conscious, behind a hedge in front of an apartment building.

The guy was greasy and sweaty and overweight. He ripped Ansel's pants off and held his arms down. But Ansel fought, he fought as hard as he could, scraping and kicking. This guy wasn't as strong as the first and couldn't pin him. Ansel broke two fingers fighting but he won. Eventually, the guy got up, "You ain't worth losing my dick over, but just remember, I's letcha off this time." He zipped up his pants and ran back to the truck. Ansel lay, listening to the ignition, and heard the truck's gears grind as they raced off at a stupid speed. He doesn't remember walking home or his mother calling him that morning.

"You did well, Mr. Williams. You did extraordinarily well," the nurse said with tears in her eyes. "Let's talk to the police about this, can you do that, Mr. Williams? Only if you consent. But it sounds like you not only saved yourself but maybe saved some others too."

Agnes had to excuse herself; she patted Ansel's arm and said cheerily, "I'll be right back, ok honey?"

Out in the hallway bathroom, she locked herself in a stall and screamed hard in her pocket book. She thought she had felt pain before but nothing like this. She was murderous with rage and choked with sadness. But this wasn't about her, it was about Ansel. Strangers had gone after her baby and it was the most helpless she ever felt. It was one thing for it to be her, but her child? The world went dark. Her legs shook beneath her as she gasped for air. Breathe, she thought, breathe. Her brain searched for someone to call, but she could think of no one. Traumas were lonely events, isolated. But she would be there for Ansel; she was not about to leave him alone.

Agnes did call Asher later but told him nothing. She asked crisply for him, or his secretary, to book the largest suite at the Ritz Carlton. He didn't ask questions. Ansel talked to the cops and was released with copious amount of pain meds.

They went straight to the Ritz and didn't leave the room for a week. They watched old movies, ate room service and didn't talk about the incident. Day by day Ansel healed, and his mother watched, worried and took care of him. She didn't drink or even sneak a Vicodin. She kept asking if he wanted to see Arthur or Abby, but he just shook his head. Agnes understood.

"Mom, this would kill them. They took care of me, they always protected me, this would make them feel like shit. Looking at you is hard enough, my god, you look like someone killed a pack of puppies."

"Oh Ansel, I just…"

"I know, Mom, this isn't fun for either one of us. But, let's just keep it between us. I am so glad you are here, I am so glad you are my mother. I mean only you with zero respect for other people's boundaries would demand a jet from Dad and bust down my door. Seriously, Mom, you are the hero in this story."

Agnes cried. She cried for so many reasons. Seeing Ansel's pain, so similar to hers. There was no protecting him from what happens to a lot of people. People are unjustly attacked. They were part of a club now and she knew it would forever change him. But he fought and she never fought enough. How to express she was proud of him for being stronger, better than her?

Agnes spent another week in Miami before they were both sick of each other. Ansel quit The Palm and focused on day jobs. Not long after, he got a job at an art gallery and had no idea that his life had actually changed for the better. Agnes sent the Ritz bill to Asher's office and never said another word.

Now dying, Agnes' only regret was leaving her children behind, unprotected by her mothering. Her own life had become nothing, a waste, a garment to discard. But their lives, she wanted to protect so they could live forever.

TWENTY FIVE

"Where is she?"

"Who?"

"Number three."

"Play nice."

"Have I ever? Why start now."

"You asked me here, remember?"

"Do you know who you are talking to? I apparently can't remember anything."

"Fair enough."

"I'm dying, Ash."

"I know, love."

"I didn't mean for it to get this bad, I just couldn't stop."

"I know, love."

"Do you hate me? Do the kids?"

"I could never hate you, Aggie, and the kids, they love you, they get a little angry at you, at us, but they love you."

"They love you too."

"Really?"

"Well sort of, as much as they can."

"I'm sorry I wasn't better for them."

"I'm sorry I didn't make you better."

"It wasn't your job to make me a father."

"I didn't make my own father a father either."

"It's the cards we're dealt, I suppose."

"I'm sorry."

"Don't be. But I'm sorry too."

Silence.

"I saw Sabine a few years ago."

"Oh?"

"She wanted to tell you she regretted hurting you. She is sorry too."

"Well, aren't we a sad lot? But I don't think about it much anymore. We were young and I've made plenty of mistakes since then."

"I suppose that's just life."

Silence.

"I hate leaving the kids but it hurts too much to stay, Ash."

"We know and they, we, don't want you to hurt any more."

"Make sure you take the dining room table, if the kids don't want it."

"Of course. Anything else?"

"Is all the paperwork done, split between the three of them?"

"Yes."

"And you won't be a shit, you'll leave everything to them when you go, not the teenager?"

"She's my wife, but yes, the kids are taken care of."

"I loved you, you know. You and I made a great team once."

"It was the best. You know what they say, you don't know

what you've got until it's gone."

"Did you love me? I mean really love me?"

"Yes, from that moment when I first saw you, there was no other like you, Aggie."

"Good."

"I have missed you. None of them were ever as clever as you or as beautiful."

"Maybe I shouldn't have divorced you. I was angry."

"That's neither here nor there."

"Before I go, can we be like we were Asher, Asher Williams? Can we go back to that?"

"Yes, my love, of course, whatever you want. But I have to tell you I'm in trouble."

"Well that doesn't surprise me. Do you need help?"

"Yes, Aggie, yes, I'm sorry to say I do."

"Tell me."

—

Agnes always remembered the day, the time, the year, every detail about when she found out Asher started to cheat on her. The irony was never lost on her that it was April 1st and she was the fool. It was before Asher's graduation from business school and there was a school function to celebrate the graduating class. She remembers walking into the party with a foolish sense of pride and the crushing humiliation later.

Sabine had given her a gorgeous emerald chiffon dress to wear. Green felt like such a daring color but when Sabine approved fashion, it was like Vogue had all but blessed the damn dress. The party was at the Canterbury Club, an upscale West Side jazz club, in honor of the graduates before they walked across the stage. Asher was in a good mood, thinking about his future. He had already been offered and accepted a job at McMillon. Agnes found a sitter and was glad for a night's reprieve from the children. She had been feeling so tied to them; aside from Sabine, she had no other life except them.

Wearing a dress and makeup felt like a vacation, her normal life left behind if only for a few hours. Asher was attentive; he liked seeing her without the kids and dressed up. It wasn't hard to read his pride.

At the party, Agnes knew most of the other wives and girlfriends; they had endured many of these functions together. Usually it was boring small talk about fashion and children, but Agnes would take it as long as she didn't have to get someone an apple juice or wipe food off the floor.

Into the evening, dancing had begun and Asher took her for a couple of spins. He paid attention to her and she appreciated it. She noticed a group of men over at a table, and she winked at Asher. It was okay, he could go on over. Like a school boy, he kissed her cheek and left.

"Can you believe them?" Agnes recognized the deep voice. It wasn't sultry but an irritating baritone. It always grated on Agnes.

"What, Kinsey?" Agnes said, frustrated immediately. Sabine rolled her eyes in commiseration. Sabine could not stand Kinsey Thoman. Kinsey was set to marry Andy Cotswald, certainly the richest, most snobbish and dullest man in their class. Kinsey and Sabine had gone to school together and Sabine always said there wasn't a camera Kinsey wouldn't jump in front of, especially if it put her in the newspaper. *Lord knows she didn't have any attributes but hair and teeth,* Sabine would say.

"Well, look at those men after last weekend, all smug and cozy," Kinsey sounded like a tuba.

"What trouble are you starting, Kinsey," warned Sabine.

"What? I mean it certainly wasn't my Andy. He would never … but how you girls put up with it, I will never understand."

"Kinsey, for once, shut up," Sabine said sternly.

"What? Everybody knows … I mean they hired those hookers …"

"Shut up."

"Fine, but I wouldn't be married to a man…"

"And you aren't, are you? So go away and plan your wedding. Should be easy with nobody attending."

"God, Sabine, you have always been such a bitch!" Kinsey stormed off and grabbed Andy's arm.

Sabine laughed, "Even he looks annoyed with her. See how long that lasts."

"What was she talking about?" Agnes asked Sabine, her heart racing.

"Nothing, don't listen to her. The poor girl has been jealous her whole life. She doesn't have an original thought in her head."

"Yeah, but what was she referring to? What hookers? What husbands?" Agnes's heart was beating hard and fast.

Sabine looked at her. "Sometimes it's better not to ask questions you don't want the answers to. Or as my mother taught me, only ask the questions you have answers to. Do you understand?"

"Did my husband, does my husband…" Agnes stammered.

Sabine grabbed her wrist hard, "Agnes, I don't know. Many of them do, few of them don't. I just assume Eric does, it makes it easier not if, but when, I find out. It's their way, I suppose. I know it doesn't seem right, but can we fight it? Where does that leave us? Our mothers dealt with the cheating, I know my mother did, and I am supposed to too. I was raised to be seen, not heard." Tears welled in Agnes's eyes.

"Don't cry. I don't know about Asher, maybe he's different?

Okay? He certainly loves you, loves you way more than Eric loves me. I am jealous sometimes when I see you two. Asher covets you. Me, I feel dispensable, a doll to play with, but you, you are his partner. Maybe he runs off now and again but he comes home to you. I don't know. Life isn't fairy tales. Maybe I am jaded, but – Agnes, look at me."

Agnes was trying hard not to cry. She could see Asher laughing and smoking a cigarette across the room. He looked so handsome, so confident. Her heart swelled for him, but she looked at Sabine.

"It's a choice and a compromise, that's what marriage is. You choose to be with them and the compromise is for good or for bad. Just hope the good outweighs the bad." Sabine grabbed a champagne off a tray from a waiter, "Here, drink this and everything will be okay."

Agnes had already suspected Asher slept with other women; this was just the confirmation she had longed to avoid. No woman, as a wife or a mother, wants to acknowledge the betrayal. It had happened weeks ago. His shirts smelled of perfume, the late nights, the refusal of sex for days or worse, sex when he wasn't excited. There was one night he came home late and reeked of embarrassment. He wouldn't look her in the eye; he showered and feigned sleep. Asher Williams had never been tired in his whole life. All the little, unusual signs piled into one and Kinsey Thoman lit the match on the bonfire.

So would she be righteous, stand on her marital vows and leave him? Ha. That was a laugh, she agreed with Sabine on that. It wasn't principle at all. It was because she loved the asshole. She loved him with all her heart and could not imagine loving another man. Asher was the smartest in the room, the most handsome and the most charming. When he made love to her, she felt alive. He gave her womanhood, her children, her life, the very life she wanted. Agnes understood every word Sabine was saying, it was a choice and it was a compromise. She dried her tears and looked at Sabine.

"Thank you," Agnes said and went to go stand next to her husband.

———

Asher brought the paperwork to Agnes' house along with lawyers and a notary. Bev didn't like strangers coming in the house; they might upset Agnes. She had become protective of her ward.

"Mr. Williams, this is not the time. Agnes didn't get much sleep and she needs a shot."

"Bev, shoo, I mean it. Go busy yourself with something else. You can give her the damn drugs in a minute, but right now, I have business. So if you don't mind, let us be."

"Mr. Williams, don't you test me," Bev stared hard at him, but Asher just stared back. Wall Street wolves couldn't best him, so neither could a testy nurse. She relented. "I'll be right outside." Bev glared at the army of suits.

"I won't be long, I promise," Asher said reassuringly. "Have her shot ready."

Agnes's signature was barely legible. Her hands trembled but slowly she signed each piece of paper, then they were notarized. After the last one, Asher's team left and waited outside.

"Thank you, love."

"You know I better be going to heaven after all this," Agnes laughed a little.

"It's what's best for the kids, just know that and that's all I care about, I'll be fine."

"If you went to prison, how long would that be?"

"I don't know, it's all just begun. It shouldn't be too bad.

They only have me on minor stuff, maybe about $200,000 and that was less than they had on Martha Stewart. I'll cut a deal," said Asher nonchalantly.

"When are you going to tell the kids? Won't it be on the news?"

"I've got a couple of days before it breaks. They are trying to get me to squeal on some others at McMillon, but I won't. I'll take the hit. Hell, who hasn't done insider trading nowadays? Good god."

"You were never much of an up and up guy." They both laughed. "Arthur will be hurt, he hates trouble. Abby won't care so much, she is the forgiving one, but Ansel, I'm afraid this will just set Ansel off more…"

"Set me off how?" said Ansel as he swung through the dining room door glaring at his parents. "Bev just said there were men in here making Mom sign papers? What did you do, Dad? What did you make Mom sign?"

"Oh, I can't, Asher. You have to handle this one. It's time. You explain." She turned to her son, "Can you get Bev? I need my shot."

"Handle what?!" Ansel roared and he father shoved him out of the room.

They went into Agnes' back office and Ansel paced, huffing and puffing.

"What did you just con Mom out of? What did you make her sign?" Ansel was being protective.

"Calm down, Ansel. Just calm the fuck down."

"Don't tell me to calm down."

Bev stuck her head into the office "The both of you hush now, Agnes is sleeping, and he's right, Ansel, calm down. I don't want to have to use an Epi pen on you." She left, shutting the door.

"Sit down, son, and I will explain," Ansel managed to say

quietly. "Your mother and I decided together that we would move a majority of my money to a trust in her name that will be bequeathed to you and your brother and sister."

"Why, Dad? Why your money and why now?"

"Well, son, seems the feds have gotten wind of some of my extracurricular business activities and in order to protect the family's assets, this is what Agnes and I decided to do."

"In English, Dad."

"I know this will give you great pleasure to hear, but I might have to do a little prison time. Just a little insider trading, not like I am the only one doing it, I mean, it's as popular as cocaine on Wall Street, I tell you."

"Dad, seriously, Mom is dying and you tell me you are going to jail?"

"Well, don't make such a big deal out of it, son, I'm not the first or the last to get my hand caught in the cookie jar." Asher sat at ease in a wing-backed chair.

"Dad, you need to answer me honestly. What did Mom really sign?"

Asher stared at his son. He blinked a few times.

"Dad?"

"Okay, you got me, some of the holdings were put in her name so if I was prosecuted they would have to go after her and let's face it, she won't be around too much longer…"

"DAD! Jesus Christ!!"

"Son, I have to say it was her idea. I mean she wanted to put her death to some use."

"Oh my fucking god, the pair of you. Since the day I was born I have never understood you two. The father who couldn't show up to a little league game and a mother who drank like Churchill." Ansel continued to pace while Asher calmly fiddled with the fringe on a throw pillow.

"Son, you were never in little league," said Asher evenly.

"NOT THE POINT DAD. You scammed your way out of being my father and you are scamming Mom out of a decent death."

"Now, hold it son, I was a decent dad. I cared as much for you kids as myself. Maybe I wasn't affectionate but all that huggy-feely stuff, that was your mother's department. I admit I could have spent more time with you all, especially when your mother got sick, but I did my best."

"Mom wasn't just sick, Dad, it wasn't the flu. You left us to take care of her and we were just children."

Asher was quiet. He knew Ansel was right.

"Do you remember when I told you I was gay?"

"No, not really."

"You didn't say anything to me, nothing, no talk, nothing. It was like I told a wall. It was a really big deal for me and you ignored me."

"Wait, son, hold on. Don't you think I always knew you were gay? Hell, it was so obvious. But it wasn't a big deal, not to me. Not that I didn't care but *I didn't care*. Gay or not, you were my kid and that's what mattered. You were a smart kid, too sensitive and moody, but smart. I knew you would be okay. Look at you, your gallery gets written up all the time. The Miami Herald loves you, they call you the number one gallery in town. Who the fuck cares if you're gay? You're a Williams and in my book, that's far more important. You are just like me, good at business. People respect you, son, and I couldn't be prouder."

Ansel's mouth gaped open. When did his father read about his gallery?

"It wasn't that I didn't care, I just never knew how to say I cared, that's the difference Ansel. I got a slew of women who could explain that to you. And you were always so angry at me, nothing I could do was ever right. I always felt like you were the one who couldn't accept me, you were the one who didn't like my... *peccadillos.* "

"*Peccadillos,* Dad? Really?! Oh my god, you and mom have got to be the worst parents on the planet."

"Hold on. No, I won't accept that. Look how wonderful the three of you are. You aren't alcoholics, you aren't going to jail. You make your own money, and Hector – you landed a doctor, son, that's not easy. I think you've done a great job. Look at Abby, she and Jake, how many years together? And those kids, sure they smell a little but they are cute and she's happy. And Arthur, I'm surprised he didn't become a mass murderer with how much we put on his plate. But he is the most honest, decent man anyone could ever meet, certainly not from my doing."

"Since when did you have a come-to-Jesus moment?" Ansel looked incredulous.

"Well, I gotta say Christie Three really opened my eyes; yeah, I know what you kids call her." Asher looked his son in the eyes to end the showdown.

"So what happens now? Are you going to jail? I mean this is pretty piss-poor timing with Mom and all."

"Let me worry about that, son, it's my bed and I gotta lie in it."

Ansel immediately called Arthur and Abby to have a family meeting. Abby still didn't feel well from the surgery and they found her lying on the couch looking tired.

"Why do you two look like cats who swallowed the canary?" said Abby suspiciously.

"Gampa!" It was hilarious, it was like little Eli could sense how uncomfortable their grandfather was with children and honed in on him. While Asher sat on the couch, Eli crawled on top of him, smashing bits of a granola bar into his Burberry sweater.

"Seems you have a fan club," said Ansel, smirking.

Felix climbed on top of his brother as Asher writhed underneath the smell of damp diapers and baby shampoo. Everyone let him suffer for a minute or two before Jake took the boys into the bedroom so they could talk.

Arthur brought Harry as requested and Ansel poured them all drinks.

"Dad has something to tell you guys," Ansel started, "And brace yourselves." He made a face like he had just seen an old lady mugged.

After Asher was done telling them, Abby sat up on the couch. She picked up a stuffed animal giraffe and threw it at his head. Asher dodged it but didn't say a word.

"Our mother is dying and you and you and you..." Abby couldn't stop, she was seething.

Jake sternly said to her, "Calm down, don't hurt yourself."

"Why?! My parents do it enough already? Jesus Christ, do you people know how fucking tired I am? Do you have any idea how exhausting this is?" Abby waved her arms all around. "I can barely handle Mom, I can barely handle myself. I am in pain, physical goddamn pain. I have two small children who need me and now you are going to be on CNN doing a perp walk?!" Abby started crying, everything breaking in her. She picked up another toy and threw it at Asher. She couldn't stop. Her brothers had never seen her this angry. None of them moved.

Jake tried to go to her, but she just pushed him away. "I can't, I can't do this. I can't take care of this, I just can't take care of any of you any more..." she screamed as she stormed out of the room.

The men were left looking down, ashamed. It was true they hadn't been taking good enough care of her.

"She'll be okay," Jake reassured them, but did not sound

convinced. "The surgery was harder on her than we imagined. She is in pain, and it's starting to hit her hard about her mother. It was easier when Agnes was drunk and mean, easier to hate her, but now she has been like her old self. It's dawning on Abby what she is really losing. Asher, you couldn't have picked a worse time." Jake sounded pissed too.

Practical Arthur asked questions. He wanted to know every detail about the indictment and possible outcomes. But Ansel kept quiet about Asher putting money in Agnes's name, fearing it was too much for Arthur to handle. It was time he protected his big brother.

They left Abby alone in her room to rest. The men ended up talking for hours and Jake ordered pizzas. They planned what to do if and when Asher was arrested. Arthur and Ansel reasoned that if they could come together for their mother all these years, after all her indiscretions, they could do the same for their father.

TWENTY SIX

New Year's arrived and none of them was up for it. Days had now stretched into weeks and Agnes kept hanging on. Surprisingly, Eve stepped in. Her boys would be at friends' and otherwise she would be alone. Arthur did not understand what was developing. After years of marriage, Arthur had no game.

"Arthur, your family is having really just a terrible time, why don't you invite them to your new house for a New Year's dinner?"

"I don't cook. And they wouldn't want to come anyway."

"Haven't you been spending a lot of time at Abby's? Then have them over to your new house, it would do you all a bit of good. I love to cook and I don't really have anyone to cook for any more. It seems to be better when all of you are together than apart. You seem – she paused – happier?"

Arthur wasn't opposed to showing his family his new home. He wanted to show them his change since Janine. When he and Janine were together they rarely had people over, family or friends. In fact, he couldn't remember the last time he hosted anything.

And he did love his new house, so did Harry, even though it had only been a couple of weeks. And his mother always loved New Year's. When they were little she would wake them up at midnight with a kiss and a hug. Later when they were older, she would buy hats, decorations and play music all night. There was no bedtime. It's when they were teenagers the fun stopped, Agnes unable to stop them from growing up and moving on. And he wasn't opposed to having Eve cook; in fact, it sounded quite pleasant to have her around too.

"I warn you, they are a terrible bunch. There will be a fight, some tears and if all goes well, everyone will be too drunk to remember what happened the next morning."

"As long as they like my cooking." Arthur laughed out loud. He suspected Eve might be flirting with him, but it hard to reciprocate. He felt his emotions being drawn all over the place and had no inclination to throw another human, especially a woman, into the mix. He appreciated Eve, even thought she was sexy, but now was definitely not the right time.

Hector stayed in Connecticut, already an honorary member of the family in such a short time. Abby and Jake found a sitter, their neighbor Emalyn Mercer. Ema was a crazy sort who sat in trees when they were going to be torn down and shouted at town hall meetings about local politics. Abby loved her because she was so unlike their mother. Ema drove a convertible and traveled with just a backpack and loved children. Ema would spend the night just so Abby and Jake could have a good time. Abby couldn't help but wish Agnes was more like Ema, but when she thought that, with Agnes dying, she felt guilty.

Harry was torn. To stay or go out with his friends? Arthur insisted he was only 17 once and not to waste it on his family. He sent him on his way. Eve and he played music, made food and waited for the family to arrive.

Everyone loved the house and it was cozy and perfect for entertaining. Arthur and Abby knew about the surprise; it was rare when they could actually give Ansel something he wanted. When she came in, all eyes were on Ansel. She looked smart, pretty and was holding a bottle of Veuve Clicquot.

"Well, I found myself in the bloody woods after all, Grandma."

`Ansel turned and laughed when he saw Kerry. Abby whispered to Hector, "You did good, boyfriend."

"Thanks, *Hermana*."

Hector arranged for Kerry to come up for a couple of nights to see Ansel and her family.

"But who is watching the shop?"

"Well, it's closed tomorrow, duh, and Liz will watch it for the next couple of days."

"Liz, our hairdresser?" They shared the same hairdresser and both adored her.

"Yeah, she gets ten percent of anything she sells."

"But you get only five?"

"Thus she is extremely motivated."

"Well done, you," said Ansel. "I missed you."

"Not as much as I missed you." Ansel and Kerry sat on the couch and caught up on all the South Beach gossip, Hector hadn't seen Ansel this happy in a while. Arthur came over and politely introduced himself. Brazen Kerry responded, "Good to see someone is more handsome and polite than Ansel. The guy is just full of himself sometimes." Arthur turned bright red at being called handsome.

Ansel turned to Kerry, who was grinning like a cheshire cat. He whispered in her ear, "Don't...you...even...think ...about...it."

She smiled at him, held up her hands, mouthing "What?" and asked Arthur for a tour of the house.

Asher knew his family was all together on New Year's. Arthur informed him but didn't extend an invitation. With the indictment coming down and how upset Abby was, Arthur said they needed a break. He was being protective and Asher respected his dedication to the family. He knew he was putting them through too much and accepted his punishment. Christie had dozens of invitations for them that evening but Asher didn't care about any of them.

Instead, he thought of Agnes and her morphine in a hospital bed. How the yellow wallpaper with flower vines would be dimly lit. Her room would be soft and cozy, peaceful, not chaotic like every other place in the world that night. It made him smile to think of her safe and protected, Bev bustling around her, keeping her comfortable. And his children, he didn't mind them being mad. They, too, were safe and happy at Arthur's and that was all he could ask. He poured himself a single malt and flicked the TV on the Food Channel – aside from news, it was his favorite, still. He was in luck: Ina Garten was making a chocolate cake for her faux New Year party. He could only imagine how much she wanted to lick the spoon.

Asher's cell phone vibrated in his pocket. Like a millennial, he could never turn it off. Anything could be important, business phone calls happened at all hours, but he was surprised to see his grandson's phone number. Asher wasn't stupid; if his grandson was calling him at nine pm on New Years and not his father's phone, there must have been a good reason.

"Grandpa, ummm," Harry was a little slurry. "I'ms neeedz your help."

Asher and Christie were about to go out for the evening but he wasn't going to refuse Harry. Even if it was getting his grandson out of jail, which was so ironic given the circumstances. Christie understood and kissed his cheek. She loved him even more for going to rescue him.

Asher made it to the Westport police station in less than an hour to find his teenage grandson slumped in a chair at a detective's desk. Asher was surprised that he was neither angry nor annoyed with the scenario. If anything, he was curious how his delightfully straight and good mannered grandson had gotten himself in this mess.

"Son," he said smiling as he approached the officer's desk.

"Hi Grandpa, I figured you were the one to call, you know because…." Asher laughed because he was a con now, too?

"You are his grandfather? Can we ask where his mother or father are?"

"Let's just say they are enjoying the festivities. Asher, Asher Williams, so do tell what happened? I am awfully curious."

Officer Clement, well into his golden years, took a deep breath and began to tell the story. It was hard for him to hide his own amusement. It began with Harry, along with three other male friends, deciding to start celebrating a little early that evening.

Harry, obviously embarrassed, sank a little further on the police chair and wouldn't look at Asher.

"Mr. Williams, after copious amounts of beer, as you can tell from the smell," Harry burped as if to accentuate the point and the odor of stale beer permeated the precinct. "The boys went on a joy ride. No worries, your grandson was not driving, far as we can tell. None of the boys would confess who was."

"Nope, wassssn't me, i wouldnz do that." Harry burped again. Asher shook his head at his grandson.

"The kids decided to go to the Long Acre Country Club and hijack a golf cart. They proceeded to drive it to (Officer Clement checked his notes) a Mr. and Mrs. Michael and Megan

Beirmann's house nearby, looking for their daughter, Bridget, who happens to be in the same class as Harry and his friends. You can see where I am going with this… " The officer said. Asher nodded.

"Yes, but please, do go on." He was loving it.

"Upon arrival at the Beirmanns', it seems young Harry here decided to pull a 'Say Anything.'" The officer looked at Harry. "Son, do I have that correct?"

"Yes, sir," said Harry sheepishly.

"Harry had a sound system or commonly known as a boom box from the '80s, and held it up to blast Peter Gabriel's song '*In Your Eyes*'. According to the boys, this was a scene made famous by a John Cusack in the movie *Say Anything*."

"That's a really good song, son, nice choice," Asher said to Harry, surprising his grandson.

"Yes, I have to agree, good choice, son, songs nowadays don't make any sense," agreed Officer Clement.

"At that point The Biermanns – who want it on record they too enjoyed the movie – let the shenanigans go on but when they went outside to sadly inform Harry that Bridget wasn't home, the boys ran away. Mr. Biermann recognized each of them because he had coached them all in soccer when they were ten.

"Then the boys proceeded to take the golf cart back to the Long Acre clubhouse. Deciding they were hungry, they tipped over several vending machines in an effort to get snacks. This is all caught on video, by the way. After they tipped the vending machine, one of them found in his pocket a few one dollar bills and eventually just bought the snacks. While the snack machine was on its side, mind you. If you care to see, again, we have video."

Harry groaned.

"We have them on camera drinking some more beer, perhaps smoking some form of cigarette but we will just leave it at that. Then the boys got the bright idea to go skinny dipping in the pond on the tenth fairway. At this point a security guard caught wind of the situation and called us. We gathered up their clothes and waited for them to get out of the pond. Two of the boys attempted to run naked down the fairway but got lost in the dark and had to come back."

"They are extremely bright children, aren't they?" Asher was snickering.

"Yes, I have nothing but faith in our future." Officer Clement deadpanned. "We have decided not to press charges, as I am too old for New Year's Eve paperwork and we have encouraged the golf club to contact all the parents for any retribution or damages. They have each child's name and address. The Biermanns would like to also relay that they recorded Harry with his boom box and will be playing it for their daughter later." Harry groaned louder.

"Officer, we can't thank you enough for helping serve our community and when yearly donations are needed, please add my name to the list of grateful citizens to contact."

"Oh, we already have, Mr. Williams," Officer Clement smiled.

Harry was allowed to go with Asher, deeply embarrassed and remorseful and smelling like a swamp.

"You hungry, son? I'm in the mood for some Swanky Franks."

Asher was whistling as he drove his grandson to the decades-old diner off of Connecticut's I-95. They nestled themselves in a booth and Harry was quiet.

"Now, son, I can't be more proud of you. Finally someone is a chip off the old block. Your dad never was."

"What do you mean, Grandpa?"

"Well Arthur was always so good, never let loose, never got in trouble. Nice to see someone has a little chutzpah in the family."

They ordered two large cheeseburgers and fries. Asher was thrilled, since Christie watched what he ate. No kale tonight.

"I was stupid, I shouldn't have drank. I shouldn't have listened to those other idiots. Now Bridget will never talk to me."

"Oh, son, don't be so hard on yourself. From where I am standing, seems like you had a pretty good time. If golf club mall cop hadn't busted you, you would be with your buddies right now laughing about it."

"Yeah, but Grandpa, everyone is going through a hard time right now and I shouldn't have been so stupid."

"Son, we all are always going through a hard time. It's our job as adults, but that doesn't mean you don't get to be a kid. If anything, Aggie would have roared at this story."

Asher watched his grandson tackle his burger with one hand. He was so natural, his body had adapted without a second limb. It was easy for Harry to live without something he had never had. Of course, everyone had offered him a prosthetic arm, but he reassured them he was fine without it, and he was. Asher admired Harry for his ability to accept the lot given to him without pity or resentment.

"Grandpa, I just feel like everyone is broken right now. Aggie's broken, so broken, Mom, Dad, everywhere something is wrong with everyone. I mean, you're going to jail. And I am broken, I came broken and it wasn't fair to Mom or Dad."

"Harry, you listen to me. You're right, all of us are busted up in one way or another, I'm not going to sugarcoat that, son. Some, like you, came into this world broken and some, like your grandmother, were broken by other people. Lord knows I did my fair share of damage to my children, I own that. I have a few ex-wives who have used the term 'emotionally stunted' when it comes to me. Seems I came into this world crippled too, just in a different way," Asher paused to look at his grandson in the eyes.

"How come you never talk about your parents? Dad always tells me to not ask," Harry looked down at his plate; he didn't want to hurt his grandfather by bringing up the subject.

"I suppose you would be curious about them. After all, they were your great-grandparents, but they are gone now."

"Dad said he never met them."

"Actually he did, but he doesn't remember, he was too young," Asher's voice got quiet. "We had just moved back to Connecticut and your dad was seven or eight, I think. My parents lived outside of Hartford and I invited them to come over to see our new place. I was pretty proud. I was a small-town kid, made all my money on my own. I had a beautiful wife, three crazy kids and a new house. In my mind, I had made it. But my dad, well, he felt different. He was a modest man, a mechanic. He always had grease under his fingers and hard opinions in his heart. I could tell as soon as he stepped out of the car, he didn't like the house. I could read his face, it was too flashy for him. He looked at it, the jewelry on Agnes, everything, and I tell you, he couldn't hide his dislike. To have a father not be proud of his son's accomplishments, well that's just hurt.

"Mom, she was a lovely woman. She was soft spoken and submissive, the complete opposite of Aggie, let me tell you, but she didn't say anything either. She never wanted to upset my Dad.

"I remember asking him as he sat at my dining table, eating my food 'So Dad, what do you think?' and he just stared at me, cold as ever and said 'Not my life' and he shook his head like it all disgusted him. So we finished lunch and they went back to Hartford. Mom got cancer soon after. I visited her alone a couple of times and went to her funeral. I didn't bother to bring Aggie or the kids. As far as I was concerned, they were "my family", not my parents anymore. I was beholden to them, not him.

"After Mom died, I tried to call Dad a couple of times but

he really didn't have much to say to me. He died in a nursing home. A lawyer called and told me he had very little left, he was so frugal. What did remain, a couple of thousand dollars, went to a cancer charity in Mom's name. And that was that. I learned just because you share the same blood doesn't make you family. And I just didn't want to talk about it with my own kids.

"Maybe my dad was broken or maybe it was me, but certainly our relationship was. That's how I learned it's what we do with brokenness, how we adapt to it, change it, hell, sometimes just ignore it. Like you getting up every day, brushing your teeth, doing your homework, walking, talking just like the rest of us, and it doesn't matter in the least whether you have one hand or two. Now does it?"

Harry shook his head. Asher continued.

"I thought for a long time, life was about fixing problems, but it's not. Some things you just have to accept and move on. My heart breaks for Aggie but she made her choices and I have to respect them. And you have your choices, and a lot of them ahead of you, some will be right and some will be wrong, but it's up to your parents and me to accept them."

"I made a fool of myself in front of a girl tonight and in front of her parents."

"Yes, you did, you most certainly did. But I'm still proud of you. Being foolish can be a form of bravery. I wish I had taught your dad that; he needed more foolishness in his life and I needed less foolishness, but that's another story for another time."

"Ten, nine, eight, seven, six ..." The diner waitresses started the New Years' countdown. The year 2010 began and they toasted with sodas in cheap plastic glasses. Looking to his grandson with immense satisfaction, finally Asher understood there were some things money couldn't buy.

TWENTY SEVEN

Reed Thompson was the third man to enter Agnes's life and the last romantically affiliated one to disappoint her. The world was reeling from 9/11, especially in Connecticut where most people knew someone, was related to someone, or knew of someone related to someone who unnecessarily died. No one could turn away from the steady stream of smoke rising from New York City like a post-apocalyptic state. The daily flow of commuters stopped from the hurting city to its beloved suburbs. Residents chose sides and hunkered down. Those safe in suburbia sighed with relief and those in the city wept, feeling defensive and defenseless. Wherever or whoever they were, people were nervous and unprotected. Agnes was all too familiar with the feeling.

She had been living alone for years now and her own vulnerability was a magnet. At 52, she was still beautiful but she had put on weight and wrinkles had formed delicately around her eyes. Agnes liked being older; she had found her youth and the expectations that came with it too exhausting. Now, she could settle into herself, be herself without apology. Abby often was embarrassed by her bold nature, but frankly, she really didn't give a damn any more. Having done the best she could with her children, Agnes couldn't stop them from living their lives the way they wanted. Janine was to forever be a thorn in her side, unworthy of Arthur or Harry. But as long as her son did nothing about it, neither could she. Ansel was happy in Miami. He had put his tragedy, that awful beating, on a shelf and moved past it. Agnes took credit that he learned that from her. They never spoke of it again, but it didn't mean she didn't worry every time she called. It was a relief when he purchased an art gallery. It was a safe place for him and she could proudly brag about him to bridge club. And Abby, since the wedding, they had never been the same. Abby was Jake's now and not hers. Agnes prayed for grandchildren so she would have an excuse to be more in their lives, whether her daughter wanted it or not.

She tried to keep her drinking under control. It was hard. The temptation seemed everywhere. It was in the silence of her house. The apathetic clock ticking through every day. Without distraction, she had nothing but susceptibility. Get a job? But what would she do? She certainly didn't need the money. Charity work required working with others and Agnes was too stubborn for that, she could never take orders from another. She always had a variety of invitations for cocktail parties and whatnot. They had become unappealing in their very volume and sameness.

At her age, she was neither young nor old and she didn't quite know what to do with it. Thus a door opened for someone like Reed Thompson to step through so boldly, he might as well have planted a flag.

"Excuse me, I believe you forgot these." He was holding her Chanel sunglasses.

Agnes was getting in her Mercedes after having lunch at

The Palm with a couple of ladies from her tennis group.

"Oh my, thank you!" Reed had an award-winning smile, teeth so perfectly aligned it put Hollywood to shame. He was wearing smart jeans, a beautifully designed cashmere sweater and his thinning hair combed to look dapper. Agnes immediately was struck.

"I couldn't help but overhear you ladies discuss erecting some sort of memorial for 9/11 victims who lived here or had family. I think that sounds like a wonderful idea." He still smiled and held her gaze.

"Oh, well, yes, it's just an idea at this point. Did you know someone?"

"Oh, many people, some close, some friends of friends. Such a tragedy."

"Yes, yes it was. I'm Agnes Williams, by the way, thank you so much for saving me the trouble of looking for my glasses all afternoon."

Reed laughed deeply, "Yes, my lady. And I am Reed Thompson."

"Oh are you related to the Thompsons on Acorn Way?"

"Most likely not, I only moved up from the city a while ago."

"Seems quite good timing."

"Yes, indeed. I heard you ladies discuss tennis, is there a good racquet club you recommend?"

Their conversation went on like this for a while until Agnes invited Reed to have lunch the following day. She was going to help him get sorted out, the ins and outs of Fairfield County.

Agnes felt excited every time she saw Reed. He was ten years younger than she, but she thought if Asher could date harpies from yoga class, then a decade was nothing but decent. And Reed was completely attentive. He was on time for all their dates, he held her car door and stood when she left the table. And he told her often how charming she was.

Reed was from California, nowhere Agnes had ever heard of, and he had traveled the world as his education. He vaguely explained that he was an investor, mostly in internet companies, and worked from home. Agnes didn't ask too many questions, he was too much fun to be around. They laughed over silly things like how the youth today were so lazy and why were movies so "action packed?" Reed had been married once a long time ago and never wanted children. He enjoyed women Agnes's age because they were forceful and settled. Everything thing Reed said to her was a compliment.

Agnes didn't tell him about her past, she kept that to herself. She let him mix her martinis and he always drove her Mercedes home for her. Agnes knew he was taking care of her and she liked it. She liked it a lot. She could tell he didn't have that much money, it was fairly obvious. So Agnes paid for their dinners, which was easier than discussing finances; she had more than enough.

Reed suggested trips to Boston and Montreal. He would book five-star hotels and cater to all of Agnes's needs. And he made love to her over and over again. Was Agnes in love?

"Mom, how come I haven't met the guy?" asked Abby one day. "You seem to be spending all your time with him."

"Oh don't worry honey. You will, you will. We are just having a bit of fun right now. No need to muck it up with Williams family drama."

"Mom, we aren't that bad. C'mon, let me meet your suitor."

"In due time, dear." Agnes became good at putting them all off. Arthur was preoccupied with work and Ansel was in Miami, it was really only Abby pestering her. And why didn't she introduce him?

Agnes was feeling selfish, they had all gone off and formed their own lives without her. And after Abby had that miscarriage and had the gall to get mad at her for sharing it with her friends, well, why should Agnes share anything with her? Reed was her friend, her life and she didn't want to hear anyone else's opinion about it.

That wasn't going to stop Abby from being suspicious. She called Mrs. Blacksmith.

"Stella, have you met this Reed? Who is he?"

Stella laughed," Well, yes I have and let me tell you he is quite a looker. But that doesn't surprise me, your mother always attracts the good ones, whether she admits it or not. Anyway, he came to a party with her just a few weeks ago."

"Tell me more, what did you think?"

"They both were very chummy; he waited on her hand and foot. And I have to say, she did look radiant. They certainly are having fun in the bedroom," Stella laughed. "But I don't want to cause any trouble."

"Since when?"

"I suppose you are right. Okay, my feeling was he was a bit young."

"Young…"

"Well, he is ten years younger, if not more."

"Really … keep talking."

"I am not really sure about his intentions. BUT I have always told your mother to just have fun, and if that is all that it is, no harm. It's okay for your mother to get her jollies, just as long as she is safe. I mean, she just needs to keep the Birkins and jewels in the safe, if you know what I mean."

"Yeah, but Mom has never proven to be overly cautious."

"That, unfortunately, is true, too."

"Thanks Stella, but let's keep an eye on her."

Weeks turned into months, and Reed was often with Agnes. Eventually, Abby did meet him and wasn't that impressed. He creeped her out, acting like Agnes's butler more than a boyfriend. She tried to ask more questions about his past, his parents, family, work, but his answers were vague. Abby couldn't find any trace of him on the internet. She told her brothers how weird the relationship was, but they weren't around to see it.

"Mom, is Reed living with you?" Abby blurted one day.

"Oh no, dear, he has his own place. It's just convenient for him to stay over."

"Well, where is his place?"

"I don't know, somewhere over in Greenfield Hills. You know I don't drive that far."

"Mom, how much do you know about this guy?

"Abby, I don't like your tone. This is my business, not yours. I can see who I want, when I want. Your father can do whatever he wants and you don't bother him!" Agnes angrily responded.

"Mom, it just…"

"You better stop talking right now, young lady. You wanted me to stay out of your life, even stay of your wedding, so you stay good and hell the way out of mine." Agnes slammed down the phone.

Abby erupted in tears. She thought she was used to her mother's anger but this wasn't normal. Her mother being mean and irrational; it was usually a sign she wasn't well.

Jake got upset when Abby cried and stormed throughout the house. The Agnes roller coaster always affected them. The mother and daughter wouldn't speak for days, and Abby would go into a depression, blaming herself, wondering what she had done wrong. Jake couldn't stand the situation because they were trying so hard to have a child. Whenever Abby was consumed with her mother's problems, then it was unlikely they would get pregnant that month. Sometimes Jake hated the Williams family and blamed them for being so fucked up.

Another couple of weeks passed and no word from Agnes. Abby was torn into knots. She wanted to know her mother was safe but she didn't want to endure her wrath again. She didn't deserve it. It was Jake who decided to fix the situation.

He went to Agnes's alone. He always marveled at Agnes's house, the long manicured driveway filled with bushes perfectly set. The grand entrance and, beyond, sweeping views of Long Island Sound. In so many ways, it was idyllic. But as he approached the front door, he couldn't help a foreshadowing feeling something was wrong. Along with Agnes's four door Mercedes in the driveway, there was a two door, sportier Porsche. It was black and very shiny, brand new. Whose Porsche could it be?

It took a while, almost too long, for the knob to turn and the door open. Jake was rapidly becoming more on edge.

"Hi, can I help you?" It was a handsome man in a bathrobe at one in the afternoon.

"Where is Agnes?" Jake voice sounded forceful, he didn't like what he was seeing.

"Oh, and who are you?" Jake figured this must be Reed. He was inhaling a cigarette like an asshole. Jake hated people who took long drags and exhaled slowly, like they had nothing better to do.

"I'm Jake."

"Sorry, *Jake*, but I don't know a *Jake*."

"Because I didn't come to your house, I came to Agnes's and I am coming in." Jake, who never had shown aggression toward a mosquito, pushed through the door. Reed tried to hold it for a second, but lost his footing and swiveled back into the foyer.

"Aggie, Aggie where are you?" Jake was frantic, rushing from room to room. He found her on the couch. She was also in a bathrobe and it looked dirty. Everything looked dirty. The coffee table was littered with ashtrays and half-filled glasses. Clothes lay on the floor, flowers rotted in a vase. With a Bloody Mary in her hand, Agnes foggily looked at her son-in-law with glassy eyes. With greasy hair and no makeup. Every alarm went off in Jake.

"Agnes, it's me," he leaned down close so she could focus on him.

"Jake! Darlingzz, soooss goodz to sees you. Where is Abby? Abby, darling, are you herezz?" He could smell she was dead drunk. He looked up to see Reed standing there arrogantly still puffing on his cigarette.

"So you're the daughter's husband. See, she's fine." Reed waved a hand over Agnes. "Just chill man, Agnes is cool. We're just having a little party."

"Did you give her drugs?"

"Relax, man, she's fine. Just some Valium, what's the big deal? She likes vodka anyway. She's not into any other shit."

"And you?"

"Fuck, man, what do you care what I like?" Jake guessed the guy probably really like cocaine and any prescription drugs he could get his hands on. Jake stood thinking. He wanted to grab Agnes and run but that would leave this creep in the house. Really he wanted to punch Reed and slam him against the wall but that was illegal. And face it, Jake wasn't a fighter. There was only one plan.

He stormed out without saying anything to Reed, but heard behind him, "Bye dude, and take your freak show with you," with a chilling laugh.

Jake went straight to Arthur's office. Arthur listened as Jake paced and explained the whole situation. Arthur calmly rose and said, "Let's go."

Without much thought, the two men returned to Agnes's.

Arthur, with his big frame and broad shoulders, slammed the front door open. He walked briskly down the front hall until he saw Reed sitting, still in a bathrobe, on the couch opposite his mother. He didn't even look at her. Grabbing the bathrobe in one hand, he punched Reed hard and squarely on the jaw. Reed, intoxicated, fell like a tree in the woods. Arthur lifted up his fist again but Jake screamed.

"No! We get him out!" Arthur was blinded with rage and took a second to grasp Jake's meaning. Another blow could do damage or kill him; they didn't need that. Reed saw the fist still hovering over him and began to scramble like a ferret. Slipping across the marble floor, he shuffled to the front door as fast as he could with Arthur looming over him the whole way.

Blood spewing from his mouth, he jumped in the Porsche, which, fortunately for him, had the keys in the ignition. He shut the door with a piece of his bathrobe caught dragging on the ground. Arthur winced as the beautiful car's gears were ground into submission. Reed raced down the driveway.

"Holy shit, Arthur! Damn, who knew you were such a bruiser?" Jake slapped him on the back and Arthur, finally calming down, shook the pain out of his unclenched fist.

"What a piece of shit."

The men went back in to find Agnes sitting up on the couch, relatively unfazed.

"Is he gone? Oh, thank you, boys. He had gotten tedious and I just didn't know how to tell him to go away." They could tell Agnes was still drunk and most likely she wouldn't remember anything. "Can I get you guys something, a drink?" She paused and looked far away. "No, I think I need to go to bed, good night, boys." And she wandered off to her bedroom without looking back.

They left. Arthur went to the office to simmer down. He

had access to his mother's accounts and checked them. She had bought the Porsche three days ago. The con artist wasn't going to get away with it, not on Arthur's watch. He called the police, who found it locked and abandoned at a strip mall. He guessed Reed was too afraid to keep it. *Ha, that's right you piece of shit, don't mess with me,* Arthur thought boldly. He had the car returned to the dealership, put the money back in his mother's account and saved her the embarrassment of ever talking about it again.

Jake narrated the whole story to Abby. She hugged him with all her might and told him he was extraordinary. But she packed a bag and ran back to Agnes'. She would move in for a few days to help her mother get back on her feet. Because that's what a daughter does for her mother, a moth to a flame.

TWENTY EIGHT

"Is that your Dad? He's handsome!" Kerry exclaimed as they all gathered around the TV. The feds came on New Year's Day. Asher was dressed and ready; he looked at ease as they led him from the building to a waiting squad car. Of course, the paparazzi were on hand for the visuals. Another Wall Street mogul taken down. Asher made sure Christie was tucked away at her parents' house in New Jersey.

"Kerry, that's my Dad," said Ansel.

"Well, I would do him."

"And he you, most likely."

"Will the press bother us?" asked Abby.

"Hope not," Arthur said glumly. He knew he would have to explain all this to his clients. CNN had the video on a loop, calling the arrest the first of many and a major coup against insider trading.

"They are being a tad dramatic, he didn't give anyone up," Abby said sarcastically. "Good old Dad, always knows how to keep his mouth shut."

"Amen to that," said Ansel.

The phone started ringing.

All of them screamed, "Don't answer it!" Jake leapt and took the phone off the hook. Anyone who needed them knew their cell phone numbers.

Ansel and Abby traditionally wore pajamas on New Year's Day and the others followed. All of them nursed hangovers of sorts from Arthur's party the night before. At some point there was dancing, too much champagne and no one could recall what time they made it home or to bed. In other words, it was fun.

They called Bev to keep Agnes off CNN or any news station. She softly conveyed their mother wasn't feeling herself today, more pain than usual. She urged them to stay home and get some rest. Bev helped them not feel guilty, knowing they had a lot on their plate.

Arthur had Harry retell his News Year's Eve adventure to everyone. The family howled with laughter, happy for the distraction.

"So Dad took you to Swanky Franks?" asked Ansel.

"Yeah, he was pretty great about everything," said Harry. It helped all three of the Williams siblings to hear about Asher being a good grandfather. It humanized him while his face flashed across the TV screen.

Asher called a while later; he had only gone to jail for a few hours. His lawyers arranged for him to be released after the fingerprinting and press photos. He reassured them he was fine and headed to see Christie in New Jersey. No one urged him to come home.

"Who knew Dad getting arrested could be so much fun?" said Ansel with a touch of merriment.

Hector said skeptically, "Isn't it just a bit *loco?* Your Mom, you know in her state, and your dad in jail and all of us here having a *fiesta*?"

"Hector, I hate to tell you, but it's how they roll, *muy loco*," said Jake, twirling his index finger by the side of his head. Abby and Ansel just shrugged.

Honestly, it was festive. No one let Abby lift a finger and she was grateful. Not one to complain, but it felt like she had been kicked in the stomach by a horse. Her insides ached but at least the physical pain offset her emotional roller coaster. Quietly, she sat and watched her family with admiration and awe. Kerry and Hector were making food. Harry played with his little cousins and Ansel and Arthur waited on their sister hand and foot. Even in the strangest times, they came together, supported each other, loved each other, faults and all. For a moment Abby felt content, until of course, Ansel burst the bubble.

He had seen it. It was just a two-second look between Arthur and Kerry and Ansel knew.

"No, no, no, no, dear god, no!" he shouted.

"What?! What is it?!" asked Hector. Everyone looked at the TV, expecting another bad news report.

"Do you both think I am stupid? THIS, NO, THIS cannot be happening!" Ansel was glaring at Arthur and Kerry like a disappointed parent. He put both of his hands on his hips like their mother. The couple looked shameless. Arthur blushed while Kerry just smiled.

"OOOOOhhhh!" exclaimed Abby, delighted by the turn of events.

Hector caught on, "Ansel, calm down, they are two consenting adults."

"No, they are my brother and best friend. They are not adults, they are selfish, stupid, frivolous children. It's incestuous!"

"Ansel…" Arthur started to speak, but Kerry stopped him.

"What's incestuous?" asked little Eli. Harry laughed and whispered something to him that made him giggle.

"Ansel, breathe for god's sake," demanded Kerry. Ansel looked like a toddler, red-faced with his hands in fists at his sides. Kerry continued, "It was a one-night stand and it was fun." Now Arthur turned the color of a beet.

Harry started chanting "Go Dad, Go Dad." Abby laughed along and fist-pumped the air.

"What about that Eve woman? We all had bets on her!" whined Ansel.

Arthur shrugged, "She went home right after midnight."

"Wait, I saw you kiss her at midnight?" said Abby, loving all of it.

"Yeah, I did." Arthur looked down.

"You dirty dog, you. Well done, big brother," Abby winked at him. She got it. He just needed to dust off the cobwebs with Kerry before going for Eve.

"You have nothing to worry about," said Kerry. "We are not in a relationship of any kind. It was New Year's and we wanted to start the new year with a bang. I can't see anything wrong with that. " She was unapologetic, almost enjoying Ansel writhing. Arthur sheepishly left the room.

Harry was still chanting, "Go Dad, go Dad."

"You heathen, vixen, infidel, whatever!" Ansel screamed at her and stormed off.

Kerry laughed, "Takes one to know one!!"

"*Mi Dios*, he is so passionate about everything!" Hector laughed and followed after him.

Abby turned to Harry, "Well that certainly was a delightful plot twist."

Kerry found Arthur nursing a ham sandwich in the kitchen. She kissed him on the cheek and told him last night was fun.

He smiled. "It was, wasn't it?" Arthur had only grateful thoughts when it came to Kerry. She was just the start of a new chapter in his life without Janine. It was true, he did like Eve, but he wasn't ready for her, either. And his baby brother could get over it.

Awhile later, Jake shouted "Got it!" with zeal, coming in from the cold. No one had noticed he was gone. He had gone to Ema's for one specific thing. Ema, their crazy neighbor, loved movies and had a vast DVD collection. It only took a few minutes of searching for him to find it.

Jake called everyone into the living room and held up a copy of *Say Anything*. Ansel and Abby screeched with happiness.

"Really, guys?! Ah, come on…" said Harry, shaking his head.

"Well I've never seen it," said Arthur.

———

It was snowing outside, a light dusting, a settling of sorts to begin the new year. January, with its cold, dark days ironically never felt like the start to anything. The yellow dining room was somber with the cold light of winter. Abby sat with Agnes quietly and thought about all the things unsaid. But did she really need to say them? Agnes rustled around in the bed a bit and stared at Abby. Neither spoke. Her mother reached out her withered hand and Abby held it ever so softly. Abby wondered, *was it time?* as her mother drifted off to sleep.

Watching her, she thought about the last few years. They had been one nightmare after another since Agnes found the lump. Now Abby understood her mother pulling away. Or was it she pushed her away? For the sake of her daughter, she had started the separation process for them.

At the hospital, the lumpectomy had gone well and surprisingly fast. Now looking back, Abby remembered her mother asking her to leave the room anytime the doctor entered. That was when she started being secretive and furtive about her health.

After the surgery, she felt her mother shift, change, palpably before her. Agnes began refusing Abby's help of any kind. She complained the lumpectomy had gone wrong, she blamed the doctors, got angry at them and said they had failed. She wouldn't return to them, calling them "quacks" and unqualified. Abby tried to suggest new doctors, even set up appointments, but Agnes found excuses to ignore her.

Abby, Ansel, and Arthur pestered her about radiation or chemo. But Agnes was vague. She told them she was taking radiation pills. They had no way to disagree; she was showing signs of fatigue and vomiting. But Agnes was still drinking, so it was harder and harder to assign which symptom to which illness. Abby saw the empty vodka bottles hidden in her mother's closet but said nothing. Little symbols of shame. Agnes couldn't quite bring herself to throw out.

And the episodes, the drinking and driving as if her mother was pushing everyone to their limit. Even the cops were ashamed by the situation, her mother's sadness too pitiful.

It was Stella who told Abby what really happened at the French restaurant.

"Oh dear, your mother was fit to be tied that night. She had just been politely kicked out of the club after throwing a knife at Mrs. Tuttle. And she knew the whole town knew about it, which they did. And unfortunately, that night there were many members at Pierre's. I am sure all she felt was shame and embarrassment walking through the dining room. Just everyone knew she wasn't allowed back at Southpoint any more," said Stella ever so gently. "I didn't know what to do with her, she just kept drinking and getting louder. She was arguing with everyone-me, the waiter, even Senator Harris at the table next to us. I suppose I should have tried to get her to leave, but your mother had a force to her that was hard to stop."

"No, no, she wasn't your responsibility," Abby reassured. "Mom was like a bull in a china shop, don't feel guilty, please don't." She had seen that look in many of her mother's friends' eyes. They wanted to help but didn't know how. But they also secretly wanted no part in it either. That's why they felt guilty; they felt like they were abandoning their friend, but really, they wanted to go.

What was anyone to do? Agnes was out of control and no one had the answer.

It was like the day Abby would never forget. The day she walked out on her mother.

After the Reed Thompson incident, Abby stayed with her mother for days and Agnes quit drinking, at least for the moment. Allowing a man to take advantage of her jolted her into sobriety. Abby stood by her, like her mother had done when she had run home from New York. Not since her wedding had she felt close to her mother. And then Abby learned she was pregnant with Eli.

Jake and Abby were ecstatic but the thrill of the pregnancy was dampened by caution. Still, they sailed through the first three months, keeping it to themselves, encouraged by every doctor's visit and a strong heartbeat. Finally when they could tell everyone, Abby wanted to tell her mother first.

They invited Agnes out to lunch, offered to pick her up and arrived promptly at the house at noon. But the front door was locked. They rang the bell and their mother's car was clearly in the driveway. Abby began to worry, maybe her mother had hurt herself? Jake could see the panic in her eyes and jumped into action. He climbed the fence and scrambled into the back yard to get to the back door. Abby's heart raced, imagining her mother falling down the stairs and hitting her head.

Jake got into the house and opened the front door. Before he could say the word *wait* Abby rushed through.

"Mom, Mom where are you?" She turned to Jake.

"Abby, honey, maybe we should just go, come back another time," he tried to say as gently as possible.

"What? What are you talking about?" He didn't want to tell her; she had been so excited this morning and now it would all disappear because of damn Agnes.

Abby read his face and he could see the curtain fall. Anger gleamed in her eyes and she shouted "Mom!" He pointed upstairs.

Abby went up and saw her sitting on her bed. Her mother was struggling to put on her shoes, dead drunk.

"Abbbyzz dear, let me just getz ready. I'm sooo sorryyy I forgot about our lunch." Abby watched her tip over and try to right herself.

"It okay, Mom, we are not going," Abby hissed. Fury rose in her like molten lava. "Just stay here."

"No, no, don't be so dramatic, dear," her mother said snidely, which only infuriated Abby more.

"Really, can you see yourself, mother? I think this is enough drama for the both of us."

"Leave me alone Abby, leave me the fuck alone. I don't need your pity."

"Okay, sure. Nice, Mom, that's right, get mad at me. I am the horrible daughter." Tears welled in Abby's eyes.

"Go away."

"I came here to tell you I was pregnant, Mom. I wanted to tell my mother I was pregnant. It's healthy and I wanted you to be the first to know." Abby sounded like a whining child.

Her mother just stared at her blinking, too drunk to process what was happening. Abby's heart tore in two. Here was the second happiest time in her life, like her wedding, and her mother was incapable of having any part of it. Her alcoholism, her pain, winning again.

She felt hands on her shoulders, they were Jake's. He was guiding her away.

"We can't leave her like this, what if she hurts herself?" Abby said outside.

"Then she hurts herself, but I won't have her hurting you or my child any more." Abby shook with grief and fear and anger as Jake put her in the car and they drove away.

But Abby could never really cut herself off from her mother. Sober or drunk, Agnes would reach out to her daughter over and over, whether she could help it or not. Sometimes it was in kindness and sometimes hatred. It was who she was. It was who they both were, attached to each other in a never-ending dance.

Like all the other instances, the women never spoke about that day but simply moved on. But every time something happened, Abby imagined a strand of string breaking in the thread cable between them. And she wondered what would happen if all strands broke and the tie between them was gone? Would she ever not feel tied to her mother, ever free of the anger and disappointment, both hers and her mother's?

When Agnes found her lump and first used the term cancer, Abby cried. But deep down, she asked, would this finally be the end? After all these years of alcoholism, would the irony be that cancer would take her? Worse, did she secretly wish her mother would die? Sometimes yes, but her death still terrified her all the same.

Finally, the state had taken her mother's driver's license away a year ago. That was the hardest time for Abby. At home, she had Eli and baby Felix. She was immersed in motherhood, caretaking, and yet her own mother wanted no part in the process. Years ago, she would have thought Agnes would have wanted to be the world's best grandmother. She had always loved children. Instead, Agnes did nothing but avoid Abby and the kids the best she could. Abby arranged lunches and trips to the park but Agnes would have an excuse to cancel at the last minute. Her mother not loving Eli and Felix drove a nail into Abby's heart.

But Agnes wanted Abby's attention all the same. Calling her at all hours to drive her someplace, getting mad at her if she was distracted by the kids. She sneered at Abby's refusal to hire help with the kids, so unlike the Agnes of decades ago.

Abby pitied and hated her.

Agnes communicated more and more through emails. She stopped accepting invitations and canceled plans more often. Friends had to go to her house to see her. She complained she was in pain for some ailment or another and told people she didn't feel well daily. It was easy to blame a cancer that rightly didn't exist; no one dared to question it.

Agnes was pulling away from life itself, but no one realized at what severity.

For Agnes, it was easier to keep Ansel and Arthur at bay; they had their own lives, like men did. But Abby was harder to shake; she loved her mother stubbornly, as was her nature. They all worried about her, but children's worry is different. Agnes never forgot she was the parent and wasn't about to let her children have any control over her situation. No matter how bad it was getting, their mother stubbornly tried to stay in charge.

From her dying mother's bedside, Abby felt her thoughts meander, in no hurry, coming to rest on an ending. Their mother had loved them with all she had, but loving someone is not the same as loving yourself. Her mother wanted to go, leave her physical body to ashes and dust. She had no love for it any more. Agnes wanted to be as light and free as the snow. Who could fault her for that? She had probably wanted that for a very long time but chose the hardest road to get there. It was time they let her go.

TWENTY NINE

They kept Asher's arrest away from Agnes. She was declining rapidly. The doctor said two weeks but they turned to Bev, who just shrugged, who really knew? Maybe days, maybe minutes.

It became even more painful to look at Agnes, lifting her limbs like they were weighted down with cement. Her eyes were heavy and enlarged, her cheeks shallow and her skin sagging off of the bones. Her physical body was in purgatory, somewhere between two worlds. No longer a replica of any photograph, she was perishing and a portrait no one wished to remember.

"I'm dying," she would tell whoever was in the room. "We know," someone would respond kindly.

Her brain had become a partially functioning organism. Memories and clarity waned. Emotions broiled. Reduced to the purity of life, like an animal only needing comfort and food. Sometimes Agnes would howl, not words but a guttural pain both physical and mental. Bev and Valerie were used to it, but when others were around, the sound frightened them.

There were only flashes of Agnes left.

Bev knew this stage, it was getting closer, it was in the air around her. Like most of her other patients, she never saw them for their skin, their hair or decaying bodies. Instead she saw their shimmering souls hovering and waiting for release. They were like birds waiting for a gust of wind to move on.

Bev's mother always knew her daughter was special and could see what others could not. From the moment she was born, her mother believed her to have the family gift of healing. Growing up in the back country of South Carolina, spirits of their ancestors, some slaves, some not, echoed around their family. Bev's father, a well off rice farmer, didn't believe in such nonsense but Bev's mother kept the family lore alive. It was known that Bev's great-great-grandmother was a witch doctor of sorts, able to heal ailments throughout the county. White and black folk alike knocked on her cabin door day or night to help with childbirth, fevers and even death, for decades. Her name was Beverly March, the daughter of two slaves who managed to die long after the Civil War.

Back then, Beverly lived her whole life in her parents' cabin on ten pristine acres of Carolina country. As a young girl, she met and married a musician. He wasn't home much but gave her three healthy sons to look after. The musician ended up dying from a heart attack somewhere in Mississippi while touring with a music group. The death wasn't much of a shock as she was used to being alone raising their boys. But her own parents had passed and Beverly had never had to earn money in her life until now.

So she started healing. It came by instinct as she had never seen a medical book in her life. Fevers needed some good herbs and anybody could deliver a baby if they just had some common sense. It wasn't hard to find clients because doctors were scarce in the low country. People who were sick were always desperate for any remedy and soon they came knocking on the cabin door through word of mouth. Beverly charged just enough to feed her sons and keep the cabin. Her sons in turn watched their mother's kindness and heroic feats keeping the community healthy. They became honorable men with good careers and kept the family growing from generation to generation.

It was the sons' wives who revered Beverly like their own mother. Her daughters-in-law kept an oral history of all the people she had helped and made sure the memories were told to every generation. Beverly had saved a white woman who had three babies come at once. She saved an old farmer who cut off his hand and only she knew how to stop the bleeding. Bev could mend the chicken pox and sit with people through scarlet fever. She was a legend in the county and the family took great pride in her.

To heal so many only incited country folk to suspect Beverly had supernatural powers. Loved ones swore when she entered the room, the dying went limp and calm. It was if she gave them permission to be at peace. For that kindness, everyone rang for her when their time had come. For lack of a better term, the country people called her a witch doctor, but they knew to be gentle when they said it.

Beverly lived to a ripe old age of 106. And when *her* daughter gave birth to her first daughter, she knew immediately to name her Beverly as well. Young Bev would grow up listening to every story of her namesake. Eventually, she had no doubt that same blood in her great-great-grandmother's veins traveled through hers. Empathy and healing came naturally to Bev and she did not fear death. There was little she found to be afraid of, even when her own strong father passed away, shriveled from cancer. It was Bev at 17 who tended and nursed him to his passing. From then on, she knew what she had to, could do, to help people. It wasn't a job, it was a calling as natural as learning to run after walking.

But unlike her great-great-grandmother, Bev wanted to travel. She had an itch to see past the rice and tobacco fields. She wanted more than the musty smell of swampland and small-town Carolina life. At 18, she left home and went to nursing school in Raleigh, North Carolina. After she graduated, her first job led her to Fredericksburg, Virginia and from there on she kept going. Every couple of years, she changed cities and states, working her way up the coast.

Families of all types took to her. She learned about different religions, from Jewish ceremonies in New Jersey to Catholic rituals in Pennsylvania. She helped city families who were poor and knew nothing but a hard life; she helped the middle class, who wept as if their worlds were collapsing in the suburbs. She had seen arguments and fistfights over the newly dead and so many final goodbyes. Bev had held hands, wiped tears and allowed strangers to use her for comfort countless times over. None of it fazed her, it all seemed so human. She was in her early thirties, now, but sounded much older than she was. Maybe it was her country blood or just her experience.

So nothing about the Williams family rattled her, not their money, which was quite a lot she guessed, or their family dynamics. If anything, Bev found them more amusing than most. Arthur was big and sweet and she always felt the need to reassure him. His struggle with showing his emotions was as plain as a Carolina sunset. It was as if only she could see his grief teeming below his skin like fireworks. She was cautious and gentle with him, wanting him to be comfortable around his mother.

Abby was the easiest for Bev to be around. The girl wanted to lean on a strong woman like her mother would have been. Lord knows surrounded by all the men, she needed backup. So Bev stood a little taller around Abby so she could slump and wilt in her own sadness without fear of someone noticing. Bev would be her backbone.

And that Ansel, well, he just made Bev laugh. His sarcasm tickled her. He was so emotionally charged, he filled a room. For men like Ansel she wanted to make a plate of cookies, sit him down and say "hush, it will all be okay."

And that father of theirs, well, he certainly was a piece of work. She could tell Asher loved his ex-wife, he couldn't stop. He didn't need Bev to help him with anything; he could handle this all on his own.

And Agnes, *dear Agnes*, thought Bev. It took a while for Bev to get the full picture of her but once she did it was like a bright, colorful painting. When the house was still, Bev would wander looking at photographs and collected things. Maybe she was a bit of a voyeur but she couldn't help studying her patients. Their homes were treasure troves of artifacts that Bev could hold and study, getting to know the soul about to leave this earth.

Agnes was special, Bev could tell. Her photos weren't the usual stark family pictures. They captured her sons laughing or her daughter looking unaware. They were intimate portraits, each one of them, and showed the lives they had led. Bev could feel Agnes wanted to relive those moments when Ansel first laughed or Arthur stumbled on a skateboard. Agnes photographed them for who they were, their beauty in being unaware. And there were many photos of Asher; he really had been her true love.

And Agnes loved artwork. Interesting paintings hung everywhere, from birds to boats to dramatic landscapes. They filled the home like portals to other worlds. Bev could get lost in one easily, that special something Agnes saw drawing her in as well. Small sculptures rested on her tables, something interesting an artist had made and was probably thrilled to sell. Nothing was without intimacy.

But Bev's favorite collection of Agnes's was tucked away in an antique glass cabinet. They were tiny porcelain boxes, no bigger than matchboxes, hand painted and each a different theme. Bev dared to pick them up and saw the word Limoges. She looked online, and read about their history. Created in France in the 18th century, exclusively in the city of Limoges, the boxes were used by royals for needles, snuff and pills. Bev had never heard of such a thing, but she laughed at herself and thought *crazy white people.* But each box was so humorous and unique and she adored them for their decadence. One was a champagne bottle, another a blue crab, and another a tiny suitcase with painted stickers on it. There was an ornate birthday cake and tiny pineapple, all made from delicate porcelain with a small gold hinge. She couldn't help herself, Bev opened each one of the 15 or so Limoges, but found nothing in them. Agnes had collected them solely for their frivolity.

But Bev liked to wonder why Agnes had chosen each one. Maybe they were tiny talismans for her and brought her luck? And looking at all the objects in her home, these personal choices that Agnes had made, they beamed a portrait of the woman herself. Bev could see Agnes for her strength of mind and fearless choices. She could feel her love of beauty and how she cherished things thoughtfully created. Agnes had no shame in putting on display her love for her children and family, as if to remind herself how special it all is or was or would be.

When the picture of Agnes came into focus, Bev could finally help her. Now she could see her birds, beautiful and bright circling above, and Bev called to them like angels. She whispered permission for them to fly away and imagined her great-great-grandmother there to receive them.

—

No one would ever know what happened the night Agnes tried to drink herself to death. November had ushered in short and dark days like a bellman. There was melancholy in the air and Agnes could not escape it. In just a few days, she would be hospitalized. Unknowingly, she was alone at home for the last time. Her family would never learn she had no intention of reaching a hospital or staying alive a minute longer. That fall day filled with a whimpering sea wind and heavy set clouds, she had decided, would be her final day. In actuality, for five straight days, she had decided it would be her last. But Agnes was not the type to take a bunch of pills or use a gun; she wouldn't even know where to begin with such things. Without any forethought or planning, she simply began to drink, morning, noon and night, straight vodka. Her system, already compromised beyond measure, was bound to break, she had ensured that with years of chipping away at it one glass at a time.

Why now? She was in pain. Her sides hurt, her back hurt, the itch was unbearable. She threw up Tylenol or aspirin; there was no relief. But none of it compared to the pain she felt in her heart, the seething rage at the man who had destroyed her, held her down and took away whatever chance she may have ever had.

It was a bouquet of flowers. They came like a Trojan horse into the house, carrying all that was rotten in the world.

The card read: *It has been a long time, I never forgot you. You were so beautiful in every way. I heard you were sick with cancer, wishing you all the best. Yours, Eric.*

Agnes's hands trembled with fear. As if it was yesterday, the thought of him caused bile in her throat. She felt alone and terrified. How had he found her? Why was he hearing about her? All of her darkest demons pulsed through her veins. Had he loved her? Had she done something to deserve what he did? Was he delusional about what happened or was she? He raped her and got away with it. Was he flaunting that fact or did he believe what had happened between them was permissible, acceptable? He had robbed her of her sanity, her dignity, her marriage, her motherhood, and worse, her spirit.

Under his weight, she was a trapped animal, not human. And now, was the memory of that some sort of conquest for him to cherish? Agnes threw the vase against the wall. In a rage she stomped on the flowers, tearing at them with hatred. After she was done, she found a garbage bag and threw every last petal away.

But the note had a number written on it. A telephone number, he wanted her to call. Agnes began drinking. And somewhere before the point she couldn't remember, she dialed.

"Hello."

"Eric, it's Agnes."

"Oh, did you get my flowers? How are you feeling?"

"You raped me." she said stonily.

"No, Agnes. What are you talking about? We had fun in the woods that night. We got even with Sabine and Asher."

"Got even?" she slurred.

"Heck, they divorced us anyway. She was such a bitch. But you and I, that was a bit of fun."

"A bit of fun?" Agnes couldn't believe what she was hearing, almost as if she was underwater.

"Yeah, I wish we kind of followed up on it. I would have liked it to last longer."

"You raped me, you held me down, I couldn't move. I said no."

"I don't remember it like that! No, Agnes, you liked it."

"I had an abortion."

"What?!"

"The idea of seeing your face on my child made me want

to throw up."

"Listen, Agnes, I don't know what's going on with you. Maybe you are on some sort of medication or something. But nothing like that ever happened, at all. So I am just going to wish you well and go."

"GO TO HELL!" Agnes screamed as she slammed down the phone. That was the last thing Agnes could remember clearly before the paramedics came days later.

When the bleeding started, it terrified her. Blood gushed from her mouth and she could see red everywhere in her bathroom. Although it was what she wanted, the reality was too brutal, too scary even for her. Deep in her consciousness, it couldn't end this way. It wasn't right. It was her animal instincts that fought for survival. She found the phone and called 911.

While alone with Bev, Agnes confided in her.

"Bev, it was a man," she said.

"Mr. Williams?" Bev asked, not sure what Agnes was saying, if she was lucid or not.

"No, not Asher. Another man, he was very rich and very powerful and he was the one who broke me," Agnes revealed. Bev was gentle; she was used to bedside confessions with her job.

"Broke you how, Agnes?"

"The way only men can break women, with force and vileness and delusion."

"How long ago?" Bev asked, knowing all too well what she meant.

"When the kids were little. I let it change me. I hate that. I hate how it changed me."

Bev rested her comforting hand on Agnes's shoulder and she could feel the woman's breath soften.

"It has changed many women, Agnes. You can't blame

yourself."

"But I did, and now look, look at what I have done." Agnes started crying and even Bev couldn't help her own tears.

"I know, Agnes, it's easy to regret looking back when knowing there is no looking forward. But don't do that to yourself. It's better to accept, it all happened and happened for whatever reason."

"The man, the man who hurt me, he found me and called," Agnes was really crying now, "And the pain of everything that has happened since that night hurts. It has always hurt. I just wanted it over."

"Shhh," whispered Bev. "Agnes, there isn't a soul that I haven't helped that didn't want the pain to be over. It's okay to want that."

Agnes listened and felt a little more relieved. "The kids...."

"Listen, your babies are just fine, trust me." And Agnes did.

Then Agnes started to chuckle, "When he called, or wait, I called him." She smiled at Bev remembering, "I told him to go to hell."

"Atta girl," Bev said and wrapped her in a blanket.

THIRTY

There was no way society didn't relish the taking-down of Asher Williams. Disgracing a family had become a national pastime in America. Bernie Madoff was headlining the news and a witch hunt had begun on corporate America. News audiences frothed at the mouth for a bad guy in an expensive tie and Asher delivered. Coming and going from his apartment, the cameras caught him smiling and relaxed, further fueling the social fire against him. How dare he look unrepentant on the nightly news.

But Asher Williams didn't care. He was still the same boy who weaseled out of homework and charmed his way through college. Maybe it was his age or the fact he had taken a physical punch or two in his lifetime, but a few federal prosecutors were like flies in his way. They were not what he was thinking about morning, noon, and night.

Not that Asher wasn't without a conscience for his bad deeds, but it wasn't the deeds people thought. It was his family. Thoughts of Agnes consumed him. The image of her wasting away in bed woke him in the middle of the night. Sweating and turning, he couldn't help but feel vulnerable to one thing, and one thing only, guilt. He wouldn't admit it to his children because he barely could admit it to himself, but he had been the catalyst to her demise.

But the worst thought, the thought that truly stemmed from Asher's narcissism and arrogance, was this: could it happen to him? Would his lifetime of achievements be reduced to a soiled hospital bed? It was shameless to be so self-pitying, but it was true. Looking at Agnes was an awful reminder of the possibilities in life, and not all of them were good. Ask a man what he truly fears and it is not his death, but his demise. His own flesh becoming his worst enemy.

He admired Agnes, how she didn't seem to fear death. She had years before, when she refused to see doctors and refused treatment. Perhaps she thought the problem would go away by simply not acknowledging it. Or did she run toward it with open arms and say, sure, my time is now. These thoughts invaded Asher's head like grenades, jarring him to his core.

When not with Agnes or at his lawyer's office, Asher sat in his study hour after hour to counteract the chaos in his life. Out of character, he did not attempt to work. For the first time in his adult life, he ignored the stacks of papers on his desk, avoided board meetings and had his secretary at the office "handle" everything, including things that needed his signature. His money made money without him even getting out of bed in the morning, so why bother?

Instead, Asher woke and dressed in comfortable clothes, shunning his usual expensive ensembles. He didn't even know he owned sweatpants before now, but found them marvelous. He would drink Christie's smoothie and go to his study. She assumed he was working from home and left him alone. As soon as he heard the penthouse door shut after she left for the gym, he turned on the

TV.

It started after Agnes came home from the hospital. Asher, expecting a phone call any time about her death, stopped going to the office. But day after day, she muddled through. They were in an incessant holding pattern and in order to take his mind off it, he turned on his beloved food network.

Ina Garten tickled him and Giada De Laurentiis was a catch to watch. Unknown celebrities were doing wonderful things with barbecue and risotto and cakes. If Christie was watching his diet, then he indulged with TV food. Cooking contests were hilarious, with housewives pitted against each other and amateur chefs arrogantly using nitro to freeze things. Old chefs, with rounded bellies, made orgasmic noises over their own food. It was fascinating to Asher, the idea that the rest of the world did these things.

But then one day, Asher turned the channel to HBO and found *The Sopranos*. He was hooked. Hour after hour, he was enthralled by what he thought could actually be real-life characters. He was convinced Tony Soprano existed. Then he found *Breaking Bad* and Walter White. TV shows were more glorious than they ever had been, the *Leave it to Beaver* days in his childhood long gone. Asher was thrilled he had finally found his kind of people. Tough guys, guys like him, guys who sacrificed and did what they did for their family at all costs, against all rules.

Asher stopped wanting to leave the house. He would go visit Agnes but rush straight back to catch whatever was the next episode or take a break from Tony and Walter and watch Ina make a chocolate cake. Days turned into weeks.

Christie wasn't immune to her husband's depression. She saw it for exactly what it was and let it be. She loved TV herself, her generation was raised on Nickelodeon, and subtly began to join him for hours on end. She didn't tell him to snap out of it; instead, his wife made him healthy food and made sure he got enough sleep. After this was all over, she didn't want a full-fledged couch potato on her hands.

Christie knew she would never get the credit from the Williams family for taking care of their father. But in her heart, she didn't need it. She loved Asher, and some days she didn't even know why, she just did with her whole heart. She understood him. He trusted her with his vulnerability and showed her a side no one else in the world would ever see. She felt honored and protective over it. The idea of him going to jail terrified her but she, like him, had faith they would get through it.

Her friends and parents urged her to get out of the marriage. Worse, the press harassed her anytime she left the apartment. From Agnes's dying to her husband being a criminal, life was hard with Asher, and she spent a fair amount of time doubting her commitment. But when they were together, alone on the couch laughing or having sex, Christie was happy, happier than any other time in her life, and so was Asher. If the outside world would just go away, they would be fine.

One of Christie's habits, learned from her grandmother, was knitting. It calmed her. So as they watched TV on those long afternoons, she knitted sweaters and blankets to give to friends or charity. Asher diligently watched her and one day grabbed two needles and began to knit as well. The two of them with balls of yarn and needles clicked away peacefully in front of the tube. They would go on outings to the yarn store and splurge on the finest angora and cashmere, all to give away. Then they would knit sweaters for the women's shelter on 86th and baby hats for the foster center on 54th. In an unspoken pact, they told no one of their hobby. It was theirs and theirs alone, making the best of a horrible time.

"Why don't your kids like me?" she asked one day, pulling

out a pretty lavender ball of mohair.

"It's not you, love. It's me they don't like."

"I mean, I like get it, Ash, you weren't the best dad but you changed. I think you have changed. I, like, wouldn't have married you if you were some asshole."

Asher smiled, "It's true, I am different around you." He held up a turtleneck sweater he had been working on through season two of *Breaking Bad* to make his point.

"I just wish they liked me, that's all."

"Then let them get to know you. Stop letting them run you over. Hell, those three could run over Mother Teresa and the Pope and still have an excuse as to why they did it. Stand up to them, show them you got balls, babe." He held up two balls of yarn and they both started laughing.

Then Christie got serious, "I know how much it hurts you to see Agnes." It had been on her mind. Asher said nothing but looked away.

"It's okay, Ash. I get it, she was your first love and, like, that is beautiful. I would never ever try and make that ugly for you, okay? So you love her as much as you have to before she goes, all right? Because I would want you to do that for me."

Asher grabbed her hands and looked into his beautiful young wife's eyes. He cried for so long, time seemed to stop. Light shifted in the room, clouds went by the window but there was no noise except Asher's sobbing. Christie held him, and whispered over and over again, "I got you, love. I got you."

———

It's called *the surge* and none of them knew about it. Why would they? They had never watched a loved one die before. Technically some say "terminal lucidity" but that's awfully formal.

Basically, sometimes the dying can rally or come alive right before death and can last a day or several days. The patients seem clear, awake and alive. Memory can return and even energy. The dying briefly become the best versions of themselves. For those unaware, it becomes a strange juxtaposition to the weeping and anguish they had been feeling for days, weeks and months. The surge is like nature's last gift to those who had been wringing their hands, desperate for the mourning to begin. Loved ones get one last glimpse of their beloved before they are destined to mourn them forever.

Bev had seen it dozens of times. Old men sitting up in bed demanding to watch the game on TV or old ladies trying to get into the kitchen to make dinner. Families get excited, the tension temporarily lifted and hope restored. But it was false, fleeting, a clever deception from Mother Nature to soften the blow of the inevitable to come. Bev recognized it immediately in Agnes.

"Bev, could you be a dear and make pancakes this morning and bacon, and sausage? I know I shouldn't, but what the hell, right?" Agnes looked bright through her yellow eyes. "I think my itch is getting better – well, it didn't bother me last night. Can you call the kids? I can't see the phone numbers. And Asher, I want to see them all today. Tell them I'm having a good day and want a visit." Agnes's cheer and lucidity broke Bev's heart.

Bev patted her and said yes. Today Bev would say yes to everything. The birds were preparing for flight.

Everyone arrived in due time, including Asher.

"It's been a long time since it was just the five of us," noted Agnes. She was even sitting up.

"Wow, you're right, Mom," said Ansel looking around.

"So Asher, how was jail, did you have to eat in there?" asked Agnes. All their mouths gaped open.

"Who told your mother?" said Asher sternly.

"Oh, no one did," said Agnes. "Haven't any of you realized I know everything about you. My little ducks, please don't worry about your father. He will be fine, I know it." She smiled. For a minute they could all see her again, her dimples, her love shining through like a light.

"Okay, I have something unpleasant to say to all four of you," they listened. "You all only have each other now, I won't be here. Please be kind to one another, love one another and dammit, support one another, even your father. You are my people, remember that. I raised you all to be better than others – you too Asher – so dammit, do it. Be Williamses, be my ducks, stay together." No one could talk.

This was Agnes's farewell. In her forthright manner, with her strength, her resounding truth, she was telling them goodbye. She was going to let them go, not the other way around. They had always been in her command, in her control and now she was releasing them, telling them to go on without her but stick together.

It was clear to all of them what was happening, this was an ending, and it wasn't dramatic, it wasn't shocking. If anything, it was right.

"Now, I want to go someplace," Agnes said factly. Everyone looked around, *what?* Bev came in, "Where would you like to go Agnes?"

"Ah Bev, get me a blanket, my family is taking me to the beach." She did just that and Arthur, big Arthur carried his brittle mother, weighing nothing more than a wet kitten, out to the car.

They put her in the back of Asher's Mercedes, and Abby and Ansel sat holding her. Asher drove slowly as if he might break her.

"Lord, Ash, I don't have all day," Agnes screeched from the back. The kids couldn't help but giggle.

"Remember that trip to Martha's Vineyard?" Ansel.

"Oh yes, that was a horrible vacation." Abby.

"That's because you had to leave that acne-faced boyfriend behind!" Ansel.

"God you were awful at 13." Arthur.

"Like you were any better at 15. You were mad because you couldn't play Dungeons and Demons with your friends." Asher.

"Dragons." Arthur.

"What?" Asher.

"It's Dragons, not Demons." Arthur.

"Nerd. Didn't I get stung by a jellyfish?" Ansel.

"It was a man o' war. We had to take you to a hospital where they gave you drugs and you talked like you were drunk." Abby.

"That was hilarious." Arthur.

"Dad, didn't we get a flat tire?" Abby.

"Yes, and your mother had to ride in a truck with some hillbilly to a gas station." Asher.

"Oh he smelled, I remember he was missing a tooth. I cursed your father the whole way." Agnes.

"I ate chocolate and it melted on Arthur's math book. Arthur, you were pissed." Ansel.

"But the house was right on the beach." Asher.

"Didn't I take surfing lessons? That was cool, I was cool once." Arthur.

"You'll never be cool, Arthur." Ansel.

"At least I didn't wrap a Scyphozoa around my face." Arthur.

"Only you would say Scyphozoa." Ansel.

"I worried about all of you in the waves. I remember you were all so fearless." Agnes.

"That scared me too, love, seeing them crashing about. Thought I would have to swim out to sea to rescue one of you idiots." Asher.

"But we were ducks, we could swim!" Abby.

"Yes, you were my ducks." Agnes.

They pulled into the beach with the Haven Jetty Agnes loved. The day was clear and what vague winter sun existed was shining. With little wind, the deep green sea looked peaceful lapping at the edge of the beach.

"Someone get me out," ordered Agnes.

This time Asher nudged Arthur out of the way, he wanted to carry her. Gently holding Agnes, he walked her out onto the jetty. They all stood feeling the sunlight, the salt air crisp and clean. Agnes breathed in and out but didn't speak. None of them did. The horizon was a guide. It was as if it told them where to go next, somewhere into the future unknown.

"Mom," Arthur.

"Yes, dear."

"We're going to miss you." He wouldn't look at her but remained focused on the horizon. He didn't know that was the one thing he wanted to tell his mother before she died. None of them could speak. Arthur had said everything for them.

"Good," Agnes said sweetly. "Now, let's go home."

They settled Agnes back in her bed but she didn't seem tired, so they stayed. Bev made southern fried chicken and biscuits for everyone. None of them talked about death or alcoholism or anything bad. Instead they told stories about the time Asher tried to fix a window and fell through it, or when Ansel got kicked out of the school art contest by copying Asher's Playboy. There was the time Agnes had a costume party and Abby and Ansel came as their parents. Or when Arthur got into Harvard and was so excited he fell down. They went over as many good times as they could before Agnes became tired.

Bev stood in the kitchen listening to the laughter, the voices filling the room with memories and love. Her heart was full and ready for what was about to come.

The next day, Agnes stared out the window, not speaking. She was tired and wanted nothing. She watched the bare branches sway in the wind like skeletons. They were like her, cold, stark and barely alive.

When the doctor told her it was her liver, with graphs and numbers and medical terms, Agnes went numb. The idea that she was going to die frightened her to the point she could not speak. He must have been wrong. She feared death; hearing she was going to die paralyzed her in an incomprehensible way. He outlined a plan to transform her entire life but when she got home, she pulled the vodka from the shelf and changed nothing.

That same day, Abby appeared out of nowhere, saying she was pregnant. But there were waves of fear and pain washing over Agnes and her daughter was far away, opaque. Abby was yelling, angry, but it did nothing to affect Agnes. Her conscience had shut down.

Agnes knew one simple truth, she wouldn't stop drinking. It was too hard. She may or may not die because of it and those were terms she accepted. She understood she wouldn't be there for her children or her grandchildren but she could not help it. When she admitted that very incomprehensible truth, it got easier. She could push them away.

Agnes could see it on their faces like writing on a wall. They were frustrated with her, even hated her, but letting her demons take over was so much easier than fighting them. And really, if the children hated her, wasn't that far less sad than loving her?

Since she had already had time with Harry, saw him grow, she was happy with the man he would become. But Eli and baby Felix, they were unknown to her. They represented everything she would never have – time, youth, their love – so she let them go first. If she kept them away then they would never become attached. She wouldn't become attached. She wasn't going to allow them to love a corpse.

Asher was easy. He would love her regardless, to the day she died. She had pushed him away a long time ago, but he never knew how to let her go.

Her children were the only ones who mattered. But Agnes knew in her heart, so deeply, that they were good and kind and would ultimately forgive her, her sins and her trespasses. They were grownups and it was time they be the bigger person. She was tired of the martyrdom parenting requires. Exhausted, she was done.

I did the best I could was Agnes's last real thought before she succumbed to nothing.

THIRTY ONE

Endings are just that, endings. Although the human mind finds it hard to go against all hope and faith by believing them to be final. But they are. Finality is nothing more than a period at the end of a sentence. When Agnes died, only Bev was by her side. Her children soundly slept in their own beds, next to their loved ones. There was no last gasp, no final plea; their mother went before dawn as if one more day was too much.

People talk about going toward a light but Bev thought quite the opposite. It's about the light leaving the body. The soul taking it and going elsewhere so there could be darkness and peace. It was like a flash, so subtle but as powerful as electricity. Bev always saw it.

She waited until the pink haze of the sky filled the room to call Abby. No need to remember death in the dark but give it light and bring it out into the open. When Abby's phone rang, she knew. She lay there in bed, her cell phone in her hand and she knew. She could see her mother's home telephone number on the caller ID and tears streamed down her face.

She answered and barely could say, "Thank you Bev, I'll tell the others." Jake held her tightly as she cried tremendous tears. Everything in her felt awash in sadness, in finality and yes, in relief. Ansel was asleep over the barn and Jake went to get him. Abby called Arthur.

When you think you have prepared for a moment, you haven't. There is nothing that can prevent that feeling of having had something and the terror of having lost it. But when you know it's coming, there is no banging of the drum, no shrieks or hysterics, just a release of emotion so overwhelming it feels like drowning.

Arthur went to their mother's to help Bev and Valerie arrange for her body to go to the funeral home. Abby and Ansel couldn't handle it. It was, of all people, Ansel who called Asher; he insisted. Not much was said, Asher grew quiet, letting his own tears fall in silence. He would drive up later.

Life is a marathon of sorts from beginning to end. At least theirs' felt like it. Letting go of Agnes was crossing a finish line, with both heartbreak and happiness that the race was over.

Later in the day, the family gathered at Abby's as usual. Jake poured wine and they all sat rather numbly. The general feeling was, what next? Agnes's body would be cremated but they needed to plan a funeral. None of them felt up for it, exhausted from the past two months.

It was January 5, *such a strange date, 1/5/10* thought Arthur. There must be some sort of astrological significance but he didn't believe in such things. When Bev told him his mother passed away at 5:10 a.m., Arthur couldn't help but think it was her parting gift to him. Numbers, she taught him numbers, and these seem like the exact appropriate numbers for him to remember her by, a nice even sequence. *Thanks, Mom.*

For Abby, she looked to the weather. It was a gray winter day with the possibility of snow on the horizon. Her favorite kind of day, one where she could nestle near a fire with a book. A day to feel safe, warm at home and she thought her mother left her with the most comforting of circumstances to grieve.

For Ansel, it was family. Hector, who had just flown home three days before, had spontaneously come back, having the feeling Agnes's end was coming. His mother died when Ansel was surrounded by all the people he loved the most. He had his nephews, his siblings, his father and the love of his life. Ansel didn't feel alone and that was his mother's gift. Even Kerry texted every hour with wholly inappropriate death memes and jokes; it helped.

Everything was feeling settled but they all forgot the one fundamental rule; they were Williamses and nothing ever was settled.

"Okay, kids, we gotta talk," said Asher. Everyone assumed it would be about the funeral or Agnes's house. Frankly, they thought it was a bit premature; couldn't it wait? Jake went to go put Eli and Felix in front of the TV, yet another showing of *Finding Nemo* to their delight.

"I'll just go in with the kids," Hector said, trying to excuse himself.

"Nope, Hector. Sorry, you're in the family now, so you gotta hear this too." Everyone began suspiciously looking at one another.

"This is not the exact time I wanted to tell you guys, but hey, you know me and my timing, ha ha, right?" Nobody was amused by Asher's joke.

In fact, if anybody looked at Arthur, Abby and Ansel they could have seen them bracing for what they instinctively knew whatever it was, was going to be bad

"Well, I decided to cut a deal with the Feds. It was the best option, no court, no excessive trial, press, you know, the whole circus. I wanted things to be easy for all of you. You know, so we could all just get past this."

"What are you saying Dad? I feel like you haven't told us the 'but'..." said Ansel suspiciously.

"Yeah, but ... the deal requires me to report to prison in two days."

"What?!" Abby exclaimed.

"Wait, what if Mom didn't die today, then you would have been in jail?!" screamed Ansel.

"Are you telling your kids and family that you are going to jail on the day our mother died?!" Even Arthur was in disbelief.

"Now, hold up kids, I didn't plan this. Just take it down a notch and you will see it's okay. I told your mother. Does that help? She knew and thought it was a good idea to just get on with it."

"Unbelievable," said Ansel.

"Okay, you guys are disappointed in me. I accept that."

"You are actually upstaging Mom's death," said Abby, who starting to laugh. It was an unnatural wheezing sound, like she couldn't get air, but it was certainly laughter.

Then Jake started laughing, "Quite honestly, I never knew which one of you was more narcissistic, you or Agnes, and turns out, it's still a tie!"

"I know, right?!" said Ansel, who started laughing as well.

"Okay, okay, very funny guys. Your mother called you ducks but you are acting like goddamn hyenas." Asher was getting frustrated with them. At that, Arthur began to laugh too.

"Stop, just stop it! Don't talk about my husband like that!" It was Christie. "This has been, like, the hardest time in his life. He loved your mother, loved her more than maybe another woman's husband should, but he did. And now he has to go to jail, and his children are laughing at him. Do you all not hear yourselves? Agnes is gone but he is still here. He is still here for you and the baby."

The room went silent immediately. Everyone heard what she said.

"UUUm, excuse me, BABY?" said Arthur. No one moved.

"Yes, baby. I am only six weeks along but doctor says it looks good, so you guys, you are having a brother or sister in about eight months. So your father decided to go to jail now, in order to get out in time. He learned from his past mistakes."

"BABY?!" shouted Ansel.

"Are you deaf?" said Christie. "Yes, Harry and Felix and Eli will have an Aunt, you guys will have another sibling."

"*baby*....?" said Abby dubiously.

"And here is what I expect of you three," said Christie seriously. "You are going to love this baby like it is one of your own, because it is. Sometimes the world, like, works in really weird ways and sometimes when you lose someone you gain someone else. No, this baby won't replace your mother but it will be another, a different part of this family. So just, like, deal with it."

Ansel looked at Hector, like check out the *cojones* on this one. Christie did impress Ansel when she stood up for herself.

"So Dad, how you feel about all this?" asked Arthur. "And just to clarify: our mother died today, you are going to jail and you're going to be a father with an AARP card. Am I missing anything?"

"Terrified, son, absolutely terrified." Asher said quietly.

Just then Arthur's phone rang with the Imperial Death March, no doubt it was Janine calling to offer condolences about Agnes.

Duh duh duh DUN DA DUN, DUN DA DUN. Everyone stopped and looked around, honestly believing Darth Vadar might actually walk in and take over the family at this point. Realizing the absurdity of the situation, one by one each of them erupted in hysterics again. Arthur was laughing too hard, fumbled and couldn't find the button to turn it off until it went to voicemail.

Finally everyone settled down.

It was Ansel, "Okay, I guess it is what is Dad. These things are beyond our control so there is no point in letting it get to us. We're here for you. For you and Christie," he nodded in her direction, "and for the baby."

Asher looked at Ansel with visible disbelief. Arthur and Abby looked shocked as well. "What did you say, son? That is entirely too sane and positive to be coming out of your mouth."

"Me!" said Hector, wildly pointing at himself. "I taught him that!"

"Well, *gracias*!" said Asher.

"Okay, that's very funny," said Ansel, embarrassed. "But what does this mean about Mom's funeral? We   can't have it without you."

"Does anyone object to waiting?" asked Asher. Honestly, no one did, they were all too tired.

Later that night, when the others had gone to bed and Asher and Christie left, Arthur, Abby and Ansel sat at the kitchen table with a bottle of scotch, a bottle of wine, and some cigarettes. They were exhausted, but none of them wanted to sleep. The fact of the matter was none of them wanted to be without the others.

"How old is Dad , 60-what?"

"64, I think."

"Mom would have been angry about this."

"Yes, but does that mean we have to?"

"I don't want to be angry anymore. I'm too tired."

"Me too."

"So we are having a baby brother or sister."

"Think of it this way, maybe she or he will be worse than

all of us and let us all out of the doghouse."

"Yeah, right."

"Mom didn't seem to be angry in the end."

"Nope, she was just Mom."

"So can we just remember her that way? The good Mom?"

"Yep."

"And stop being so pissed off at Dad?"

"Yeah."

"I am going to get sappy."

"Please dear god, don't."

"I love you guys."

"Fucking cheers to that." And they toasted their glasses.

"To Mom."

"To Mom."

"To ducks who don't give two fucks…"

"Ansel…"

THIRTY TWO

"Abby didn't want to come?" Arthur asked Ansel.

"No, Abby has become so maternal, she stayed behind to watch over Christie . Did you know they talk all the time? So weird. Christie didn't come because she was afraid the paparazzi would photograph her pregnant." Ansel made a face only men make when talking about female body parts. "She's *really* big."

"Be nice," warned Arthur and Ansel rolled his eyes. He was glad it was summer in Connecticut. The trees were leafy and green, the air buzzed with cicadas. It was a different heat than Miami but it was heat all the same.

"How's Hector in the new gig?"

"Oh, they love him, of course. But everyone loves Hector." Hector had joined a private practice as a general practitioner and naturally, he was the most popular doctor at the office.

"Do you get jealous people like him so much?" Arthur nudged his baby brother to tease him. Ansel would never ever admit that, yes, he did get jealous but he was so proud of Hector, so proud to be with him. There were worse problems. They had moved in together – well, Hector had moved into Ansel's because he was too spoiled to give up his own place. There were noises about marriage and children but Ansel didn't want to plant that seed in Arthur's head. Arthur would tell Abby and then they would both pester him.

"How's Kerry?" Arthur grinned. Ansel had just made Kerry full partner in the gallery and business was booming. They were going to open a second branch in Ft. Lauderdale soon.

"She is fine but not for you to ask about. How would Eve feel?" Ansel smirked.

"Eve wouldn't feel a thing because she does not know what happened and never will."

"Well, color me surprised, mister uppity up," Ansel laughed.

Finally, Arthur and Eve started dating a few months ago and it was, surprisingly, very easy. For the first time in his life, Arthur could finally claim he was falling in love.

"Why does this take so long, can't they just release the gates?" Ansel said with a pinched face.

"Gates, really ? This isn't *Gladiator*, " said Arthur.

Ansel looked at him like *whatever.* "Since when have you seen *Gladiator*? Oh, let me guess, Eve lives in the 21st century and watches movies."

Finally a door did open and Asher came gliding through like the triumphant return of a weary soldier. But he wasn't weary or a soldier. He looked bright, thin, and groomed in a smart purple sweater set.

"You look like you are getting out of a spa," Ansel said as he hugged his father.

"Not so bad in there, gotta say." Asher was sentenced to the cushiest lowest security prison in Danbury. "Got some new friends named Iggy and Bruno, brushed up on my poker game which had gotten weak, hit the gym. Food was terrible though, I even missed Christie's kale salad."

"So are you on parole? Do you need to report today?" asked Arthur.

"Son," Asher shook his head at Arthur, "Sometimes you just gotta stop with the details. Look at the sky, it's a beautiful day, let's just enjoy it. I hope I am seeing all my grandchildren today?" Asher could not have been more pleased. He had only served eight months in the end; the case against him was weak. He even started an investment portfolio for the warden out of boredom and knitted 46 sweaters for charity.

Asher wasn't really gone long enough for anybody to notice but that didn't stop all three kids from wanting to see him when he got out. Without Agnes, it was hard not to have Asher around, but in a strange way, it was good for everybody as well. They grieved on their own in their own ways. Now that Asher was free, they could finally have Agnes's funeral.

Abby was at home waiting for her brothers to bring her father back. The food was ready and she had set up tables outside. It would be a nice day with everyone.

While waiting she stared at the cursor on her computer screen.

"Mama," said Felix as he crawled up onto her lap. He smelled like goldfish again. She could tell Jake and Eli were behind her.

"Don't feed them, I have tons for lunch." She tickled Felix until crackers spewed out his mouth.

"I know, I know, but who can stop them?" Jake laughed. The boys did eat a lot.

"Mom's writing something. Whatcha writing, Mom?" Eli nestled up against her leg. She thought about how smart he was and hugged him.

"That's right I am. I am writing about your grandmother."

"Aggie, but Aggie is gone." said Eli.

"Yes, and that is how I am going to remember her. I am going to write everything down that I can remember and then someday you two can read about her too."

She could feel Jake's hands on her shoulders, encouraging her.

Dolores from The Chronicle popped into her head. She had told Abby people would only see her for where she came from, not for who she was. But who she was, was where she came from. *Fuck them*, as Dolores would say, and she laughed quietly to herself.

"Go on and get ready boys, Grandpa is coming home from the slammer!" Abby joked and Jake laughed.

"Slammer! Slammer! Slammer!" Eli and Felix chanted.

Here's what nobody could say out loud: they all felt better. Since Agnes's death each of them felt more alive than ever before. Ready, able to tackle their dreams, do what exactly they wanted without worry or fear. They were going to do exactly what their mother taught them to do, to live a better life. They finally learned how to breathe and it could have only happened without her.

The funeral was the following Saturday, August 2. Abby arranged a small church service and the family took up all the front rows. Abby, Jake, Felix, Eli, Arthur, Eve, Harry, Ansel, Hector, Kerry, and Asher and Christie. Even Janine came, which Arthur and Harry appreciated. Stella and other ladies from the club filled many pews, having somehow magically forgotten Agnes's misdemeanors. Even the chief of police stood quietly in the back. Turns out he had a soft spot for Agnes and how many times she got in trouble.

It was decided Ansel would speak for them all:

"I realized you don't just sit down and write about Mom; it doesn't work like that. It's Agnes and that is so much bigger than any of us can grab hold of. Thoughts, memories, feelings about her flood like the tide rising and swelling. All these years, Arthur, Abby and I were like boats and she was our captain. We weathered the storm together and no matter how rough the seas, we made it to shore time and time again. Mom, in her very unorthodox way, taught us not just to swim but to sail. To chart our own course in a way that she never could, survive the worst of storms, never give up, and discover our own new worlds.

"Mom urged us to stand up for ourselves, even though sometimes it meant standing up to her. In the end, I'd like to think that is what she wanted for us – to be a stronger, better version of her. They say you can't describe a person with one word, but with Mom it was about finding the right one. I keep coming back to 'bright'. Mom was very, very bright. She was radiating, vivid, brilliant, quick-witted, intelligent, clever, lively, illustrious and, at times, luminous. It was undeniably her best quality. But with brightness there was darkness and she lived both in the spotlight and the shadows. As the saying goes, those who shine twice as bright, burn half as long."

When Ansel was done, he looked out over the audience and one radiant face stood out with tears in her eyes but smiling so loudly, it made his heart sing. Her purple dress shone like a jewel in a crowd of muted colors. It was Bev. Ansel grinned stupidly back at her.

After the reception and the niceties – no one brought up Agnes's many indiscretions – the Williams clan gathered. Arthur, Abby, Ansel and Asher climbed into his menacing black Mercedes again, this time with Agnes's ashes on the front seat. They drove to the Haven Jetty just like she asked. The sun was setting and the summer sky was lit up with brilliant bands of red, oranges and yellows. The sun appeared to melt in the horizon. It was perfect.

When they walked out to the end, to the point they could only see the horizon, they stopped. Arthur held the box. He took off the lid and found the plastic bag with what remains of their mother was left.

"Umm, well, this is weird. Does anyone have any scissors or a knife?" he asked.

"What in Sam Hill? Oh Jesus Christ, we have to open a plastic bag?!" said Asher.

"Abby, do you have any toenail clippers or something?" asked Ansel. She looked at him like he was an idiot.

"Do I have a purse? And who would carry toenail clippers in purse? You don't go out in public and clip a few off." They started searching their pockets and the four of them looked like they were being robbed out at the end of the jetty by no one.

"Use your keys," said Ansel.

"What?" said Asher confused.

Ansel grabbed his father's keys and made a slit in the bag. He learned immediately the second most terrifying thing in life next to hospitals was the remains of a human in a plastic bag. He was totally grossed out.

"Okay, are we finally ready?" said Arthur, annoyed.

Abby grabbed the box but before she spread the ashes in the water, she said, "Are we sure about this?"

"Oh for god sake, do you idiots ever stop joking." Asher rolled his eyes.

Ansel and Arthur said together, "No."

Abby smiled and turned back toward the horizon, "Love you, Mom."

"I love you, Agnes."

"Mom, I love you."

"Bye, Mom."

And it was over.

Agatha (the Greek name meaning "Good") Williams was born in September. Asher asked Christie if she was sure about the name; he was surprised that she chose one with an "A." She just smiled. "Our daughter is a Williams, after all, but hopefully more *good* than *bad*. And well, she is named after me, Agatha Christie, get it?" She laughed at herself, even Christie (No. 3) had learned to joke.

Years later, it would be Agatha's friends who would nickname her Aggie. No one in the family minded.

The End

ACKNOWLEDGEMENTS

I have so much gratitude for my team Mike Howie editor, Irene de Bruijn designer, and Sara Matthis, editor, mentor and extraordinary friend. The endless encouragement and support over the past few years has resulted in so much more than we could have imagined.

To the City of Key West- thank you for being a great fan club of my journalism and novels. It has been my great pleasure working for you.

To Kerry Gallagher, Alisa King, Leslie Johnson, Nina Venus and Stephanie Mitchell- you have been my crutches and my cheerleaders these past few years, there is no way I would be sane without you ladies.

To the McIntosh Family- Tosh was with me every step of the way.

To my German family, Julia & Birger and all the Blinckmann/Engels.

Dad- for supporting my career choices.

To my sister Buffy Trott Hanschka, we ran the ironman together and made it. Mom would actually be proud of us.

Lastly to my true loves, my husband Jan-Marten, and my sons, Hugo and Max - may I always find the words to tell you how much I love you.

This book is in memory of my mother, Jeannie Goodman McIntosh.

ABOUT THE AUTHOR

Hays Trott Blinckmann is a writer, journalist and painter. She has a Bachelor of Arts from Tufts University and a Bachelor of Fine Arts from the Museum School, both in Boston. Hays Blinckmann lives in Key West, Florida with her husband and two sons. Her first novel, *In The Salt*, is also available on Amazon.com.

If you enjoyed this book please review it on Amazon .com. This is a self-published novel and with your help reviewing and recommending it online and on social media, Where I Can Breathe can reach a larger audience. Thank you.

Made in the USA
Columbia, SC
23 January 2020